The
Other Brother

The
Other Brother

Brandon Massey

Kensington Publishing Corp.
http://www.kensingtonbooks.com

DAFINA BOOKS are published by

Kensington Publishing Corp.
850 Third Avenue
New York, NY 10022

All Kensington Titles, Imprints, and Distributed Lines are available at special quantity discounts for bulk purchases for sales promotions, premiums, fund-raising, and educational or institutional use. Special book excerpts or customized printings can also be created to fit specific needs. For details, write or phone the office of the Kensington special sales manager: Kensington Publishing Corp., 850 Third Avenue, New York, NY 10022, Attn: Special Sales Department, Phone: 1-800-221-2647.

Dafina and the Dafina logo Reg. U.S. Pat. & TM Off.

ISBN-13: 978-0-7582-1072-2
ISBN-10: 0-7582-1072-8

First trade paperback printing: July 2006
First mass market printing: November 2007

10 9 8 7 6 5 4 3 2 1

Printed in the United States of America

Acknowledgments

I would first like to thank the Creator, for giving me the gift of writing and the opportunity to share it with others.

Thanks to my family and friends for the support and encouragement over the years.

Thanks to my agent, my editor, and the entire staff at Kensington, for your efforts on my behalf.

Thanks to the booksellers, for hand-selling my books in your stores and making them available to your customers.

Thanks to the many book clubs that have discussed my novels, and, in many instances, invited me to participate in the discussions, including—and certainly not limited—to: Nia Imani Bookclub in Sacramento, California; GAAL Bookclub, in Atlanta; Sisters Turning Pages, in Atlanta; Imani Literary Group, in Atlanta; Ladies of Color Turning Pages, in Los Angeles; S.T.Y.L.E.S Bookclub, in Atlanta; Circle of Friends (and all of your wonderful chapters); R.A.W. Sistaz (all your chapters, too!); The Cushcity.com Bookclub and Circle of Essence, in Texas; and so many more.

And thank you very much to the readers, without whom I would be unable to do this as a career. Keep on reading and spreading the word. Peace.

Standing at his bedroom window, watching a thunderstorm building in the evening sky, Isaiah Battle touched the glass and thought about death.

Death comes stealing like a thief in the night, he thought. Death came without warning, without preamble, invading suburban mansions and inner-city housing projects, taking away the young and the old, the feeble and fit. No one was spared. And no one was safe.

Not even him. Especially not him.

For most of Isaiah's life, the veil separating life from death had been as thin as the cold windowpane on which his fingers rested.

He pursed his lips, took his hand away from the window. Ordinarily he did not contemplate such macabre thoughts. But today he couldn't avoid them.

It was like that when you expected someone was coming to kill you.

He was dressed in a gray button-down shirt, loose-fitting Levi's, and black Timberlands. The ends of the shirt flowed over his waist, concealing, he hoped, the bulge of the Glock nine-millimeter handgun he wore holstered on his hip.

Mama knew he owned guns, but she didn't like for him to carry them around the house. Tonight he didn't dare walk unarmed for a moment, not even while in his own home.

There was a rap at the door. Isaiah spun, quick as a cobra, hand flicking to the Glock.

"Dinner's ready," Mama said behind the door.

He relaxed. "Be there in a minute."

He turned back to the window.

The churning April sky, resembling the face of a wrathful god, offered him no comfort. The brewing storm made him edgy. And the urban wasteland beyond the glass—the dilapidated houses, trash-strewn sidewalks, and pothole-riddled streets of Chicago's Southside—fired up an old, familiar anger that simmered in his chest like heartburn.

We deserve a better life than this. We never should have been here.

A battered desk stood beside the window. Photographs—clippings from business magazines and newspapers—covered the desktop.

Many of the photos depicted two black men standing together, dressed in expensive suits, clearly father and son, the consummate family entrepreneurs. Other pictures featured only the son, a dapper guy in his late twenties who had life by the balls, and his wide grin showed that he knew it, too.

Resentment rippled through Isaiah.

Another photograph, framed and standing at the edge of the pile, showed the father from the other pictures, in his youth, and a pretty black woman with an Afro. They sat at a table in one of those Japanese hibachi restaurants, smiling as if they would be young and beautiful forever.

He didn't know why he'd pulled out the pictures. Looking at them had the predictable effect of stoking his anger. He supposed that he was in an introspective mood, ruminating on his life and how it was so unfair that it had turned out this way.

He picked up the framed photograph. It was wallet-sized, and the glass front was cracked. It had been damaged when, in a rage, he'd flung the photo against a wall.

He double-checked that his shirt covered his gun and then left the bedroom, tucking the picture in his pocket. He checked in both directions along the dark hallway. Looking for a hidden intruder. No one was in there.

It was just him and Mama, like always. Mother and son against the world.

Mama sat at the kitchen table, smoking a Newport. The table was set for dinner. But she hadn't eaten. The aromas of fried chicken, greens, cornbread, and other foods rose from the battery of pots and pans on the counter and stove.

Mama's gaze flicked across the bulge underneath his shirt. Disapproval flared in her eyes. Mama was a long way from stupid.

Isaiah moved his hand to conceal the gun. "You didn't have to wait for me, Mama."

"It's Sunday," she said, as if that explained everything. And it did. Mama believed in sit-down family meals on Sundays, and he obliged her.

She believed in attending church services on Sundays, too, but he refused to go along with that. He believed in God, but he no longer believed God cared about people like him. His initial realization of God's indifference to his plight came during his first stint in juvenile detention, when two teenage bullies, beating him because he was new, laughed mockingly when he cried out for God to help him.

And his faith hadn't been helped when, as a teenager, he'd seen the pastor of their church—a married man with three kids—hurrying out of Mama's bedroom one night, yanking up his slacks around his waist.

Fifty-two years old but looking much older, Mama hadn't

lured any philandering pastors or other men of note into her bedroom in a long time. She was a short, slender woman, with chestnut skin and almond-shaped, copper-brown eyes. Her brittle hair, dyed red but showing stark gray roots, was pulled back into a severe bun. She wore a shapeless blue dress, like an old church lady.

Isaiah remembered when, back in the day, brothers driving by Mama would honk and yell crude come-ons. She was far removed from the pretty, vibrant young thing who'd posed in the photo at the Japanese restaurant. Although black women tended to age well, years of hardscrabble living, cigarettes, and drinking had taken the luster off her complexion, added a net of wrinkles to her face, slowed her stroll, and drawn dark circles underneath her once lively eyes.

Mama, too, deserved a better life.

She rose, bones creaking, and began to fix plates for both of them. She didn't always get his food for him. But ever since he'd been released from state prison at the beginning of the year, she'd given him extra care and attention, as if he were a wounded bird that required TLC before he could spread his wings again. He didn't have the heart to tell her he'd never flown.

He didn't like for Mama to cater to him, but she'd snap at him if he resisted, so he sat at the table and waited. He looked around at the fancy new things she'd recently bought. The oak dining set. The bone china and silverware and glasses. The new microwave, food processor, rotisserie oven, and mixer.

And he thought about the stuff in the other rooms: the Queen Anne furniture, the opulent draperies, the antique vases, and crystal bowls. The kind of luxuries she'd always wanted, but never had been able to afford.

The expensive items were pathetically out of place in their cramped, crumbling home. They'd inherited the house six years ago from his grandmother, moving there from the roach-infested apartment in the infamous Robert Taylor Homes, where he'd spent his youth. Grandma's house didn't need new furniture and appliances; it needed to be renovated, and extensively at that. The hardwood floor was missing boards, dents marred the walls, the roof leaked, and in the winter, the wind whistled like a banshee through the rooms, the result of poor insulation. Packing the place with fine new things was as ludicrous as putting ten-thousand-dollar rims on a rust-bucket car fit only for a junkyard.

But who was he to tell her what to do with her money? When he'd given her the check for fifty thousand dollars—guilt money from his dad—Mama had shrieked so loudly you would've thought she'd won the lottery.

He hadn't taken any of the money for himself. He didn't deserve it. Mama did. She'd sacrificed so much trying to raise him right that she deserved fifty grand times a thousand.

A rumble of thunder barreled through the night, clinking the dishes on the table. Wind tested the windows, like fingers trying to pry inside.

Isaiah cocked his head, listening for sounds of forced entry, aware that the thunderstorm might provide covering noise for intruders. But there was nothing. Yet.

Mama returned to the table with his plate. She'd heaped it with fried chicken, spaghetti, turnip greens, and a hunk of cornbread. Good, old-fashioned soul food. She took a glass pitcher out of the refrigerator and filled his tumbler with the extra-sweet, Kool-Aid lemonade he'd loved since he was a kid.

"Thanks, Mama," he said. "Looks good."

"Tastes better," she said—her customary response. She got her own plate and sat across from him. Reaching for his hand, she bowed her head to pray.

He bowed his head, too, but only for her benefit. He'd given up praying after his first beating in juvie detention.

Thunder rocked the house as his mother prayed in a steady voice. He never understood how she managed to pray, as if she were so *certain* that God actually listened to her and gave a damn. He wanted to shake her sometimes, scream at her that she was wasting her time. But he kept his mouth shut and allowed her to nurture her illusions. Everyone had to believe in something.

She concluded the prayer and picked up her fork. He reached into his pocket and placed the photograph on the table.

Mama scowled. "Why'd you bring that in here? You know how much I hate that damn picture."

He shrugged. He wasn't quite sure why he'd brought it, just as he wasn't sure why he'd dragged out all those other photos on his desk. Maybe he was indulging in self-flagellation, or feeling angry at life, as he was prone to do sometimes.

On other occasions, Mama would look at the pictures he'd clipped, too. She'd pay special attention to the photos of the son, as if wondering why Isaiah's life had not followed the same track as his.

"Put it away," she said.

But he left it sitting there. "Do you ever wonder how things might've turned out if you'd married him?"

She did not look at the photo, or at him. Her gaze drifted to the wall, and her eyes hardened as though she didn't like what she saw there. "Never. He was married to another woman, you know that."

"But what if he'd left her for you?"

"Then we'd be living in the lap of luxury in Atlanta, wouldn't we? You would've gone to school instead of prison, and I'd be spending all day getting my nails done and shopping at Bloomingdale's. Right?" She turned to him. Fire flashed in her eyes, and he caught a glimpse of the feisty woman she'd been before life had beaten her down. "I'm gonna tell you one last time—put that picture away. It makes me so sick I might lose my appetite."

"Sorry, Mama," he said. "Sometimes I just wonder, that's all."

"Ain't no use in wondering. Shit. We'd better be happy he

gave us the money that he did. It ain't fair, but that's life, huh?"

He wasn't satisfied with her answer, but there was no other answer to be found. He reached for the photo.

Thunder cracked again, and it almost masked the sound he'd been preparing for: the front door banging open as if struck with a battering ram.

He slid his hand to the Glock.

They had arrived.

"They" were a couple of thugs with whom he'd gotten into a scuffle at a party last Friday night. Held in a cramped project apartment, it had been a typical ghetto house party: a two-dollar cover charge to get in, dark as midnight, music so loud your head pounded in sync with the beat, blunt smoke thick in the air, drinks being passed freely, and wall-to-wall brothas and sistas, their horny bodies emanating cologne, hair grease, and funk.

He had been talking to a fine sista with cocoa skin and a luscious body, and she was digging him, encouraging him, devouring his words as if they were the sweetest taffy, when suddenly a guy with dreadlocks popped up and claimed to be her boyfriend. Dreads ordered Isaiah to step the fuck back or he'd knock him flat *on* his back. Never one to back down from a fight or allow another man to disrespect him, he'd gotten in Dreads's face. Threats flew, followed soon by fists. He punched Dreads in the jaw; someone slammed a fist into his ribs; Dreads's bald-headed partner came at him, and Isaiah dropped Baldie with a blow to the kidney. Then someone in the background drew a gun and fired, shattering a window— and the party goers fled the apartment like roaches caught under a lamp.

The party was over. But that hadn't been the end of it. On the streets, grudges didn't die—they multiplied. He'd known that Dreads and Baldie would be coming for him. It was only a matter of when.

All because of a woman. It was stupid and petty, but that

was typical. In prison he'd once seen a brother get shanked because another guy thought the dude was cheating on a PlayStation game. Black men killed each other over trivial machismo bullshit every day.

Footsteps hammered across the floor. From the kitchen, he couldn't see the intruders, and they couldn't see him either. The kitchen was at the end of the hall, and the table was in the corner, tucked away from the doorway.

But they would soon find him.

Mama looked at him. Fear shone in her eyes.

Isaiah hated that she'd been pulled into this situation. He could have stayed with a lady friend, laid low for a while. But the danger in doing so was that these guys might hurt Mama in order to get back at him. He'd seen it happen too many times. He had to stay home to protect her.

"What have you done?" she asked in a whisper that nonetheless held a note of accusation.

He hadn't told her anything about the fight at the party. Trouble had shadowed him all his life. Mama would know from bitter experience that he was mixed up in another mess.

"Go down to the basement," he whispered. He motioned to the narrow door behind the table; it led to the cellar. "I'll handle this."

She shook her head. Tears trickled down her face. How many times had she wept for him? It amazed him that she had any tears left.

"I'll call the police," she said.

"You know I'm still on parole," he said. "Those clowns might arrest *me*."

Mama only looked at him, and a surprising thought hit him: That was what she wanted. She was sick of him and would rather have those assholes send him back to prison.

He couldn't say that he blamed her. He had been a burden for her since the day he was born.

But he wasn't going back to jail, ever again.

"Please, Mama," he said. "Downstairs. Hurry."

Choking back a sob, Mama quickly pushed away from the table. She opened the cellar door and descended into the darkness beyond.

He heard the thugs at the front of the house, overturning furniture and tearing through the bedrooms. Something shattered. Probably one of those expensive vases Mama had bought.

His hands tightened into fists. Mama didn't deserve to suffer for his deeds. He was going to take care of these motherfuckers.

Standing, he lifted his shirt and closed his hand around the Glock's cold grip. He'd paid a lot for this piece. Now it was time to see what it could do.

He moved to the kitchen doorway and peered around the frame.

One of the thugs was coming down the hallway. He was a black man, wide as a refrigerator, a doo-rag capping his dome. It wasn't Dreads or Baldie, but a different brother, another member of the crew. Doo Rag's eyes were slits of onyx.

Doo Rag had a gun, too. The gun in his hands looked like a cannon at first, but it was really a shotgun, sawed-off, probably a twelve-gauge, nonetheless an absolutely lethal weapon.

Doo Rag spotted him and pulled the trigger.

So did Isaiah.

The gunfire was deafening in the house, underscored by a boom of thunder.

Buckshot plowed into the door frame, splinters flying—and part of the buckshot spray ripped into Isaiah's shoulder. He screamed and staggered sideways, knocking against a counter.

He quickly regained his composure. He'd been shot before; this was only another battle in the ongoing war of his life. He didn't feel much pain yet, but he knew it was coming, an express train of agony on the way.

Looking into the hall, he noted with satisfaction that he'd drilled the thug between the eyes. Doo Rag lay sprawled on his back in the hallway, lips parted in an unfinished prayer. Dead.

Isaiah felt nothing—no sorrow, no pity. Although it wasn't the first time he'd killed a man, each time he did it he felt less for his victim, and in his moments of introspection, that bothered him, made him wonder if he'd lost his humanity.

But he didn't have time to think about that right now. There were, by the sounds of it, at least two more men in the house. One of them poked his head into view at the end of the corridor. Baldie.

He fired at Baldie, and the thug jumped out of sight. He'd missed him.

Pain gnawed deep into his shoulder. He looked at his wound, saw dark blood soaking his shirt.

Dizziness swam through him.

I can't go out like this.

But he was fading. His legs buckled and he spilled onto the linoleum like a drunken uncle. He hooked his hand around the table leg and pulled it, fuzzily thinking he could use the table as a shield. The table tilted to the floor, hot food and lemonade spattering around him.

Isaiah hauled the table in front of him, propped his back against the row of cabinets, and positioned the Glock atop the edge of the table to steady his aim.

His vision was beginning to get blurry.

Gotta focus.

Ahead of him, the hallway was empty. But he knew they were out there. He felt their cruel eyes on him. They were waiting to make a move.

Gotta hold on.

A door creaked open. Mama rushed out of the basement to his side. Her eyes were red from crying.

"Get away," he said, but his voice came out as only a ragged whisper.

"I'm not letting my baby die," Mama said. She wrapped

her arm around his waist and started to drag him across the floor toward the basement door.

"Mama, no." He tried to resist her, but he was too weak. They had moved from behind the table, making themselves easy targets.

Mama's jaws were set. "I'm not leaving you out—"

Gunfire rang out. He squeezed his eyes shut, certain the bullet was going to find him.

Warm blood sprayed against his face. But he felt no pain. *Mama.*

"No!" he cried.

She slumped against him, her body as limp and heavy as a sandbag. He tried to hold her against him with his good arm, but he lacked the strength. She slid out of his grasp and thudded to the floor. Blood pooled around her lips, and for an absurd moment, it looked as if she were okay, as if she'd merely fallen asleep wearing red lipstick.

Isaiah wanted to believe that she was only asleep. The urge to deny what had happened to her was nearly overwhelming.

He touched her chest. She was still; she wasn't breathing. She was gone.

Grief clenched his heart like an iron fist.

The photo of Mama and his father, happy during their brief affair, lay nearby, mocking him with the dream of what could have been.

He reached out and snagged the picture in his quivering fingers. He fixed his gaze on his father.

This is your fault, and I'm going to make you pay.

If his father had done right by them, they never would have been here. They wouldn't have been living in the ghetto, he wouldn't have grown up plagued by trouble, and Mama never would have led such a hard life. None of this would ever have happened to them.

No matter what, I'm going to get you for this.

A booted foot materialized from out of nowhere and caught him under the chin. He flipped backward and hit the floor, the photo flying out of his hand. He blinked groggily.

Two faces swam into view above him: Dreads and Baldie. They were grinning.

Thunder roared, and lightning flashed, shadows jumping crazily around the two men, as if they were not simply two thugs there to settle a score, but were the devil's minions, come to deliver his soul to the foulest depths of Hell.

Snarling like a bad actor in a gangster movie, Baldie ground the photo under his heel.

"Payback's a bitch, ain't it, motherfucka?" Dreads said.

Isaiah tried to raise his hand and fire the Glock, and discovered that he couldn't move his arm. He no longer had the gun, anyway. He'd dropped it somewhere.

But Dreads still had his gun. It looked like a nine millimeter. Once you were popped with something like that, your ass wasn't getting back up.

Dreads aimed the weapon at his chest.

Isaiah thought about his father again.

No matter what, I'm going to get you . . .

Dreads pulled the trigger.

Isaiah spiraled into darkness, his promise of vengeance following him into oblivion.

No matter what . . .

Part One

FAMILY MATTERS

All happy families are alike, but an unhappy family is unhappy after its own fashion.
—Leo Tolstoy

Chapter 1

On Gabriel Reid's thirtieth birthday, he looked Death in the face for the first time. It wouldn't be the last.

Monday, June 6, began cold and dreary in metro Atlanta. The temperature stalled in the fifties, twenty degrees lower than normal at that time of year. Tombstone-gray clouds gathered in the sky, signs of a coming storm. A bracing wind blustered out of the northwest, forcing residents to don jackets and sweaters and complain of the unseasonable weather, and reminding transplanted Yankees of what they'd left behind.

Standing at the panoramic office window overlooking the green spaces and wind-rippled lake at Reid Corporate Park, Gabriel felt a chill, too. In spite of the heated air blowing into the conference room and the wool Hugo Boss suit he wore, coldness sank into his flesh, settled deep in his bones.

Shivering, Gabriel rubbed his hands together.

The chill lifted suddenly, as if it had been a brief touch by a ghost.

Birthday jitters, he thought. He turned thirty today. His life was going so well for a thirty-year-old man—a thirty-year-old *black* man, especially—that he couldn't help feeling anxious. Undeservedly blessed. As if someone in power was going to decide he didn't deserve his good fortune, and would snatch his life from under his feet without warning.

Unlike many successful people who'd battled through difficult circumstances on their climb to the top and feared falling to the bottom of the ladder, Gabriel never had tasted rough times. His anxiety had no basis in past struggles. He led a charmed, enviable life, always had. T.L. Reid, his father, had made sure of that. Pops had vowed that no child of his was going to endure the troubles he'd faced on his own path to prosperity. Gabriel and his baby sister, Nicole, knew nothing but good times and happiness.

Still, each new birthday brought deep reflection on the state of his life, and reflection led to worries that a hammer was going to fall and smash everything he prized to bits. Gabriel didn't understand the source of the anxiety. But it sat on his stomach like a sour, undigested meal.

A knock at the door pulled him out of his brooding. His father stepped into the room.

Looking at his father was like viewing himself after a twenty-five-year, digital age progression. They shared the same lean, six-foot build. The smooth, mocha complexion. The unusual eyes—a shade of gray, like tarnished nickels. They both had close-cropped haircuts and neatly trimmed goatees, too, though streaks of silver ran through his father's hair.

The main difference was in their facial features. Although they were a handsome pair, obviously father and son, his father's face was all sharp angles, while Gabriel had a soft, baby face.

Folding his arms over his chest, Pops leaned against the long, mahogany conference table. "Morning, Gabe. Still in here thinking about the fortune you're going to be earning us?"

Reid Construction offered services in real estate development, general contracting, program management, property management, and construction. It was one of only a handful of black-owned corporations of its kind in the United States. His father, Theodore Lee Reid, known in the community as T.L., had founded the company twenty-seven years ago, building it from a one-man operation to a nationally recognized firm that employed a hundred and fifty people and had enjoyed revenue in excess of fifty million dollars last fiscal year.

Gabriel had worked in the company, in various capacities, for much of his life. He'd been promoted to vice president of operations two years ago, upon completing his MBA at Emory. According to their succession plan, he would assume the CEO mantle in five years, but the truth was that since Gabriel had been a toddler, his dad had been grooming him to become the leader. Everything he'd learned about the business, he'd learned at his father's feet.

To hear Pops tell it, Gabriel was already filling his father's giant footsteps. In the client meeting that had concluded fifteen minutes ago, Gabriel had closed a deal that would add nine million dollars in revenue to the coffers of Reid Construction. A massive project for terminal renovations at Hartsfield-Jackson Atlanta International Airport, it was the most lucrative contract Gabriel had ever steered from inception through completion without his father's guiding hand.

"Thanks, Pops," Gabriel said. "But you know I couldn't have done it without you."

"All I've done was help you stretch your wings. You've been soaring on your own for a while now. I'm proud of you."

Gabriel smiled, but something in his smile must have looked false, because Pops approached him, his brow creased.

"Something wrong?" Pops asked. "You look as if the deal has fallen through."

Gabriel glanced out the window. The stormy sky swirled like a whirlpool. A fine drizzle had begun to snap against the glass.

"I just feel *too* lucky sometimes," Gabriel said. "As if things can't keep going this well for me. You know what I mean?"

"I'd never let anything bad happen to you." Pops put his arm around Gabriel. "I take care of my family. Since when have I let you stumble?"

Gabriel knew the answer: never. Pops took care of his family, like he said. That was his father's primary duty—to ensure that his wife and children were taken care of, in every sense. The family home was an estate in a secluded neighborhood, the mansion full of every conceivable creature comfort. Gabriel and his little sister had attended the city's best private schools. They'd taken exciting family vacations twice a year, and Gabriel had seen more exotic locales by the age of twelve than most people saw in a lifetime. When Gabriel reached college age, he attended Morehouse College, Pops's alma mater, to complete his undergrad work, and, of course, a lucrative position at the company had been awaiting him upon graduation. He'd never even worked for anyone other than his father.

But Pops's attention to Gabriel's well-being went further than that; he was there whenever the winds of ordinary life threatened to blow Gabriel in the wrong direction, too. When a bully had taunted Gabriel in sixth grade, Pops had placed a call to the principal and gotten the bully's parents involved in remedying the situation. When Gabriel failed to make the cut for the freshman high school basketball team, Pops had talked to the coach, and, miraculously, Gabriel found himself suiting up for games. As recently as five months ago, when Gabriel had been ticketed for speeding on I-85, Pops had called a judge—a golf buddy of his—and the ticket was thrown out and a warning issued to Gabriel instead.

No problem was too minor for Pops's benevolent involvement. Once, Pops had been visiting Gabriel and had opened the refrigerator to get a beer. He'd apparently been dissatisfied with the amount of food inside, because when Gabriel came home the next day, the refrigerator was stocked with enough provisions to feed a family of five, and a note attached to the door said, "My boy has to eat well."

Gabriel appreciated his father's concern, but he often thought Pops went too far. He was a thirty-year-old man, for God's sake. When was Pops going to realize that and stop intervening whenever he hit a pothole in his life?

"I've never let you fail," Pops said. "Is that a true statement?"

Gabriel wanted to tell his father to back off, but he couldn't. He loved his dad, and his father only wanted the best for him. He didn't want to spurn his father's assistance and hurt his feelings.

Gabriel summoned a smile. "That's true."

Pops squeezed his shoulder. "Anyway, why are you hanging around here? It's your birthday—your *thirtieth* birthday. Why don't you take the rest of the day off?"

"I've got work to do, Pops. I've got another meeting at eleven; then I need to put in a call to—"

"All that can wait, man. I'm not asking you to take off. As your boss, I'm *ordering* you." He grinned. "My boy's not gonna spend his thirtieth birthday working all day."

"Well, if you say so. Thanks."

"You've earned it, son."

Pops's words echoed in Gabriel's thoughts as he walked to his office to retrieve his belongings. *You've earned it, son.*

Had he really earned anything? Or had he only been lucky to be born into the right family?

His executive assistant was an elegant, silver-haired black woman affectionately known as Miss Angie. She smiled at him as he passed by.

"Someone's got a delivery from a certain young lady," Miss Angie said.

"Is that so? Let me check it out." He walked inside his office. It was a cavernous space, clean and orderly, full of polished mahogany furniture, comfortable leather chairs, vibrant art work, and lush plants. Pops had hired an interior decorator for him.

A vase full of colorful lilies, tulips, and roses stood on the large desk. A Mylar balloon announcing HAPPY BIRTHDAY! floated above the bouquet.

He read the card attached to the vase.

Happy Birthday, Babyface, the card read. It was signed, *Love, Dana.*

She'd had flowers delivered to his job. His fiancée sure knew how to surprise him.

He called Dana's number, but got her voice mail. Dana was a pediatrics resident at Emory and probably was in the midst of making her rounds. He left her a message asking her to call him back on his cell phone.

As he left, he told Miss Angie he was going home for the day and asked her to reschedule his meetings.

"T.L. already told me," she said.

"Oh, okay."

Pops was always one step ahead of him.

"Have a great birthday," Miss Angie said. "Tell Dana I said hi."

When Gabriel pushed through the glass double doors to exit the building, the rain was coming down harder. He opened his umbrella.

Reid Construction was headquartered in a sprawling, slate-gray, two-story building on a hundred-acre plot of land located near Cascade Road in southwest Atlanta. Lots of big windows, shady trees, and meticulous landscaping lent the headquarters an air of quiet professionalism.

The vast parking lot, full at this time of morning, offered

three reserved spaces in the row nearest the entrance. The first slot, for the CEO, was occupied by his father's black Mercedes-Benz S600 sedan; the second one, vacant, was for the chief financial officer, who was out on vacation; the third spot was for the vice president of operations, Gabriel. Rain drummed against his white Lincoln Navigator.

Driving away from the building, windshield wipers clicking across the glass, Gabriel switched on the radio. On V-103, a news reporter talked about a forecast for heavy rains and potential flooding, and cautioned drivers to slow down.

Slow down—yeah, right, Gabriel thought. *You'd have a better chance of negotiating world peace than you would convincing Atlanta drivers to slow down.*

He switched to another station. Jill Scott was singing "Golden," a midtempo groove about living life to the fullest.

Tapping the steering wheel in time with the beat, Gabriel started to feel better. His life was good; better than good, it was wonderful. He should be thankful and enjoy it. Stop waiting for disaster to strike. After all, a lot of people would kill to be in his shoes.

He pulled into a Shell gas station. As he refueled the Navigator, ruminating on the good old days of cheaper gasoline and trying to keep from getting wet, his cell phone rang.

"Hey, Birthday Boy," Dana said. "How's your day going?"

Although rain was falling in sheets, hearing Dana's voice was like sunshine breaking through the clouds.

"Great," he said. "Thanks for the flowers. That was a nice surprise."

"I'm glad you liked them. You still at the office? It sounds like you're outside in the rain."

"I'm going home. I closed the airport deal, so I took the rest of the day off. Pops's orders."

"Hmph. How nice of him."

Dana made no secret of her dislike for how much influence his father had on him. Dana and Gabriel had argued only once—happy couples didn't argue, in Gabriel's opinion—but the single argument they'd had came from her opinion that Gabriel was his dad's puppet. Her accusation had infuriated him. He loved his father, admired him, wanted to be like him. But he was ultimately his own man and made his own decisions. How could she say such a thing?

That argument had nearly ended their relationship. Since then, she tread carefully around the subject, but rarely passed up an opportunity to hint at her displeasure.

"He means well, Dana," Gabriel said. "I'm his only son."

"He tells you what to do as if you're a kid. You aren't twelve. You're thirty years old."

Gabriel clenched his teeth. She'd voiced the same thoughts he'd had earlier. But he didn't dare share that with her. It would be like siding against Pops.

"I don't want to talk about this right now," he said. "It's my birthday, remember?"

"Sorry," she said. "Anyway, congrats on closing the deal. That's great news."

"Thanks," he said. He almost added, *Pops was impressed, too*, and decided against it. He didn't want to give her a chance to take another cheap shot at his father.

"I'm really looking forward to tonight," she said. "Eat light today because I plan to fatten you up."

She was coming to his house that evening to cook dinner. She was such a fabulous cook that he'd been anticipating the meal for almost a week.

"You still haven't told me what you're cooking," he said.

"It's a surprise. One of many surprises I've got in store for you."

"Is that so? How about a hint?"

"Let's just say this: after the surprise dinner, you'll get another surprise that'll help you work off all those excess calories."

"Really? You giving me a Bowflex or something?"

"Not telling. But . . . some flexing is involved." She giggled.

"Hmmm. Now you've got my imagination running wild."

"See you tonight, sweetie. I've gotta run. My little ones need me."

"Love you," he said.

Dana smooched the phone and then hung up.

Although they'd been dating for three years and had been engaged for four months, Dana had never verbally said, "I love you." She'd written it many times on cards and notes. But she'd never spoken the words.

Everyone had issues.

Gabriel left the gas station and took Cascade Road to I-285, known by locals as the Perimeter because it encircled a major portion of the Atlanta metro area. The highway would take him to his home in south Fulton County.

In spite of the downpour, cars zoomed past at speeds in excess of eighty miles an hour. Gabriel moved into the far right-hand lane.

Wind gusted. The rain came down harder, thrashing the elm trees that flanked the highway and assaulting Gabriel's Navigator like machine-gun fire.

Gabriel turned the wipers to the fastest speed, but they couldn't sweep the glass quickly enough to give him a clear field of vision.

"It's like something out of the Old Testament out here," he said under his breath.

Cars and trucks rocketed down the highway at murderous velocities. A handful of other drivers, the smart ones, had slowed and turned on their hazard lights.

He hit a puddle of water and the Navigator's tires lost their grip on the pavement for a beat, sending nausea wriggling through his stomach.

Okay, time to slow down. Let the rest of these speed racers risk their lives out here.

He decreased his speed to about forty. Water, spewed in the wake of the car ahead of him, blanketed the windshield. He lowered his speed a little more, to increase the distance between his vehicle and the one ahead.

At this rate it would take forever to get home, but he wasn't in a hurry. He planned to spend the day napping and, later, preparing for Dana's arrival.

He was immersed in an erotic fantasy of what he and Dana might do later that night when he noticed the cars ahead of him slowing, brake lights flaring. From the looks of it, they were braking because of a pool of water spread across the pavement, a mini lake produced by the highway's poor drainage in that area.

He gently applied the brakes.

There was an eighteen-wheeler in the lane on his immediate left, a car length ahead of him. The faded logo on the trailer, advertising a bakery company, proclaimed, LIFE IS DE-LICIOUS.

The truck, also attempting to slow, began to hydroplane. The trailer swayed dangerously.

"Hey, man." Gabriel tapped the horn to let the driver know he was there.

Water spraying from its tires and coating Gabriel's windshield, the truck rumbled closer, the gigantic trailer looming like a wall.

"Hey!" Gabriel mashed the horn.

The truck kept coming.

Gabriel pumped the brakes and wrestled the steering wheel, aiming to direct his vehicle to the shoulder of the highway. But the semi slewed into his lane and banged against Gabriel's SUV, and the effect was like a giant swatting a fly. The collision sent Gabriel spinning toward the guardrail, out of control, the steering wheel tearing through his fingers violently enough to scorch his skin.

Terror seized the pit of his stomach.

I'm gonna die, he thought with piercing clarity. *This is how it ends . . .*

He didn't even realize he was screaming.

The Navigator hurtled over the guardrail and plummeted down the embankment beyond.

Chapter 2

I'm gonna die. . . .
Crashing over the guardrail, hitting the muddy embankment, rolling end over end, Gabriel wanted to close his eyes and avoid witnessing his own demise. But fear had peeled back his eyelids.

The world spun. One second, he made out trees, the low gray sky spitting rain, and houses huddled against the storm. A second later, everything was upside down, as if he were traveling through a corkscrew loop on a roller coaster. His stomach lurched, bitter bile filling the back of his throat. He banged against the door and ceiling, pain spinning like broken glass through his body.

The air bags deployed and blew into his face, burning his skin.

In spite of the clamor of the rolling SUV, Gabriel heard the radio. Smokey Robinson was singing about cruising with someone you loved. Dana's face flashed through Gabriel's mind, and he felt a swelling of bittersweet love.

He was never going to see her again.

He was never going to see anyone again. This was the end.

Visions of his life paraded before his eyes. Snap shots of his youth, the good and the bad.

Faces floated through his mind's eye, too. He saw living relatives: Pops, Mom, his sister, his aunt, his uncles. Their eyes were teary, grieving.

I don't wanna die.

And then the dead charged into his thoughts: his grandparents, his best friend from high school who'd also died in a car wreck. Their arms beckoned to him, and they whispered, *Welcome.*

No, I don't wanna die . . .

As if from far away, he heard a crash, the groan of crushed metal, the tinkling of shattered glass.

The truck stopped rolling. He was upside down, his head mashed against the ceiling. He sensed rather than felt his twisted limbs.

Something wet seeped into his eyes. Too warm to be rain. Blood? His blood? Where was it coming from? He was numb, couldn't feel any of his injuries, couldn't so much as flex a finger.

The wetness suddenly faded. He felt himself drawn . . . *out.* As if he'd slipped outside of his flesh, like a snake shedding its skin. He moved away from the vehicle, floated away from the rain-torn day, and drifted into a nebulous realm of shadows.

Where am I?

Somewhere ahead, the fog cleared. A doorway of brilliant white light shone in the distance.

There really is a light on the Other Side.

He didn't want to die, but the white light seemed to exert a gravitational hold on him. It pulled him toward it.

I'm not ready to die, please.

Before the light absorbed him, a hulking, faceless humanoid form, as bright as lightning, emerged from the doorway. It pushed him away.

He was catapulted backward, like an astronaut marooned in outer space.

The shimmering portal closed.

Darkness enveloped him. Deep, complete.

Chapter 3

Gabriel awoke.

He blinked. The world was blurry; soft, warm light surrounded him. He smelled antiseptic odors, heard shoes squeaking against floors somewhere in the distance. Was he in a hospital?

As his eyes slowly focused, he saw that he was correct. He lay on his back in a bed, covered with crisp sheets. He wore a patient's gown, and a plastic I.D. bracelet on his wrist read GRADY MEMORIAL HOSPITAL.

Funny, he was a "Grady Baby," had been born at this very institution. Right now he felt so disoriented he might have just been birthed again.

He tried to sit up, and a hatchet of pain cleaved across his skull. He lay back on the pillows, cautiously touched his head. A thick bandage encircled his temple.

The left side of his rib cage ached, too. As he drew breaths, a sharp pain poked between his ribs, as if a dagger had been jabbed into his flesh.

What had happened?

The last thing he remembered was driving in the rain on

I-285, swerving to avoid an eighteen-wheeler, the truck smacking his Navigator and sending him flying toward the guardrail . . . and then his memory lapsed into darkness.

But it was easy to put the pieces together: he had survived the accident, and paramedics had brought him here.

He flexed his fingers, arms, and legs. His tendons were sore, and his muscles ached. But he didn't wear a cast, and felt no broken bones. He had only the assorted pains and a throbbing headache.

He was lucky. He could have been dead.

Although he'd awakened feeling as though his head were stuffed with down feathers, now his senses suddenly seemed heightened: colors were more vivid, noises were louder, scents were more intense. A bitter, medicinal flavor lay on his tongue; it was so sharp that he nearly gagged.

He looked around. The door was partly open; the bed on the other side of the room was vacant. A beige jacket lay folded on the upholstered chair next to his bed, along with an Octavia Butler paperback.

Dana's stuff. She must have stepped out of the room. He turned to the window and saw the night-shrouded Atlanta skyline beyond, lights twinkling in the skyscrapers.

How long had he been unconscious? The bedside digital clock read nine-forty, but he wasn't sure how much time had elapsed while he'd been unconscious. It could've been several hours. Or days. Even months.

Panic rose in his chest. He had to talk to someone. The call button for the nurse dangled beside his bed. He reached for it—and then pulled back.

He felt something strange. A cool, tingling sensation on his hands. As if he were running his palms across a blanket laden with static electricity.

He raised his hands to his face. They were the same long, slender fingers he'd always had, his palms were unmarked, and his hands were steady, not trembling.

Still, his fingers tingled. It was a pleasant feeling. He

felt—and it was weird to think this—but he felt *powerful*. As if magic resided in his hands.

He rubbed his palms together.

The prickly feeling passed.

What had that been all about? A blood circulation problem? Maybe. Or maybe nothing.

Light footsteps approached the doorway.

"Oh, thank God, you're awake," Dana said.

Gabriel couldn't remember ever being so glad to see her. Although Dana was simply dressed in jeans and a pink sweater, she had never looked more lovely to him.

Dana rushed to the bed and wrapped her arms around him. He held her close, buried his nose in her hair, inhaling so deeply of her clean, sweet scent that he got slightly dizzy.

Stepping back, Dana gave him a once-over. Her large brown eyes were tinged with red.

"How're you feeling?" she asked.

"I've had better days." His voice was raspy. Dana picked up a bottle of water from the bedside table and brought it to his lips. He sipped eagerly.

"Your parents and sister left barely ten minutes ago," she said. "They'd been here for a couple of hours, waiting for you to wake up. I was planning to stay for the rest of the night."

"How long have I been knocked out?"

She checked her watch. "Almost twelve hours." She gave a small smile. "It's still your birthday."

"Where's my gift?"

Her smile faltered. "Well . . ."

He grinned. "I'm kidding. Seeing you again is the best birthday gift I could ever have."

Dana sat on the bed with Gabriel, holding his hand, and filled him in on what had happened.

"Your truck went over the guardrail," she said. "You rolled

over five or six times on the way down the hill. Needless to say, the car's been totaled."

"Damn, I loved that ride."

"But you, Gabe . . . all you sustained were a few minor scratches, bruised ribs, and a concussion. No broken bones, no internal bleeding, no damaged organs. It's a miracle." She dabbed her eyes with a Kleenex.

He decided to avoid mention of his tingling fingers. She'd been worried about him; telling her something that might worry her further would serve no useful purpose, especially since he was almost certain that it was just a temporary, blood circulation problem. His hands had fallen asleep or something.

But it hadn't really felt like that, had it?

He touched her cheek. She held his hand against her face, kissed his fingers.

"You have no idea how scared I was," she said softly. "I thought I was going to lose you. I couldn't handle that."

When Dana Stevens was eleven years old, riding to a family reunion in Memphis with her dad, mom, and little brother, a drunk driver had struck their minivan. Her family had died on the way to the hospital; Dana had survived the accident with only a scar on her neck. Her more profound injuries were of the spirit.

Like many individuals who used tragedy to motivate themselves to achieve ambitious goals, Dana channeled her energy into academics. She graduated valedictorian from high school. Summa cum laude from Spelman. Top of her class at Morehouse School of Medicine. When she graduated from medical school, she chose to stay home and pursue her residency in pediatrics at Emory University, which would enable her to work in medically underserved communities throughout metro Atlanta. Places where she could help children in need—other young Danas in the world.

In spite of the fulfillment she found through her work, Gabriel knew she resisted forming close emotional attachments. She had a couple of friends from college, and a handful of relatives she spoke to regularly, but that was all. Her grandparents, who had raised her after the accident, had died, too, soon after she completed med school.

She and Gabriel had met at a Fourth of July cookout, hosted by a friend of his father's who'd been one of Dana's professors at Morehouse. Always looking out for his son, Pops had slyly hooked them up. Dana had been slow to open up to Gabriel, but he had persisted, initially because—truth be told—she was gorgeous. She was five-six, with soft cocoa skin, the toned body of a dancer, short and curly dark hair, dreamy cinnamon eyes, and a gentle smile, as if you and she shared an intimate secret. He was immediately hooked.

And he quickly learned that she had much more than beauty to offer. She had depth, intelligence, spunk, character. After one month of dating, he knew he'd met the future Mrs. Reid. But he took it slow; because of what she'd been through, Dana was a slow-track kind of woman, and rushing things would have driven her away.

But after three years, they finally were on the path to marriage, with an October wedding in the works. Nevertheless, Dana still couldn't bring herself to say that she loved him, out of an irrational but unshakable fear that once she said the words, she would lose him, just as she'd lost so many others close to her.

"I'm here, all in one piece, doc," he said. He tried to sit up, winced as pain stampeded across his head. "But I think I could use some Tylenol or something. My ribs hurt and I've got a killer headache."

"I'll have a nurse bring you something for that." She pushed the call button. "Meanwhile, I'll call your folks and let them know you're okay."

"I love you, Dana," he said.

She smiled, kissed him, and then picked up her cell phone to call his family.

* * *

A nurse gave Gabriel a couple of ibuprofen tablets to ease his pain, and checked his vital signs, all of which were satisfactory. After she finished, the physician on duty, Dr. Boone, came in to examine him. Dr. Boone was a thirtyish, ruddy-faced guy with reddish hair and an Alabama accent. He performed a physical exam on Gabriel under Dana's watchful eye.

"Lookin' good here, Gabriel," Dr. Boone said. He capped his pen and closed Gabriel's file. "I gotta say, after hearing about your wreck, you're one lucky fella. But we'd like to keep you here till the morning, for observation."

"Cool. Maybe I'll go to work tomorrow."

Dana glowered at him. But he was serious. He wanted to get back into his routine.

Boone noticed Dana's look. "You might wanna take it easy for a few days, Gabriel. You're gonna be in some pain for a while. You need lots of rest."

"Okay, I hear you," Gabriel said, mostly to pacify Dana. He tapped the bandage around his head. "So, when can I take this off? It feels like I've got a turban on my head."

"The swelling and bruise should go away within a week, two weeks at the most," Boone said. "Schedule a follow-up appointment with your primary-care physician. He'll take care of it for you."

"Or I will," Dana said, putting her arm around Gabriel protectively.

Boone looked from Dana to Gabriel. He grinned. "Like I said, you're a lucky fella. Any more questions, Dr. Stevens . . . Gabriel?"

"We're all good," Dana said. "Thanks, doctor."

"Take care of that guy," the physician said, and winked at Dana.

When the doctor left, Dana closed the door.

"I feel so much better," Gabriel said, "knowing I'll be married to a physician who'll take care of my every need."

"Yep, *every* need, babe," Dana said. Sitting on the bed,

she slipped her hand underneath the covers and cupped his manhood through the thin gown. He quickly grew erect. "Hallelujah. This definitely wasn't injured."

He pulled her down onto the bed until their noses were touching. "Can I get my birthday present now?"

"I'd love to, but something tells me there's a rule against a doctor getting her freak on with a patient in a hospital room."

"Betcha that's not in the Hippocratic oath."

She kissed his nose. "Tomorrow night, Birthday Boy. Promise."

"It's a date. Meantime, I need to take a piss."

"Spoken with all the crude charm of a man." She grasped his hands. "Come on. I'll help you up."

She helped him climb out of bed. His knees wobbled. She put her arm around his waist, steadying him, and walked with him to the restroom.

"I've got it from here," he said. He closed the door behind him.

After he emptied his bladder, he stood in front of the sink, gazing in the mirror. The bandage resembled a grotesque headband. His face, usually soft and chubby, looked a little gaunt, and there were red patches on his cheeks, thanks to the air bags smashing into his face. There was a cut on his chin the size of a dime.

But all in all, he felt good. His life had been turned upside down, but it was a mercifully brief shake-up, and when he went home tomorrow morning, everything would be back to normal.

He turned on the faucet. He washed his hands, bent over, splashed cool water onto his face.

When he rose, face dripping, and was about to reach for a towel, a shadowy figure stood in the mirror watching him.

He gave a startled yelp, stumbled backward, slipped, and fell to the floor on his butt. Pain fanned through his tailbone and rippled through his injured ribs.

"Gabe?" Dana knocked on the door. "You okay?"

Breathing hard, Gabriel looked around the restroom. It was barely larger than a shower stall. He was alone—of course.

"I'm fine," he said thickly. "I slipped."

"You need me?"

"No, I'm okay."

Heart knocking, Gabriel looked up at the mirror. He didn't get a full view of the glass from where he sat on the floor. He wasn't sure he wanted one.

What the hell had he seen?

He grasped the lip of the sink. Groaning, he pulled himself to his feet, checked in the mirror again.

He saw only his damp face. No one else.

It was his imagination, he reasoned. Post-traumatic stress disorder. He'd been through what could have been a fatal accident, and was badly shaken. It should come as no surprise that his brain was a little loopy.

He reached for a towel. Then he stopped. He felt the cool tingling on his fingers again.

This time the sensation faded after a few seconds.

He mopped his face dry.

Something was happening to him, and he was beginning to wonder whether the theory that he was experiencing normal aftereffects from the accident was adequate.

It seemed stranger than that. Much stranger.

Chapter 4

Night. Although the day's rains had passed, tatters of silvery clouds littered the sky, pieces scudding across the fat, pale moon.

The smoke-gray, 1970 Chevy Chevelle SS with Illinois plates devoured I-75 South, roaring out of Tennessee and across the Georgia state line. The custom-built V8 engine growled like a wild thing; the chrome, twenty-inch Letani wheels spun like circular saws. The Chevelle tore through the night at ninety-five miles an hour, far above the posted speed limit of seventy.

Isaiah Battle didn't care about speed limits. Especially today.

Today, June 6, was his birthday. He'd turned thirty.

The Alpine stereo blasted a song called "Gangsta Gangsta," recorded by the seminal West Coast rap group, N.W.A. Ice Cube, a member of the act in his pre-Hollywood days, spat out savage, profanity-laden lyrics. The speakers, strategically positioned throughout the car, enveloped Isaiah in a cocoon of bone-rattling beats.

Isaiah rapped along with Cube. He didn't consider himself a gangsta or a thug or a street soldier—though he had once fit the description of such a man. He'd grown up in the Robert Taylor Homes, which had used to be one of the roughest projects in Chicago. He'd lived his life in and out of the penal system. He'd committed heinous crimes—armed robbery, assault with a deadly weapon, even murder.

But that was in another life.

He was a different person, if not on the surface, then at least in spirit.

Still, he had an abiding love for hip-hop and urban culture. Some things hadn't changed.

His appearance hadn't changed, either, and that was a good thing. He was a lean, muscular six feet. Bald head. Clean-shaven. Handsome, sculpted, matinee idol features; women often said that he favored the actor Morris Chestnut. And he had those eyes. They were gray, and gleamed like shards of worn steel.

His stomach rumbled. He hadn't eaten since he'd left Chicago that morning. He saw an exit for Dalton nearing, and he took it.

He parked in front of a Waffle House. A few dusty pickup trucks and old cars sat in the parking lot. A couple of the trucks had Confederate flags plastered proudly to the rear bumpers.

Welcome to the Deep South. Rednecks in effect.

There was a bite in the evening air, so he shrugged into his leather jacket and then went inside.

The aroma of meat and potatoes sizzling in grease greeted him. A few leathery faced men turned from the counter and looked at him hard, as if he had interrupted a Ku Klux Klan powwow.

"Evening, folks," he said in his best Southern drawl.

None of them answered him.

Isaiah sat in a booth in the corner. A pretty, redheaded waitress, smacking bubble gum, came to the table to take his order. Her name tag read SUE ANN. Figured.

He ordered four soft scrambled eggs, a double order of hash browns "scattered, smothered, and covered," a side of waffles, and sides of bacon and sausage. He requested coffee and orange juice, too.

It was enough food for two people, but he was ravenous. Besides, no matter how much he ate, he didn't gain an ounce of fat. He'd always had one of those supercharged metabolisms, like a jungle predator.

He loved breakfast food, too, especially late at night. It reminded him, pleasantly, of his childhood, and how he'd sneak into the kitchen in the wee hours of the morning to get a bowl of Cheerios. He'd sometimes eaten those same Cheerios for dinner, too, if Mama was strapped for cash.

"Hungry tonight, ain't you?" Sue Ann asked. Her green eyes sparkling, she swayed closer to the table. "I like me a man with a big appetite."

He arched his eyebrows. This white girl was flirting with him.

It didn't surprise him. Women loved him. Based on his appearance, they thought he was a bad boy, and women loved men like him, even though logic dictated that they shouldn't. People were rarely logical, especially when sex was involved.

Her gaze never leaving his face, Sue Ann blew a bubble, sucked it in expertly, and smiled at him.

He gave her a deliberate once-over. She was probably in her early twenties, part of that generation of white kids that thought black hip-hop stars and athletes were the coolest creatures to walk the earth. She had a slender build, long legs, firm titties. One eyebrow was pierced, and he glimpsed a tattoo of a red rose on her chest, underneath a spatter of freckles.

He started to reply, and then hesitated. The diner had fallen silent. He felt the hot gazes of the rednecks on him, watching their exchange, wondering why Sue Ann was talking to this black guy for so long. *He better not be trying to flirt with her, goddamnit, or else we'll show him, just like those good old boys in Mississippi showed Emmett Till.*

Isaiah sensed their rising anger, their envy, their hatred. It rose off their auras like sour sweat, promising danger if he dared to tread further.

But none of these people knew what kind of man he was.

He gave Sue Ann a bright smile. "My appetite isn't the only big thing I've got."

"That so?" She didn't blush. She met his gaze, a sure sign that she'd been around. "I saw that nice car of yours. You from Illinois?"

"Chi-Town," he said.

"That so? You headed to 'Lanta?"

He nodded. "I'm going to a . . . I guess you could call it a family reunion."

"That's nice; wish my family did stuff like that. . . ." She blinked. "Hey, I better put your order in, huh? You so hungry, you liable to eat me up."

"And you'd love it," he said.

She giggled. "Be right back." She sashayed away. Damn, she had a booty like a sista. He noticed more and more white chicks sporting sista-girl asses these days. Maybe they were getting implants down there or something.

The rednecks hunched over the counter watched him and Sue Ann, displeasure evident on their faces. After Sue Ann put in the order with the cook, she went to refresh the guys' coffee. One of them, a tanned, Mt. Everest of a man, grabbed her arm and whispered choice words in her ear. The giant redneck kept his gaze on him as he spoke to the waitress, as if to say, "Yeah, I'm talking to her 'bout you. What you gonna do about it?"

Isaiah calmly sipped his coffee. Sue Ann finally slipped out of the guy's grasp, massaging her arm. Although she'd promised to be right back, she avoided him until she brought his food.

"So," he said as she spread the plates in front of him, "your boyfriend scare you away from me?"

"Bo ain't my boyfriend, but he wanna be," she said. "He don't like black people too much, neither, no offense."

So the guy was named Bo. How typical. Had his parents picked it out of the *Book of Redneck Baby Names?*

"No offense taken," he said. "I figured as much."

"I wanna talk to you some more, but we can't do it here. You want my number?"

"Sure."

Smiling secretly, she wrote her number on a napkin and slid it to him. The big guy, Bo, leaned back on his stool, watching them.

"Bo's breaking his neck peeping us," he said.

"Butthole." She rolled her eyes. "Call me, 'kay?"

"Promise." He tucked the napkin away in his pocket. He had no intention of calling her—he would be too busy in Atlanta—but why tell her that? Better to let her fantasize about what might have been. If nothing else, it would drive her redneck friends crazy.

Isaiah shoveled down his food with single-minded attention. The meal contained enough fat to clog the arteries of a gray whale, but it was delicious. He cleaned his plate. When you grew up in a household where you might not know when the next meal was coming, you learned to fill your belly at every opportunity.

He left a generous tip, got up, and walked to the cash register. Bo and two of his buddies got up, too, trailing behind him.

He felt the familiar tightening in his stomach, the precursor to violence. How far would this go?

He paid the bill and pushed through the exit, emerging into the chilly night. He shoved his hands deep into his pockets and began to walk to his car.

He heard Bo and his homies following. He didn't glance over his shoulder. Let them assume he was afraid to look behind him.

But he clenched his hands into fists.

I wish they would try something. I wish they would.

"Hey, boy!" one of them called.

Near his car, Isaiah stopped, his spine rigid. These guys were a trip. They were like a parody of that old white supremacist flick, *The Birth of a Nation*. Had he been unwittingly placed in a time machine and transported into the nineteenth century?

He turned around. Bo stood in the middle of the parking lot. His buddies flanked him, like pet dogs. Bo crossed his thick arms over his broad chest. His eyes were blue ice.

Facing Bo, any other man would have been quaking in his shoes. But Isaiah only said, softly, "My name isn't Boy."

"He say his name ain't Boy," Bo said. He laughed and his pals joined in. Bo's laughter died and his face hardened. "Then maybe your name is Nigger."

All he'd wanted was to grab a hot meal at the tail end of his drive. But trouble followed him, like exhaust fumes.

"We don't like niggers talking to our women," Bo said. He glanced at the Chevelle, saw the Illinois plate. " 'Specially Yankee niggers."

Isaiah had heard enough. Time to set it off.

"I'll talk to any woman I want, you stupid redneck," he said to Bo. "It's not my fault your woman prefers big dicks and dark meat."

Bo's lips parted in disbelief. Hesitation passed over his face. *This boy's a little too cocky*, he knew Bo was thinking. Maybe he's got a gun in that jacket of his.

Isaiah slid his hands out of his pockets to show that he carried no weapons.

"You gonna let that Yankee nigger talk to you like that, Bo?" one of the buddies said. "I think you need to teach him a lesson."

Bo wiped his mouth, looked around. Confidence returned to his face as he saw that his boys had his back and realized that this black guy was defenseless. He flexed his big muscles and thundered forward.

"I'll show you how we handle niggers in Georgia," Bo said.

Bo swung his fist at him, a wild haymaker.

Isaiah didn't try to evade the blow. He spread his arms and took the hit. Bo's fist slammed into his marble-hard slab of abdominal muscles. Isaiah stumbled backward and fell to the asphalt on his butt.

That was nothing, he thought.

He drew in a breath. His heart beat at a tranquil *lub-dub-dub*.

But a thick vein began to pulse in the center of his forehead. Energy stirred at the base of his spine, grew hotter, stronger, like lava in a volcano set to erupt.

This feeling, this *power*, was part of his new life, but it felt as comfortable to him as something he'd been doing since he was a child, like riding a bicycle.

Focus.

Isaiah looked up.

Bo charged forward.

The energy rushed up his spine and exploded into his brain. He trembled in anticipation.

Command.

Bo had started to draw back his leg, probably to kick him in the ribs with one of his muddy construction boots.

"Freeze," he said to Bo in the strident tone of a master commanding a dog.

Bo's eyes widened.

The redneck stood stock still, as if he had been flash frozen like a side of beef.

Although he had issued the command to Bo, his friends paused, too, confusion on their faces.

Isaiah moved fast.

He propelled himself to his feet in one fluid motion,

bringing his fist upward. He smashed the heel of his hand into Bo's nose, breaking it, driving shattered cartilage into the man's brain.

Bo shrieked like a girl. He flopped to the pavement. His limbs twitched. Blood oozed from his nostrils.

Bo's buddies looked at their fallen leader, looked at him.

Isaiah stepped toward them. "Want to try me?"

They turned and fled.

He gazed down at the redneck. The guy looked comatose. In fact, he might die.

Isaiah spat on him.

"My name isn't Boy, or Nigger," he said. "My name is Isaiah Battle."

Isaiah turned on his heel, climbed into his car, and drove away into the night.

Chapter 5

On Tuesday morning, Gabriel was discharged from the hospital. He shuffled out of the lobby wearing jeans, a button-down shirt, and sneakers, clothes Dana had brought for him the previous night. His head, wrapped in a fresh bandage, ached intermittently, and his ribs were still sore. He planned to pop painkillers all day, to keep his discomfort at bay.

He hadn't experienced another episode of tingling hands—or glimpsed another dark figure in a mirror. Barring another occurrence, he'd decided to store both strange incidents in the Do Not Open room in his mind, and forget about them.

But if something unexplainable happened again . . . well, he would try to avoid thinking about it.

June weather had returned to Atlanta. The sun shone brightly, the temperature was in the low eighties, and the cloying humidity made stepping outdoors like going into a steam room. He loved it.

His mother had arrived to pick him up. She waited in front of the hospital in the late-model, silver Jaguar coupe Pops had bought her for their thirtieth wedding anniversary.

Gabriel opened the door and tossed his bag on the backseat.

"Hey, Mom." He kissed her on the cheek. "Thanks for picking me up."

"Let me look at you." Scrutinizing the bandage on his head, she turned his face from one side to the other. Marge Reid had a degree in elementary education and no formal medical training, but she examined him with the keen gaze of a physician—Dr. Mom. "They sure booted you out of there fast. Are you positive you feel okay?"

"I'm all right. My head throbs a little, and I'm kinda sore, but the doctor said that'll go away soon."

"Hmph." She looked skeptical. "What does Dana think?"

"She's fine with it. Really, Mom, I'm okay. I came out of that accident unscathed. It was a miracle."

At the mention of miracles, the doubt finally left her face. She nodded. "Yes, indeed, it was a blessing from the Lord." She pulled the car away from the hospital.

Gabriel had to smile at his mother's concern for him. He was the elder of his mother's two children, and her only son, which naturally made him a prime candidate to be a mama's boy. When he was growing up, she'd baby him as much as Pops would allow—which wasn't much. "Don't do that, Marge, you're gonna spoil the boy," had been his father's constant refrain. Mom had often nurtured Gabriel in secret, away from his father's stern eye. She'd let him sleep late when school wasn't in session; Pops believed in rising at dawn every day, even on the weekends. During the summer, she'd let him and his best friend spend all day at Six Flags Over Georgia, an amusement park—at times when she would tell Pops that she planned to keep Gabriel at home to help her with housework. She'd give him a ride to school whenever he missed the bus, and never tell his father. Pops despised tardiness and would have been incensed that Gabriel had missed his ride.

Pops had spoiled him, too, but in a way he thought was

appropriate for a boy: Pops would pay him for working, but the compensation was sometimes out of proportion to the labor Gabriel had actually performed. Ten dollars for taking out the trash. Fifty bucks for cutting the lawn. A hundred for raking the autumn leaves. It was as if the mundane tasks Gabriel performed were an excuse for his father to slip some money into his pocket.

Pops was similarly generous with Gabriel's sister, and with Mom, especially. "A man is only as successful as his wife looks" was one of Pops's axioms, and he'd made sure that Mom had the best of everything. This morning Mom wore a navy-blue Gucci business suit that complemented her reddish-brown complexion and slender frame, and Ferragamo pumps. Her long, dark hair, streaked with regal strands of gray, was impeccably styled, and her nails were manicured. She wore understated, but very expensive, gold jewelry, and her diamond wedding ring, which Pops had recently upgraded, was a flawless, three-karat rock in a platinum setting.

The irony was that Mom was the least materialistic person Gabriel knew. She allowed Pops to shower her with fine things because it made him feel good, as if he was doing his duty as a husband, but the reality was that Mom was more concerned with spiritual matters. She was a highly active member of their local Baptist church, teaching a Bible class for teenage girls, singing in the women's choir, and serving in shelters for the homeless. You never caught her without her Bible close at hand, and she quoted scripture so fluently that Gabriel sometimes couldn't be sure which of her spoken words were hers and which ones she'd culled from the Good Book.

As they drove through downtown, strains of Mahalia Jackson filtered from the stereo. Mom sang along softly. She had a good voice; her singing reminded Gabriel of when he was a child, a time when she would often coax him to sleep with a lullaby.

They approached the entrance ramp for I-85/I-75, the

downtown connector. Although it was almost ten o'clock in the morning, after rush hour, traffic crawled like a wounded animal.

"I wonder where this congestion is coming from," Mom said. "After I drop you off, I'm meeting some of the Link sisters for brunch. I don't want to be late."

His mother was a longtime member of the Links, an international organization of black women that aimed to advance civic, educational, and cultural agendas for their respective communities. Mom had been a grade school teacher when she and Pops had married, but the success of Pops's business had enabled her to leave the classroom so she could focus on raising their children and pursuing outside activities. Her Links chapter was one of her many interests.

As they inched forward through traffic, Gabriel saw flashing blue and red lights ahead, the telltale signs of a wreck.

Like ice water, dread spilled over him.

The victims of the accident were strangers to him, but the sight resurrected the memory of his own glimpse of Death's face.

Although he didn't want to, he thought of his tingling palms—and of the figure in the mirror. The thoughts flew like bats through his mind, hooked their teeth deep into him. Forgetting about that stuff was impossible. He was deluding himself if he thought he could.

"Oh, Lord, it's an accident," Mom said. "I hope no one's hurt."

"Me, too."

Mom must have picked up on his tension. She touched his arm, worry stamped on her face. "You okay, Gabriel?"

"I'm okay," he said. But he went on. "Remember that time you had a concussion? When you and Pops were driving to visit Uncle Bobby and got in an accident?"

"Yes—goodness, that was years ago." She shook her head. "What about it?"

"How'd you feel afterward? Did anything . . . strange happen?"

"Strange?"

"Any bad headaches, anything like that?"

"I do remember having an awful headache for a day or two. But that's not strange for someone who's had a concussion. What's wrong, Gabriel?"

He never should have asked the question. Mom was ready to drive back to Grady and demand that the doctors reevaluate him. He'd been hoping that she would admit to weird side effects. A pins-and-needles sensation in her hands. Maybe seeing visions in mirrors. No such luck. It was time to change the subject, or else she would worry further.

"I'm fine, Mom," he said. "I guess seeing that accident up ahead kinda shook me up."

"Brought back bad memories?"

"Guess so."

"Bless your heart." Mom patted his arm. "After your father and I had that accident, I was nervous riding in a car for about a month. But if you're feeling ill—"

"Mom, I'm okay. Seriously."

"You know I love to mother you, baby. I miss that sometimes, what with you living in your own house and about to get married."

"I'll always be your son. I'd better be, 'cause I don't wanna give up your peach cobbler."

"Can Dana make cobbler?"

"Dana's cobbler is good, but it's not the same as yours. Don't tell her I said that, by the way."

"It'll be our little secret." Mom smiled and then redirected her attention to the traffic.

They drove past the accident. An Oldsmobile and a Mustang had collided, both of the vehicles looking as if they had been smashed in a giant trash compactor. Paramedics rushed a gurney toward an ambulance, the gurney's white sheet concealing a victim's prone body. Or corpse.

That could've been me yesterday.
Shuddering, Gabriel looked away.

Mom pulled into the driveway of Gabriel's house. A dark blue Corvette convertible was parked in front of the two-car garage. It was his dad's weekend, cruising ride.

"Is Pops here?" Gabriel asked.

"He left the 'Vette for you to drive since your car was to-taled." Mom dug a set of keys out of her purse and dropped them in his hand. "Keep it until you get the insurance and whatnot with yours squared away."

"He didn't have to do this, Mom. I was going to rent a car."

"You know your father. He's always looking out for his boy."

Gabriel formed a fist around the keys. Once again his father had reviewed his situation, diagnosed a problem, and provided a solution. Gabriel loved and appreciated his father's concern, but sometimes he overstepped his bounds. Couldn't Pops allow him to handle anything on his own?

"Your father only wants to help," Mom said, as perceptive of his moods as ever. "It would hurt his feelings if you don't take the car."

"I'm a grown man. I don't need him to do everything for me."

"Fine. Give me back the keys. I'll tell him you don't appreciate his help."

"I didn't mean it like that."

"You should be grateful that you have a father like him," Mom said. "Do you know how many young men don't have their fathers in their lives? Do you know what they would give to be blessed with a father who loves you as much as yours does?"

Gabriel wished he had kept his mouth shut. Mom was his dad's biggest champion, always had been. She was from the old school, believing that it was a wife's duty to submit to her husband's leadership and support his position on important family matters. She wasn't going to side with Gabriel over his father. He should have known better.

"I'll keep the car," he said.

"And you should call your father and thank him for providing it. Honor your parents."

The only way to settle this was to agree with her.

"You're right. Thanks for the ride, Mom. I'll see you at the party this weekend."

He was having a birthday bash at the 755 Club, a ritzy establishment located inside Turner Field. Pops—big surprise—was funding the celebration, while Dana, Mom, and his sister were organizing it.

"Stop by to see me before then," Mom said. She winked. "Maybe I'll have some of that peach cobbler, just for you."

"I'll be there."

Chapter 6

Home sweet home.

Gabriel lived in Glenwood Mills, a golf community of spacious brick homes with well-tended lawns. An eighteen-hole golf course wound throughout the fringes of the neighborhood. Gabriel's own house was a four-bedroom, two-story model sitting on a half acre of verdant Bermuda grass that overlooked the fairway for the sixth hole.

He'd lived there for three years, and he and Dana planned to stay there after they wed in October. Due to traffic congestion and high real estate prices on the northern rim of metro Atlanta, the south side was booming, and he wanted to keep the house for a while longer to enjoy the increase in equity.

True to form, Pops had offered to give him the down payment on the property, but Gabriel, in a rare display of independence, had come up with the funds on his own. This place was *his*, purchased with his own money, and that made him especially proud.

He unlocked the door and went inside.

Perhaps it was due to his close call with death, but he

looked around his house as if he were a first-time visitor. It was tastefully furnished with contemporary furniture, in earth tones. Hardwood floors. Stainless-steel appliances. Granite countertops. Cathedral ceilings. Colorful, jazz-themed prints on the walls. Lots of framed photographs filled the rooms, many of them showing Gabriel and his family, others featuring him and Dana.

He truly had been blessed. Even a collision with an eighteen-wheeler and a vicious tumble down an embankment had failed to ruin his good life. It was as though a magic spell had been cast on him at birth, to ward off misfortune.

As he walked to the master bedroom on the main level, the house seemed unnaturally quiet. He felt out of place being home on a Tuesday morning. He'd rather go to the office. But his physician had advised him to take the day off and rest, and Dana would chew him out if she found out that he'd ignored the doctor's orders. He would have to stay home all day.

A cool breeze had been blowing outdoors, so he opened several windows to let fresh air circulate. He leafed through his mail. Turned on the TV and channel surfed; saw nothing of interest. Dug inside the refrigerator, only to discover that he had no appetite. Logged on to the Internet to check his e-mail and found nothing but enticements for porn sites and online casinos.

This isn't going to work, he thought. Like his father, he was a chronic workaholic. He was happiest when he was engaged in productive activity.

He called his insurance company to follow up on the claim for his wrecked vehicle. But after sitting on hold for twenty minutes, he hung up and decided to call back later.

Out of ideas, he decided to simply do some cleaning. Dana was coming over that evening to cook a birthday dinner for him—something she'd planned to do last night until his accident intervened—and while the house wasn't a pigsty, it could use some straightening up. He got a bottle of Windex and a roll of paper towels, and he went to the master bathroom to start cleaning in there.

The wind, blustering through the opened bedroom windows, slammed the bathroom door behind him. Startled, he almost dropped the window cleaner.

Gabriel laughed, a little uneasily, at his jumpiness. *Relax, Gabe.*

He approached the large mirror. Last night's vision—or hallucination—flashed through his mind.

But he was the only person reflected in the glass. As expected.

He looked away, and then quickly turned back to the mirror. The same baby-faced mug, a little more gaunt than usual, a bandage on his head, stared back at him.

"You're nuts, man." He laughed at himself.

Realizing that he needed another cleaning solution for the toilet, sinks, and garden tub, he turned away and walked to the bathroom door. He reached for the knob.

The knob twisted. The door swung open.

Before he touched it.

Gabriel backed away from the door so rapidly that he nearly tripped over his own feet. He moved all the way to the other side of the bathroom, the small of his back mashed against the hard edge of the vanity.

He stared at the half-open door. He tried to detect movement on the other side, a shifting shadow, anything. But he saw nothing.

"Who's there?" he asked. His voice crackled.

He heard only his shallow breaths, and his racing heartbeat. No intruder's footstep. He *felt* alone in the house, too.

So how had the door opened?

His hands, clenched in fists at his sides, began to tingle.

He studied his fingers. They looked normal, but it felt as

though cool sparks danced across his skin—the same curious sensation that had occurred last night.

What was going on?

As he contemplated the question, the tingling subsided.

Gabriel wiped his hands on his pants and returned his attention to the doorway. He stepped forward and looked behind the door. There was no one there, of course.

A breath of wind whispered inside the room and teased the curtains.

"The wind did it," he said.

But he didn't really believe it; it was a woefully inadequate theory, the equivalent of slapping a Band-Aid on a gunshot wound. The wind could not have twisted the knob like a corporeal being and opened the door.

That left him with only two possible explanations.

The first: his house was haunted. He thought that was as likely as the theory that the world was flat. He was a man of reason and logic. He didn't believe in ghosts, hauntings, any of that superstitious nonsense.

So that left him with the second, and far more disturbing and plausible, possibility: he had hallucinated the whole thing, which meant he was losing his mind.

Chapter 7

On Tuesday, Isaiah performed reconnaissance.

He'd arrived in metro Atlanta late last night. After checking into a Days Inn located off I-75 in Marietta, he was asleep within three minutes of hitting the mattress.

Nightmares tormented him. Dreams of gunfire, death, and eternal darkness. Fearsome visions plagued his sleep every night, and though they visited him daily, they were no less terrifying. It was the price he paid for his history of violence; he'd suffered such dreams since he was a teenager.

As he showered, he ignored the scar tissue on his chest. The mark of the bullet that had nearly stolen his life.

Dressing in jeans, a black T-shirt, and Timberlands, Isaiah kept his attention on a photograph he'd placed on the nightstand: a snapshot of his mother and father, smiling as they dined at a Japanese restaurant in Chicago, so many years ago.

It was the only keepsake he'd taken from Mama's house after she was murdered.

Isaiah took the photo with him as he left the hotel. He

kept the picture on his person at all times. To make sure that he always remembered his promise.

No matter what . . .

He took I-75 South into the heart of Atlanta. He wanted to take in the skyline of this so-called City Too Busy To Hate, this monument to the New South—and his new home.

Skyscrapers jutted into the hazy morning sky like giant blunt knives, sunlight coruscating along their edges. Gigantic billboards flashed enticements for air travel, lotteries, and Braves games. Opiates for the masses.

But at road level, highways I-75 and I-85 merged, creating an ugly traffic snarl. Drivers chatted on cell phones, weaving in and out of their correct lanes. Others cut off one another with impunity and switched lanes with reckless abandon, not bothering to use turn signals. A soccer mom in a Honda Odyssey swerved in front of Isaiah, nearly clipping his bumper, and when he tapped his horn to alert her of what she'd done, she shot her hand out the window and gave him the finger.

Isaiah cursed under his breath. These people had lost their damn minds.

He was thankful when he inched out of the clogged traffic and made it to the exit ramp for I-20, which would take him to southwest Atlanta.

Twenty minutes later he turned into the entrance of Reid Corporate Park.

It was an impressive sight. Gently winding roads flanked with elms and dogwoods. Lush, manicured islands of grass. Walking trails curving around a gleaming lake and shady trees. The headquarters, located near the middle of the park, was a gray, two-story structure with lots of windows.

The building looked exactly as it did in the pictures he'd examined for so long.

Late-model cars filled the parking lot, as though everyone employed there was earning lots of money—or saddled with debt.

Isaiah cruised along the front of the building. There was a row of three reserved parking slots at the front. Expensive foreign automobiles occupied the spots belonging to the CEO and CFO.

Isaiah's gaze lingered on the black Mercedes sedan parked in the CEO's slot. The Georgia license tag read HNIC.

Head Negro in Charge, huh? We'll see about that.

The third parking slot, for the VP of operations, was vacant.

Isaiah frowned.

He parked in the far corner of the lot, dialed a number on his cell phone.

A woman answered, "Good morning, Reid Construction. How may I direct your call?"

"May I speak to Gabriel Reid, please?" Isaiah said, using his best Corporate America voice.

"Mr. Reid is out of the office today. Would you like his voice mail?"

"Oh, he is? Gosh, I'd wanted to chat with him about the proposal he submitted," he lied. "Do you know when he might return, ma'am?"

"Tomorrow, hopefully," she said. "He had a car accident yesterday and he's home recovering."

"I'm sorry to hear that. I hope he gets better soon."

"What did you say your name was, sir?" the woman asked, no doubt realizing she had shared personal information with a complete stranger.

"Pardon me? My cell's breaking up. . . ."

As she repeated her question, Isaiah hung up.

Gabriel Reid had gotten into a car wreck on his thirtieth birthday. What tough luck.

But Isaiah would continue with his plan. It was time to make his next stop.

Gabriel Reid's house.

*   *   *

Gabriel Reid lived in a subdivision that oozed buppie money. Big brick houses and large, trimmed lawns. Driveways full of Cadillac Escalades, Benzes, Lexuses, and BMWs. He knew black folks lived in these cribs because the license-plate frames boasted colleges such as Morehouse, Spelman, Florida A&M, Howard, and Tuskegee, and Greek organizations such as Alpha Phi Alpha, Delta Sigma Theta, Alpha Kappa Alpha, and so on, ad nauseum.

Isaiah curled his lip. Uppity-ass Negroes. Why did they have to advertise their educational backgrounds and Greek affiliations for the whole world to see? It proved that no matter how much money they made, they were still insecure.

He cranked up the volume on his Alpine car stereo, to let these bougie folks know that someone outside their caste had invaded their precious real estate. The speakers pumped out an early song by Cypress Hill, "How I Could Just Kill a Man." An anthem to homicide and ghetto insanity.

Nodding his head to the bass, he drove past Gabriel's house. His brick home was impressive for a man who lived alone and had just turned thirty.

A blue Corvette convertible was parked in front of the garage. The Georgia plate read MYVETT, which seemed, to Isaiah, insufferably conceited. "My Vett." As if he'd earned it.

As if he'd earned anything.

Isaiah completed a pass of the house, busted a U-turn, and parked against the curb, a couple of residences down from Gabriel's house. Since Gabriel was apparently home, he would keep a safe distance.

There would be plenty of time, later, for face-to-face conversation.

He opened the duffel bag that lay on the seat beside him. He removed a pair of Bushnell high-powered binoculars. He focused them on the house.

He spied Gabriel through a window on the first level.

The man was sweeping the floor. A bandage was wrapped around his head.

Isaiah's hands shook.

He had seen Gabriel before, in pictures, but viewing photos hadn't prepared him for the experience of seeing the guy in the flesh.

He and Gabriel looked so much alike, it was almost as if he were viewing a film of himself.

They had the same complexion, the identical lean, six-foot-tall build. Similar facial features.

He zoomed in for a closer look.

On closer scrutiny, he noticed differences. Gabriel's face was pudgier than his, as if storing deposits of baby fat. Gabriel had a short fade haircut, too, and a goatee, while Isaiah was clean-shaven and his dome was completely bald.

Isaiah wondered if they shared the same gray eyes. He couldn't be sure; the binoculars weren't powerful enough to allow him to discern eye color.

Gabriel moved differently, too. His movements were slow, a bit lazy—the movements of a man lulled by a sedentary, privileged lifestyle. Isaiah moved with the quick, economical grace of a man who'd spent his entire life on the edge.

As Isaiah watched, Gabriel set the broom against the wall and picked up a cordless phone. A grin spread across Gabriel's face. He rubbed his belly.

It was the perfect tableau of a man gorging himself on the good life.

"Spoiled motherfucker," Isaiah muttered.

Grinning and laughing as he talked to someone on the phone—probably a woman—Gabriel shuffled out of sight, disappearing deeper into his luxurious house. He reappeared moments later in the living room. He sat on a sofa and propped his feet on an ottoman. He sipped a glass of iced tea. Still yapping on the phone.

Isaiah had to restrain the urge to explode out of the car and rush to Gabriel's house.

"Patience," he advised himself. "Patience."

But patience wasn't his strong suit. He hated waiting, for

anything. That was one of the reasons why he'd committed so many crimes back in the day. Why work a minimum-wage job and sock away pennies in hopes of purchasing a new television, when you could easily break in someone's house and just take the damn thing? When every day might be your last, you learned to take the things you wanted to satisfy your desires immediately—because tomorrow might never come.

But he was a stronger person now. More disciplined. He had to stick to his plan.

So Isaiah quelled his turbulent emotions by imagining that he was the one sitting on Gabriel's sofa in that huge house. Sipping iced tea. Talking on the phone to a fine woman who was begging, eager to come over and fuck him.

I could live that life, Isaiah thought. *It could be mine.*

He continued to watch Gabriel, and his imagination was so vivid that, soon, he *was* sitting on that sofa, living that lavish lifestyle, and he looked out the window of his tastefully appointed living room and saw Gabriel Reid, standing in the front yard, bedraggled and beaten—and Isaiah waved at him, snapped the curtains shut, and poured himself another delicious glass of tea.

Chapter 8

After the episode in the bathroom, Gabriel cleaned the house thoroughly. As he put things in order and sanitized and swept various surfaces, he felt as though he were putting his thoughts back in order, too. By the time he had finished cleaning, he'd reached a conclusion about what had happened.

It was a fluke.

Everyone, at some time, experienced an event that could not easily be explained. For example, you think of your friend and how you'd like to talk to him, and a minute later your phone rings and it's him calling. Or you start humming a favorite song, and you switch on the radio, and lo and behold, that very song is playing. Or you decide to drive a different route to work, just for a change, and you find out later that by taking an alternate route you avoided a three-car wreck.

Or a bathroom door appears to open on its own. . . .

Those things happened to everyone once or twice in a lifetime. Those incidents were coincidences, and could likely be explained by statistics—or, in his case, by someone with a strong grasp of physics.

A fluke. He wasn't losing his mind. It was nothing worth dwelling on.

While cleaning, he talked on the phone with friends and family, and when he finished his housework, he took a long nap on a couch in the finished basement, the coolest part of his house during the summer.

While napping, he had a strange dream. He dreamed that he'd somehow been kicked outside of his house. His keys didn't work; the locks had been changed. When he went to a window, he saw someone who looked like him, yet was different in some indefinable way, lounging on his furniture, and when Gabriel pounded the window and demanded to be let inside, his twin pressed a button on the sofa arm and an electrical shock sizzled through Gabriel. . . .

Gabriel woke up shaking his head. What a weird dream.

Around seven, Dana arrived. He greeted her at the door with a kiss. She put the plastic grocery bags she was carrying on the floor and hugged him.

"How're you feeling?" she asked. She carefully touched his head bandage.

"Almost normal again." He smiled. "I almost went to work today."

"Better be glad you didn't," she said. "If I'd found out, you would've been in big trouble."

"Is that right? You would've spanked me?"

"I might've sent you out back to get a switch," she said.

"Hey, I can do that. Just give me the word."

She laughed. "I see you are back to normal, with your freaky self. Come out to the car and help me get the rest of these groceries."

As Dana went to the kitchen to put away the bags she'd brought in, he went to her Honda. A few Publix bags waited in the trunk; a red gift bag was nestled among them, the contents concealed by frizzy crepe paper. His birthday present? He started to stick his hand inside.

"Stay outta there," Dana said, hurrying to him. "I knew you'd go in there first. You can't open it until after dinner."

"After dinner? Come on, Dana, technically my birthday was *yesterday*."

"True, but we're celebrating it *today*."

"So I'll get all my gifts today?" He rested his hand on her hip, rubbed it.

"All of 'em—and then some." She gave him a quick kiss. "But not until after dinner."

"Then let's hurry up and eat."

"Patience, tiger." Dana tucked the gift bag under her arm and walked to the house, swinging her hips. She looked over her shoulder, saw him watching, and gave him a sexy wink.

God, he loved her. Sometimes he felt as if he didn't deserve the love of such a special woman. In his life full of blessings, Dana was, by far, the most treasured. She meant more to him than any amount of money or lofty career title ever could.

He was, indeed, the luckiest man alive.

Talk about adding insult to injury.

Isaiah had spent hours spying on Gabriel. He'd been there throughout the afternoon, had left for a couple of hours to grab a bite to eat, and then returned around six in the evening. At seven, a woman pulled into Gabriel's driveway in a red Honda Accord coupe.

When she strolled up to Gabriel's house carrying grocery bags, Isaiah sat up straighter in his seat and fumbled to get the binoculars on her.

Watching her, his heart stuttered.

She was *fine*.

She was probably five-five, five-six at the most. Dark hair

styled in a short, curly do. Smooth brown skin. Big, pretty eyes. She wore a yellow blouse and a denim skirt, the clothes showcasing a body that belonged front and center in a hip-hop video—or wrapped around a pole at one of Atlanta's finer gentlemen's clubs.

"Hell, naw, she *can't* be your girlfriend," Isaiah whispered. "You're a lucky bastard, but you ain't *that* lucky."

He got confirmation a couple of minutes later. Gabriel shuffled outside to get something out of the woman's car, and then she rushed up to him. As they talked, Gabriel put his hand on her booty, possessively, and she kissed him on the lips—gestures that told Isaiah everything he needed to know.

Gabriel was, truly, the luckiest motherfucker on the planet.

The woman strutted back inside the house, shaking that lovely ass of hers. Isaiah lowered the binoculars. He wiped his lips, which suddenly were dry.

He had seen enough for one day.

He started the engine, mashed the gas pedal, and thundered down the street. Gabriel glanced at him as he drove past. Isaiah pressed the accelerator harder, making the engine bellow like a lion.

He had to go somewhere else. Vicious waves of energy churned through him, and he needed to channel the forces in an alternate, more positive direction.

As he drove away, he thought his course of action proved that he was a different man. A wiser, more patient man.

In the past, he would have killed Gabriel right then.

As Gabriel was taking the rest of the groceries inside, a car sped past.

It was an old-school, smoke-gray Chevy Chevelle with supersized chrome wheels. Tinted windows concealed the driver. The car streaked down the road, orange-red sunlight shimmering on the rear window as though the interior of the vehicle were afire. The car veered around the corner at the end of the block and rumbled out of sight.

For some reason, the car sent a shiver tipping along Gabriel's spine.

Weird. It was an ordinary car, driven by God knows who.

But the chill clung to him until he went inside the house and closed—and locked—the door.

Chapter 9

For dinner, Dana cooked some of Gabriel's favorite dishes: cream of spinach soup. Pan-seared salmon with sour cream and dill. Twice-baked potatoes. Steamed vegetables. A tossed salad with balsamic vinaigrette dressing. And for dessert, she'd prepared cheesecake.

They had dinner by candlelight in the formal dining room. Soft jazz, broadcast from a satellite radio station, played on the stereo system that dispersed music throughout the house.

Gabriel could not help but reflect on the amazing flow of events. Last night he had been unconscious in a hospital after a car wreck. Barely twenty-four hours later he was in the comfort of his home, enjoying dinner with his fiancée. What a trip. When they said grace, he spent an extra minute with his head bowed, giving thanks to God for the many blessings.

"This looks delicious," Gabriel said. He filled Dana's wineglass with chardonnay, and then his own. "Best birthday dinner ever."

Dana raised her glass. "I want to make a toast. Happy thirtieth birthday to you, Gabriel Joseph Reid, the most wonderful man I've ever met, my future husband—and future baby daddy." She cracked a mischievous smile.

They clinked their glasses together, took short sips of the wine, and began to eat.

"You know," Gabriel said, "we can get started on the baby daddy part tonight if you want."

"Uh-huh, I bet," she said. "We're not married yet."

"Okay, I was kidding about starting tonight. But we can start when we go on our honeymoon."

"You know that's not the plan," she said.

"But wouldn't it be cool to have a Gabe Junior running around?"

"How do you know the first one will be a boy? It might be a girl."

"The first one will be a boy, trust me," he said. "Then we'll have our baby girl, Kaya."

They had already selected names for the children they planned to have. They believed—well, Gabriel believed—that they would have two children, a boy and a girl. Just like his parents had had him and his younger sister.

"One year," Dana said. "I'm not carrying any babies before then."

"There you go."

Along with picking names for their future children, they had discussed their plans for starting a family. They had agreed—well, Dana had *decreed*—that they would begin attempting to have children only after they had been married for at least a year. Although Dana was twenty-nine and the ticking of her biological clock got louder by the day, she insisted that it was important for them to spend a year as a married couple without children, bonding.

Gabriel went along with Dana's wishes and saw the validity of her position—but he didn't want to wait. He was eager to be a father and excited about the challenges and joys of fatherhood. Why wait? He and Dana already had been dating for three years and spent time together nearly every day. If they hadn't "bonded" by now, they never would.

"We've discussed this," she said. She stabbed a broccoli spear with her fork. "Sometimes I wonder why you're in such a rush to have kids."

"I'm thirty years old. I don't want to be an old man, hobbled with arthritis, when Junior wants me to play ball with him."

"Yeah, that's what you always say. I feel like the gender roles have been reversed. Usually the guy wants to put kids on hold so he has more time to enjoy his wife while her body is tight."

"Is it so wrong for a man to want to have children with his wife? Seems like a natural, good thing to me."

"Like something your father would approve of, huh?"

He laid his silverware against the plate. "What's that supposed to mean?"

"Forget it." She shrugged. "How's your salmon?"

He stared at her for a beat. Dana studied her wineglass and took a bite of food, avoiding his gaze.

It was enough.

She didn't buy his explanation for why he wanted to have children so soon, and he wasn't prepared to confess his honest motives, either. The truth? Having children of his own, in a way, would make him feel like Pops. Gabriel loved children, was excited by the thought of being a dad. But . . . being a father would nudge him that much closer to living in his father's vaunted image.

But was that such an awful thing? His father was a good man—a great man. Pops was Gabriel's hero and role model, always had been. Shouldn't a son emulate his own father and not some immoral and arrogant pro athlete or rap artist, as so often happened nowadays?

Dana just didn't understand, and he didn't want to discuss it with her further. His adoration of Pops was already a source of tension between them.

Gabriel chewed a piece of the fish. "The salmon is delicious."

"Good." She took a long sip of her chardonnay and then held out her glass. "Mmm. Pour me some more, please."

"Looks like someone's gonna get lit tonight." He reached for the wine bottle, which was an arm's length away.

His hands began to tingle. Pins and needles attacked his flesh.

Gabriel snatched his hand away from the bottle and buried both his hands in his lap.

"What's wrong?" Dana asked.

"Nothing." He rubbed his palms against his jeans, trying to make the prickly feeling go away.

"I'm not stupid. You were about to get the wine and then you jerked your hand away—and now you're hiding your hands under the table. What's wrong?"

"It's nothing. I felt a chill, that's all. It startled me."

"I know you better than that, babe." she said. "Please, tell me what's wrong."

He felt his resolve faltering. He couldn't continue to tell himself that the weird things happening to him were flukes. This was the third time his palms had gotten that electric, crackling feeling. Coincidences didn't happen in threes.

The sensation faded. He put his hands on top of the table and spread them as though for a palm reading.

"Gabriel," Dana said. "Please."

"Okay," he said. "I'll tell you."

He told her everything.

He told her about the tingling that had thrice struck him at unexpected moments. He told her about the humanoid shape he'd seen in the mirror at the hospital. He told her about the door that evidently had opened of its own accord.

As he talked, though he had no answers for anything that had happened, he began to feel better. It felt good to share his troubles with someone who cared, and he berated himself for not telling Dana earlier.

"I wish you hadn't kept this from me," Dana asked. "I might've been able to help you."

"Do you know what's going on?" he asked.

"Off the top of my head? No. But I'll research it. I think it's connected to your accident. You may have sustained some kind of nerve damage to your hands."

He nodded. That made a lot of sense. But there was more. "What about me seeing the shape in the mirror?"

"That happened to you shortly after you awakened last night, right? After you'd suffered a major concussion, remember? Seeing a fleeting glimpse of something, a brief hallucination or misinterpreting a shadow—not so unusual."

"I can buy that," he said. "And the bathroom door opening?"

Her brow furrowed. "I'm not sure about that one. I'm inclined to think that the door wasn't closed all the way and it sort of bounced open when you moved toward it. Probably was blown open by the wind."

"But I saw that knob *twist*, Dana. I know it."

"Like you saw the shape in the mirror?"

He pursed his lips. She smiled a little. She had him.

"So I imagined that, too," he said.

"I prefer to say 'misinterpreted,'" she said.

"Whatever you call it, it worries me. Going around having hallucinations, misinterpreting things, as you say? That makes me sound like a head case."

"Let's not jump to any hasty conclusions, babe. First things first; you need to see your doctor."

"Why do I have to do that? You're a doctor. You help me."

"I'm a pediatrician, Gabe. I treat children—though sometimes you behave like one." She smiled.

"Ha-ha."

"Seriously, you need to see your own doctor. I'll see what I can find out, but a second opinion never hurts. I want you to make an appointment tomorrow."

He groaned.

"I know, you hate going to the doctor," she said. "But this is important. We can't put it off or try to brush it under the rug and hope it goes away. You already said your hands have gotten that pins-and-needles feeling three times since yesterday."

"You're right," he said. He examined his hands. They felt normal. For now. "I'll make the appointment tomorrow morning, see if he can fit me in right away."

"Good boy," she said. "Let's finish dinner before it gets cold. We won't let this little thing ruin the rest of the evening."

But the mood already had been altered, irrevocably, in Gabriel's mind. Even as they finished dinner and indulged in their dessert . . . even as Gabriel opened his birthday present and discovered that Dana had given him a beautiful Movado watch . . . even as they cuddled on the sofa to watch a Will Smith movie and Dana interrupted the film to climb on Gabriel's lap and slip out of her blouse . . . even as they began to make love . . . even as, afterward, they lay together in bed and drifted to sleep . . . even as all these things happened, the question of what was happening to him lingered over him . . . like a storm cloud waiting to give birth to thunder and lightning.

Chapter 10

That night, Isaiah decided to get a woman of his own.

The Days Inn at which he was lodging in Marietta was located near Dave & Buster's, a massive entertainment complex that featured arcade games, billiards and shuffleboard tables, a restaurant, and bars. Isaiah strolled into the place around nine o'clock.

It was a space as vast as an airport hangar, bedecked with glitzy lights and abuzz with electronic sound effects, music, chatter and laughter, and bar-food aromas—enough sensory stimulation to scramble your nerves. Which was most likely the intended effect. Customers satiated with stimuli were more likely to keep guzzling drinks, gorging themselves on fatty food, and pumping money into games. Fun, fun, fun.

Wishing he had a pair of sunglasses and earplugs, Isaiah sidled up to the Viewpoint Bar, aptly named because it was situated to allow customers to scope out the action in the restaurant and billiards area. A twenty-screen video dome displayed an Atlanta Braves game and news clips of the day's other sporting events.

The Latino bartender, a dead ringer for Ricky Martin, came to take Isaiah's order.

"Double shot of Hennessy, on the rocks," Isaiah said. He added, "VSOP."

"You got it, man," the bartender said.

Mama, whenever she drank, was partial to Hennessy. Isaiah had his first try of the cognac—without her knowledge, of course—when he was twelve years old. One taste had hit him like a punch to the chest, but he'd loved it. He wasn't a big drinker, didn't like how alcohol robbed the mind of control, but when he chose to indulge, Hennessy was his preferred poison.

He was drinking tonight because he needed time to locate a lady, and a man sitting at a bar drinking a nonalcoholic beverage looked, quite frankly, like a pussy. In society, perception was reality. He wanted to come across as a man with an edge, even though, with his appearance and bearing, he didn't exactly *need* a drink to do so. But a little extra emphasis never hurt.

The bartender quickly delivered the cognac. Taking a slow sip, Isaiah checked out the scenery.

There was a group of red-faced white guys in Dockers and polo shirts sitting at one end of the bar, knocking back Budweisers and talking about their boring corporate jobs. A trio of white girls on the other side of the counter, drinking wine and laughing too hard. An overweight sista with a cute face, and her friend, a bigger girl with an ugly face, sitting near the corner, both of them glancing at him and then turning to whisper to each other in the childish way some women do.

A scan of the restaurant and billiards room yielded no prospects either.

He was about to get up and check out the arcade area on the other side of the complex when he spotted someone walking along the corridor past the bar, on the way to the restaurant ahead.

He saw her from behind, and what a sight she was. Big booty fighting the seams of her designer jeans. Tiny waist. A purple halter top that showed her lean, bronzed back to perfection, her mane of brown hair swishing over her slender shoulders.

But she wasn't alone. A tall, dark-skinned brother with an Afro walked beside her, his New York Yankees jersey dragging down to his knees like a skirt. Although the guy didn't see Isaiah, he wove his hand possessively around the woman's waist, as though to announce to onlookers: *Don't even think about it.*

But Isaiah had already decided that she was the one.

He kept his attention on the couple as they went to the restaurant. After the hostess seated them, Afro Bro got up and walked to the restrooms, a cell phone pressed to his ear.

Big mistake.

Within twenty seconds, Isaiah was at the table. The woman's front was just as fine as the rear. She bore a strong resemblance to Beyoncé, and from the way she carried herself, you could tell she knew it. She had confidence. He liked that.

Isaiah slid into the booth in front of her.

She blinked. "Umm, excuse me, that seat is taken."

"It sure is," he said. He sipped his drink. "By me. Afro Bro committed a fatal error: never leave a beautiful woman alone in public."

His boldness earned a flickering smile from her. That flash of a smile, and the fact that she didn't immediately tell him to get stepping, told him she was interested.

"I'm Isaiah." He offered his hand; she shook it, and he held on for a second longer than was necessary. "It's a pleasure to meet you. And you are?"

"Why should I tell you? You come sitting here uninvited. You might be a psycho or something."

"I might. Or I might be the man you need tonight."

"Hmph." But she still didn't ask him to leave.

"How about you tell me your name after I get rid of Afro Bro?"

She laughed. "You gotta lot of nerve."

"Is that what they call it? I call it confidence."

"You think he just gonna let you sit here? Akili ain't no punk like that."

"Here he comes. Let's see."

The guy came striding down the aisle, Afro bouncing. He stopped at the table and scowled at Isaiah, and then looked at the girl.

"Who dis?" he asked Beyoncé.

Beyoncé looked at Isaiah, striving to contain a grin, and he realized that she liked to see men competing for her attention. "He said his name is Isaiah."

"You know him?" Afro Bro asked.

"Nope," she said. "He sat here and started talking to me when you was walking away, talking on your cell and stuff." She rolled her eyes.

Afro Bro turned to Isaiah. His eyes hardened. "All right, brah. Get up and push on."

"I'm more comfortable here." Isaiah drank his cognac. "Why don't you go play some arcade games while I get to know the pretty lady here?"

"What?" Afro Bro stiffened. "Wanna step outside?"

He was a big man, with large fists, and probably knew how to use them, but Isaiah wasn't going to let it come to that. He disliked hand-to-hand combat—his beating of the redneck at the Waffle House notwithstanding. Fisticuffs were barbaric, something the old Isaiah would have done. These days he was better than that.

Beyoncé leaned back in her seat, her pretty eyes glimmering with amusement as she measured them, pondering which man would win her hand.

Isaiah fixed his gaze on Afro Bro.

The guy glared at him, ready to rumble.

Focus.

A fat vein in the middle of Isaiah's forehead had begun to throb. Energy stirred at the base of his spine, spread throughout his body, like currents of heat.

"You heard me," Isaiah said.

Command.

"Get out of here and go play some games," Isaiah finished. And he added, "Sucker."

Afro Bro's lips parted as though he were in a trance. His eyes glazed over.

Then, lowering his head, he shoved his hands in his pockets and walked away. He didn't look back.

"Oh, snap!" Beyoncé said, turning in her seat to watch the guy disappear in the games pavilion. "You scared the hell outta him!"

Isaiah casually sipped his drink.

"Now, sweetheart, you were going to tell me your name?"

Later, Isaiah clawed his way out of a nightmare: a dream of being a child again and watching his mother being beaten by one of her knuckle head boyfriends—and he was too small and weak to help her.

Leave my Mama alone. . . .

Climbing out of sleep, Isaiah exhaled, blowing the images out of his mind's eye.

On some nights, more so than others, the past clung to him like an old, heavy coat.

He switched on the bedside lamp. The clock read four forty-two A.M. He'd slept for about three hours. Long enough.

That was another dimension of the new and improved Isaiah: he didn't require much sleep. Before, he was notorious for sleeping eleven or more hours, well into the afternoon, which had driven Mama nuts. These days, about three hours was all he needed to be refreshed and sharp.

He'd placed the old photograph of Mama and his father next to the clock. He picked it up. He traced his finger across his father's features.

They looked so much alike, no one could ever deny that they were father and son.

His eyes grew teary. He wiped them, angrily, and put the photograph facedown on the nightstand.

"Turn off the light, baby."

He turned around in the bed. The woman from Dave & Buster's lay beside him, blinking groggily.

What was her name? Yolanda, Keisha, something like that. Her name didn't matter; once you got past the video-vixen body, there was nothing memorable about her. She was like too many women Isaiah knew: adrift on the sea of life, pre-occupied with clothes and shoes and hairdos and nails, hold-ing her breath for a man to come along and infuse her world with meaning and purpose. Even the sex had been ho-hum, a session of merely going through the motions, like a boring exercise routine.

Isaiah suspected that Gabriel's woman was nothing like that. He was sure Gabriel's girl was a singular woman of substance and passion.

Gabriel got the best of everything. This unfulfilling one-night stand of his served only to emphasize the disappoint-ing divide between his life and Gabriel's.

What's-her-name rubbed her eyes. "What time is it?"

"Time for you to get out."

That woke her. She sat up, scowling. "You kicking me out?"

"I got to handle some business."

"This early?" She pulled the bedsheets to her bosom, covering herself. "How am I gonna get home?"

"Call a cab." He peeled some bills out of his wallet and tossed them at her. "I'm gonna take a shower. When I come out, I want you gone."

"Damn, why you gotta be so mean to a sista? I thought we had a nice time."

"Please. I would've rather done some push-ups."

She started to open her mouth to spit some venom at him, evidently thought better of it, and shut her trap. She threw aside the sheets and grabbed her clothes, her lips poked out in the universal feminine sign of anger.

But she didn't cuss at him. No doubt she remembered how he'd ordered Afro Bro to take a hike. In spite of her obvious anger, she was afraid of him. Smart girl.

He walked to the bathroom, closing the door behind him.

As the door swung shut, he saw something in the mirror. A human silhouette, the size of a man. Centered in the glass.

He whirled around. There was no one behind him. He pushed open the door. The woman was on the other side of the bedroom, talking on the phone to a taxi company. It hadn't been her.

Isaiah ducked back inside the bathroom and flicked the light switch.

The figure in the mirror had vanished.

He shut the door. Leaning over the sink, he stared at the mirror. The phantom did not reappear.

He was certain he'd not simply seen his own reflection. The shadowy form had been fixed in place, like a statue, whereas he had been walking forward, into the bathroom.

What had it been? A hallucination?

He could not accept that answer. He was too well grounded, mentally, to succumb to illusions.

Perhaps, then, it had been a vision. That seemed a far more likely scenario to him. In his prior life, of course, the notion that he'd witnessed a vision would have been ludicrous. But now he lived a different reality. Phenomena such as clairvoyant apparitions could be part of it.

But it had been an apparition of . . . what?

Or who?

Gabriel awoke from a dream of funhouse mirrors and objects manipulated by invisible forces.

He lay in bed, breathing hard, drenched in cold sweat. The dream images receded into the mists of his unconscious.

Within a minute, he could barely recall what the dream had been about. But whatever it had been, it had left behind a residue—a pervasive sense of dread that made him peer fearfully at the dark corners of the bedroom, as though something malevolent watched him.

Snap out of it, Gabe. Everything's cool.

And it was. Dana was the only one in there with him. She slept next to him, nude, the warm globes of her hips resting against his leg. She felt so good that he didn't want to move; but his bladder had other plans.

Gabriel climbed out of bed and shuffled to the bathroom, keeping the lights off so as not to awaken Dana.

A murky, humanoid shape was moving in the mirror.

Gabriel let out a cry. He flipped on the light.

Nothing was in the mirror. There was only him, gaping at his reflection with puffy, frightened eyes.

"Gabe?" Dana asked in a scratchy voice. "You okay?"

No, I'm not okay, baby. I'm seeing shit in mirrors, and it's not a damn misinterpretation of anything.

But he said, "I'm okay, sweetheart. Go back to sleep."

"Thought I heard you shout. . . ."

"I . . . stubbed my toe on the door," he said. "I'm fine."

"'Kay," she muttered.

He didn't enjoy lying to her. He wasn't sure, in fact, why he lied to her. Maybe he was really lying to himself. The truth had nothing to do with nerve damage to hands, concussions, and misinterpretations of what he was seeing.

Something deeply unusual was going on, and their theories could not explain it.

Chapter 11

Isaiah arrived at Reid Construction at seven o'clock in the morning.

The parking lot was already half full. Early birds striving to beat morning rush-hour traffic.

The parking slots for the CEO and VP of operations were vacant. He'd been counting on that. Perfect.

Today was a big day, so he'd taken care to dress appropriately. He wore a gray Armani suit and polished loafers. The last time he'd worn a suit had been five years ago—when he was in court on an armed-robbery beef. The jury had convicted him, and he'd served five terrible years at a maximum-security penitentiary in Stateville. So much for the idea that clothes made the man.

The *mind* made the man. He knew that now. But visual impressions could be important, in the beginning.

The spacious lobby was as nice as he expected. Soft lighting. Oak paneling. Marble floors. Potted ferns. Award plaques hanging on the walls. He noticed framed magazine articles from *Black Enterprise*, *Ebony*, and other magazines, some of the same ones he'd clipped and saved over the years, which made him feel oddly familiar with this world of suits and ties, though he'd never worked a day in corporate America in his life.

A black woman sat behind a marble counter. Perhaps in her midtwenties, she had bedroom eyes, muffin-brown skin, long, dark hair, and full breasts that filled out her green business suit. Did fine sistas grow on trees in ATL? He wondered if Gabriel was doing this girl on the side.

The woman snapped shut her makeup compact, looked him up and down in that measuring way sistas do, decided he was worth a smile. She had cute dimples.

"Good morning, sir," she said. She had a husky Georgia accent. "How may I help you?"

Although Isaiah possessed talents that would have enabled him to manipulate this woman as easily as a child toying with Play-Doh, he'd learned that when dealing with a woman, charm and a winning smile could often secure whatever favors he wanted.

He grinned. "Good morning, sista. I'm here to see Gabriel Reid."

"I'm sorry, Mr. Reid isn't in the office yet. What time is your appointment?" She reached for the visitors' log on top of the counter.

"Oh, he's not here yet?" he asked, as though surprised. "That's fine. I'll go make myself comfortable in his office."

"Excuse me?"

"My name's Isaiah," he said. "Gabriel and I are family. I'm sure you can see the resemblance?"

"Matter of fact, I was thinking that you and Gabe do favor a *lot*," she said, losing her businesslike pose and giving him a glimpse of the earthy Georgia peach underneath the professional veneer. "You two could be brothers, seriously."

He approached the counter. He leaned forward and smiled as though they were co-conspirators. He swore he could see the flush in her cheeks. She was digging him.

"What's your name, sweetheart?" he asked.

"Rhonda," she said, and blushed.

"Can I trust you to keep a secret, Rhonda?" he asked. "Gabe doesn't know I'm here. I'd like to surprise him."

"Your secret's safe with me, Isaiah," she said, and winked. "Where are you from? You sound like you're from Chicago."

"You got it."

"I like Chi-Town brothas. Y'all know how to treat a lady." Her dimples reappeared in full force.

Perhaps he needed to rein in his charm a little. This girl was ready to leap over the counter and get it on. She was a beauty, but he didn't have time to deal with a woman. He had too much work ahead of him.

Still, he didn't want to turn her down cold. He winked at her slyly and asked, "Where's Gabe's office?"

"Second floor, far right corner off the stairwell. You can't miss it."

"Cool. Remember our secret, Rhonda." He felt her watching him as he strode away.

She'd been so impressed she hadn't asked him to sign the visitors' log.

As Isaiah strolled along the carpeted hallways, head held high, he smiled and said, "Good morning," to everyone he passed. The worker bees cheerfully returned his greetings, and he could tell from the way they looked at him that they thought he was a man of influence, and probably assumed that he was a blood relative of Gabriel's, too.

If only they knew the truth.

He found Gabriel's office. There was an oak door with a frosted-glass window on which GABRIEL REID, VICE PRESIDENT, OPERATIONS was engraved in black. A silver-haired, fiftyish black woman sat at a large desk outside the door. She had to be Gabriel's executive assistant. What a life.

Isaiah paid her a smile, too. "Good morning. I'm Isaiah, a relative of Gabriel's. I'm going to wait for him in his office."

"Hi, honey, Rhonda said you were coming up," she said. "I'm Angela, Gabriel's assistant. You can wait out here for him, he should be in soon." She indicated a couple of chairs in a waiting area on the other side of the corridor.

His smile froze. "I'd prefer to wait in his office, Angela. We're family."

"I understand, but that's his private office, Isaiah." She sweetened her refusal with a light laugh. "Those chairs over there are quite comfortable. Can I get you anything? Coffee, juice?"

Isaiah's lips formed a firm line. He stepped toward the woman.

Sometimes charm and an affable smile could take you only so far.

He fixed his gaze on the woman . . . and a thick vein began to throb in his forehead.

Focus . . . command.

"Open the door to Gabriel's office, Angela."

Angela's smile quivered. Her eyes grew clouded.

Then she rose from her chair, like a robot, went to the door, and opened it.

Isaiah walked past her and entered the office.

"Thank you, Angela," he said. "Now fetch me some coffee. Lots of cream and sugar."

Smiling at him like a child eager to please a parent, she hurried away.

Isaiah clicked on the overhead lights. It was a huge, airy space, with numerous windows that offered a view of elms and dogwoods, blooming shrubbery, and rolling vistas of grass. Mahogany bookcases lined one wall, full of boring business texts. Another wall could have served as the Wall of Rampant Ego. From it hung Gabriel's framed degrees from Morehouse College and the Goizueta Business School at Emory University, photos he had taken with celebrities like

Magic Johnson and diplomats like Andrew Young, and a handful of meaningless community award plaques.

A thirty-gallon aquarium stood in one corner, in lieu of a window. Colorful fish swam the clear waters. Isaiah bent and studied the mild-mannered creatures.

You could learn a lot about a person from studying their pets. People tended to choose animal companions that reflected their own personality. A man who kept a calming collection of fish in his office was a man who likely avoided conflict and danger.

In other words, Gabriel was the polar opposite of Isaiah.

Angela entered the office. "Here's your coffee, sir."

He took the steaming ceramic mug, sipped. Smiled.

"That'll be all for now, Angela. Go back to your desk and resume working. Close the door as you leave."

Angela obediently left and closed the door behind her. No one could see him clearly through the frosted glass. Good.

He went to Gabriel's desk. It was a massive slab. An entire tree probably had been sacrificed so Gabriel could place his crap on top of it. A fragrant bouquet of flowers stood on the edge of the desk; a Mylar balloon attached to the vase proclaimed HAPPY BIRTHDAY!

Isaiah read the card that lay beside the vase.

Happy Birthday, Babyface. Love, Dana.

"How sweet," he said.

The desk featured the requisite photos of Gabriel's hottie girlfriend—now he knew her name was Dana—and other pictures of Gabriel and his family.

Isaiah began to open the desk drawers. One of them stored a collection of CDs—old school jazz albums by artists such as John Coltrane, Miles Davis, Duke Ellington. Damn. Was Gabriel thirty years old or seventy?

In another drawer he found an expensive silver Mont Blanc pen in a leather case. There was an elegant monogram on the pen: G.J.R. Gabriel's initials.

The pen occupied a prominent position in a top drawer,

evidence that Gabriel used it often to ink those big-money deals. Isaiah held the pen in his hands and closed his eyes. He drew several deep breaths. Concentrated.

Yes. This would do just fine.

He slid the pen into his pocket.

Gabriel's computer was missing; a couple of cords lay on the desk like severed appendages. Mister hard working vice president must have taken it home with him.

He sat in the roomy leather chair. It was like sitting on a throne. All he needed was a crown.

Looking around the desktop, he picked up a photograph of Gabriel and his girlfriend. Gabriel wore a tuxedo, and Dana was ravishing in a black cocktail gown. Probably attending a thousand-dollar-a-plate dinner or some pompous affair buppies wasted their money on in order to feel important.

He dropped the photograph and selected another. This one featured the old man and Babyface on a fishing trip. Wearing clothes straight out of an L.L. Bean catalog, they proudly displayed their fresh catches in front of them.

Heat warmed Isaiah's face.

He had never been fishing.

He'd never been to a black-tie dinner with a woman, or even alone, for that matter. Red Lobster was the swankiest restaurant in which he'd ever dined.

He picked up another photo. This one showed Gabriel, the old man, a woman that had to be Gabriel's mother, and a younger lady that had to be his sister at a graduation ceremony. Gabriel wore a black gown and that silly flat cap with the tassel. All of them wore shit-eating grins. Had to be Gabriel's college graduation.

Isaiah had never been to college. He'd dropped out of high school in the tenth grade; had never gotten his GED, either.

Blood pounded in his temples.

One person was responsible for him missing out on so many opportunities.

Isaiah picked up the photograph of Gabriel and the old man on their fishing trip. He clutched the frame in his hands. He squeezed it so tightly his knuckles turned bone white. Rage contorted his face.

The frame cracked.

Chapter 12

Gabriel was eager to return to the office. He was looking forward to immersing himself in the safe, predictable world of conference calls, staff meetings, contract proposals, and deals. He left the house at seven-thirty, earlier than usual.

Self-conscious about his head bandage, he wore a felt hat to cover it up. Although it was much too formal to wear around the office, he preferred being overdressed to resembling an accident victim on the mend.

It was another sweltering, hazy morning. Although Pops could be overbearing sometimes, Gabriel was thankful that he'd loaned him the convertible Corvette. He drove with the top down to bask in the balmy breezes. He pulled into Reid Construction's parking lot a few minutes after eight o'clock, humming the final notes of "A Love Supreme" by John Coltrane.

A gray Chevy Chevelle with tinted windows and big chrome wheels occupied Gabriel's parking space, as though one of ATL's many hip-hop artists had mistaken the Reid corporate office for a recording studio.

"What the hell?" Gabriel muttered.

Had he seen this car before? It had Illinois plates . . . no, he was wrong. He hadn't seen this car and didn't know to whom it belonged. Whoever owned it, they would have to move it out of his spot.

Gabriel parked in his father's slot beside the Chevelle. Pops had an off-site meeting and wasn't due in until after lunch.

Gabriel gathered his briefcase and got out of the car. He gave the Chevelle a closer look. Although it was a model from the seventies, it was in mint condition, with not a scratch on the bodywork. A big, mean muscle of a ride.

Cupping his hand against the glass, he tried to peer through the driver's-side window. But the tint was so dark—wasn't it *illegal* for the tint to be that dark?—that he couldn't see any of the interior.

What business would someone driving a car like this have at Reid Construction?

And parking in his reserved spot, most of all?

There had to be a reasonable answer. Maybe it was some-one making a delivery of some kind. Or maybe it belonged to a temp worker. In other words, the owner of the vehicle could be there on entirely legitimate business.

But that idea failed to eradicate the tumor of anxiety that festered in Gabriel's stomach.

He would have to get to the bottom of this as soon as he got inside. He was the owner's son, next in line to run the business, and his father was away. If someone was there who didn't need to be, it was his responsibility, ultimately, to take care of it.

Clasping his briefcase, Gabriel walked to the front en-trance.

"Morning, Gabe," Rhonda, the receptionist, said. "Wel-come back. How're you feeling?"

"Better, thanks," he said. He examined the visitors' log on the front desk. "Do we have any visitors this morning, Rhonda?"

"No, sir." But she smiled, conspiratorially.

"None?" He frowned. "But someone parked in my spot. Gray Chevy Chevelle, Illinois plates."

She shook her head, but she was grinning. "Sorry, I've got no idea."

"Why are you smiling?"

"Umm, I just think your hat is cute," she said, but he knew she was lying. She was hiding something.

He was about to ask her another question, but then her phone beeped. Rhonda answered the line, turning away from him with a slight smile.

He didn't get it. Was there a joke he'd missed?

Outside his office, Miss Angie greeted him. "Good morning, honey. I'm so glad to see you're okay after that awful accident."

"Yeah, I'm okay," he said. Looking past her and through the frosted glass, he saw the vague shape of someone sitting at his desk. "Is someone in my office?"

"Of course not. I wouldn't let anyone in your office without your permission."

"But I see someone in there."

"You do?" She looked behind her and then turned back to Gabriel. Her lips had parted into a startled expression. "I'm sorry, someone must have come in when I stepped away from my desk. . . ."

"Never mind, I'll take care of it." Gabriel opened the door.

A black man sat at his desk. He was tilted back in the chair, feet resting on the desktop, sipping coffee. He smiled at Gabriel.

Gabriel had never seen this man in his life, but a shiver coursed through him as he regarded the visitor.

The man looked so much like him, they could have been brothers.

* * *

Gabriel closed the door.

Smiling softly, the man placed the coffee mug on the desk. A closer look at him reinforced Gabriel's initial impression of their physical similarities.

Most notably, they both had gray eyes.

But this guy looked . . . maybe the right word was *harder*. His face, though strongly resembling Gabriel's, was leaner, tougher. His eyes resembled slivers of dirty ice. His suit jacket concealed the skin of his arms, but Gabriel was willing to wager that his flesh was inked with tattoos.

Ex-con, Gabriel thought. *Or someone who's otherwise come up the hard way. Someone not to be trifled with.*

But he suddenly knew this was the man who had stolen his parking spot. To see him in here, sitting at his desk as if he owned the place, only fueled Gabriel's indignation.

"Who are you?" Gabriel asked. "And why are you sitting at my desk?"

"Good morning, Gabe," the man said. He swept his arm around. "Nice office you have here. Quite befitting a successful executive such as yourself."

"Thanks. Now would you mind taking your feet off my damn desk?"

"My bad. I got too comfortable waiting for you to show up." The man removed his feet from the desktop and bounded out of the chair. "I apologize."

But he didn't appear to be sorry. He wore a gloating grin, as if he knew some secret. That grin, and his use of Gabriel's nickname, only pissed off Gabriel further.

Gabriel clutched his briefcase like a shield.

"You like fish, I see," the man said. He hooked his thumb at Gabriel's aquarium. "Myself, I'm partial to snakes. Lovely creatures."

"I *hate* snakes." Gabriel could not suppress a grimace. "Anyway, why don't we get to the point: who the hell are you?"

"My name is Isaiah Battle." He strolled around the desk. He and Gabriel were the same height and build, but Isaiah moved with silky grace, like a panther.

Isaiah offered his hand. Gabriel glanced at the man's hand but didn't shake it.

Shrugging at Gabriel's rebuff, Isaiah turned around one of the wing chairs that flanked the desk and settled into it. He crossed his legs.

"What's your business here, Isaiah?" Gabriel asked.

"Have a seat, Gabe. We're going to have a serious discussion."

"I'll stand."

"Suit yourself. To answer your question, I'm here on family business. Things have been kept under wraps for a long time. It's about time some buried secrets come to light."

"What secrets?"

"What if I told you that your father isn't the man you think he is? What if I told you he's got some skeletons in the closet that he's been hiding from you and everyone else?"

"I'd tell you you're full of shit." Gabriel tossed his briefcase onto the floor and clenched his hands into fists. "Who the hell do you think you are, man? Coming in here talking about my Pops? I'll—"

"Hear me out," Isaiah said. He raised his hands in a placating gesture. "Chill, okay?"

"I've heard enough of this, I'm getting Security." Gabriel marched to the desk and grabbed the telephone.

"Put the phone down," Isaiah said in a soft voice. "You are going to listen to me, for your own good. I'm only offering the truth."

Gripping the phone, Gabriel met Isaiah's gaze. He stared into those gray eyes.

Eyes that were so much like his.

A tremor spread through Gabriel. He didn't want to hear any more. He wanted to hit the number to call Security and demand that they haul this man out of the building. He wanted to stuff his ears with cotton and deafen himself to the words Isaiah wanted to say. He wanted to flee his office, to get away from this man who looked far too much like him.

But Gabriel did none of those things. He replaced the phone on the cradle and dropped into the chair.

He'd taken a painkiller only an hour ago, but his headache had returned with savage intensity.

"I'm only here to tell the truth," Isaiah said.

Gabriel looked away from him. He noticed that the frame containing the photo of him and Pops on last summer's Father's Day fishing trip was cracked. He wondered how that had happened, but at the moment, it seemed unimportant.

He looked at Isaiah.

"The truth," Gabriel said, and the words tasted foul in his mouth, like bitter medicine.

"The truth," Isaiah said. "Straight up, no chaser."

Gabriel was beginning to feel dizzy. But he said, "All right. I'm listening."

Isaiah leaned forward. He spoke in a whisper.

And he said the words that changed everything.

"You and me, we have the same father, Gabriel. T.L. Reid is my dad, too. I'm your brother."

Chapter 13

As a child, Gabriel had loved to play football with some of the boys in his neighborhood. They would play in the grassy field that bordered the community, and what would start as a clean touch-only game would inevitably, as the competition intensified, evolve into a rough-and-tumble tackle match. During one game, Gabriel had caught a Hail Mary pass and made a sprint for the end zone near the line of maples at the boundary of the field—when Big Benny Jones had blindsided him.

He hadn't blacked out, but he'd come close. He'd lain on the ground, unable to move, staring dreamily at the cloudy summer sky as the boys huddled fearfully around him and wondered if he was paralyzed. He hadn't been paralyzed, but the breath had been knocked out of him and several minutes passed before he got to his feet.

Isaiah's revelation was like being blindsided by Big Benny Jones.

Even though, deep in his heart where he locked away his worst fears, he'd known Isaiah would say something like this—he and Isaiah looked so much alike, they could only be blood relatives—it nonetheless snatched the breath out of his lungs. He sat in his leather chair in his lavishly appointed office, a place where he probably felt more in charge than anywhere on earth—and he felt, for the first time ever, that the ground had broken beneath him. The foundation of his life had crumbled. Below, there was an abyss, a great unknown, and it was sucking him inexorably into it.

But, falling, he still tried to claw his way to the surface and hold on to what he held dear.

"That's impossible," Gabriel said. "You're lying."

"Am I?" Isaiah casually sipped his coffee. His manner was that of a card shark who held a royal flush and knew your bluff was worthless.

"It's a lie," Gabriel said. "I won't believe it."

"You know it's true. It's written all over your face."

"No." Gabriel shook his head.

"Look, we obviously have different mothers," Isaiah said. "I grew up in Chicago. That's where my mama and our father met."

"Pops never lived in Chicago."

"He met her while he was there on a business trip. He spent two weeks in Chi-Town, back in the summer of '74."

"1974?" Gabriel was so shaken he couldn't think straight, but Mom and Pops had married in '72—he remembered that much. "No. Mom and Pops were married in '72."

Isaiah made a tsk-tsk sound. "Come on, are you really that naive? Do you think our father never messed around?"

"Pops would never cheat on Mom," Gabriel said, but his defense sounded feeble, even to him.

"You think he's a saint or something? Our dad's a man. Every man, given the opportunity, is gonna cheat."

"Not every man," Gabriel said absently. In spite of himself, he was remembering things. He'd never seen Pops cheat on his mother, never heard of such a thing happening—but he'd been lying if he said he thought it wasn't possible. He'd noticed, many times over the years, how Pops liked to flirt with women when he and Gabriel were in public together. In particular, Pops had always loved the strip clubs: Magic City, Club Nikki, Jazzy T's; when one club would close, Pops would find another spot. He'd take Gabriel with him to those places to discuss business. "Boys' Night Out," he'd call them, and while they discussed company matters, Pops would spend hundreds of dollars—sometimes thousands—on lap dances and special attention. And the dancers and club owners knew Pops well. He was a regular, a great customer whom they made sure went home happy.

Gabriel had never told his mother about their gentlemen's club business outings. He figured Mom probably knew. He'd assure himself that it wasn't as though Pops was really cheating on his mother—frequenting a strip club didn't mean he was fooling around—but Gabriel, watching how much Pops enjoyed the attention of the ladies, could not help but wonder if Pops had ever taken his fascination with other women to the next level. . . .

"You're starting to admit it to yourself, aren't you?" Isaiah asked with a knowing smile. "I see the gears turning in your head. You know our father is a player."

"I haven't admitted anything to you."

"Chew on this, Gabe. My birthday is June sixth. I turned thirty yesterday. Just like you."

Another blow rocked Gabriel. He reared back in his chair.

"How'd you know that?" Gabriel asked.

"A little research." Isaiah waved his hand to indicate the framed magazine and newspaper articles about Gabriel and his father. "You've been written up quite a bit over the years, Mr. *Black Enterprise*."

"You and I having the same birthday doesn't mean anything."

"What time were you born?"

He shrugged. "I don't know, a few minutes after midnight—"

"I was born *one* minute after midnight," Isaiah said. He grinned. "That makes me older than you; that makes you my baby brother, and it makes me our father's firstborn."

"It makes you a goddamn liar!" Gabriel shot to his feet and reached for the phone again. "I've heard enough of this shit. If you're trying to extort money, we'll—"

"T.L. already paid me."

"What?" Gabriel stopped short of grabbing the phone.

"Three months ago, I contacted our father for the first time. I'd always wanted to talk to him, but Mama would say he didn't want anything to do with me, that I'd only get my feelings hurt. But I couldn't hold back any more—I'd gone through some rough shit and had to find out the truth on my own. So I called him. Want to know what happened?"

Gabriel didn't say a word. He was feeling ill.

"T.L. paid me fifty grand to stay away from him and his family," Isaiah said. "He didn't want to meet me. Nothing. He just wanted to pay me off to stay the hell out of his life. I gave all the money to Mama. She deserved it for all the shit she put up with over the years." Anger flared in Isaiah's eyes.

Gabriel sagged into the chair.

The ground was crumbling away, piece by agonizing piece.

Isaiah rose. He dug his hands deep in his pockets and paced across the floor. "You have no idea how bad Mama and I had it. Growing up in the projects." His gaze found Gabriel, but Isaiah seemed to be looking through him, seeing other places and people. "Mama worked two jobs, sometimes three, to make ends meet. Shitty jobs, man. Cleaning white folks' houses and waiting tables and changing pissy bedpans at nursing homes for smelly-ass old people. But it was never enough. We were always on the edge. And because Mama worked so much, she wasn't around much for me, so, of course, I got into my share of trouble."

Gabriel was silent. He didn't want to hear Isaiah's story, but he sensed that Isaiah was going to continue whether he wanted him to or not.

"I got sent to juvie for the first time when I was eleven. For shoplifting. Trying to cop some steaks at the supermarket. Mama loved steaks, you know? It wasn't my first time getting busted so they sent me to juvie, and when I was there, I got my ass kicked on the regular. Kids can be worse than grown-ass cons, man."

"I'm sorry," Gabriel said. He didn't know what else to say.

"Juvie was just the beginning. I was in trouble all the time. Been to prison twice. I just got out again at the beginning of the year."

"What were you in for?"

"Murder," Isaiah said. And when Gabriel's eyes widened, he laughed. "I'm just fucking with you, man. I've never killed anyone. I was in for armed robbery. I did five years on this last bid."

"I'm sorry," Gabriel said again.

"This past April, Mama was gunned down at the crib. Right in front of me. Can you imagine that, Gabe? Watching your mother die in your arms?"

Gabriel shook his head.

Isaiah dragged his hand down his face. He reached into his jacket pocket, withdrew a photo, and tossed it onto the desk.

"There's your last bit of proof," Isaiah said. "I'll take a blood test if you want."

Gabriel picked up the picture. It was an old, faded photograph, but the subjects were clear. His father, probably in his midtwenties, sat at a restaurant table with a pretty, young black woman. Both of them were grinning in the way that Gabriel recognized from pictures he'd taken with Dana; the grin reserved for lovers only. The caption beneath read *Ron of Japan, Chicago, Illinois.*

Gabriel slid the photo across the desk, like a man paying his life savings to a debtor. Isaiah tucked it away in his pocket again.

Gabriel blew out a breath. "Okay. What do you want from us?"

Isaiah settled in the chair again. "I'd like to get to know you, man. All my life, I've always wanted a brother. And don't you have a sister? I'd like to get to know her, too."

"I don't think this is a good idea."

"We're family, Gabe," Isaiah said. "Flesh and blood. I have a right to get to know you and all my kin."

"That's all you want? To get to know us?"

"I'd love to become a VP in the company, too. Get me a big house here in ATL and a pretty girlfriend and . . ." As Gabriel's mouth fell open, Isaiah broke into laughter. "Damn, I'm kidding. Relax!"

"Let's try this again: what do you really want?"

"I want to know my roots," Isaiah said. "Do you know how it feels to be cut off from half of your family for your entire life? You don't, do you?"

"No." Gabriel sighed.

"Then you don't understand." Isaiah dropped a card on the desk. "My cell number's on there. I'm staying at a hotel in Marietta. I'm looking forward to meeting the rest of the Reid clan—my peeps."

"Give me some time to think about this, okay?" Gabriel said. "This is a lot for our family to deal with."

"My family now, little brother." Isaiah winked, turned, and strode out of the office.

Gabriel cradled his head in his hands.

The ground had broken apart completely. There was only a yawning pit beneath him.

He didn't know what to do next. There was the temptation

to do nothing, in the vain hope that he would wake up and realize that all this was a terrible nightmare.

But couple minutes later, he rose. There was one thing he could do.

Talk to his father.

Chapter 14

Edgewood Avenue in downtown Atlanta, recently dubbed "The Edge," was a neighborhood that had seen better days. Part of the Fourth Ward, it had been in disrepair for decades, rife with crumbling buildings, closed storefronts, vagrants, and crime.

But lately, like much of in-town Atlanta, investors had begun to funnel money into the area, birthing an ever-growing community of shops, loft condos, and restaurants. A textbook case of the gentrification trend that was sweeping inner cities across the country.

Pops was holding a business meeting at a coffee shop on Edgewood called Javaology; Gabriel spotted his father's Mercedes parked across the street. Gabriel had been to the café before, for a Morehouse–Spelman alumni mixer. He pushed through the shop's new wooden doors and was greeted by the pungent aroma of coffee that, in his current agitated state, only made his pulse pound faster.

The café had science-lab-style decor. Sleek track lighting. Wraparound windows. Nests of tables, comfortable chairs, and sofas. Customers enjoying caffeinated beverages tapped away on laptops—the coffeehouse provided free wireless Internet access—and talked among themselves.

Gabriel saw his father near the back of the shop, sitting at a table with a couple of white men in Brooks Brothers suits. Pops was chatting and gesturing excitedly, a sure sign that he was engaged in selling something.

Gabriel tapped Pops on the shoulder. "Hey, Pops."

"Gabriel!" Pops beamed at him, turned to his colleagues. "Gentlemen, this is my son, Gabriel. My VP and future CEO."

Introductions and quick handshakes all around. Gabriel turned back to his father. "Can we talk?"

"Right now?" Pops asked.

"It's an emergency."

Pops straightened his suit jacket. "Well, sure. We were about to wrap up, in fact. Give me two minutes."

Gabriel stepped away and studied the coffeehouse menu while Pops concluded his meeting. Although his eyes skimmed the various offerings, his thoughts were focused elsewhere. How was he going to talk to his father about Isaiah? He'd never had such a conversation with Pops, and had no idea how to broach the subject. He half-wished that he could leave and let someone else have this conversation with his father.

As he was thinking of leaving, Pops touched his arm. "I'm finished. We can sit here and chat."

Gabriel looked at the people clustered around them, and then glanced upward at the loft area, which appeared to be vacant.

"Let's go up there," Gabriel said. "We need some . . . privacy."

Pops gave him a questioning look, but followed him upstairs. They settled around a table.

"Now, tell me," Pops said. "What's wrong? Something you need me to help you with?"

Typical Pops. Always ready to solve Gabriel's problems.

Gabriel cleared his throat. He had considered a dozen different openings—and, in an instant, discarded them all and opted to cut to the chase. "I had a visitor at the office today, Pops. He said his name's Isaiah Battle. That name mean anything to you?"

Pops flinched as if sucker-punched.

His reaction answered Gabriel's question: *it was all true.*

Gabriel felt his stomach roll. "It's true then, isn't it?" he said. "He's really your son."

Pops took out his handkerchief, blotted his forehead, and then held the cloth against his lips as though trying to hold in the words that wanted to spill out.

"He said you paid him fifty thousand dollars to stay away from us," Gabriel said. "Hush money."

Pops wiped his mouth, glanced in the handkerchief, frowned. He put the cloth against his forehead again, sopping up a fresh layer of sweat.

"He and I even have the same birthday," Gabriel said. "He's just turned thirty, too. He's actually a few minutes older than I am. He's your firstborn."

Pops stuffed the handkerchief in his pocket. Drew in a breath, steepled his fingers.

Gabriel paused. "Well?"

"I never meant to hurt anyone," Pops said. "This was very unexpected."

Unexpected. Not, *I'm sorry.* Gabriel could not believe this.

"How long have you known about Isaiah?" Gabriel asked.

"Since he was born, of course," Pops said, with a trace of annoyance.

"Does anyone else in the family know?"

"No."

Jesus, Mom's going to have a heart attack.

"You've been hiding this from all of us for thirty years?"

"I never wanted this to happen, Gabriel. That's why I paid him. He was supposed to leave us alone."

For the first time in his life, Gabriel had the distinct feeling that this man who'd named him, who'd taught him how to ride a bike and shave and knot a tie, who'd lectured him about right and wrong, who'd instructed him on how to be a man . . . this man, he didn't know as well as he thought he did. This man, his father, whom he adored, was a stranger to him.

And a disturbing question lodged in Gabriel's mind like a splinter. What kind of man would bribe his own child to stay away?

"How could you?" Gabriel asked. "How could you do this?"

Pops glared at him. "Why are you so upset? What have I done to *you*, Gabe? I've given you and your sister everything you've ever wanted and needed. If anyone has the right to be angry with me, it's your mother, and, possibly, Isaiah."

Gabriel couldn't think of an adequate reply. Tears seared his eyes.

I should have known better, he thought. What kind of response had he expected from his father? A tearful confession? A heartfelt apology? He'd never witnessed his father crying, and his father rarely apologized, even if he was at fault. T.L. Reid was a man's man, and in his opinion, emotional displays were the exclusive province of women. Although Gabriel had patterned himself after his father, his mother had helped to sooth the rough edges of his heart, had taught him that it was okay to behave as something other than an emotional Neanderthal sometimes.

But Pops didn't play that stuff. Gabriel had been a fool to assume that confronting his father about Isaiah would provoke a reaction of genuine contrition.

"You've got a lot of balls to corner me like this," Pops

said. "As if I'm accountable to you for my actions. Do you know who I am, boy?"

Gabriel wiped his eyes. Now that he'd asked the questions, he had to endure the browbeating.

Don't ask something if you can't handle the answer, Pops had taught him.

"Let me tell you who I am," Pops said, squaring his shoulders. "*I am your father, Gabriel.* You may not agree with my decisions, but you have no right to pass judgment on me. You don't know the full story. I did what I did because . . . I had to. For you, your sister, and your mother. For all of us."

Liar, Gabriel thought. *You didn't do it for us. You did it for yourself.* Gabriel sniffled.

"I don't know what else I can say," Pops said. "The truth is out, and we'll deal with it as a family." He pushed away from the table. "I'm sorry you had to find out this way."

Pops walked toward the staircase. When he noticed that Gabriel didn't follow, he looked back at him.

"Coming?" Pops asked.

Gabriel turned away.

Nothing's ever going to be the same after this, Gabriel thought. *For any of us.*

His father's footsteps receded in the distance.

Chapter 15

Theo Reid drove aimlessly, thinking about secrets.

He'd planned everything so meticulously over the years. He'd fooled everyone. But as today proved, he'd fooled himself, too.

There was nothing like the power of the blood bond. The blood bond pulled people together that lived on opposite ends of the globe; it reunited families who had been estranged for generations; it never faltered, never faded. He should have known better.

Eventually, blood always won out.

When the boy had contacted him a few months ago, Theo thought he had been prepared. He'd offered the boy a substantial payoff—bribing him, essentially, to stay away from Theo and his family forever. The boy had accepted the money and agreed to the terms. So why had he come back?

And not only had he returned, he'd approached Gabriel first, as though to spit in Theo's face and make sure Theo couldn't arrange another cover-up. Theo's only alternative was to confess the truth to his family.

How could you? Gabriel had asked.

Gabriel, his sweet, innocent son. If only Gabriel knew the truth, in all its vile glory, he would hate Theo forever.

For that reason, Theo despised truth. In seconds, truth could destroy marriages, families, and multimillion-dollar corporations that had been decades in the making. Theo had learned, the hard way, that the path to success and happiness was paved not with truth, but with what he liked to consider "comforting fictions." People didn't really appreciate learning the truth, no matter how much they claimed to want to hear it. Because the truth usually hurt.

The problem was that when you dispensed so many comforting fictions throughout your life, it was easy to become tangled in them yourself, to lose your way, to *believe* them. That was dangerous. Theo had thrived for years because he'd been careful never to confuse reality with fiction.

This time, he'd screwed up. He wasn't going to let it happen again. There was too much to lose.

His hands-free car phone beeped.

"Answer," Theo said, commanding the system to open the line.

"It's me . . . Pops," the caller said, derision in his voice. "How are you?"

The caller didn't announce his name; he didn't have to.

Theo's jaw hardened like cement. "We had an agreement."

"That's something I'd like to discuss with you. Can we meet?"

Theo didn't want to meet him. He wanted to terminate the call and bury his head in the sand, ignoring the tsunami that was surely rising and rumbling straight for his family.

But the power of the blood bond conquered him, too.

"Where do you want to meet?" he asked Isaiah.

Chapter 16

In a daze, Gabriel wandered out of the coffee shop and drove to Children's Healthcare of Atlanta at Egleston, a pediatric hospital on the Emory University campus. He parked illegally and shuffled inside the building.

He found Dana in the room of a patient— a little black girl with Afro puffs, hooked up to a respirator.

"Gabe?" Dana asked. She dropped her clipboard onto a chair. "What's wrong?"

He pulled her into his arms and wept.

Alone with Dana in the hospital staff lounge, Gabriel told her what had happened. He spoke with a fistful of tissue in his hand, which he frequently used to dry his teary eyes.

He hadn't cried like this in years, not since his paternal grandmother had died. He was not the kind of man who typically showed his feelings to such a dramatic extent, but his father's confession had busted open the dam containing his emotions, and in spite of how much he despised weeping, he was unable to hold back the tears.

Dana held his hand. She looked shell-shocked, too, shaking her head.

"Oh, my God," she said. "I can't believe your father would've done that. . . ."

"He *admitted* it," Gabriel said. "He even tried to pay off his own kid to make him stay away! Fifty grand!"

"I'm so sorry, baby. I know how you feel about your dad."

Gabriel's head drooped like a lead weight, as more tears poured out of him. Dana cradled him to her bosom and stroked his hair. He held on to her tightly; right now, she was the only stable thing in his life. Everything else he prized had crumbled away.

"He's going to tell the rest of the family, right?" Dana asked.

"He said he would. If he doesn't, I damn sure will. I'm not hiding this from Mom and Nicole."

Dana grimaced. "This is going to get ugly."

"Everything we believed about Pops . . . it's all a lie," he said. "I don't know what to believe anymore. This is so fucked up."

"What does this man, Isaiah, want?"

"He wants to get to know us." Gabriel shrugged. "But something about that guy bothers me. I don't know what it is, but I don't like the idea of him being around."

"He's got every right to be around, Gabe. He grew up not knowing anything about his father's people."

"Then why come around now?"

"Put yourself in his shoes. How would you feel if you'd grown up without knowing your father?"

"If I'd known he was doing shit like this behind our back, I wouldn't want to know him."

"Don't say that, babe." Dana kissed his forehead. "I've got to get back to work. Call me later, okay?"

He drew himself to his feet. She examined his hands, scrutinized his face.

"Did you make that doctor's appointment yet?" she asked.

"Honestly, with everything going on, that's been the last thing on my mind."

"I understand, but please do it," she said. "I'm worried about you."

"I'll take care of it, promise."

She hugged him. "Everything's going to be fine. Your family's strong. You'll get through this."

"I hope so," he said.

But he didn't share her confidence.

It was a lovely day for a walk in the park.

Sipping from a chilled bottle of V8 Splash, Isaiah strolled through Piedmont Park, the largest park in Atlanta, located in Midtown. Hardwoods stretched overhead, providing ample shade, and dogwoods and azaleas scented the warm summer air.

In a meadow, Isaiah saw a father and son playing catch with a football. Envy boiled in him like heartburn.

Gabriel and their father probably had used to play catch like that.

Isaiah located his dad sitting on a bench in the cool shadows of a magnolia. Although he had never met his father in the flesh, he recognized him from the photos. He wore an expensive dark suit, loafers. A leather briefcase lay beside him. The quintessential successful businessman.

Head bowed, studying the grass as though it contained the answers to life's mysteries, his father didn't hear him approach.

Isaiah's heart banged. He had been so focused on his mission that he hadn't taken time to reflect on the weight of this occasion. *He was meeting his father for the first time.* He didn't know whether to be elated or angry. He supposed he felt a bit of both.

"Theodore Lee Reid," Isaiah said, using his father's full name.

His dad looked up.

Damn, they looked so much alike. His father might have ignored him for his entire life, but he could never deny that Isaiah was his son.

His father, too, appeared to be taken aback by their striking similarity. Isaiah wondered if Mama had ever sent his father a photo of him. There was so much his father didn't know about Isaiah's own life that it drove him crazy.

"You look . . ." His father started.

"Like your son," Isaiah finished for him. He sat next to his father on the bench. He shivered; he had goose bumps from sitting so close to this man who had haunted his and Mama's lives.

His father studied him. "Christ. I haven't seen you since you were an infant. You're a good-looking kid."

"Good-looking *man*," Isaiah said. "You can drop that kid shit. Those days are over—you missed 'em, *Pops*."

Isaiah used the address "Pops" with as much mockery as he could summon. Gabriel called their father that bougie-sounding shit. Isaiah had decided to use it, too; every time it would pass his lips, he would feel a twinge of anger and remember why he wanted revenge.

"Fair enough," Pops said soberly. "I thought about you a lot, you know. Wondered how you were doing."

"Give me a motherfucking break. You don't need to tell me that shit to make me feel better. Let's get down to business."

Pops winced, looked around as though worried who might be overhearing them. "Do you have to curse so much?"

"What? You see me for the first time in thirty years and want to criticize my foul language?"

"Forget it," his father said, "You want to talk business? All right, then. Why are you here?"

Isaiah tossed the empty drink bottle toward a nearby trashcan. It missed and tumbled onto the grass. "Damn, I'm a terrible shot. Probably because Daddy wasn't around to teach me."

"Let's not get into that. I don't have time to rehash old issues with you. I want to know why you came. We had an agreement."

"'We had an agreement,'" Isaiah said, mimicking him. "You can't buy me off, man. My life isn't one of your business deals. I don't accept payoffs."

"You took the money."

"Of course I took it. You think I'm gonna turn down fifty grand? As far as I'm concerned, that loot was like past-due child-support payments. My only regret is that it came too late for Mama to truly enjoy it."

His father wiped his lips with his handkerchief. "I'm sorry about her."

"Whatever. You didn't give a fuck."

His father looked pained. Then, "What do you want from me, Isaiah?"

"You really want to know?"

"You want more money, is that it? How much more would it take for you to leave? A hundred thousand? Two hundred thousand? Half a million?"

"*It's not about the money!*" Isaiah leaped to his feet. He was about to lose control, and he had to catch himself. This wasn't the way he wanted this conversation to go.

"If it's not about money, then what is it?" His father spread his arms. "Tell me—what is this all about?"

His father didn't get it. He thought Isaiah only wanted money, as though money alone could solve life's problems, as though money mattered now that Mama was dead.

Isaiah wished he could kill his father then. But this wasn't the time or the place.

Isaiah sat down again. Counted to ten. Slowed his racing heartbeat.

"I want to be a part of your family," he said softly. "I want to be like you and Gabe are together, want the kind of relationship with you that you have with him." *And I want everything else Gabe has, too.*

His father looked at him, measuring. "You're serious."

Isaiah nodded.

"Shit." Now it was his dad's turn to get to his feet. He put his fists on his waist, pacing through the grass.

"I'm not going back to Chicago," Isaiah said. "There's nothing left for me there. I want to stay here with you . . . Pops."

His father glanced at him, eyebrows arched.

"I have a life here, Isaiah, an image to uphold," he said. "I'm well established in the community, an elder at my church. I'm a role model for a lot of people."

"So now it's time for you to be a role model for me."

Isaiah's words seemed to hit his father like a punch to the stomach. Pops grimaced, lowered his head. Shoved his hands deep in his pockets.

"I'm not the sole decision-maker on this," his father said. "I need to talk to my wife, Gabe . . . Nicole . . ."

"Come on, you're the man of the house," Isaiah said. "Lay down the law."

"It's not that easy."

"You mean to tell me that T.L. Reid, legendary entrepreneur and millionaire, has to go to his family and ask if his own flesh and blood can be a part of his life?"

"Stop trying to play to my ego." Pops rubbed his lips, pondering. "I'll think it over. I'm going to have a talk with everyone this evening."

"Good enough. What time should I be there?"

"*You* shouldn't be there tonight. Telling them about you is going to be rough on everyone. I don't think they could handle meeting you tonight."

"Fine. Tomorrow, then."

"I'll let you know."

Isaiah would have to be happy with that. *Patience*, he reminded himself. *Take it slow.*

Now that he'd set things in motion, why rush?

He had plenty of time to destroy his father's family.

Chapter 17

Gabriel had no desire to be anywhere in his father's orbit, so he avoided returning to the office. He drove to Decatur to visit his physician, Dr. Louis Robinson. Dr. Robinson, a Morehouse man like Gabriel and his father, had a thriving family practice on Wesley Chapel Road. He'd agreed to squeeze Gabriel into his schedule on short notice.

A medical assistant weighed Gabriel and took his blood pressure, both of which were normal. When the woman asked the purpose of Gabriel's visit, Gabriel mumbled, "I was in an accident a couple of days ago. I only want to have a physical, get my head bandage checked, make sure everything's in order."

He didn't mention his tingling palms or the visions in the mirror. Now that he was there, sitting on the exam table, surrounded by the cold, logical instruments of science, he was embarrassed to admit what was happening to him.

"Gabriel!" Dr. Robinson said, stepping into the examination room. He was a bearish man in his midfifties, with a shiny bald head and a neatly trimmed beard. "I haven't seen you in a while, brother."

"Yeah, it's been a couple of years."

"How's your father? I haven't seen Theo since the Grand Boule's Centennial Celebration in Philly."

Gabriel's father and Dr. Robinson were members of Sigma Pi Phi, an ultraexclusive black fraternity casually known as the "Boule." Gabriel had pledged Alpha Phi Alpha during undergrad, just like Pops, and he'd wanted to join the Boule in a few years, with Pops paving the way for his acceptance in the by-invitation-only society.

But all those goals of his had changed as of that morning. Now he no longer cared about getting his father's help with anything.

"Pops is fine," Gabriel said and forced a smile.

"Good, good." Robinson studied Gabriel's file, looked up at him. "Says here you were in a car accident recently? How're you feeling?"

"Okay, I guess. They discharged me from the hospital yesterday. I had a concussion, bruised ribs."

"Thank God that was all." Robinson checked the bandage on Gabriel's head, nodded with approval. "Is anything else wrong? Having any headaches or dizziness?"

"No, nothing like that."

"How do your ribs feel?"

"Still sore, but I can get around fine."

"I'll write you a prescription to help ease the pain," Robinson said. He scribbled a note in his illegible physician's handwriting. "Your noggin's healing well. Drop in later next week and we'll see if we can remove the bandage."

"Will do."

"Is there anything else, Gabriel?"

"Nah. I just wanted to get a physical to make sure everything was okay."

Robinson frowned. "I've been your physician since you were knee-high. You've only come in for exams when you needed them for school. You sure you're giving me the whole story?"

"Well." Gabriel looked down at his hands. "There's this weird thing that's been going on with my hands. They . . . uh, tingle."

"Tingle?"

"Like how it feels when they lose circulation. A cool, prickly feeling."

"Like pins and needles?"

"Exactly."

"How long does that last? And how frequently does it happen?"

He shrugged. "It lasts for a few seconds. It's happened maybe three times since my accident."

"Did it happen before the accident?"

He shook his head. "It started right after."

"Any numbness, loss of motor skills?"

"Nope."

"And this is happening only in your hands?"

"Just my hands."

Robinson made a series of quick notes on his pad. "It sounds like you're experiencing a mild case of nerve damage. It's very probable that you injured your hands during the accident. Hand paresthesia is the term, if memory serves."

"Is it serious?"

"Not at all. Know the treatment? Rest those hands."

"That's all?"

"Sure, as long as there's no pain. If you begin to experience numbness—or if the tingling persists for longer than a week—then call me." He started toward the door. "But I think a few days' rest is all you need. No prolonged typing, writing, heavy lifting, or exertion. Take a break."

"I guess I can take a few days off." Gabriel slid off the table. "That was easy."

"Was that everything?" Robinson moved away from the door, seeming to sense that Gabriel was holding back.

Gabriel smiled, embarrassed. "There is one more thing. . . ."

He told Robinson about the hallucinations. The doctor

listened patiently. He didn't appear shocked, as Gabriel had worried, and he didn't push a button to summon the men in the white coats. Gabriel realized that in his time as a physician, Robinson had probably heard some of everything.

"Dana, my fiancée, thinks I'm seeing those shadows or whatever because of my concussion," Gabriel said. "She's a doctor, too."

"She sounds like a good one," Robinson said. "I agree with her. Visual disturbances—seeing bright lights or shadows, blurred or double vision—are possible aftereffects of head trauma."

"Good. So I'm not crazy."

"Of course not. But it might be worth a trip to the neurologist for a closer examination."

"They already ran a CAT scan on me at the hospital. I was fine."

"A second look won't hurt," Robinson said. "I can give you a referral to an excellent neurologist."

Gabriel loathed visiting doctors and had made this visit to Robinson only because he'd promised Dana. Now Robinson was advising him to go see yet another physician? Gabriel was beginning to regret he'd scheduled this appointment at all.

But he didn't share his dismay with the doctor. He only said, "Sure," and started toward the door.

Robinson opened the door for him. "It was good seeing you again, son. Tell my frat brother I said hello. That old dog needs to get in here for his annual checkup."

Gabriel smiled thinly. "I'll pass that along."

When Gabriel reached his car, he discovered a message on his cell phone: Pops was holding a family meeting at seven o'clock that night, and wanted Gabriel to be there. Pops spoke in a crisp, businesslike tone, as though he was discussing plans for an ordinary client meeting, not the unveiling of a secret liable to tear apart their family.

I don't want to be there, Gabriel thought, shutting off the cell phone. *I don't want to see the look on Mom's face when she finds out what Pops did.*

But he would be there, to support his mother, and out of obligation to his family.

Even though, after tonight, there might not be much family left.

Chapter 18

At five minutes to seven o'clock, Gabriel drove into his parents' subdivision.

His family lived off Cascade Road in southwest Atlanta in a gated enclave of million-dollar estates situated on giant, manicured plots of land. Inhabited exclusively by African Americans—executives, entertainers, and pro athletes—they were picture-perfect mansions, every one of them worthy of a spread in *Ebony* magazine as proof of what black people could accomplish.

But cruising along the tree-lined road with Dana riding beside him, Gabriel found himself wondering about the skeletons, the residents of these homes concealed in their spacious walk-in closets, the lies they hid behind their estates' elegant brick and stucco facades, the depths of the sins they'd buried beneath their perfectly trimmed lawns.

Gabriel knew he was being cynical, but he couldn't help it. His anger toward his father had degenerated into a bitterness that spoiled everything he viewed.

He hadn't told Dana about his doctor's visit, and she hadn't asked. She clearly sensed that he wasn't in a talkative mood. During the past twenty minutes they'd been riding in the car, they had exchanged less than five sentences.

His parents' home was located in a quiet cul-de-sac. They lived in a two-story, brick European estate sprawled across two lush acres. He rolled into the wide driveway and parked in front of the three-car, side-entry garage.

A green BMW convertible was parked in the driveway, too. His sister's car.

"Looks like Nicole's here," Gabriel said. "I don't see Isaiah's thugged-out ride. Maybe he won't come. Pops didn't say whether he was showing up or not."

"You don't want him here," Dana said. It was a statement, not a question.

"That's right, I don't."

"I hate to burst your bubble, Gabe, but he's your dad's son. He's got a right to get to know you guys."

"I don't want to know him. I want him to leave."

"Baby, I know this is hard for you, but try to be a little understanding, okay?"

Gabriel grunted.

"I'll take that as an agreement," Dana said and got out of the car.

Gabriel climbed out, slammed the door hard. The subject of Isaiah was quickly becoming a thorn in his side. He could only imagine how much the guy's arrival would disrupt the chemistry of the family, his life—everything he'd ever known and valued.

This is all Pops's fault.

Teeth clenched, he followed Dana inside.

Inside, his family's estate was even more impressive. It had a marble-floored, two-story foyer highlighted by a curving staircase with a mahogany, handcarved railing. A three-tier, crystal chandelier. Antique furnishings. Privately commissioned paintings and sculptures by well-known black artists. A two-story, grand salon with an enormous fireplace and a rear wall of windows offering a stunning view of the sparkling swimming pool and the woods beyond. . . .

As an adult, visiting his parents' home had used to soothe Gabriel, would remind him of his comfortable childhood. Now, walking through the house made him feel vaguely ill, as though there were a repugnant odor floating underneath the clean, lemony fragrance that scented the air.

Gabriel and Dana found his mother and Nicole in the library, sipping tea and chatting. If Gabriel was a younger version of his father, then Nicole was a carbon copy of his mother, minus twenty or so years. Twenty-seven years old, Nicole was a petite redbone with long auburn hair and hazel eyes framed by stylish designer eyeglasses. Nicole worked as an associate at a corporate law firm; she wore a cream business suit, evidence that she had probably come there straight from the office.

When Pops called a meeting, everyone in the family responded.

The last time the Reids had come together for an emergency meeting, it had been to discuss the deteriorating health of Grandma Vee, his father's mother. They had talked about funeral arrangements, insurance, wills, and other grim matters. It had been one of the most painful conversations Gabriel had ever experienced in his life.

In Gabriel's opinion, this one was going to be worse.

Gabriel and Dana said their greetings and took seats.

"Where's Pops?" Gabriel asked.

"He'll be in here shortly," Mom said.

He was preparing himself for the firestorm, Gabriel figured.

The library had long been one of Gabriel's favorite rooms in the house. It was full of a dozen bookcases, each of them stocked with hardcover titles. Classic works by authors such as Zora Neale Hurston, Richard Wright, Langston Hughes, Ralph Ellison, and an abundance of contemporary fiction by Toni Morrison, Terry McMillan, Walter Mosley, and many others. Comfy leather club chairs flanked a granite fireplace, and a large picture window framed a gorgeous view of his mother's garden of azaleas and roses. Growing up, Gabriel had spent countless hours in there, spinning away the summer days in the cradle of a good novel.

After tonight he would never feel the same about the library.

Clustered in a semicircle, Mom, Nicole, and Dana began chatting about shoe sales and clothes. Mom and Nicole had no idea why Pops had called this meeting, but he could see the anxiety lining their faces underneath the amiable front they were striving to present to one another. Dana, who knew the truth, was trying to keep a poker face and show interest in the superficial chatter.

After ten minutes of increasingly strained chitchat, Pops still hadn't arrived. Gabriel rose. The women looked at him, curious.

"I'm tired of waiting," he said. "I'm going to get him."

He found his father in the master bedroom. Pops sat on the king-size bed, head hanging low. He held a snifter of Crown Royal. The rich aroma filled Gabriel's nostrils, blending with his anxiety to make him slightly dizzy.

A photo album lay on his father's lap. Pops didn't look up when Gabriel approached.

Gabriel peered over his father's shoulder. Pops's thumb rested on a picture he and Gabriel had had taken together during one of their fishing trips. They were both grinning, holding up their catches. The perfect father and son.

One of the sons, anyway, Gabriel thought sourly.

"We're waiting on you," Gabriel said.

Pops looked up. His eyes were watery and red.

Gabriel took a step back. Pops had been crying? He couldn't believe it.

"We had a nice time there," Pops said, tapping the photo. "I always loved spending time with you for Father's Day."

Every year on Father's Day weekend, Gabriel and Pops would take a weekend trip to their cabin nestled in the foothills of the Blue Ridge Mountains in north Georgia. Just the two of them. They would fish, drink beer, and talk about business, politics, women, family, life. Gabriel had loved those trips, would always come home feeling closer than ever to his father.

Thinking about those happy times made the pain of his father's betrayal sink that much deeper. Gabriel had the wild urge to rip the photo album out of his father's hands, toss it into a fireplace, and burn it to ashes.

"Have I been a good father?" Pops asked in a wavering voice.

Gabriel swallowed, hesitated.

"Until . . . this happened, of course," Pops said. "Have I been good to you?"

"You were a good father," Gabriel said. He looked away. "I . . . I idolized you."

"I always wanted to give you the very best. You, your mother, your sister—all of you. Nothing but the best."

"Then give us the truth. You owe us that."

"The truth?" Pops laughed hoarsely. A cloud passed over his eyes and Gabriel had a distinct sense that his father was hoarding a treasure chest of nasty, incriminating secrets—of which Isaiah was only the first.

No, Gabriel thought. He refused to believe it. It couldn't be any worse than it already seemed. He would not consider it.

Pops drained the rest of his liquor and extended his hand toward Gabriel. Gabriel moved away.

"Okay, then," Pops said. He stood, wearily. There was a helpless look in his eyes Gabriel couldn't bear to see. This wasn't his father, the hero. He didn't know this weak, dispirited man.

"I need you, son. Don't abandon me now."

"They're waiting for you." Gabriel started walking to the doorway.

Grim-faced, hunched over, Pops followed him to the library to face his family.

Gabriel didn't sit. He stood behind the chair in which his mother sat and rested his hand on her shoulder.

She was going to need it.

Pops sat in the middle of the group. He rubbed his mouth with a handkerchief as though to force his lips to move. But he remained silent.

Everyone looked at Pops. The silence in the room thickened.

Gabriel cleared his throat. "Pops brought us here to tell us something."

Pops shot him a reproving look. But he finally began to speak.

"Thank you all for coming here this evening on short notice," Pops said. "You all know me as a man of purpose who likes to get straight to the point. That's what I'm going to do. It's the only way to do this."

Pops brought the handkerchief to his lips again.

"This morning," he said, "a young man visited Gabriel at the office. The man said that he and Gabriel have the same father—me. Gabriel came to me and asked me if the man was telling the truth. He was."

Nicole gasped. There was no reaction from Mom. She sat, frozen.

"The young man's name is Isaiah," Pops said. "He, like Gabriel, is thirty years old. In fact, he and Gabriel share the same birthday, as unlikely as that may sound. His mother lives—lived—in Chicago. She passed away earlier this year."

Nicole was shaking her head, tears flowing down her

cheeks. Dana rubbed Nicole's back, murmuring supportive words.

Mom had not shown any reaction.

"I'd always known about Isaiah, but I kept him a secret. After Isaiah's mother died, I suppose he wanted to meet me, so he's come here. I'm all he has left. He wants to know his people."

Nicole was weeping freely. Dana hugged her.

Mom was a marble statue. Gabriel put his arms around her. Her skin was clammy and her eyes were glassy.

Pops moved his handkerchief from his mouth to his eyes.

"You can't know how sorry I am that this has happened," Pops said. "I did a terrible thing, and it doesn't matter that it happened so many years ago. I'm so sorry. But I hope that we can pull together, as a family, and let Isaiah become a part of our lives. I owe him that much."

Finished, Pops leaned back in the chair and tilted his gaze to the ceiling. Tears trickled down his face.

Crying, Nicole wrapped her arms tightly around Dana. Dana rocked her, whispered to her.

Gabriel looked at his mother, who'd yet to speak a word.

She sat still, silent.

"Mom?" he asked. He shook her gently. "Are you okay?"

Mom blinked, turned to look at Gabriel.

Startled at what he'd seen in her gaze, Gabriel took a step backward.

Mom shrieked. It was a strange, tortured cry—the first time he'd ever heard her make a sound like that.

Mom pounced like a bobcat on his father.

She moved much too fast for anyone to stop her, and Pops didn't try to ward her away. As he sat there with his hands in his lap, Mom leaped on him. She was a delicate woman, but she slammed into him so hard that she knocked him off balance. The chair in which Pops sat tipped backward and crashed to the hardwood floor.

Gabriel was so awestruck that he couldn't move.

Sitting on Pops's chest, Mom dug her hands into his shirt like talons. She throttled him as if he were a rag doll. Pops's head thunked against the floor as she shook him.

"How could you, how could you, how could you?!" Mom screamed. She drew back her hand and smacked Pops so hard that a stream of saliva spewed from Pops's mouth.

Gabriel wanted to hurt his father, too. He truly did. He envisioned himself rushing to the fireplace, snagging a poker, and using it to beat his father senseless like a human piñata.

Nicole groped toward him, too, wild-eyed and weeping. Dana struggled to keep her away.

As she shook his father, Mom's screams of "How could you?" had become ragged sobs.

Pops lay there, taking the punishment like a martyr in the name of some noble cause, and it was that limp, defenseless pose that propelled Gabriel into action. On one level he was worried about Pops, concerned that his mother might seriously hurt him. But on another level that really got him going, he saw Pops's lack of resistance as just another act, another way of manipulating them to make them believe he was genuinely sorry. He had to be sorry, right, if he was allowing them to take their rage out on him like this? Gabriel didn't want to play into his hands, didn't want to be deceived, not anymore.

Gabriel hooked his hands under his mother's arms and attempted to drag her away from his dad. It was like trying to grab a knot of rattlesnakes. Mom writhed out of his grasp and fell on top of Pops, flailing her arms. One of her hands smacked Gabriel in the face, and, knocked off balance, he tumbled on top of both his parents.

Trying to regain his balance, his gaze fell on a photograph on the other side of the library. A family portrait taken when he was five years old. He had an Afro, and so did Pops and even Mom, and Nicole, all of two years old, had Afro puffs. They wore grins that looked as though they would never be erased from their faces. A moment of family bliss preserved forever.

Mom had maneuvered herself back onto Pops's chest. Her hands closed around his throat. She was squeezing. Weeping.

Pops gasped for air.

Gabriel wrapped his arm around his mother's waist and tugged her away.

Wailing, Mom kicked at Pops, her shoes striking against his ribs. Pops rolled away, still choking.

Gabriel hauled his mother to a chair on the other side of the room. He forced her into it. And then he held her there, braced both his arms around her, using his full weight to keep her in place.

"Stay here, Mama," he said. "Don't hurt Pops, just stay here."

Mom began to rock—as much as she could while trapped within the circle of his arms. "Lord Jesus help me," she cried. "Lord Jesus, Lord Jesus . . ."

Across the room, Nicole lay sprawled in a chair, limp and bedraggled. Dana had left the library.

Maybe she'd decided that his family was too crazy for her and had left. He couldn't say he would blame her.

Pops slowly sat up. He wiped his face with his handkerchief and blew his nose.

"I'm sorry," Pops said again in a tired voice. "I never wanted to hurt anyone. I hope you can forgive me. You all mean everything to me."

Mom grasped Gabriel's arms, started to peel them away. He didn't stop her. She moved with a deliberate strength that let him know she had gotten herself under control. Freed from his arms, she leaned forward in the chair, her gaze riveted on his father.

"Are there more?" Mom asked in a voice that, though full of pain, was surprisingly strong.

"More?" Pops asked. "I don't understand."

"More children you fathered," Nicole said. "That's what Mom means. Are there any more, or is this son the only one?"

"Jesus." Pops wiped his face. "Who do you think I am?"

"We don't know anymore," Gabriel said, and his mother and sister nodded.

"I can't believe you'd ask me that . . ." Pops trailed off. "No, there aren't any more, for God's sake."

"You lied to me," Mom said in a soft voice. She shook her head sadly. "How could you—after all I've sacrificed for you?"

"Marge—"

"I don't want to hear it." Mom raised her hand in a stop gesture.

Pops shut his mouth.

Mom looked from Nicole to Gabriel. "Your father and I need some time alone. Please shut the door on your way out of the library."

Mom's tone was firm and crisp. People who didn't know their family from the inside usually assumed that Pops ran the show. He did, in many ways, but in matters of discipline, Mom called the shots. "Spare the rod, spoil the child" had been her rule, and when she used that strident tone, they knew she meant business.

Gabriel and Nicole quietly left the library and closed the door behind them.

Gabriel saw Dana coming down the hallway with towels draped over her arm. Her eyes widened with alarm when she saw him and Nicole.

"What's going on?" Dana asked.

"Mom and Pops are talking in private." He took one of the towels Dana offered him and wiped his sweaty, tear-streaked face. "Shit, what a night."

Although his watch read half past seven, meaning that only about thirty minutes had passed since they had arrived, Gabriel felt as though several hours had gone by. He could never remember feeling so drained.

He ambled into the kitchen and sat on a stool near the granite-topped island. He buried his face in the towel.

He wanted this night to be over. He wanted to forget that any of this had happened. It was like someone else's life, not his.

But part of him felt as though this family catastrophe was inevitable. Hadn't he always believed that their lives were a little too *Cosby Show* ideal? Hadn't he always sensed something awful lurking just out of sight, waiting to slither into the light?

Maybe they deserved a shattering revelation like this to disabuse them of their illusions about themselves and drop them back into the real world, where there was no such thing as a perfect family.

No, this is all Pops's fault. There's no excuse for what he's done, and we don't deserve this.

He removed the towel from his face and wrung it with his hands as though choking someone.

Nicole took three Heinekens out of the refrigerator, beers left over from their Memorial Day cookout—what a happier day that had been—and handed them out. Neither Nicole nor Dana usually drank beer, but they popped off the caps and took long gulps. Gabriel sipped his, too, but he could have used something stronger to smooth the ragged edges of his emotions.

Nicole covered her mouth and belched. She leaned against the counter, closer to Gabriel. "You've met Isaiah, Gabe. What's he like?"

Gabriel started to say, "I didn't like him at all," but Dana fired a warning glance at him.

"You'll have to meet him yourself and form your own opinion, Nicole," he said. "I'm sure it won't be long before he stops by. You heard what Pops said about accepting him into the family."

"But does he look like he could be Daddy's son?" Nicole asked. "Maybe Daddy is wrong about him."

"Pops isn't wrong, trust me," Gabriel said. "The guy looks a lot like me. He even has gray eyes."

"And you and him are the same age, and have the same birthday?" Nicole said. "That's really weird."

"A bizarre coincidence," Dana said. "Isaiah is only a few minutes older than Gabe."

"Which makes him think he can call himself the first-born," Gabriel said.

But Nicole hadn't heard him. She patted at her reddened eyes with a towel. "I just can't believe Daddy would do this. I'm still shocked."

Gabriel wanted to shout, "Get over it, Nicole!" He didn't want her to be shocked. He wanted her to be angry. Was he the only one who was truly enraged at their father? To his way of thinking, *not* being angry at Pops was akin to forgiving him, and his father was a long way from deserving their forgiveness.

While Nicole and Dana continued to talk, Gabriel went back to the library. He cracked open the door.

His father was the only one in there. He stood at the window, nursing another stiff drink. He didn't glance at Gabriel.

"Where did Mom go?" Gabriel asked.

Pops shrugged. "You know your mother. After she cussed me out she went off to pray somewhere."

You need to be praying, too, Gabriel wanted to say. *For forgiveness.*

But Gabriel only shut the door.

He went to the second level and approached Mom's private study. The door was closed, but soft light glowed underneath.

He knocked. "Mom, it's Gabe."

"Come in," she said.

Mom's personal study was a book-lined room with a desk, comfortable sofa and reading chair, and Tiffany lamp. Mom sat on the sofa in the golden lamplight wearing her reading glasses; a large, leather-bound Bible lay open on her lap and a box of Kleenex stood on a nearby table.

He wasn't surprised to find his mother in there. Her uncharacteristic burst of rage notwithstanding, Mom was an easygoing woman, a devout Christian who placed great emphasis on forgiveness. She wasn't going to let righteous anger rule her. She would set aside her anger and hurt to work to heal their family. For Mom, healing began with seeking God's counsel.

"Sorry to interrupt," he said. "I wanted to make sure you were okay."

"Have a seat." Smiling weakly, she patted the cushion beside her.

He sat next to her. Mom dabbed her eyes with a tissue, sniffled, and then placed a shaky finger underneath a line of scripture.

"Listen," he said. "If you want to be alone, Mom . . ."

"Please." She placed her hand on his arm. "Sit here with me. For a little while."

"Okay," he said. He looked around the room awkwardly, not knowing what to say. Still struggling to handle his own anger, he felt incapable of comforting his mother.

"It hurts, I know," Mom said. "But we must forgive him."

"Forgive him?" He shook his head fervently. "I'm not there yet, Mom. Are you?"

"No," she admitted. "But I'm upset with your father for . . . other reasons."

"Other reasons?"

Mom blinked as though catching herself in a lapse. "Forgiveness is good for the soul, Gabriel. Although I suspect it will take some time for you to reach that point."

"You could be right," he said, nodding. "Or maybe I never will."

Chapter 19

An hour later, Gabriel drove home, Dana riding in the passenger seat.

"Mom talked to me about forgiving Pops," Gabriel said. "Ain't no way in hell."

Dana looked away from the window, where she had been contemplating the night.

"That's kinda harsh, baby," she said.

"Pops cheated on her, Dana. Then he lied to her. Hell, he lied to all of us—for years."

"True," she said slowly. "He did a terrible thing. But . . ."

"But what?"

"But I'd hate to see this tear apart your family. In spite of what your father did, you have a wonderful family. Not everyone is so lucky." Her eyes darkened, and he knew what she meant. She had lost her folks when she was just a kid. To her, he appeared to be blessed beyond measure.

Maybe she was right; maybe he was being shortsighted and immature. He couldn't deny that Pops had been a great father to him and Nicole, and a loving husband to his mother. He looked up to his father as if he were a hero, always had.

Perhaps that was why learning about Pops's lie cut so deep.

"Do you know what's going to happen next?" Gabriel asked. "After Mom is done weeping and praying and forgiving Pops? I can tell you."

Dana sighed, didn't respond.

"Pops is going to bring Isaiah over to meet the family," he said. "Wait and see. It's bad enough that he had to lie for all these years—now he's gonna rub our faces in it, too."

Gabriel's house was ahead. He turned into the driveway, too fast, and almost smashed into the garage door before it had finished opening. Calming himself, he slowly maneuvered into the garage, and switched off the engine.

He massaged the bridge of his nose. Dana sat with him, quietly. It was only half-past nine, but he was exhausted and couldn't wait to sleep.

"Your father isn't perfect," she said, ending the silence. "He's only human. He makes mistakes."

"This isn't just a mistake! We're talking about a son. He's out there fathering kids!"

"Okay, then it was a *huge* mistake. But I think sometimes you expect too much of your father."

"Expecting him to honor his vows to be faithful to my mom is too much to ask?"

"You put your dad on a pedestal. And that's okay. You should admire him, but everyone needs room to make a mistake sometimes."

"Now *you* think I should forgive Pops, don't you?"

"Whether you forgive him or not is up to you. In my opinion, forgiving is healthy. But I think you first need to accept that your dad isn't perfect."

She had verbalized the same concerns that weighed on his mind. He hated that she was echoing his feelings. Because he wasn't ready to do anything about them yet.

"This is none of your business, Dana."

"You're right, it's none of my business. Excuse me for caring."

"It's not that." He pinched his nose harder. "You just don't understand."

"Don't understand? Oh, I understand, Gabe. I understand that you idolize your father and don't want to admit that he can make mistakes like an ordinary person. You let him run your life—"

"Pops doesn't run my life."

"—and you're starting to worry that if your perfect daddy who—let's admit it—runs your life isn't as perfect as you thought, then what does that say about you? What does that say about the life you've let him create for you? Maybe it's not all it was cracked up to be, maybe it's not all so perfect, maybe it's time you learned to make your own decisions."

"I've heard enough of this shit." He flung open the car door and stomped inside the house.

Dana followed him. "Grow up! Stop relying on Daddy to do it all for you. 'Cause guess what? Daddy ain't perfect! Matter of fact, Papa was a rolling stone!"

At the door to the master bedroom, Gabriel seized the knob so tightly that his knuckles popped. "Are you finished?"

Dana stood in the hallway, fists on her waist, bosom heaving. "What, is a little honesty too much for you to handle?"

"Drop it, Dana."

"I need my husband to be his own man."

"What the hell does that mean?"

"It means grow up. Or this isn't gonna work."

There was a threat in her words. A threat he didn't want to consider.

She didn't know what she was saying, he told himself. She was emotionally drained, and so was he. Neither of them was talking sensibly.

"Look, we've had a long night, and we're both exhausted," he said. "Can we discuss this later?"

"I want to talk about it now."

"Well, I don't. Argue with yourself. Good night."

He went into the bathroom to shower. Dana's words reverberated in his thoughts, and he tried to shut them out.

I need my husband to be his own man.

He had never been so insulted. Under a jet of scalding hot water, he scrubbed his skin angrily.

When he finished showering and entered the bedroom, he found Dana sitting on the bed. She sniffled, rubbed her eyes.

"I'm sorry," she said. "I didn't mean everything I said."

"But you meant part of it?" He snatched away the bedsheets and climbed on the mattress. "I'm done talking about it."

"Gabe . . ." She reached for his arm. He jerked away.

"Don't shut down on me," she said.

"I'm just trying to act like I'm my own man," he said. He pulled up the covers and rolled onto his stomach, away from her.

He heard her sigh loudly. Then she went into the bathroom and turned on the shower.

They fell asleep with a cold, wide space between them.

Chapter 20

When Gabriel awoke at six o'clock the next morning, Dana had already left.

Dana was an early riser and often needed to be at the hospital by five A.M. But when she slept over, she never left without first waking him and kissing him good-bye.

Last night felt like a bad dream. Dana's abrupt departure proved that it was not. She was still upset. They needed to patch this up, and quickly. They'd never been at odds like this.

Happy couples didn't argue, Gabriel believed. He'd never seen Mom and Pops involved in an argument. If they ever had a disagreement—and he wasn't sure they had until last night—they handled it behind closed doors, away from him and his sister. He'd never seen them work through conflict together, never heard them discuss and resolve their issues.

He wondered if that was a good thing. Children learned so much from observing their parents. On those rare occasions when he found himself mired in relationship troubles, he felt out of his depth, like a poor swimmer tossed into a deep sea.

He would call Dana soon and handle these problems before things worsened.

He climbed out of bed and padded to the bathroom. A long, warm shower would help him relax.

He noted with satisfaction that there was nothing unusual in the mirror. Only his fatigued face.

He slipped on a shower cap to keep his head bandage from getting soaked and stepped into the shower stall.

He was soaping his body under a spray of warm water, humming the notes to a Miles Davis solo, when he glanced through the glass stall doors and saw something on the bathroom floor.

Water blurred the glass, preventing him from getting a clear view. But it looked like a snake.

"Oh, shit," he said.

Then he thought, *It can't be a snake. What would a snake be doing in my house?*

He turned off the water. He rubbed clear a spot on the glass.

It was a dark snake, its scales bedecked with light bands; a little more than two feet long, it had a thick, muscular body and a pale yellow belly.

Gabriel knew the breed, and even as his mind told him what it was, he wanted to deny it: the snake was a cottonmouth water moccasin. A member of the pit viper family. One of the deadliest snakes in the world.

Barely four feet away from the shower stall, the serpent slithered across the marble floor. It quested along the edge of the vanity, rose, slipped out its forked tongue to taste the air, and then whispered into the shadowy crevice underneath the sinks, behind the small trash can. Gabriel saw only the faint sparkle of its scales.

He stood stock-still, disbelieving what he'd seen. The water left on his skin felt like shavings of ice.

How the hell had a water moccasin gotten into his house?

There was a large lake in the subdivision about a half block away from his home. He'd seen lizards scampering across the lawn from time to time, and once a turtle had crept across his driveway. He'd heard rumors of water moccasins lurking in the waters. But he'd never, ever seen one.

And now there was one in his bathroom.

Had Dana left a door open when she'd left? How had this happened?

It wasn't enough that his dad had confessed to fathering a son outside the marriage and that his family had been turned upside down; it wasn't enough that he was plagued by visions in mirrors and tingling palms and doors that opened for no apparent reason; to add the icing to the cake, he had a lethal snake in his house, in his bathroom, when he was butt naked in the shower.

Gabriel could have dealt with almost any other kind of threat. Spiders, rats, wasps—anything. But not a snake, and certainly not a lethal one.

He vividly recalled the time a water moccasin had bitten him in north Georgia. His right calf began to throb, as though remembering the horrifying pain inflicted by those fangs. He'd been rushed to the hospital and had been lucky (yet again) to survive.

He didn't want to get out of the shower. But he couldn't stay in there, naked and defenseless.

He came up with a plan.

He had to contain the snake. If he could get out of the bathroom without disturbing the reptile, he could close the door, trapping the snake within until a pest-control expert arrived to remove it.

It wasn't a brilliant strategy, but it would have to do.

With a trembling hand, he slowly pushed open the door.

He didn't dare to take his attention away from the crevice beneath the sink. The snake was motionless. But he felt it watching him.

Water dripping off his body, he stepped outside the stall and steadied his feet on the floor. He drew in a couple of breaths. He was on the verge of hyperventilating.

To get to the door, he had to pass the sinks. He would rather have walked across a bed of burning coals than to move anywhere closer to that snake, but there was no way around it.

There was a towel hamper beside the shower. It was as high as his waist. He decided to use the hamper as a shield. He gripped the edges of it and lifted it off the floor.

Keeping his gaze on the dark space and the resting reptile, Gabriel began to creep across the bathroom, holding the hamper between him and the reptile's lair, trying to be as silent and smooth as possible.

The snake sprang out of the crevice like a jack-in-the-box. Hissing angrily, it came at him.

Gabriel screamed. He heaved the towel hamper in the direction of the charging snake, thinking vaguely that it could knock the snake away and maybe buy him a second or two to escape, but as the hamper crashed against the floor, the reptile fluidly vaulted over it as though it had coiled springs in its body. The snake surged toward him in a dark flash. Too far away from the door to make it out safely, Gabriel whirled and ran back to the shower stall. He half leaped, half stumbled into it, banging his knees and elbows painfully.

He grabbed the handle and slammed the door just as the snake drew back to strike.

The water moccasin pressed against the glass. Its narrow yellow eyes found Gabriel and glared at him with pure hatred.

Gabriel's blood froze and his lips parted in a garbled scream.

The snake's mouth snapped open, revealing two wicked fangs dripping with venom.

Gabriel mashed himself against the wall, as far away from the door as possible.

"Jesus, Jesus, Jesus," he said. He shivered so violently the entire stall shook around him.

The snake stared at him a moment, as though warning him, and then it moved away. It undulated across the floor to the doorway.

"No," Gabriel said. "Stay out of there!"

The snake crossed the threshold and disappeared in the bedroom, blending into the shadows.

Now the reptile could wind up *anywhere* in the house. His half-baked plan to trap the snake in the bathroom had been worthless.

He waited about a minute. The water moccasin did not return.

Warily, he opened the shower-stall door again and got out. He picked up a towel off the nearby rack and wrapped it around his waist.

Then he moved to give himself a line of sight into the bedroom.

The bedroom was quiet, and full of shadows, too, thanks to the blinds he kept shuttered on the windows to keep sunlight from leaking inside. He wished he'd opened those blinds as soon as he'd gotten out of bed. The reptile could be hidden anywhere out there.

He wasn't going to try to find the snake. His only wish was to get out of the house alive. Someone else could hunt down and trap the damn thing.

Gabriel moved closer to the doorway. The snake did not spring out of the shadows. Wherever it had taken refuge, it was well hidden.

He grabbed the bathroom door and swung it shut.

Before he went anywhere, he needed to dress. He hurried to the walk-in closet off the end of the bathroom and quickly threw on jeans, a T-shirt, and athletic shoes.

He wished he kept a telephone in the bathroom. He would have called someone and never taken the risk of leaving until the snake was captured.

He found a baseball bat in the corner of the closet. It was a Louisville Slugger, a relic from his days in Little League. Dust coated the wood. He wiped off the bat with a towel and hefted it in both hands.

"I've got something for you now," he said.

His confidence ebbed when he remembered how the agile snake had evaded the towel hamper. If he swung at the water moccasin and missed . . .

Don't think about that, Gabe.

Clutching the bat, he returned to the bathroom door and slowly pushed it open.

He didn't see the snake. But he was sure it was still concealed somewhere.

To escape the bedroom, he had to pass by the foot of the bed. He worried that the snake was hidden in the darkness under the bed—and that it might strike him as he ran by.

Or it could be waiting for him in the hallway, outside the bedroom.

Or it could be in the kitchen.

Or it could be . . .

He shook his head. Thinking of the numerous, dire possibilities had temporarily paralyzed him.

Do something, he thought to himself firmly. *Stop thinking and move.*

A phone stood on the nightstand along the path to the doorway. He could pluck the phone off the cradle as he got out of there, too.

Okay, so do it, Gabe.

Cold sweat crept down his spine. He redoubled his grip on the bat.

Then he lowered his head and sprinted across the bedroom. He refused to pause, refused to look around him or behind him, because if he did that, he was convinced he'd see the reptile, poised to deliver a fatal bite, and that would be the end of him.

As he ran, he snatched the phone off the nightstand.

He made it safely to the door. The snake had not appeared.

He slammed the door behind him. In case the water moccasin was inside, it would be imprisoned in there.

The hallway was empty. But there were rooms branching off the hall, and they were cloaked in shadows and could be hiding the reptile.

He had no plans to explore any of the rooms. He just had to get to the front door.

Brandishing the bat, he hurried down the hall to the front of the house.

The water moccasin lay coiled on the hardwood floor, no less than a foot away from the door and freedom. It rose, hissing.

"Shit," he said.

He raced to the garage. He threw open the door, stumbled inside, punched the button to raise the large sectional doors. He dashed across the garage and ran outside so quickly that his head brushed against the bottom of the still-opening doors.

He turned around and backpedaled all the way to the mouth of the driveway. He was panting, his lungs aching.

He expected—he hoped—to see the snake slither out of the garage and away from the house. It didn't.

He dialed the first number that came to mind: his parents' house. Pops answered on the third ring.

"Hello," Pops said. He was breathing hard, too, but Gabriel knew that his father ran on the treadmill in the morning before heading to the office.

"Pops, I need your help," Gabriel said. And as he told his father what had happened, he didn't consider the terrible and dishonest acts his father had committed. He was a boy again, seeking his father's assistance and calm assurance that everything would be okay, and it hit Gabriel that Dana was right: she did need her husband to be his own man. And he wasn't yet such a person.

Chapter 21

The representative from Metro Wildlife Control arrived at Gabriel's house shortly after eight o'clock that morning. Pops had called the company on Gabriel's behalf and requested emergency service. Pops himself promised to come soon.

Gabriel was still angry with his father, but grateful for his help.

Gabriel met the wildlife control expert in front of the garage. He was a tall, husky white man with unruly brown hair barely contained underneath a Florida Gators cap. He wore a T-shirt with a poster image from that Russell·Crowe flick, *Gladiator*. The colors were so faded that Gabriel guessed the guy had washed and worn the shirt a hundred times. Was this man really an expert on removing snakes?

The guy introduced himself as Fisher.

"Saw a cottonmouth in your house, huh, dude? Bet that scared the shit out of you, didn't it?" Fisher said. He went to the bed of his Chevy pickup. The truck bore huge mud splashes, as though he'd been ripping through the Florida Everglades.

"Of course it scared me," Gabriel said. "But I can't figure out how it got *in* there."

After he'd talked to Pops, Gabriel had called Dana to tell her what had happened and to ask whether she'd seen a door or a window open when she'd left that morning. But she hadn't answered his call. He'd left her a brief message, asking her to call him back ASAP.

"Snakes usually slip inside your house if your home makes a good habitat for 'em," Fisher said.

"I can't believe my house would be a good habitat for snakes. I've never had this problem before."

"Anyway, they're sneaky little creatures," Fisher said sagely. "Might've gotten in when you opened a door or a window, or found a little hole somewhere." He shrugged. "I'll check for that stuff while I'm here, so you'll be cool, buddy."

Fisher lifted a couple of items out of the truck: a long steel rod with a pair of large metal tongs at the end, and a voluminous white sack made of a tough material.

"Snake tongs; snake bag," Fisher said with the formality of a Catholic priest conducting Communion.

Carrying the sack in one hand and balancing the rod on his shoulder, Fisher approached the front door.

Gabriel hung back. "Be careful, man. It was sitting right in front of that door when I last saw him."

"No problem, dude. Is the door open?"

Gabriel stepped forward, unlocked the door, and then quickly moved away.

"Go ahead," Gabriel said.

"You'd prefer to wait out here, huh?" Fisher said. "I was hoping you'd come in with me and hold him down with your hands while I slip the bag over him."

Gabriel gave the guy a *you must be out your damn mind* look.

Fisher laughed. "Just kidding with you. Sit tight. I'll whistle if I need you."

"Sure."

Gabriel had removed a lawn chair from the garage and parked it in the cool shade of a maple tree in his front yard. He'd driven to the local QuikTrip gas station and picked up the day's *Wall Street Journal* and two bottles of water, too.

He wasn't going inside his house until Fisher captured the snake, and while he waited, he might as well be comfortable.

As he sat in the shade reading the newspaper, his cell phone chirped. It was Dana.

"Hey," she said with minimal enthusiasm. "I got your message. What's up?"

"Well, good morning to you, too," he said. "I didn't see you before you left."

"I didn't want to wake you," she said curtly.

He hated the tension between them. They were better than this.

"Listen, Dana, about last night—"

"I can't talk about that right now. It's busy here."

Shot down. Fine then. He would be all business, too.

"Did you see an open door or window before you left?" he asked.

"No. Why?"

"There was a snake in the house. A water moccasin."

"What?" Her standoffish tone fell away. "Are you serious?"

"I saw it in the bathroom when I was showering. It was on the floor."

"Oh, my God. Are you okay?"

"I got the hell out of there without being bitten. A wildlife control guy is in the house now to catch it. Needless to say, I'm waiting outside."

"Jesus," she said. "I didn't see anything before I left, Gabe. If I'd seen that thing, I would have screamed my head off."

"You think I didn't? You remember how I was bitten when I was a teenager?"

"I remember you telling me about that. I'm so glad you're okay."

"I'm taking care of it," he said. He didn't dare confess that he'd called his father for help. That was the last thing he needed to let her know.

"I need to go, Gabe, but call me and let me know how it goes, okay?"

"Will do." He hung up.

Gabriel stared at the phone. At least he and Dana were talking, though they hadn't dealt with the real problem yet. Perhaps they could talk about it tonight face-to-face after their emotions had settled some more.

However, he wasn't sure what he would tell her. *You're right, I'm not my own man yet. I need Pops to help me live my life.* She wasn't going to let him off the hook about that; he sensed that it was so important to her that it could very well determine the fate of their relationship.

As if he didn't already have enough to be worried about.

About fifteen minutes later—there had been no word from Fisher—Pops pulled into the driveway. He was dressed for work in a charcoal suit, and his hair was freshly trimmed. He looked nothing like the beaten-down man who'd confessed his sins to his family last night.

"They catch the snake yet?" Pops asked.

"He's still in there looking for it."

"Helluva way to start off the morning."

"You're telling me. You know how I feel about snakes."

Fisher exited the house through the garage. Gabriel noted that the snake bag fluttered loosely, as though empty.

"Are you the guy who called us?" Fisher asked Pops.

Pops nodded. "I am indeed."

Fisher looked from Pops to Gabriel. "There's no snake in there, dude." His eyes were downcast, as though he'd been robbed of an exciting adventure. "The premises are all clear. I don't even see how a snake would've gotten in there. There're no entryways unless you left a door wide open. But you say you didn't."

"I'm positive," Gabriel said. "The snake has to be in there. I told you it was by the front door!"

"Home's clean," Fisher said. "I looked everywhere. I'm telling you, dude, there's no snake in there."

Gabriel pinched the bridge of his nose. He was beginning to get a headache. None of this was making any sense.

Fisher removed a long cardboard box from his truck.

"I'll set a trap," Fisher said. "I'll leave this box in there; there's glue in it. If he comes back, the trap'll catch him. Just give me a ring and I'll come pick it up."

"Fine," Gabriel said.

Fisher disappeared in the house again. Pops took a call on his cell phone; a business issue, from the sounds of it.

Gabriel walked to the front door just as Fisher was coming out.

"You're all set, buddy," Fisher said.

Nodding absently, Gabriel pushed open the door, looked down the hallway. He didn't see the water moccasin. But it might have hidden somewhere, eluding Fisher's probing eye.

The thought of going inside and taking a closer look didn't appeal to him at all.

When he returned to the driveway, Pops was writing a check to pay Fisher for the visit.

"Pops, I've got it," Gabriel said.

Pops waved him off. Fisher gave him a receipt, loaded the tools of his trade in the truck, and drove away.

"What next?" Pops asked. "You want me to call someone else, get a second opinion here?"

"I guess it must've slipped out before he got here," Gabriel said. "If he says it's gone, I'll take his word for it. But I'm going to keep my eyes peeled."

What he didn't tell Pops was that he was going to do more

than keep his eyes peeled. He was going to search the house from top to bottom. He had to do it for his own peace of mind.

"You want to stay with us for a couple days?" Pops asked.

It wasn't an entirely unattractive offer, but Gabriel would have a tough time regaining Dana's goodwill if he accepted it.

"I'll manage here," he said.

"Our door is always open," Pops said. "You know your mother and I love having you around."

"How is Mom?"

Pops smiled tightly. "We're working it out, son. Speaking of which, I'd like you to come to the house again tonight. Seven o'clock."

"Why?" Gabriel asked, but he thought he knew the answer.

"I'm going to introduce Isaiah to the rest of the family."

Chapter 22

Isaiah went shopping.

Atlanta was known for its shopping malls, and Lenox Square, in Buckhead, was one of the crown jewels of the metropolitan retail scene. Anchored by Bloomingdale's, Neiman Marcus, and Macy's, Lenox offered more than two hundred specialty shops that sold everything from shoes to designer clothing to furniture to sporting goods, and much, much more.

But more than that, it was a people watcher's paradise. Celebrity spottings were common there. Celebs parked in the valet's driveway—beside which sparkling luxury automobiles were lined up as though for a car show—and vanished inside to be spotted by their adoring public. Tourists prowled the mall, cameras dangling around their necks, ready to take a snapshot of a beloved superstar. Scantily clad beautiful women of every ethnicity flocked from store to store, perhaps the wives—or mistresses—of said celebrities. Or gold diggers hoping to snag a man of means.

People watched Isaiah, too. Dressed in a black T-shirt that displayed the tattoos on his arms for all to see, strutting with a slow, brother-man stroll, and wearing a platinum-encrusted chain, he might have been a rap star, dropping in to spend a few grand on some clothes.

He was there to purchase clothing. But that was only a small part of his shopping list.

In an upscale men's clothing store, he purchased a couple of sport coats, shirts, slacks, and loafers. Casually elegant wear.

Then, after going to his car and securing his purchases in the trunk, he returned to the mall to buy the other items on his list.

Three hours later, laden with several bags of merchandise, he visited a restaurant in the mall for a late lunch. The place was called Prime, and they specialized in steak and sushi. Although it was located in the mall, the muted lighting, thick white table linens, and spotless contemporary decor made you feel as though you were floating in an epicurean fantasyland.

Isaiah was not accustomed to dining in nice restaurants. This visit was a rare pleasure, a splurge to celebrate the launching of his mission. He was a bit surprised when the hostess showed him to a corner table without blinking twice at his casual wear. She definitely must've pegged him as a rapper or music producer of note.

Within a minute of Isaiah taking his seat, a gorgeous Asian waitress arrived. She introduced herself as Amy, and her gaze lingered on the rattlesnake tattoo twined around his muscular forearm.

"That's a beautiful tattoo," she said.

"Thanks. You like snakes?"

"I love them, actually," she said. "Does that make me weird?"

"Not at all; it makes you unique. But you're right, not many people like snakes. My baby brother hates them, for instance. They scare him to death. Poor kid."

"What a shame," Amy said, and smiled at their perceived common bond.

Isaiah smiled, too—though for an entirely different reason.

Poor Gabe.

Part Two

HOME INVASION

Home is where the heart is.
—Anonymous

Chapter 23

Gabriel took the day off from work.

Although he had important tasks at the office that required his attention, he stayed home. He spent the day examining every potential snake hideout in his house: underneath beds and tables and furniture, behind curtains and desks and dressers and televisions, inside closets and pantries and cabinets and drawers, and within every shadowy niche and crawl space.

As he searched, he carried his Louisville Slugger, ready to knock the reptile senseless.

But the only living creatures he found were a couple of small spiders that he trapped in a napkin and flushed down the toilet. No snake. He'd looked everywhere, multiple times.

It was impossible. But the wildlife control guy hadn't found the creature either.

He would have to accept that the snake had escaped. That bothered him. If the serpent had eluded him, that meant it was on the loose.

That meant it could come back.

He remembered how the reptile had showed its fangs to him.

The snake would return; he had no doubt. The damned thing seemed to harbor a malicious intent toward him, as absurd as that sounded. And what if he wasn't so lucky during their next encounter?

He wouldn't be able to relax in his house again for a long time. His home, previously his sanctuary, had become a nest of horrors.

His father's offer to stay with them for a couple of days had never looked more attractive. But if he accepted, he would never live that down with Dana. When he'd talked to Dana again and told her that the snake apparently had escaped, and invited her to the family meeting that evening, he'd tried to sound calm and in full control of the situation. Like the kind of man she wanted her husband to be. He couldn't stand the thought of losing her respect any more than he already had.

He would have to stay home and tough it out.

After a fitful nap—he could barely keep his eyes shut because he kept imagining the snake lurking nearby—he had begun yet another sweep of the house when he glanced at a clock in the kitchen and realized it was a quarter to seven. Pops had scheduled the family meeting for seven o'clock. He wanted to "introduce Isaiah to the rest of the family," as he'd put it.

As far as Gabriel was concerned, it was like trading one snake for another. There was something about Isaiah he didn't like. But he couldn't put his finger on exactly what it was.

Gabriel was grimy from crawling around the house all day and didn't have time to shower. He washed his face, put on a clean T-shirt, and hurried to the car. He wanted to get to his parents' house before Isaiah arrived. That seemed important, for some reason.

He just didn't trust that guy.

When Gabriel pulled in front of his parents' house fifteen minutes late, he saw that Isaiah had beaten him there. Isaiah's Chevelle was parked in the driveway in the same spot Gabriel usually parked his car when he visited his family.

First Isaiah had taken his parking space at the office. Now he'd done it at the family home.

Dana and Nicole's vehicles were there, too. Everyone invited was already there, actually. He was the last one to arrive.

Gabriel didn't like that, not at all. He couldn't articulate why. He just didn't like it.

He parked at the end of the driveway and hurried inside.

Gabriel found everyone gathered not in the library or grand salon, as he'd anticipated, but in the formal dining room. Silver platters heaped with food covered the long oak table: fried chicken, corn on the cob, barbecued rib tips, collard greens, potato salad, coleslaw. Pops sat at one end of the table; Isaiah sat at the opposite end (Gabriel's normal spot); Mom, Nicole, and Dana sat around the men.

Everyone had already begun eating.

"Nice of you to join us, son," Pops said. He grinned. "We've got a full spread here—grab a seat and dig in while it's still hot." Pops tilted his head toward Isaiah. "You've already met your brother, of course."

Isaiah rose. He was stylishly dressed in dark blazer, silk shirt, and slacks. Gabriel, clad in his dusty cargo shorts and wrinkled T-shirt, felt pathetically underdressed.

Isaiah extended his hand. He was smiling so hard that it looked painful.

"Please don't leave me hanging this time, Gabe," Isaiah said.

Whatever, Gabriel thought. They shook hands briefly. Isaiah's skin was dry and cold, as though ice water pumped through his veins.

Gabriel sat in the chair next to Dana. She gave him a brief smile that made it clear that matters still had not been repaired between them.

"Who cooked all this food?" Gabriel asked. He looked at

his mother questioningly. But she only shrugged and nodded at his father.

"I had the food catered in," Pops said. "I wanted to give your brother a proper welcome home."

"Welcome home?" Gabriel asked.

"That's right," Isaiah said. "I've been away for a long time, little brother. My whole life, isn't that right, folks?"

Nods and murmurs of agreement all around the table.

A knot of resentment swelled in Gabriel's stomach. And what was up with that "little brother" shit?

To Gabriel, Mom and Nicole appeared to be trying too hard, smiling too much and hanging on Isaiah's every word as if he were the Dalai Lama or something; they were determined to present a friendly family pose. Dana seemed interested, too, but that was to be expected, since she was friendly to everyone. Pops was leaning back in his chair, beaming proudly, and that annoyed Gabriel. Springing a thirty-year-old son on your family—that was nothing to be proud of. And Isaiah . . . he was far too comfortable here, sitting in that chair, *Gabriel's seat*, as though he'd been there his entire life.

Is there something wrong with me? Gabriel asked himself. *Why am I the only one who seems to be pissed off?*

"Eat something, Gabe," Dana said.

"I ate before I got here," Gabriel lied. "I'm not hungry."

Dana frowned at him, as though she knew he was lying, and then went back to eating.

"Actually, now that Gabriel is here with us, I'd like to make a speech," Isaiah said. He pushed away from the table and stood. He clasped his hands together, dipped his head as though in deep thought.

Everyone stopped eating. They watched Isaiah expectantly.

Gabriel bristled. What line of bullshit was Isaiah about to feed them now?

Isaiah raised his head, swept his gaze around the table.

"I've been waiting my whole life for this day," Isaiah said. "The day when I would finally meet my father's wonderful family. I can only imagine how difficult this has been for all of you, since, until yesterday, none of you even knew I existed. But I can see, already, that you're charitable, compassionate people. I'm humbled by your hospitality and kindness."

"It been hard on us," Mom said. She touched her sad eyes with a tissue. "But you're my husband's son. That makes you family."

Give me a break, Gabriel thought. *This is ridiculous.*

Pops approached Isaiah and wrapped his arm around his shoulder. He wiped his eyes with his handkerchief. "Thank you, Marge. You don't know how much it means to me for you to accept him."

"I never thought I'd have another brother," Nicole said. She was beginning to cry, too. "And you and Gabe look *so* much alike."

"I know," Isaiah said. He grinned. "But I'm older."

Everyone except Gabriel laughed appreciatively. Gabriel twisted a napkin in his lap.

"Seriously," Isaiah said. "God works in mysterious ways. I honestly believe that it took losing my mama—may her soul rest in peace—for me to truly appreciate the value of knowing the rest of my kinfolk. When God closes one door, he always opens another."

"Amen," Mom said. She touched the gold crucifix that hung on her necklace. "He's an awesome God, yes, He is."

"I am thankful to all of you," Isaiah said. "It's my desire to become a valued member of this family. I won't lie; I've lived a rough life and done some things I'm not proud of—"

"We all have," Nicole said.

Gabriel was shaking his head.

"But God has been so good to me, so patient with me," Isaiah said. "And after many trials and tribulations, I've finally wised up and realized what's most important in life. Faith. Family. Honesty. Integrity. Compassion." Isaiah nodded at Pops and Mom. "The same qualities both of you in-stilled in your children."

"We tried our best," Pops said.

"I could go on and bore you, but I won't," Isaiah said. "All I want to say is thank you. This means everything to me . . . if only you knew . . ."

Isaiah's eyes began to water. Drying his eyes with a nap-kin, he sat. Pops massaged Isaiah's shoulders. Nicole reached across the table and took Isaiah's hand, and Mom was whispering praise to God.

Dana glanced at Gabriel. Her brow crinkled when she saw the angry expression he couldn't keep off his face, and she lip-synched the question, *What's wrong with you?*

Gabriel couldn't hide his feelings. Isaiah deserved an Oscar for that dinner speech.

"I need to get some things out of my car," Isaiah said. He rose again. "I'll be right back." He left the dining room.

With Isaiah temporarily away, the focus shifted to Gabriel.

"Why are you acting like this?" Dana asked.

"You look upset, honey," Mom said.

"What's the deal?" Nicole said.

"Anything I can do for you, son?" Pops asked.

"Look . . ." Gabriel started. He wanted to be diplomatic, but it was difficult. "I think we need to take things slow, that's all. We don't know enough about Isaiah to be welcom-ing him into the family with open arms."

Mom turned a stern glare on him. "We know about his in-carceration, Gabriel. Isaiah shared his unfortunate personal history with us before you got here. Why don't you give him a chance?"

"It's not that, Mom," he said.

"Then what is it?" Pops asked.

Gabriel struggled to find the words to express his worries without sounding like a jackass.

"Gabe's upset because he's not the only son anymore," Nicole said. She spoke in a high-pitched, singsong voice that used to annoy Gabriel when they were children. "He's spoiled rotten, like I always said he was—"

"Will you shut up, Nicole?" Gabriel said.

"Don't tell me to shut up, boy," Nicole said. "I'm a grown woman. You aren't my daddy."

Gabriel ground his teeth. This wasn't going well at all.

"Why don't you like him?" Dana asked. "Give us the truth."

"Look, it's a gut feeling that I have, okay?" Gabriel said. "I don't trust him and I think we need to be careful. That's all I'm saying."

But everyone's faces were full of doubt. They thought he, not Isaiah, was the one with the problem.

"I expected you, of all people, to handle this better," Pops said. He shook his head sadly, but then his voice turned to steel. "I know this has been hard for you, but I want you to keep an open mind here, understand? I'm not allowing this change to fracture our family. We need to all be on board with this. Hear me?"

Anger and embarrassment stung Gabriel's face. He regretted opening his mouth in the first place.

"Got it?" Pops asked.

"Yeah, whatever, Pops," Gabriel said.

Watching him, Dana only shook her head. He could feel this discussion pulling them further apart.

Isaiah returned to the dining room. His arms were heaped with brightly colored gift bags.

"I've got presents for everyone," he said. "It's the least I can do to express my gratitude for your hospitality."

The women melted, and Pops smiled that goofy, proud grin again.

Damn him, Gabriel thought. *He's got everyone fooled. But not me.*

After dinner, Gabriel stood outside on the covered flagstone patio, leaning against a pillar and watching moonlight glimmer on the swimming pool. He was nursing his second Heineken, and because he hadn't eaten dinner, the alcohol had gone straight to his head; a warm buzz had settled over him.

Gabriel wanted to stand out there alone for the remainder of the evening. The family was in the grand salon, going gaga over everything Isaiah said and exclaiming about how wonderful his gifts to them were. Isaiah had bought gaudy trinkets for the women, Crown Royal for Pops, and, for Gabriel, a wooden statue of a snake winding around a man's body.

A snake statue, for God's sake.

Although, thankfully, no one told Isaiah about Gabriel's recent experience finding the snake in his house, Isaiah already knew Gabriel despised snakes. When they had first met in Gabriel's office, Gabriel had told him about his loathing for the reptile.

Isaiah's flagrant disregard for his feelings only proved to him that the guy was up to no good.

But how could he convince his family that Isaiah had devious motives? He lacked any hard evidence. He mostly had, as he'd told them, a gut feeling. But he couldn't reasonably expect them to take his intuition seriously—especially since, thus far, Isaiah had been the perfect gentleman.

Gabriel was ruminating on those thoughts when he heard footsteps behind him.

He looked over his shoulder. It was Isaiah.

"What's up, little brother?" Isaiah said. "Okay if I chill out here with you for a few?"

"It's up to you."

Why had Isaiah come out there? If Isaiah thought he was going to win him over like he'd charmed everyone else, he was wasting his time.

Sipping a beer, Isaiah strolled across the patio. He motioned for Gabriel to follow.

Grudgingly, Gabriel shuffled forward. Isaiah wandered toward the koi pond, which was nestled in a grotto on the other side of the immense patio. A small waterfall cascaded into the pond, water sparkling like silver in the moonlight.

"What kinda fish are in there?" Isaiah asked, pointing with his beer bottle.

"Koi," Gabriel said. "Japanese fish."

Isaiah chuckled. "You've gotta be kidding me. So now black folks got Japanese fish?"

"It was my mom's idea," Gabriel said. "Gives the land-scaping a touch of class. But you probably don't know any-thing about that."

Isaiah only smiled at Gabriel's jibe.

"I love your family, man," Isaiah said. "They're great people. You were blessed to grow up in a place like this, around folks like them."

"Yeah, it was nice," Gabriel said. "I feel very protective toward my family, you know."

"You should. What good son wouldn't?"

"Even if that means I sometimes have to do things my fa-ther doesn't want to do. It's only to keep my family safe. That's what matters most to me."

"Sounds fair."

"Look." Gabriel tossed his beer into a nearby trash can. "Let's cut the bullshit, okay? I know why you're here."

"Really? So why am I here, Gabe?" Isaiah appeared to be amused.

"Come on, man. Do I need to say it? My dad's a million-aire; we've got a booming business—a business *I've* worked in my entire life. You think you're going to pop up on the scene and get your piece of the pie. That fifty grand he paid you made you greedy for more."

"So it's all about the Benjamins, you think?"

"I'm not gonna stand back and let you do it," Gabriel said. "I want you to stay the hell away from my family. My dad is feeling too guilty to do the right thing, but I'll be damned if I let you come in here and fuck up everything we've built together."

"You've got me all wrong. It's not like that, little brother."

"I'm not your little brother, asshole. This conversation is over. Remember what I said. You've been warned."

Gabriel spun to leave. Isaiah clapped his hand on his shoulder. He squeezed, stabbing his finger into one of Gabriel's nerves.

Gabriel let out a soft cry. His legs turned mushy.

Isaiah pulled Gabriel beside him in what would have appeared to be a brotherly gesture to onlookers—but fury bunched his features.

Fear swelled like a balloon in Gabriel's chest. He wanted to fight back, but the agony in his shoulder had immobilized him.

"I've had enough of your smart mouth, motherfucker," Isaiah said. "You don't know who you're talking to. Do you know what I could do to you?"

His forefinger dug deeper into Gabriel's nerves. Gabriel bit his tongue to keep from howling.

"You're wrong—I don't give a fuck about your family's money," Isaiah said. "If I wanted to, I could go into the house right now and tell your daddy to write a check out for me for a hundred grand, and he would do it. Believe that."

He drew Gabriel closer. Their faces were only a few inches apart. Gabriel smelled the beer on Isaiah's hot breath.

"But I don't want money," Isaiah said. "Know what I want?"

Trembling, pain shrieking in his shoulder, Gabriel shook his head.

"*I want to tear your family apart,*" Isaiah whispered. "Starting with you, you spoiled fuckin' brat. Daddy's given you everything you've wanted for your entire life. What did he ever do for me? You don't deserve anything you have. And I'm here to take it all away—including that fine piece of ass in there you call your fiancée."

"No," Gabriel said weakly.

"When I'm through with you, I'm going to take care of your daddy," Isaiah said. "I want him more than I want you.

I'm going to get him for what he did to Mama and me. I swore on her grave that I would get him, no matter what. I'm keeping my word."

"Leave us alone," Gabriel said.

"Oh, I'll leave your mama and your sister alone," Isaiah said. "The way to destroy a family is to take away the men. That's been happening to our people for generations, you know."

"I'm not gonna let you get away with this."

"You can't stop me," Isaiah said. "They won't believe a word you say. Want to try it?" He released Gabriel's shoulder and pushed him aside. "Run in there and tell them everything I just said. Go ahead."

Gabriel moved away, massaging his aching shoulder. But he didn't run inside the house and share Isaiah's evil machinations.

Because Isaiah was right.

His family wouldn't believe him. Isaiah's plan was too bold, too malicious to be believed. His family, already aware that he didn't trust Isaiah, would suspect that he was spreading lies to turn them against him.

Isaiah smiled. He sipped his beer and belched.

"Taking it all away, little brother," Isaiah said. "Piece by piece."

"I'm going to stop you."

"How're you gonna do that? Daddy's not gonna help you this time."

Gabriel turned away.

"Daddy's on my side." Isaiah laughed.

His laughter followed Gabriel all the way inside the house.

Chapter 24

Soon after his encounter with Isaiah, Gabriel announced to everyone that he was leaving. He claimed that he had a stomachache, which was true. Isaiah's threats had induced a sickening dread in his gut.

From the moment he'd first met Isaiah, he'd known the guy was trouble. First impressions were never wrong.

But what was he going to do about it? He still had no answer. Isaiah, who'd masterfully charmed his family, held the upper hand.

As Gabriel walked out of the grand salon to a scattered chorus of good-byes, Isaiah winked at him.

Dana left with Gabriel. Although they had not resolved last night's argument, seeing him so obviously ill at ease had likely summoned her mothering instincts.

"I'm sorry you don't feel well," she said as they walked to their cars. "Want me to sleep over so I can keep an eye on you?"

Gabriel thought about the snake, possibly roaming loose somewhere within his house.

"You mind if I stay at your place?" he asked.

"Worried about the snake?"

"Honestly? Yeah."

"I don't blame you. Sure, you can stay with me tonight."

They got in their cars. As Gabriel backed the Corvette out of the driveway, Isaiah and Pops stepped outside the front door. Pops put his arm around Isaiah's shoulder. They held drinks in their hands, like hard-partying frat boys.

Daddy's on my side.

They grinned and waved at him.

For his father's benefit, Gabriel returned the wave—albeit, halfheartedly—and then drove away.

Dana lived in a sixth-floor condo in Atlantic Station, a trendy live-work-play community just north of downtown. Formerly the site of a steel mill, the district was touted as a city within a city, with an abundance of retail and entertainment venues, wide sidewalks, narrow streets, and vast underground parking areas. The in-town condo market had been booming of late, as well-heeled residents migrated from the suburbs to the city. Using money bequeathed to her by her deceased parents, Dana had snagged the property before prices had rocketed into deep space.

Dana's dog greeted them at the door. It was a lively Bichon named Mandy. Mandy scampered around Dana and Gabriel, yapping happily.

"Hey, pretty girl," Gabriel said.

Dana scooped up the dog in her arms. "I'm taking her out to potty. Why don't you lie down and relax?"

Dana talked to him so sweetly that he could almost believe she'd forgotten about last night. He sat on the sofa and stretched out his legs.

Dana had decorated the two-bedroom unit with cranberry-colored draperies, earth tone accent rugs, cherry-wood furniture, and numerous Annie Lee figurines, many of them depicting children at play. Reflections of the happy childhood Dana had lost. Nevertheless, it was a tranquil place, and as Gabriel rested his head against the cushions and gazed out the floor-to-ceiling windows at the dazzling Atlanta skyline, he felt some of the day's stress drain out of his body.

Then Isaiah's leering face invaded his thoughts.

I want to tear your family apart.

Gabriel switched on the television and channel surfed, trying to find something that would distract him from his worries. He settled on a rerun of *Law & Order*; he liked the show. The good guys usually prevailed in the end.

Dana returned. Mandy bounded across the floor and hopped on Gabriel's stomach.

"Ouch," Gabriel said, sitting up. He scratched Mandy behind the ears and the dog whined with pleasure.

"Careful, Mandy, you're going to hurt Daddy," Dana said. She sat next to Gabriel and removed Mandy from his lap. "You want something for that stomachache?"

"Nah, I'll try to sleep it off."

"I knew you'd say that." She looked at him closer. "What's really wrong?"

"A stomachache, like I said."

"It's your brother, isn't it?"

"He's not my brother."

"Biologically speaking, that's what he is," she said. "I don't know why you don't like him. He seems like a really nice guy to me, so down-to-earth and humble."

Isaiah had fooled Dana, too. This was as bad as Gabriel had feared.

"Dana, that guy is bad news, trust me."

"Trust your gut feeling, like you said earlier?" She looked doubtful. "But I like him, and so does the rest of your family. So why are you the only one with this 'gut feeling' that he's so terrible?"

Gabriel pinched the bridge of his nose. He wanted to tell her what had happened. But he kept his mouth shut. It might start another argument.

"Are you jealous of him, like Nicole said?" Dana asked.

"What?"

"Are you upset that you aren't the only son anymore?"

"That's bullshit," he said. "Do you really believe that about me?"

Dana leaned against the sofa cushions, Mandy on her lap, wagging her tail.

"When it comes to your relationship with your family, I don't know what to believe about you anymore," she said. "We still haven't talked about this hero-worship thing you have with your father."

"I don't want to get into that tonight."

"And I can't help thinking that you're *threatened* by the idea of another son stealing your father's attention away from you."

"Damn it, it has nothing to do with that, all right? Do you know what Isaiah told me? He said he wants to tear my family apart. Starting with me. He wants to take away everything I have—including you. Yes, you." He pointed at her.

She stared at his finger, skepticism forming in her eyes.

"And when he's through with me, he wants to take care of Pops."

"Take care of him?" Dana asked.

"I don't know what the hell he meant. Kill him? I don't know. But Isaiah told me that tonight, and I know he was serious."

"Why would he say something horrible like that?"

"Revenge," Gabriel said. "He wants revenge for Pops abandoning him and his mother, leaving them to have a rough life. He vowed on his mother's grave that he'd get revenge."

Dana pursed her lips, her face troubled. Gabriel got an awful plummeting feeling in his stomach.

"Do you know how ridiculous that sounds?" she said. "He wants revenge? *How about he just wants to know his family?* Do you have any idea how it feels to grow up without your family? Do you?"

Shit, Gabriel thought. He'd unknowingly touched a raw nerve. He'd momentarily forgotten that Dana's parents had died when she was a kid.

"I can't believe you'd make up some shit like this," Dana said. She got to her feet. She was shaking; Mandy spilled out of her arms and scrambled across the floor, seeking cover.

"I didn't make it up," he said. "Do you think I'm lying?"

Her upper lip quivered. She wouldn't look at him.

"Look at me, Dana. Do you think I'm lying to you?"

Reluctantly, she looked at him. Tears shone in her eyes.

"I don't know what to think," she said. "The weird way you've been acting . . . I don't know anymore. I'm sorry."

If their relationship had been represented by a stone sculpture, a jagged fracture would have cracked down the middle at that moment.

Gabriel could not think of anything to say. He wished he hadn't said anything. Why hadn't he kept his damn mouth shut?

Dana marched past him and out of the living room.

"Dana, come back," he said. "Let's talk about this."

He heard her opening a door, grabbing something, closing the door.

I've really screwed up, he thought. He wanted to repair the situation, but didn't know how; everything he said seemed to be the wrong thing. He and Dana had never been so out of sync with each other.

Dana came back, carrying a pillow and a blanket. She dumped them on the sofa beside him.

"What's this?" Gabriel said.

"You're sleeping out here tonight," she said, and went back to her bedroom and slammed the door.

Chapter 25

The evening had gone even better than Isaiah had planned. While he had expected his charm, humor, intelligence, charisma—and dashing good looks—to eventually win over the Reid clan, his reception was warmer than he had anticipated. The Reids were so determined to present themselves as a charitable, Christian family that they made his task immeasurably easier. He was quite certain that the mother, Marge, was outraged over his very existence; and he figured that the daughter was shocked; and he understood that his father was ashamed. But they were willing to set aside their private pains in order to do the right thing and welcome him into their circle.

He couldn't help but admire them. They were, indeed, a picture-perfect family, so remarkable that it seemed unreal—a living, breathing cast of characters from a TV show, like *Father Knows Best* or some other outdated program that espoused moral values that no one cared about anymore.

But Gabriel . . . now, he was something else. His little brother was fast becoming the black sheep of the clan.

Isaiah sat in the Reids' enormous, sumptuously decorated

grand salon, sipping cognac just like his father, who sat beside him. His stepmother, or whatever she was to him, was
drinking chamomile tea, and Nicole nursed a Coke. They
were filling him in on their lives and asking him questions
about his background and his plans.

They asked: Are you moving to Atlanta?

To which he responded: Maybe. I'll stay here for a few
weeks and see how I like it.

The real answer, which he kept to himself: *I'm here to
stay, folks. You aren't getting rid of me.*

They asked: What kind of work do you do?

His answer: When I was incarcerated, I learned how to work
in a print shop, so that's what I've been doing. I love to work.

Real answer: *Please. I'm a hustler. I haven't worked a
legit gig in years and I'm not starting now.*

They asked: Do you have any children?

His answer: No, I haven't been blessed with any kids yet.
I'm waiting to meet the right woman to marry first.

Real answer: *I've got several kids, so I've heard, but I've
never seen them, and don't care if I ever do. Those women
were having babies to try to trap me.*

And on it went. Sometimes he gave them the unvarnished
truth; sometimes he gave them the truth, with embellish-
ment, for the sake of dramatic effect.

But most times, he lied shamelessly.

Throughout, they listened as if he were a soothsayer,
smiling and nodding.

Life was so funny. Last year he'd been sharing a prison
cell with a serial rapist, facing a murky future. Now, look:
his rich father's family was entertaining him at their multimillion-dollar estate, listening raptly to every word he spoke.

If only Mama could have lived to see this.

He could imagine what Mama would say, in her raspy,
smoker's voice: *"Ask that rich-ass daddy of yours to give us
some money. Shit, he ain't never done nothing for you. He
owes us."*

Isaiah sipped his Rémy Martin and smiled at his new family.

I'll get something better than money, Mama. I'll get justice.

When the tall, ornate grandfather clock in the corner—the damn thing probably had cost several thousand dollars, Isaiah thought—struck eleven, Isaiah drained his cognac, placed the snifter on a nearby marble table, and stood.

"It's time for me to go back to my hotel," he said. He faked a yawn. "It's been quite a day."

Pops looked at his wife and she nodded, almost imperceptibly. Clearing his throat, Pops turned to Isaiah.

"We'd like for you to stay with us, son," he said. "It wouldn't be right for you to stay in a hotel."

Isaiah wanted to laugh. These people were a trip.

But he said, "I appreciate the offer, but I can't do that. You weren't expecting a houseguest. The hotel is fine."

"What hotel are you staying in?" Marge asked.

"It's a Days Inn, in Marietta," he said.

"No son of mine is staying in a Days Inn when he could be staying at my estate." Pops said. "You're staying here with us, Isaiah, and that's the end of it." He softened his words with a smile.

"He could stay in Gabe's old room," Nicole said. She glanced at her parents. "Right?"

"That's exactly what I was thinking, dear," Marge said.

"Well, well." Isaiah gave them his best *aw, shucks* grin. "I guess I'd better go get my stuff."

A few minutes later, Isaiah returned inside the house with his suitcases. Nicole met him in the gigantic, soaring foyer; the area was nearly as big as the project apartment he and Mama had used to live in.

"You had your luggage in your car?" Nicole asked, head cocked.

"I don't believe in leaving personal belongings behind," he said. "A habit I picked up from living in places where your stuff could be stolen. I keep my things close at hand."

"Oh," Nicole said. Her look of surprise was so genuine that Isaiah had to choke back a laugh. This girl, a bona-fide black American princess, probably would only have consented to roll through Isaiah's old hood in a police-escorted, armored truck. She had no street smarts whatsoever, no idea of how people lived in the real world.

But to her credit, she *was* cute, so he could cut her some slack. Short and slender with a gymnast's firm figure, she was a redbone, with auburn hair and hazel eyes. She wore dainty glasses and had the manner of an intellectual—or a nerd, even. She was the kind of girl who'd want to visit a science museum on a first date.

But in Isaiah's experience, girls like Nicole, the geeky girls, often were the biggest freaks. All that bottled-up brainpower found its truest expression in the bedroom.

"I'll take you to Gabe's room," she said. "Follow me."

"Lead the way," he said.

As she ascended the curving staircase, he admired how her tight ass worked in the khaki shorts she wore. He wetted his lips. He'd like to get his hands on that booty.

A stern voice in Isaiah's mind admonished: *She's your half sister, man. You shouldn't be looking at her like this.* But Isaiah smothered the voice. He didn't know this girl. If he'd met her on the street before today, he'd have had no idea that they were related, and neither would she. So who cared?

"This is a beautiful house," Isaiah said.

She shrugged nonchalantly. "I'm glad I don't live here anymore. It's too old."

"Too old?"

"Yeah, thirty years old or something like that. I keep telling Daddy he needs to buy something more contemporary, but he's settled here, looks like."

Isaiah was perplexed. This girl had grown up in an elegantly appointed mansion, and all she could say was that it was too old?

If she'd been his mama's daughter, Mama would've slapped the shit out of her for saying something stupid like that.

He followed her down a hallway so wide he could've driven his Chevelle across it. African-American art in gold frames hung on the walls, each of them expressing a familial theme. Isaiah would've bet his right testicle that they were originals, not replicas.

They arrived at a door. Nicole went inside first and switched on the light.

"Wow," Isaiah said.

The bedroom was probably the size of the entire first floor of Grandma's home. A Chinese sleigh bed dominated one area; large windows offered views of the dark woods beyond the house; a big television and stereo system took up space on another side; a bookcase packed with titles stood near the bed. A computer and printer sat on an oak desk.

"Will this be okay?" Nicole asked.

Are you serious? This is the nicest room I've ever stayed in in my life!

"This will be great, thanks," he said.

She went to another door off the bedroom. "Here's the bathroom."

It was a full bathroom with a shower stall, double sinks, and whirlpool tub. He'd never been in a whirlpool tub. He might be drawing a bath tonight.

He went back to the bed and, out of habit, slid his luggage underneath, drawing a strange look from Nicole.

"I'll go get some fresh towels for you," she said. "Be right back."

He sat on the bed and ran his hand across the duvet. It was as silky as a dream.

Nicole returned, her arms laden with fluffy towels. "Here they are," she said. She headed to the bathroom. "I'll put them in here for you."

Isaiah went to the bedroom door and closed it. Locked it.

He was about to do something dangerous. He didn't want any interruptions.

Nicole strolled out of the bathroom, running her fingers through her hair. She didn't notice that he'd shut the door.

"Anything else you need?" she asked.

He sat on the bed.

Attempting to do what he planned was risky, but he thrived on risk, danger.

He inhaled a deep breath.

Focus.

Psychic energy flickered at the base of his spine, developed into a current of power that surged up his back and burst into his brain. A vein pulsed like a small heart in the center of his sweat-filmed forehead.

Command.

He fixed his gaze on Nicole, who watched him expectantly.

"Actually, I do need something else," he said. He made a come-hither gesture with his index finger. "Get over here."

She did as he ordered, walking in front of him. Her eyes settled on something behind him, a vacant look to which he was accustomed when exercising his talent on people.

She wore a pink halter top, the fabric outlining her round, perky breasts.

He licked his lips. He put his hands on her breasts. He squeezed.

She sighed softly.

"Feel good?" he asked. "Tell me it feels good."

"It feels good," she whispered. Her eyelids fluttered behind her lenses.

Isaiah's erection throbbed against his slacks. Although Nicole's shapely body was a turn-on, what titillated him even more was exercising power over her. This woman was his. She would do anything he wanted. *Anything.*

He slid his hands to her hips, kneaded them between his fingers.

"Hot body like yours, I know you're a freak," he said. "But you hide it behind those glasses and your little geek-princess attitude. You can't fool your big brother."

She only stood there, blinking slowly, allowing him to feel her up.

He loved, loved, *loved* this.

He rose off the bed.

"Get on your knees," he said.

She hesitated, as though some small part of her consciousness was alert, resisting him.

He concentrated, drilled his gaze into her eyes.

"On your knees," he said firmly.

She knelt in front of him. His rock-hard dick was only inches away from her face.

He cupped the back of her head in his hand. He pulled her head forward against his groin.

"Feel that?" he said. "It's going to be in that sweet pouty mouth of yours in a minute."

She whimpered. A sound of anticipation or fear? He didn't know. Didn't care.

"Unzip my pants," he said.

Hands shaking slightly, she grasped his zipper, tugged it down. His dick strained against the confines of his boxer shorts.

Isaiah was about to command her to open her mouth—when he heard footsteps creaking along the hallway outside the bedroom.

A knock tapped against the door.

"Are you kids in there?" It was Marge.

Isaiah quickly zipped his slacks. He focused on Nicole. She gazed up at him, face placid as a pond, awaiting instruction.

"Stand up," he said. And she did.

"Once I snap my fingers," he said, "you'll remember none of this. You'll be feeling just fine again. Okay?"

She nodded. He hurried to the door. Looked back at Nicole and snapped his fingers.

Nicole blinked.

"What happened?" she said.

"You were showing me around." Isaiah opened the door. Marge stood outside with an inquisitive expression and Isaiah reasoned that motherly intuition had brought her there.

"Nicole was about to give me a tour of the rest of the house," Isaiah said. "Ready, Nicole?"

"Sure." Shrugging, Nicole came out of the bedroom. "Follow me."

Isaiah smiled at Marge, who hesitated, and then returned the smile. He followed his little sister on a tour throughout the rest of the estate.

It was so wonderful to be a member of the family.

Chapter 26

Gabriel tried to get comfortable on the sofa and close his eyes to fall asleep. That didn't work, so he tried to watch TV until his eyelids grew tired and slid shut. That didn't work either. An awful fact boomeranged through his mind, keeping him awake.

Dana didn't trust him anymore.

Realizing her doubt in him was like being slugged in the face. He was tempted to leave, without warning, and go home, a passive-aggressive way of letting her know how deeply she'd hurt him. But he didn't do that; it seemed cowardly, equivalent to giving up on their relationship. He loved her too much to leave and let this problem ruin what they had together.

They would work this out, somehow, just as he would work out this issue with Isaiah. He had to believe it. At this point, faith in a better future was all he had.

Mandy cuddled on Gabriel's lap. She looked up at him with adoring eyes.

"You haven't given up on me, have you, girl?" Gabriel said. "You know I'm telling the truth."

Mandy licked his fingers.

Gabriel rested his head against the pillow. He watched the spinning ceiling fan and began to count the revolutions. . . .

Sometime later he jerked awake with a crook in his neck. The room was dark except for bands of coppery streetlight that filtered through the blinds. Mandy snored softly at the opposite end of the sofa, her body a white bundle in the darkness.

The TV was off. Dana must have switched it off while he'd been sleeping. The digital clock on the fireplace mantel read one fifty-three.

Gabriel rubbed his aching neck. He started to stretch his legs into a more comfortable position—and then noticed something moving on the floor barely five feet away. A dark, serpentine shape.

Terror clawed up his throat.

It was a snake.

Logic wanted to deny what his eyes told him. He was in Dana's condo, in the middle of the city. There were no snakes there. It was impossible. He was imagining this. He was dreaming.

Then he heard a soft hiss.

That evil hiss pressed a panic button in his brain. He began to tremble.

This was really happening. Again. It wasn't a dream.

He reached toward the lamp on the end table. He turned the power knob.

It was a water moccasin. It was identical to the snake that had terrorized him at his house.

The snake lay coiled on the hardwood floor between the fireplace and the glass coffee table. The table was the only object separating them, and it was no protection at all be-cause the snake could slither beneath it.

The snake watched him, muscles taut, challenging him to move.

How could this be the same snake? Had it hidden in a bag or something he'd brought there?

No, that couldn't be. He hadn't brought anything from his house other than the clothes on his back—and he sure as hell would've known if a two-foot-long pit viper hitched a ride with him.

He didn't know where it had come from, but he had to get away from it, or, failing that, contain it somehow until someone else could take care of it.

He looked around the room, frantic.

At the end of the sofa, Mandy continued to slumber, dead to the world. It seemed weird that the dog didn't smell or hear the water moccasin, so close by, but, then again, Mandy was a house dog whose hunting instincts had been dulled by years of pampering. If she'd been awake she would only have barked and perhaps driven the snake into a deadly rage. Better for her to stay asleep.

He grabbed his pillow. He held it in front of him. Rising slowly, he edged away from the sofa, toward the kitchen.

He wanted to get his hands on a weapon of some kind. Like a knife. Even a broom would do. Anything that would keep this creature away from him.

The water moccasin shifted, watching him. Light glimmered dully on its green-black scales.

This was far too detailed to be a dream. His heart felt as if it were at the back of his mouth. His clammy hands dampened the pillow so much he could've wrung sweat from it.

A chest-high, granite counter separated the kitchen from the living room area. He reached the counter, looked around the kitchen, saw the trash can, got an idea.

The snake charged forward in a liquid blur.

Gabriel scrambled around the counter. He dropped the pillow on the floor, grabbed the edge of the trash can and flipped up the lid. The can, lined with a white bag, had recently been emptied. Good.

He raised the can.

As the snake slithered around the corner, Gabriel slammed the can downward, aiming to trap the reptile underneath.

He missed.

The snake evaded the trap, smoothly flowing out of the way. Hissing, it came at him again.

Gabriel backpedaled so frantically he almost fell down. He banged against a door, realized it was the pantry, reached behind him, and twisted the knob. He moved aside and flung the door open as the water moccasin writhed toward him.

The door thwacked into the snake's head. The reptile collided against a cabinet and lay still, momentarily dazed.

Gabriel snatched a broom out of the pantry. Like a hockey player whacking a puck, he swung at the snake. The bristled edges whooshed across the tile and swept the twisting snake into the depths of the pantry against a large bag of Purina dog food.

"Gotcha!"

Gabriel closed the door.

Then he noticed the gap between the bottom of the door and the floor. It was less than an inch high, but he didn't want to take any chances. He hurried to the pillow he'd dropped on the other side of the kitchen. Kneeling, he stuffed the pillow in the gap, imprisoning the snake inside the pantry.

The reptile thumped against the door, hissed angrily.

Gabriel moved away. Cold sweat drenched his face and back. He couldn't stop shaking.

It's over, man. You're safe.

He turned to the sink to get some water and calm his nerves.

Dressed in her pajamas, Dana stood at the edge of the kitchen. He was so startled to see her that he almost screamed.

Dana regarded the upended trash can on the floor.

"What are you doing in here?" she asked.

"There's a snake in here," he said, his voice quivering. He hooked a thumb behind him. "But I trapped it in the pantry."

"What? A snake?" She stared at the pantry door. "Are you serious?"

"It was a water moccasin like the one I saw in my house. Looked like the same one, matter of fact. But I caught that joker this time. I need to find an emergency number for that wildlife control company." He grabbed for the *Yellow Pages* directory stored in a niche near the wall phone.

"Hold up." She raised her hand. "I can't believe you found a snake in my condo, Gabe."

Gabriel flipped through the phone book. "Believe it or not, it's in there. It was trying to get out a minute ago, but it's quieted down now."

"Are you sure you weren't dreaming?"

"You don't believe me?" He dropped the phone book on the counter. "Do you think everything I say now is a lie?"

She flinched as though he'd slapped her.

"That's not what I meant," she said. "But I think the episode at your house today frightened you, and maybe you had a nightmare."

"It wasn't a nightmare! The damn snake is in there. You wanna look for yourself?"

"And remember those visions you were seeing in the mirror? Those hallucinations?"

"This isn't the same thing. This is real."

"As real as the other snake that was at your house—but that the wildlife control guy couldn't find?"

"It got away, hid somewhere."

She walked toward the pantry. He caught her arm.

"Don't open that door," he said. "You'll let it out. It's a poisonous snake, Dana."

"Stand back, then." She shrugged off his hand, knelt, and yanked away the pillow from the door.

Gabriel went to the far side of the kitchen.

Dana opened the pantry door.

The pantry was full of canned goods, dog food, and other nonperishable items.

No snake.

Chapter 27

"I'm *not* imagining things," Gabriel said to Dana for the tenth time. "A snake *was* in here, and it *did* attack me. I know that for a fact."

They sat at the dinette table. Dana sat on the other side of the table, watching Gabriel with what he recognized as her "MD look"—an intense yet detached gaze, as though he were one of her patients at the hospital—and he hated that. The way she looked at him, it was as though she'd already made up her mind that he was a nutcase who needed psychiatric care. He couldn't make her understand that there was nothing wrong with him.

"We searched the entire pantry," Dana said. With a wave of her hand, she indicated the pantry's bare shelves and the items they'd pulled out and stacked on the floor. "There was no snake in there."

"It got away. Slipped through a crack in the walls or something."

"That's stretching it, don't you think?"

"Then you think I hallucinated seeing the snake at my house, too. Don't you?"

Sighing, she ran her fingers through her hair, looked away from him.

"Dana, come on. This is your man talking here. You know me better than that. You know I've always got it together."

"I'm worried about you, Gabe."

"There's nothing wrong with me."

"I want you to make an appointment with that neurologist Dr. Robinson referred you to. I'm worried that your concussion is the source of these symptoms."

"But my head hasn't been hurting." He tapped his temple; against his doctor's orders, he had removed the head bandage that morning, tired of how it made him look like a patient. "No headaches or anything. I feel fine."

"All I'm saying is, go see a neurologist, have a few tests run, an MRI—"

"I'm not going to another doctor," he said.

"Why do you have to be so damn stubborn?" She spread her hands on the table, pleading. "I only want to help you!"

"You want to help me?" He smiled bitterly. "Start taking me at my word again."

She didn't flinch this time. She leaned forward, her eyes scalding hot. "I *am* trying to help you. I care about you enough to tell you what I honestly think. And you know what? I'll be damned if I indulge you for the sake of protecting your feelings—especially when your health is at issue."

Gabriel cradled his head in his hands, silenced. Dana's words began to gnaw at him, eat away his confidence.

Had he really seen a snake? Could it all have been a hallucination?

He remembered the snake's terrible hiss, its murderous glare.

There's no way I imagined that. That was real.

Mandy lay near Gabriel, sleeping. Gabriel recalled that when he'd spotted the snake on the floor, the dog had remained asleep, which had struck him as odd.

Maybe Mandy had not awakened because there never had been a snake in the condo to begin with.

A finger of ice tapped the base of his spine.

Was this how it felt to go crazy? Were you aware of gradually losing your grip on your sanity? Did you watch helplessly as the walls of logic crumbled and gave way to madness?

"I thought it was real," he said, and to him, his voice sounded hollow.

Dana came around the table and put her hand on his shoulder.

"I know," she said. "Please, go see the doctor, baby. I'll go with you. We'll go tomorrow, together."

Gabriel had begun to voice another weak opposition—claiming that he had to go to work tomorrow and get caught up on business—when he glimpsed something in the mirror that hung over the fireplace in the living room. A large, dim shape.

It propelled him to his feet.

"Look!" He pointed at the mirror and rushed across the living room. "See this? This is the same thing I've seen before!"

It was a tall, man-sized figure—almost like viewing himself, albeit in a blurry, dust-filmed mirror. He could not make out any specific details of the figure's appearance. But he saw that the apparition was motionless.

This excited him. In previous incidents the shadow had faded as abruptly as it had appeared.

Dana came to stand beside him. "I don't see anything, Gabriel. I see the two of us reflected."

The mysterious figure stood between Gabriel and Dana in the glass, like a dark pillar.

"But it's right there!" He put his index finger on the mirror. "Can't you see it?"

"Baby." Dana gently took one of his hands. "Please sit down."

He turned away from the mirror and looked at Dana. Fear glistened wetly in her eyes. But it wasn't fear of what he saw in the glass. It was fear for him.

Everything he'd seen was all in his mind. Hallucinations.

He glanced at the mirror again. The silhouette had vanished.

"It was there," he said. "I'm not crazy."

Dana took him by the elbow and guided him to the sofa, as though he were a senile old man in a nursing home.

"I'm not crazy," he said.

Dana pulled him into her arms, held him tightly. He felt his body go limp. A shudder rattled through him.

"I'm not crazy. . . ."

Gabriel's voice broke and he started to cry.

When Isaiah did not dream of being a child and watching, helpless, as his mother suffered at the hands of abusive men, he dreamed an even more disturbing dream.

He dreamed of being murdered.

"Payback's a bitch, ain't it, motherfucka?"

The thug standing over him spat those final words, aimed a gun at Isaiah's chest, and pulled the trigger.

Darkness passed over Isaiah, swallowing him, plunging him into oblivion. . . .

Isaiah awoke with a start, clawing at the air as though it were the smothering darkness in the dream and could be torn away like wallpaper.

I don't wanna die, not yet. It's not time.

When Isaiah realized that he was alive and safe in his father's home, he dropped his arms to the mattress. He drew in deep, invigorating breaths. He used the bedsheet to blot the sweat on his face.

He hated that damn dream. It reminded him of how his life used to be.

He'd taken steps to rectify that aspect of his past, too.

He'd murdered those thugs who had gunned down Mama and had tried, unsuccessfully, to kill him.

Why, then, did he still dream of being shot?

Troubled, he checked at the bedside clock. It was a few minutes past three o'clock.

He'd been asleep for barely an hour. He'd stayed up late, working.

He switched on the lamp.

He reached underneath the bed where he'd stored his duffel bag and other luggage. Although the bedroom included a huge walk-in closet, Isaiah liked to keep his most important belongings within easy reach. Old habit.

He unzipped the bag. It was full of battered paperbacks he'd purchased from a used bookshop in Chicago. Titles such as *The Art of War*, by Sun Tzu; *The Count of Monte Cristo*, by Alexandre Dumas; *The Prince*, by Niccolo Machiavelli; *The Autobiography of Malcolm X*.

He'd read all of them, most of them twice.

His bag also contained other, more esoteric books. Books about near-death experiences; developing your psychic abilities; telepathy; mind control.

He'd read all those, too.

All his life, he'd been a voracious reader. In prison, especially, there wasn't much else to do. Mama hadn't been much of a reader—her Bible was the only book that interested her—so he wasn't sure how he had acquired the love of books. Maybe it had been embedded in his genes. Some people were genetically predisposed to be brilliant; other poor souls were destined to be idiots.

He preferred to read nonfiction: texts about politics, war, business, martial arts, crime, history. Books about facts, not fiction, not make-believe. Fiction was for women and soft men; Gabriel probably enjoyed fiction.

Reading had refined his raw intelligence, had equipped him to survive on the streets and in prison. *The mind made the man.*

He dug under the books and retrieved his journal. He'd clipped Gabriel's expensive Mont Blanc pen, which he'd stolen from his office, to the front cover.

When Isaiah had taken the pen, he hadn't planned on actually writing with it, but it had proven a splendid writing instrument.

Of course, the pen served other purposes for him, too.

He uncapped the pen, found a fresh page in the journal, and began to write:

> *Friday, June 10. 3:07 A.M.*
> *I've awakened again from the nightmare of being murdered. I don't understand why I keep having this dream. What does it mean?*
> *I have a suspicion about what it might mean, and it worries me.*
> *Am I living on borrowed time?*

He paused and removed the old photograph from his wallet. He studied the picture. Mama and Pops.

No matter what. . . .

He wrote:

> *If my days in this world are limited, I only want enough time to finish what I came here to do. It's going so well that it would be a shame if I didn't finish.*

Pen poised above the page, he smiled.

Little brother's starting to lose his mind.

Chapter 28

The next morning Gabriel visited a neurologist, Dr. Gulati, in Decatur. Dr. Robinson's office had called Gulati and managed to secure Gabriel an appointment on short notice.

Dana accompanied him. While they sat in the waiting area, Gabriel perused a recent issue of *Fortune*. Dana was reading another of those suspense thrillers she always carried around. The one she was currently reading was titled *In the Shadows* or some such thing.

"Hmph," Dana said. She tapped the cover of the paperback novel. "One of the main characters in this story is going to a neurologist because he's been having hallucinations and other problems. Isn't it weird that I'd happen to be reading this right now? Serendipity."

"Do they decide that the dude is crazy?" Gabriel asked.

Dana skimmed the page. "Doesn't look like it."

"Then I'll take that as a good sign."

A nurse called Gabriel's name and beckoned him into the exam area.

Gabriel underwent a cranial CT scan, a test to evaluate the brain for abnormalities and to visualize vascular masses.

According to the scan results, there was nothing wrong with him. But Dr. Gulati, alarmed at Gabriel's confession of suffering intense hallucinations, scheduled an MRI for the following Monday.

When they left the physician's office, they went to the Flying Biscuit Cafe, a restaurant in Candler Park, for a late breakfast. Candler Park was a historic neighborhood of big elms and maples, winding streets, and charming bungalows and Cape Cods festooned with kudzu. An eclectic hodgepodge of businesses—cafés, an antiques place, a bridal shop, and a used-record place that still sold vinyl albums—lined the stretch of McLendon Avenue where Gabriel parked his car.

The Flying Biscuit Cafe was a cramped, New Age–style spot that attracted a diverse, loyal clientele. A sunflower-themed mural that looked as though an artist tripping on acid had painted it decorated one wall. Mismatched tablecloths covered a maze of tables that stood on creaky legs on the unfinished floor. The cheerfully inconsistent decor would have spawned nightmares for the president of a chain restaurant, but the quirky ambience—and superb food—kept the safe packed.

Their waiter was a tall, slender black man with a nose piercing who clearly had a lot of sugar in his tank, as Gabriel's mother would have said.

Gabriel ordered the Smoked Salmon Scramble—three scrambled eggs with salmon and dill cream cheese; Dana had an omelette with cheese, mushrooms, basil, and tomato coulis. Each of them had the fluffy biscuits and apple-cranberry butter for which the restaurant was famous.

"So it looks like going to the doctor was a waste of time," Gabriel said.

"It wasn't a waste of time," Dana said, slathering butter on a biscuit. "We've just narrowed down the possibilities. Medicine works that way quite often. You rule out one diagnosis and search for another."

"I still don't understand any of this. Why is it happening to me? Why the figure in the mirror? Why snakes?"

"The snakes probably come from your fear of them," Dana said. "You were bitten by a water moccasin, you know."

"I get that. But what about this shape in the mirror? Am I secretly afraid of blurry shadows?"

"Are you?" She gave him a probing gaze.

"I was joking, Dana."

"Well, I don't know why you see that stuff. But we'll figure it out soon."

Gabriel looked out the windows. His breakfast and coffee were growing cold, but, disturbed by his thoughts, he'd temporarily lost his appetite.

"Earth to Gabe," Dana said and waved her hand in front of his eyes.

He blinked. "I think we're going down the wrong road here. Gut feeling."

"Elaborate please."

"I think the real answer has nothing to do with my concussion. It's something . . . else."

"What?"

"I don't know."

"I've got to approach this from a scientific standpoint," Dana said. "I'd be doing you a disservice and dishonoring my profession if I resorted to gut feelings instead of verifiable medical evidence. I deal in facts, baby."

"What about my opinion? We're talking about my personal situation here, not some case in a lab book."

"I know that. Your opinion is important, but . . ."

"But what?"

"You're having issues right now. You're not thinking logically all the time."

Anger brought a wave of heat to his face. Did she realize she'd just insulted him?

She grasped his hand. "Let's do this my way. I'll do research; we'll get the MRI done on Monday, and more tests, if necessary, and that's how we'll get to the root of this. No more of this talk about gut feelings and all that. Okay? Will you trust me?"

"I'll trust you when you start trusting me."

"Right." Dana slid her hand away from his.

He had hurt her feelings, but he didn't want to apologize. He'd meant what he'd said. How could he trust her if she didn't trust him? Trust was a two-way street.

Dana pushed her plate aside, though half her meal remained. "I'm ready to go. I've got to go to work."

"Yeah." He looked away from her. "Me, too."

After a few minutes, Gabriel dropped off Dana at her condo, and he drove home. It was a few minutes past eleven. He planned to shower, dress, and arrive at the office by the end of the lunch hour.

He tried to avoid thinking about Dana. When she'd climbed out of his car, she hadn't even kissed him.

He began to wonder if he should have apologized for what he'd said, to keep the peace. But apologizing would have meant going along with her plans, and he sensed, intuitively, that she was wrong.

And she wasn't willing to admit that she might be incorrect either. He loved her, but she could be stubborn sometimes. Just like him.

Along with everything else that had happened that week, their impasse on the matter was serving only to unravel their relationship thread by thread. He didn't know how they could mend it—or if they could. Thinking about the possibility that their relationship was heading toward the end was so painful that he had to put it out of his mind.

Although he couldn't articulate his feelings about what was happening to him as anything more descriptive than an intuitive sense, he knew he was right. His problems would not be solved by CT scans and MRIs and the like. There was something else going on here. He was as certain of that as he'd ever been certain of anything.

He mulled over those thoughts as he parked the Corvette in his garage. He walked to the mailbox near the end of the driveway. With all the things going on lately, he hadn't checked his mail in a couple of days.

It was a hazy, sweltering day, in the low nineties. Twenty seconds outdoors was sufficient to wring sweat from his pores. He wiped his forearm across his face as he reached for the mailbox door.

The door dropped open with a soft creak.

But he hadn't touched it.

It's happened again.

His palms began to tingle. He raised them to his face.

"What the hell is this?" he whispered, desperately.

He clenched and unclenched his hands. The prickly sensation didn't go away.

He looked at the mailbox. Envelopes and fliers bristled from the slot. He extended his hand forward.

The mail slid out of the box and into his fingers.

Gabriel stepped back quickly, dropping the mail. The pieces fluttered around him like birds.

He bent, peered into the mailbox. It was empty. There was no miniature gremlin inside shoveling paper around.

His palms were still tingling.

He moved one hand toward the mailbox door to close it.

The door creaked shut on its own.

No, not on its own.

He examined his palms.

He understood, finally, what was happening.

He was doing this.

He ran back inside the garage, forgetting the mail on the ground.

A button that controlled the garage-door opener was mounted on the wall near the door that led inside the house.

Gabriel raised his hand as though intending to touch the button, but stopped his fingers about three inches away.

The button depressed with a soft click. The garage door began to clatter to the floor.

I can't believe this.

He dug his hand in his pocket and took out the key to unlock the door. He started to insert the key in the hole—and then moved back. He poised the key about three inches away from the lock. He released the key.

The key floated forward, as though guided by invisible fingers, and slid into the keyhole.

Gabriel rotated his hand clockwise in the manner of a puppeteer manipulating a marionette.

The key turned, and the lock disengaged.

He turned his hand again. The doorknob twisted.

He made a pushing gesture with his other hand.

The door bumped open.

Gabriel laughed—a giddy sound, like a child who has pedaled down the sidewalk on a bicycle for the first time without training wheels.

He felt as though he had been dropped into a movie. Like *Star Wars*. He was like a Jedi Knight, using the Force to manipulate objects around him.

Use the Force, Gabe.

Laughing, he rushed inside the house to explore his newfound power.

Chapter 29

Isaiah was at Reid Construction on Friday. Schmoozing with his father.

Because of the lies he'd told the night before about learning the printing trade in prison, Pops initially took him to the company's print shop, clearly intending to offer him a job. Isaiah feigned interest in the work, but then told his father, "I'd like to learn about what you and Gabriel do. Indulge me."

"You're ambitious, aren't you?" Pops grinned. "I'm sure ambition runs in your blood like it does in mine. Come on, let's go to my office."

They holed up in his father's huge second-floor office, and Pops gave him a rundown on the construction business. Isaiah asked several perceptive questions and shared plenty of insights that surprised his father; after all, Isaiah had been following his father's growing corporation since he was a teenager, reading about it in periodicals he had found at the library. He knew as much about the company as any outsider possibly could.

"You've got a sharp head on your shoulders," Pops said.

They lounged on leather chairs in a comfortable sitting area, sipping coffee. Pops drank from a white mug on which *World's #1 Dad* was stenciled in green type. A gift from one of his bratty kids. *World's #1 Dad*? Isaiah wanted to snatch that cup out of his father's hands and bash it against his skull.

But he checked himself. Patience.

"Thanks," Isaiah said. "Guess it runs in the family, huh?"

"As a matter of fact," Pops said, "I think I'd like to offer you a position in the company—and not in the print shop, either."

"Oh, I couldn't accept that," Isaiah said with as much modesty as he could manage. "You've got people with MBAs and years of experience here. I didn't even graduate college."

"Neither did Bill Gates," Pops said. "Did that stop him from building Microsoft into one of the most successful and influential companies in the world?"

Isaiah gave him another *aw, shucks* grin.

"For starters, you've got street smarts," Pops said. "That's more important in a corporate setting than you may think. This can be a cutthroat industry, son. You have to be able to scope out the competition and strategize a way to stay one step ahead of them."

"I know all about that," Isaiah said, one of the most truthful statements he'd made all day.

"Sure you do," Pops said. "You're a quick learner, too. A good businessman has to be able to size up a situation quickly and make a smart decision. You can only do that if you can swiftly absorb facts. I think you can do that."

"I'd try my best," Isaiah said.

Pops moved to the edge of his chair. "All your innate talents notwithstanding, as your father I *owe* you a shot here. I did that for Gabriel." He studied Isaiah intently. "I can do the same for you, if you're interested."

Isaiah set down his coffee and stroked his chin. Acting as if he were considering the outrageous offer.

"What would I be doing?" Isaiah asked.

"You'll shadow me, Gabriel, and other leaders in the organization for a few weeks, attending meetings and conference calls and whatnot, to gain in-depth exposure to our operations. After that, I'll expect you to create a proposal outlining how, with your unique talents and perspective, you can add maximum value to our firm. We'll use the proposal as the basis to design a position for you in the company—with a salary and benefits package commensurate to the role."

"You're telling me I can make up my own job here?" Isaiah could not conceal his genuine surprise.

"I'm telling you that your future is in your hands," Pops said. He leaned back in his chair and grinned. "You can go as far as you'd like here. Maybe even to the CEO's suite, but don't tell Gabe I said that." He chuckled.

Isaiah laughed, too, but he was sure that his laughter was for a different reason than his father's. This guy was willing to let an ex-con work in the boardroom? Was he out of his mind? The average ex-con couldn't land a gig flipping burgers at McDonald's, what with all the background checks companies conducted these days and that infamous question on job applications, inquiring about past felony convictions. A prison record was a scarlet letter that stayed on you for life. And people wondered why so many thugs wound up back in the joint.

His father was either a sentimental fool or a brilliant tactician who recognized Isaiah's talents and was determined to use them to enhance the bottom line.

"What do you say?" Pops asked. "Remember—think fast."

"I'm honored to accept your offer."

"Excellent." Pops shook Isaiah's hand. "I'm excited to have you with us. We can get started now. We have a one o'clock meeting with a prospective client flying in from Charlotte. An important discussion. Gabriel, another executive, and I will be there—and you. We need to bone up on their file."

"Then let's get to work," Isaiah said. He followed his father out of the office.

I'm starting to like this guy, he thought. *I almost regret having to kill him later.*

Almost.

Gabriel spent the next couple of hours exploring his talent, like a bird that had just learned how to fly, soaring through the sky.

He went to the kitchen and used his power to swing open the refrigerator door. Then he used his talent to remove a Budweiser, twist the cap, and bring the cold bottle to his lips. He took a few deep gulps and burped.

"Ah," he said and laughed.

He wandered throughout the house. Opening and closing doors. Turning on the TV and the stereo. Lifting the telephone off the cradle and punching in buttons with a phantom finger.

It was impossible. It was incredible. But it was real.

At the moment, he was too caught up in testing the ability, too drunk on the sheer pleasure of his powers, to speculate how and why he'd gained this gift. It was like being in a childhood dream in which he possessed magical talents.

He turned water faucets, flicked light switches on and off, opened windows, pushed chairs, moved silverware and plates and bowls and cups and glasses.

His palms continued to tingle, tingle, tingle.

He went to the finished basement, where he'd set up a fitness room. It was equipped with a weight bench, a barbell, several iron plates of Olympic weights, dumbbells, and rubber mats.

He attempted to lift a twenty-five–pound dumbbell. He brought it a couple of inches off the floor; then it dropped to the mat. When he tried to move it again, it budged only an inch.

Then there were some limits to his power. He couldn't lift a car in the air, for instance.

But maybe, with practice, he could.

As he started to go to another section of the house, fatigue suddenly spread through him. He was as exhausted as if he'd performed a grueling two-hour workout. Hunger pains cramped his stomach, too.

The prickly feeling dissipated—like a motor that had run out of fuel.

With great effort, Gabriel shuffled upstairs to the kitchen. He made a ham and cheese sandwich, felt his belly rumble again, and decided to make two sandwiches.

He took the sandwiches with him into his home office. Now that he'd gotten over the initial rush of discovery, it was time to seriously think about where these powers he'd acquired had come from.

He powered up the laptop computer and munched on the first sandwich, thinking.

A possibility surfaced in his thoughts: the car accident.

He remembered that when he'd awakened at the hospital, after his accident, he'd experienced the tingling for the first time. The phenomena was apparently a precursor of his being able to levitate objects. It only followed, then, that this unusual skill of his had been brought on by his accident. Basic cause and effect principle.

It was like in those horror movies when a character almost died of some kind of injury, but survived—and then discovered that he could see visions of the future. Same idea.

But this wasn't Hollywood. This was real. He needed real answers, not make-believe theories.

He logged on to the Internet. He pulled up Google, his favorite search engine, and began digging for more information.

He found a label for his talent: telekinesis, psychokinesis, or remote influencing. Whatever the name, it referred to the ability to move objects from one place to another without physical contact.

He had psychic powers. Him—Mr. Corporate. How crazy was that?

Only a few days ago he would have scoffed at this mystical stuff, would have dismissed it as superstitious nonsense promoted by loonies who had no grip on reality. But there was nothing like personal experience to change your mind. He devoured the information more eagerly than any contract or business proposal that had ever been placed in front of him.

The Web sites he visited offered various explanations for what stirred the onset of telekinetic abilities. Traumatic accidents. Transcendent experiences. Purposefully trying to awaken your psychic powers through meditation, diet, and practice.

As far as where the powers originated from, the general theory was that every human being was born with the potential to perform such wondrous feats. But most people used only a small portion—say, 10 percent–of their brain's capabilities. If you fully tapped into your brain's power, you could do telekinesis, telepathy, levitate, gain visions of the future . . . hell, you could become the real-life equivalent of an *X-Man* character.

Gabriel wanted to laugh. It was so absurd. But he couldn't laugh it off—because he knew it was true.

He wondered about the hallucinations. How did the encounters with the snake and the shadowy figure in the mirror tie in to all of this? Were they also related to his accident?

As he was constructing a new search, the telephone rang. Caller ID announced the call as coming from Reid Construction.

Gabriel looked at his watch. It was almost one-thirty.

Uh-oh. I forgot to do something at work. But what?

He picked up the phone. "Hello."

"Where the hell are you?"

It was his father. His father cursed only when he was angry.

"Umm, I'm at home, Pops," he said. "I had to go to the doctor this morning."

"That was this morning. You said you were going to be here for our one o'clock with the folks from Charlotte. Did you forget?"

Oh, shit!

"Uh, well . . . I'm on my way now."

"Forget it, Gabe. The meeting will be over within the hour. Besides, Isaiah has been filling in for you—very capably, I might add. You owe him."

"Isaiah? What?"

"I'm heading back to the meeting. We've got to wrap up. Get your ass in here, ASAP."

Click.

Gabriel slowly replaced the phone on the cradle. Shock had numbed him.

How had Isaiah filled in for him? The man knew nothing about the business and had never worked a day of his life in corporate America.

Besides, Isaiah has been filling in for you—very capably, I might add.

Isaiah was sabotaging his career, destroying his life. As he'd promised he would.

Taking it all away, little brother. Piece by piece.

Gabriel raced to the bedroom to shower and dress for work. While he still had a job.

Chapter 30

By the time Gabriel arrived at the office five minutes after two, the meeting was over.

The conference room in which the discussion had been held was empty. A large paper flip chart stood in the corner, on which Gabriel would have written ideas and feedback from the prospective client. The pages were full of writing in black marker; Gabriel read through them and guessed that they were notes from the talk.

"You missed it," Pops said from the doorway, startling Gabriel. Pops stepped inside and closed the door. He leaned against the conference table, arms folded over his chest, hands tightened into fists. "I'm very disappointed in you. If you had a problem that required you to stay home, you should have told me in advance. That's our policy. You know that."

"I'm sorry." Gabriel dug his hands in his pockets. He felt like a child again, as though he'd brought home failing grades on his report card. "I got caught up in something."

"And it prevented you from calling me?" Pops asked. "This was an important meeting. There was a lot of money riding on this deal. The prospect was expecting to talk to *you*."

How could he tell his father what was really going on? *Pops, I was at home experimenting with my psychic powers. Want to see me float a pencil?* His father, a hardheaded realist, would think he had cracked up, and Gabriel wasn't convinced that a live demonstration would sway his father—or that he'd be able to summon his telekinetic ability on demand in the first place. He was still tired and hadn't felt the tingling in his palms since he'd left the house.

He had to keep the truth to himself and endure the rebuke from his father. But it stung. In spite of his father's confessed failings, Gabriel still admired him as a business person. Hearing his father's disappointment in him was worse than being whipped with a belt.

"Pops, I'm sorry. It was an honest mistake. It won't happen again."

"We closed the deal anyway. You can thank Isaiah for that." Pops motioned to the flip chart. "He took those notes. He shared a ton of shrewd ideas, impressed the hell out of the prospect. And me, too. You should have seen him in action. You would've been floored."

"I'm sure." Gabriel smiled sourly.

"What the hell is your problem? I'm beginning to lose patience with your attitude about your brother."

If you only knew what Isaiah was planning, Pops.

But, again, Gabriel could not express his honest thoughts. There was no way his father would believe him—especially after Isaiah had apparently helped guide a lucrative contract to completion. Few things held as much influence with Pops as dollars and cents.

"It's what I said last night," Gabriel said. "I just don't trust him."

Pops walked toward Gabriel. "Listen to yourself, Gabe. Not twenty minutes ago, *this man you don't trust* helped us seal a property development contract for two million dollars.

Because you brought in this prospect, *this man you don't trust* just helped you earn a bonus check for five thousand dollars. When I offered to cut him a bonus, too, *this man you don't trust* declined it and said he was serving only as a substitute and didn't deserve the money. Does that sound to you like a man who shouldn't be trusted?"

Pops's nostrils flared. He was furious, Gabriel realized. He hadn't seen Pops this angry since he'd been in high school, when Gabriel had taken one of the family cars without permission and backed into a tree. Afterward Pops had grounded him for a month and made him pay for the damage.

"All right," Gabriel said. He had to be careful here; he didn't want to infuriate Pops further. "Isaiah helped close a deal, I'll give him credit for that. But, Pops, why is he working here—and participating in executive meetings, no less? How is he qualified for that?"

"He's my son," Pops said. "What other qualifications does he need?"

That explained it, Gabriel suddenly understood. Pops believed that merely because Isaiah was his son, he deserved an opportunity to work in the upper ranks of the company. As though Isaiah had inherited a gene from Pops that had destined him for entrepreneurial greatness. Pops had often said the same thing about Gabriel, but that had not stopped Gabriel from earning an advanced degree and toiling in every level of the organization to learn the business from the inside out. He'd paid his dues. It was only fair that Isaiah should have to do the same.

But that argument would not sway his father. Pops didn't care about what was fair. He cared about making money—and Isaiah had somehow convinced him that he could deliver.

"College degrees and job experience aren't everything," Pops said. "There's a lot to be said for natural ability, for pure management talent. Do you think everyone with an

MBA and ten years' work experience is destined to become a millionaire?"

"Of course not." It sounded as though Pops was talking about him.

"Isaiah will be shadowing various executives in the organization—me, you, and others—to gain deeper insight into what we do. Then we're going to work together to create a position for him, a role that will best utilize his talents for our company."

Gabriel couldn't believe he was hearing this. But, at this point, arguing with Pops would gain him nothing.

"Sounds as if you've got it all worked out," Gabriel said.

"We worked it out today—while you were 'caught up in something' at home."

Gabriel gnashed his teeth.

"I expect you to help Isaiah learn the ropes," Pops said. "This is business, Gabe. When we're here I could care less about whether you like him as a person, though I think you should make an effort to get along with him. He's had a rough life, but he's a good guy at heart. You could be a positive influence on him."

Gabriel said nothing. He didn't trust himself to speak without screaming.

Pops clapped him on the shoulder.

"Back to work, son. You've got a little healthy competition for the CEO mantle now."

Gabriel went to his office, but he could not concentrate on his work. He felt as though he were going to collapse underneath the weight of all his problems.

Pops was disappointed in him. His relationship with Dana was foundering. He was seeing frightening hallucinations he couldn't explain. He'd gained a psychic talent from mysterious sources and it appeared to be empowering—but it could bring unknown and harmful side effects. And Isaiah, whom everyone but him trusted and adored, was succeeding in setting up him and his family for a catastrophic fall.

Gabriel swiveled away from the computer and buried his head in his hands.

He needed a shoulder to lean on, a sympathetic ear. But there was no one to whom he could turn. He'd alienated everyone.

He'd never felt so abandoned.

"It's all falling apart, isn't it, little brother?"

Gabriel snapped up. Isaiah had entered his office. Gabriel had been so absorbed in his worries, he hadn't heard the door open.

"Get out of my office," Gabriel said.

"Hold on." Grinning triumphantly, Isaiah sat in a chair in front of Gabriel's desk and comfortably crossed his legs. "Pops told you I'd be shadowing you, studying the business from the inside. I'm here to learn."

Gabriel gripped the edges of his desk. It took all his self-control to restrain himself from bounding over the desk and strangling Isaiah with his bare hands.

"And you should be thanking me, too," Isaiah said. "I closed the deal while you were at home with your thumb in your ass. Because of me, you're five grand richer. Can I get a 'thank you'?"

"How about a 'fuck you'?"

Isaiah merely smiled.

"You keep on slipping up here and Pops is going to bus your ass down to the mail room," Isaiah said. He looked around, appraising the decor. "I'll move into this office, get rid of that boring shit you've got on the walls, maybe add some posters of Janet and Halle and some other hotties."

"You've lost your mind. You're not taking my office." But Gabriel's denial lacked conviction. The truth was that his father was so enamored of Isaiah that he didn't know what might happen. His future at the company, once assured, suddenly seemed to be in question.

"It's tough when Daddy isn't on your side, cleaning up behind you, straightening your tie, and wiping your snotty nose, isn't it?" Isaiah shook his head sadly. "Now you know how I felt my whole life. You're learning how it feels to be out in the cold with no safety net, no one to save you."

"Look, I'm sorry you had to go through that crap, but that has nothing to do with me."

"It has *everything* to do with you," Isaiah said in a low voice. Rising, he planted his hands on the desk and leaned forward. He was so close that Gabriel could smell the peppermint on his breath. "If you hadn't been around, my father would have taken care of me and Mama. He deserted us—for you and the rest of you arrogant, spoiled assholes."

Isaiah's eyes bore into Gabriel. The eyes of a psycho. He was the kind of man who would do anything to get what he wanted. Gabriel understood that about Isaiah intuitively.

But Gabriel held Isaiah's glare.

For the first time in his life, he had nothing to lose.

"I don't need Pops to take care of you," Gabriel said. "I'm going to handle you myself. You're gonna wish you never came here."

"Hear that line in a movie or something, little brother?" Isaiah smirked. "You don't know me. You don't know who you're fucking with."

"No—*you* don't know who you're fucking with," Gabriel said. "I don't have anything to lose anymore. You hurt anyone in my family and *I will kill you.*" Gabriel stabbed his finger at Isaiah, inches away from Isaiah's nose. "That's a promise."

Isaiah blinked—then he laughed. He pushed away from the desk.

"We'll discuss business later, little brother," Isaiah said. "I think I'm going to swing by the mall and buy some new threads for our birthday party tomorrow."

Gabriel's family had planned a thirtieth-birthday celebration for him at the 755 Club. At first Gabriel had been eagerly anticipating the party, but so much terrible stuff had been going on that he'd almost forgotten about it.

"Our birthday party?" Gabriel said. "It's my party, not yours."

"We share the same b-day, remember? Pops thought it would be a good idea to make it a celebration for the two of us."

"You're lying." But Gabriel knew he was telling the truth.

"Now, Gabe, you know how our father feels about me. I'm his firstborn."

Gabriel got to his feet. "Get out."

"See you at the party," Isaiah said.

Snickering, Isaiah left. Gabriel dropped back into his chair. He rubbed the bridge of his nose.

He didn't even want to think about tomorrow night, having to watch Isaiah mingle with his family and friends. The prospect was nauseating.

He couldn't stop his father from including Isaiah in the party—Pops was footing the bill for the affair—but he had to do something to prevent Isaiah from further insinuating himself into his life. But what could he do?

There was a knock at the door. Miss Angie came inside with a bundle of envelopes.

"You don't look well," she said. "What's wrong?"

"How much time do you have?" he said. Then he shrugged. "Never mind, I don't want to talk about it. What do you have for me?"

"Lots of mail," she said. "It's accumulated quite a bit with you being in and out of the office this week."

She deposited the mail on the desk. Turning to leave, she said, "You and Isaiah look so much alike. It must be exciting to discover that you have a brother like him, such a nice young man."

Gabriel forced a smile. "It was a surprise."

"Oh, certainly. But you have a wonderful family. I'm sure he's been fitting right in."

His smile faltered. "That's one way to put it."

Miss Angie, seeming to realize that she was treading on a minefield, excused herself and left the office.

Gabriel began to sort through his mail. Most of it was junk: invitations to overpriced seminars and workshops, enticements to subscribe to business periodicals, résumés from individuals who apparently had done no research whatsoever on the company. Gabriel was involved in hiring decisions, and one of his responsibilities involved reviewing résumés from management candidates.

At the bottom of the stack he found a thick nine-by-twelve envelope from Miller Investigative Research Services, Inc.

Sean Miller, an old Morehouse buddy of Gabriel's, had founded Miller Investigative Research Services. His company conducted extensive background checks on prospective employees. In these days of fraud, you could never be too careful about whom you hired. Miller would verify prior-employment history, criminal records, judgments and liens, credit reports—anything requested. Everyone's life and deeds were documented, somewhere, and your past could be used against you.

Gabriel tilted back in the chair, contemplating the envelope, though he didn't open it.

You don't know me. You don't know who you're fucking with.

Isaiah was right. Gabriel knew nothing about him. He knew only what Isaiah had told him and the family.

Could he have lied about his background?

He could have—and Gabriel was positive he most likely had.

Gabriel sprang forward and yanked open a drawer. He

looked for his lucky Mont Blanc pen Pops had given him when he'd graduated from Morehouse, but he couldn't find it. Maybe he'd left it at home.

He uncapped a Bic pen and flipped open a notepad. Then he clicked on his Blackberry and pulled up the phone number for Sean Miller.

It was time to learn the truth about Isaiah Battle.

Chapter 31

Sean Miller lived in the West End, not far from the Atlanta University Center, a group of historically black colleges that included Morehouse, Clark Atlanta, Spelman, and Morris Brown. Once a prosperous area, much of the West End had been damaged by the urban blight that plagued most of America's neglected inner cities. A long-term community revitalization project was underway to add retail and new housing, improve transportation, reduce crime, and polish the neighborhood to the urbane elegance it had once enjoyed.

Sean ran Miller Investigative Research Services out of his house, a renovated Craftsman bungalow that sat far away from the road within the confines of a large fenced yard. A BEWARE OF DOG sign was posted on the gate. Gabriel pushed through the gate and approached the front door. When he pressed the doorbell, spirited, deep-throated barking rang out.

"Wassup, chief?" Sean said, opening the door. He welcomed Gabriel inside.

Gabriel hung back, peered over Sean's shoulder. "Where are the dogs?"

"Down the hall, waiting to rip out your throat," Sean said, and when he saw Gabriel's look of horror, he grinned. "Relax, man. I'm just joining you. You know me. The hounds are in the back. They'll remember you. Come on in."

"They bite, I sue." Gabriel smiled.

He and Sean shook hands and exchanged a one-armed brother-man hug. Gabriel had to bend over slightly to do it; Sean was only five-three. Although small in stature, he had a physique that might have been chiseled from granite. He wore dreadlocks and a beard. He'd started locking his hair, Gabriel recalled, after he made his exodus from corporate America five years ago.

Gabriel followed Sean down the hallway. Artistic renderings of Bob Marley hung from the walls, and Gabriel heard strains of reggae music thumping from somewhere deep in the house.

The dogs waited at the end of the hallway, sitting patiently on their haunches. Two huge black rottweilers. They looked at Gabriel and then looked at Sean.

"Friend," Sean said.

The dogs sniffed Gabriel's slacks, tails wagging.

"I'd hate to be classified as 'enemy,'" Gabriel said.

"You certainly would." Chuckling, Sean rubbed behind one of the canine's ears. "This neighborhood is on the rise, but you never can take too many precautions. My lab is probably valued at more than the house."

Sean snapped his fingers, said, "Roam," and the dogs dutifully trotted away.

Gabriel shook his head in amazement.

They crossed the kitchen—something delicious and spicy simmered in a pot—and went to a door that led to the basement. Downstairs, Sean had erected his "lab." It was a large, brightly lit space, full of computers, monitors, printers, copy machines, file cabinets, and a couple of desks.

Off to one side, there was a lounging area with upholstered chairs, a sofa, a chaise lounge, and a coffee table. A gorgeous, dark-skinned woman reclined on the chaise. She wore a red tube top and black capris that clung to her long, shapely legs. She was reading a physics textbook.

"Kristi, this is my old college buddy, Gabriel," Sean said. "Gabriel, meet Kristi."

"Nice to meet you, old college buddy." Kristi stood and shook Gabriel's hand. The woman stood at least five-ten without heels.

"Gabriel is here on some sensitive business," Sean said. "Would you mind leaving us alone for a few?"

Kristi gathered her textbook and notebooks, and sashayed up the stairs. Gabriel whistled lowly and turned to Sean.

"Now, she's something else," he said. "Where'd you meet her?"

"At a Barnes and Noble near Georgia Tech," Sean said. "She's from Nigeria, working on her Ph.D. in physics. You know I like the tall sisters—especially the ones with brains."

"That's been your MO since back in the day."

"And she can cook her ass off. Been fattening me up with all those spicy stews. A brother might have to settle down with her. You and Dana still on track for October?"

"I guess so," Gabriel said.

"All right, I can tell from your tone that I'd better not go there," Sean said. He sat on a swivel chair and spun around. "Have a seat. So, what can I do for you? You were sounding secretive over the phone."

Gabriel sat on a nearby chair. He hadn't wanted to divulge the purpose for his visit while at the office. He didn't think Isaiah or his father would have overheard his conversation . . . but he'd begun to feel paranoid and felt more comfortable discussing the matter with Sean face-to-face.

"I need to find out about a guy," Gabriel said. "This isn't for the company—well, not completely, anyway. It's personal."

Sean had grabbed a pen and a notepad. He nodded, poised to make notes.

"It's about my family. It's kind of embarrassing. . . ."

Sean raised his hand in a stop gesture. "Hey, you don't have to tell me. I don't need to know why you need the info in order to get the goods. I'm serving as a tool, nothing more."

"Okay, thanks, 'cause I'd rather not go into all that."

"What's the guy's name?"

"Isaiah Battle. He's from Chicago—at least, that's where he claims to be from. I have my doubts about a lot of what he's said."

"Know when he was born?"

"June sixth, nineteen seventy-five."

Sean's eyebrows arched. "Isn't that your birthday?"

"It is."

"Hmm. Happy belated birthday, by the way. Big three-O."

"Thanks." Gabriel removed a slip of paper from his jacket pocket. "Here's his license-plate number. He drives a Chevy Chevelle SS, 1970, I think."

"Old school, baller whip," Sean said. He studied the note Gabriel had given him and jotted down some information. "This'll help a lot."

"Look especially for a criminal record," Gabriel said. "I wouldn't be surprised if he had a list of offenses as long as your girlfriend's legs."

"Sounds like a tough dude."

"He is." Gabriel didn't say more, though it was clear that Sean was eager to know exactly how he and Isaiah were connected, and why he was seeking this information. "That's the only concrete stuff I have on him. I'm hoping you can fill in the blanks."

"That's what I do, chief," Sean said, scribbling furiously. "When do you need this by?"

"As soon as possible. I'll pay you whatever you need to put a rush on this."

"I can start tonight," Sean said.

"And if you come across anything that really stands out, I want you to holler at me right away."

"Will do. How should I get in touch with you? I'd like to get your private e-mail addy in case I want to send you a document or something."

Gabriel used Sean's notepad to write his personal e-mail address and cell-phone number.

"Remember, Sean, this needs to stay between us—no matter what you find."

"If I didn't know how to be discreet, I wouldn't be in business." Sean bounced to his feet. "I'd ask you to stay for dinner—Kristi's cooking her banging oxtail stew—but I think I want to get started on this immediately. I get the feeling that would be cool with you, too."

Gabriel smiled tightly. "I'd appreciate it. You have no idea."

"I'll try to get back to you with something before the night is over."

Chapter 32

On Friday night, Nicole went to her parents' for dinner. Although she lived in her own town house in Buckhead, there was nothing like Mom's cooking, especially at the end of a long week. After working an eleven-hour day at the downtown law firm where she'd been practicing corporate law for the past year, she was eagerly anticipating a good meal in the company of her family.

"Hey, Mom," she said when her mother opened the door. Mom wore shorts and a T-shirt, a sure sign that she'd been involved in working around the house. Nicole gave her a kiss on the cheek.

"Hey, Nic," Mom said. "Looks like it's just you and me tonight."

"Where's Daddy?"

"He and Isaiah went out for drinks. They're celebrating a deal Isaiah helped close."

Nicole set her purse on a table, frowned. "Isaiah's working with Daddy now?"

"It sounds like it."

"Oh."

"I was as surprised to hear about it as you are." Mom shrugged. "But that's your daddy's business. You know I don't intervene."

Nicole followed her mother into the kitchen. Mouthwatering aromas drifted from the pots and pans on the stove. Nicole's stomach growled, but she held off on grabbing a plate. Mom stirred a pitcher of sweet tea.

Nicole fidgeted with a pen on the counter.

"What do you think of Isaiah?" Nicole asked. "Honestly?"

"Learning about him shocked and hurt me," Mom said. She sighed. "I'm still praying on that. But . . . he's your daddy's flesh and blood. I have to accept him, to honor my husband. It's the right thing to do."

"But what do you think of Isaiah as a person?"

"He seems like a nice boy. Respectable, well mannered, God-fearing. I think he deserves to know his father and his father's family. He's missed out on so much."

"Well, yeah, he has."

"Why did you ask me that?"

Nicole twisted her hair around her finger. "I was only wondering."

Mom gave her a skeptical look, but she didn't pursue it further. She poured a glass of tea and slid it to Nicole. Nicole loved her mother's sweet tea, but she didn't pick it up.

"I'll be back, Mom. I'm going to change out of these clothes."

Nicole left the kitchen and went upstairs. She'd been living on her own since she'd left to attend undergrad, but she still kept some clothes in her old bedroom.

She passed Gabriel's room—now occupied by Isaiah—on her way down the hallway. She moved back to the closed door, hesitated.

She'd wanted to feel out her mother before airing out her own honest feelings. Her mother, as she'd assumed, liked Isaiah. But oftentimes, Mom made such comments only because she was supporting Daddy and didn't want to cause any conflict and appear to be at odds with him. It could be difficult to know what Mom was really thinking.

But Nicole knew how she personally felt about Isaiah. She didn't like him. He gave her a bad feeling. An icky feeling.

She'd liked him fine until she had given him a tour of the house the previous night. She could not put her finger on anything he'd said or done while she'd been showing him around, but afterward, when she thought of him, she felt nauseous. It was weird.

She'd even had a dream about him last night. In the dream he made her do awful things, perverse acts that turned her stomach. When she awakened, it took her a long time to get back to sleep.

She knew she sounded as crazy as Gabriel with his "gut feeling" about Isaiah. But she couldn't help it. Isaiah creeped her out. He scared her, to be honest.

But why?

She looked down the hall to make sure her mother was not around. Mom would never approve of snooping.

But she wanted to go inside the room, to find something that would either support her fear or prove she was being silly and needed to get over it.

Satisfied that her mother was not nearby, Nicole opened the door and crept inside. She turned on the light.

The room smelled like Isaiah—a slightly woodsy, masculine scent. It would have appealed to many women. But it curdled her stomach.

The bed was neatly made; it looked as though it hadn't been slept in. None of his personal items lay on the nightstand or dresser.

What were you expecting to find? A collection of human skulls?

Then she remembered that when she had shown him into the room, he had slid his luggage underneath the bed. She recalled it only because it had struck her as odd, but she hadn't commented on it. He was from another world and his ways were foreign to her.

She approached the bed. Kneeling, she lifted the bed skirt. Two suitcases and a duffel bag lay underneath. She grasped the handle of one of the suitcases, tugged it out.

She looked behind her to confirm that she was still alone.

Turning back to the suitcase, she happened to glance at a wooden figurine on the mantel above the headboard. A carving of a man and a woman, bodies intertwined.

She had seen the statue a thousand times before—Gabriel had picked it up on a trip to Ghana when he was in college— but looking at it triggered a spell of dizziness.

She put her hand against her head.

Oh, God, what's wrong with me?

Images invaded her mind. They were so vivid that it was as though she had been plunged into a waking dream. . . .

Isaiah sat on the bed. He made a come-hither gesture with his index finger.

"Get over here," he said.

She couldn't resist him. She wanted to, but she couldn't. Her mind was like a car; he had torn her away from the steering wheel and slid behind it himself. He could drive her wherever he desired.

She walked in front of him. She didn't look at him, however. Her gaze settled on a wooden figurine behind the bed, a carving of a man and a woman.

Watching her, he licked his lips. He put his hands on her breasts. He squeezed.

"Feel good?" he asked. "Tell me it feels good."

She had to obey. "It feels good."

He slid his hands to her hips, kneaded them between his fingers.

"Hot body like yours, I know you're a freak," he said. "But you hide it behind those glasses and your little geek-princess attitude. You can't fool your big brother."

She only stood there, allowing him to feel her up. A distant part of her mind screamed, wanted to stop this violation. But he held her in his thrall.

He rose off the bed.

"Get on your knees," he said.

No, *she thought.* No, no, I won't do that. Stop it!

His gaze bore into her brain, penetrated her soul. The vise he had clamped on her mind tightened. Her head began to ache.

"On your knees," he said firmly.

She couldn't resist any longer. He was too strong.

She knelt in front of him. His erection, straining against his pants, was only inches away from her face.

He cupped the back of her head in his hand. He brought her head forward, against his groin.

"Feel that?" he said. "It's going to be in that sweet pouty mouth of yours in a minute."

She whimpered softly.

"Unzip my pants," he said.

She grasped his zipper, tugged it down.

Suddenly there was a knock at the door.

"Are you kids in there?" It was Mom.

Isaiah zipped his slacks. He looked at her. She watched him, awaiting instruction in spite of her desire to disobey, to scream until her throat was raw.

"Stand up," he said. She did.

"Once I snap my fingers," he said, "you'll remember none of this. You'll be feeling just fine again. Okay?"

She nodded. He hurried to the door. He snapped his fingers . . .

Catapulted out of the vision, Nicole gasped. She fell against the bed. Cold perspiration matted her forehead.

Dear, Jesus, what was that?

Her stomach heaved. She staggered into the bathroom and vomited.

Had that nightmare really happened, here in this bedroom? Or had it all been in her mind?

She wiped her lips with a wad of tissue and then gargled with Listerine. She washed her face with cold, purifying water.

Whether it had been an actual incident or not, she had to get out of this room. Spending another minute in here would sicken her again.

She hurried out of the bathroom, remembered the suitcase she'd pulled from beneath the bed, rushed to it, and shoved it back in place. She tried to position the suitcase exactly as she'd found it—Isaiah might be one of those obsessive-compulsive people who arranged everything just-so and would detect if something had been moved—but she was so frazzled that she couldn't remember precisely how she'd found the luggage. She shifted it under there as close to the former position as she could remember and then moved away. Her stomach was beginning to knot again.

She practically ran out of the bedroom and had to stop herself from slamming the door behind her.

When she entered the hallway, the nausea passed.

Weird things like this didn't happen to her. She couldn't simply forget about it. Whether her vision had been a recollection of an actual incident, or a piece of a nightmare, she was convinced that at some time, Isaiah had done something awful to her.

She had to talk about it with someone. Her mother, of course, was off-limits. She could only discuss it with someone who shared her suspicions about Isaiah.

And there was only one person who fit that description.

Chapter 33

Gabriel walked out of Sean's house feeling better than he had in days.

He was finally doing something proactive to combat Isaiah's invasion of his family. Instead of mumbling about his gut feelings, he wanted to present undeniable facts that would reveal Isaiah as the viper he really was.

As he approached the Corvette, crossing from the sidewalk to the street, he glimpsed something on the car's front seat. A darkly glimmering, coiled shape.

He leaned closer.

It was a water moccasin. The same one he'd seen last night at Dana's, and, prior to that, at his house.

The snake had gotten into the car. It seemed impossible. But there it was.

His mouth went dry. He kept his distance from the passenger's-side window.

Was this real? Or was he imagining this?

A breeze whisked along the street, pushing the scent of dogwoods, summer flowers in bloom, and exhaust fumes from passing cars. A rusty Oldsmobile rumbled by, music rattling the windows. At a brick house across the street, an elderly woman dug in her flower beds.

If he was hallucinating, how could his senses be so acute?

The snake slithered to the passenger's-side seat. It rose, its face sliding up the window. It watched him with its narrow, evil eyes.

There was no rational explanation for the snake winding up in the car. The only answer was that someone was stalking him, had planted the snake within his vicinity—but that mystery stalker would have had to first enter his house without his knowledge to leave the snake, then get into Dana's condo to deposit the reptile, then break into the Corvette . . .

It didn't make any sense.

The water moccasin's forked tongue tasted the air as though salivating at the thought of sinking its fangs into Gabriel.

"It's not real," Gabriel said softly. Then, more firmly, "I'm hallucinating this. There is no snake."

He half expected his declaration to cause the reptile to dissolve, like a figment of a dream. But it didn't fade away, didn't flicker. It remained as realistic looking as the pavement on which Gabriel stood.

He didn't know what to make of that.

He jingled the keys in his hand.

Think.

But he couldn't come up with another plan. Resolving to act, he moved closer to the car, grasped the passenger door handle. He pulled it, opening the door—and swiftly moved away.

The water moccasin poured to the ground like an oil slick. It glared at him, menacingly, and Gabriel jumped away, ready to bolt back to Sean's house if the snake got any closer. The snake drew backward, almost proudly, as though pleased by its intimidation of him. It slipped between the grates of a drainage ditch and disappeared.

Gabriel kicked the door closed. He hurried around the car, careful to avoid the drain, got in, slammed the door.

He'd been lucky that time.

He inhaled deeply. The car's interior smelled of soft leather and scented oils. There was nothing in the warm air to indicate that a snake had occupied the space only seconds ago. Wouldn't it have left behind a noticeable odor, a foul smell?

It would have. If it had been real.

Although common sense and even intuition told him that the snake was an illusion, he was not willing to put himself in harm's way. The evidence of his eyes held more weight than the feelings in his heart.

Faith is the belief in things unseen. . . .

Those words, part of a Biblical scripture, came to mind, and how true they were. He lacked faith. In himself.

Disturbed by those thoughts, he turned on his cell phone. He planned to leave it on in case Sean attempted to call him.

He'd received a voice-mail message from Nicole.

"Hi, it's your sister. I need to talk to you right away. In person, preferably. Give me a call on my cell, okay?"

Gabriel called her back. Nicole wanted to see him ASAP. He suggested they meet at Fellini's Pizza in Buckhead. Since Dana had not returned any of his calls—though she was at work, he knew the real reason why she was avoiding him—he assumed he was flying solo that night.

"Hurry," Nicole said. "I'll be there by nine."

What was so urgent? Curiosity was chewing a hole in his stomach.

"I'm on my way," he said.

Isaiah had been busy sowing discord and, in general, ruining people's lives.

He'd left the office early after wowing his father during the meeting and rubbing little brother's face in his feat. He made plans to meet with Pops for drinks that evening to celebrate the deal. They were going to Club Touch, a strip joint, of course—and that had actually been his father's suggestion.

But before Isaiah did that, he took care of a little business.

He stopped by Home Depot. There, he purchased a couple cans of spray paint.

Then he drove to Dana's condo. He had copied her address out of Gabriel's address book, which he'd found in his desk at the office.

People tended to leave such valuable information out in the open.

He was counting on Dana, a big-shot physician, being at work. Her condo was on the sixth floor at the end of the corridor, the door nestled within a recessed doorway. How fortunate; it would give him privacy.

A rap on the door confirmed that she was out, or sleeping, or otherwise not answering. He heard a small dog yapping, little paws scratching against the door.

"Shut the fuck up," he said to the dog. "Or I'll bust in there and kick your guts out."

The dog whimpered, fell silent.

He went to work. It didn't take long. A few minutes later he was back in his car.

Taking it all away, little brother. Piece by piece.

Chapter 34

Around nine o'clock Gabriel arrived at Fellini's Pizza on the corner of Peachtree Street and Rumson Road in Buckhead. Buckhead, known as Atlanta's upscale party district, was congested with creeping Friday-night traffic, people in shiny cars cruising Peachtree to see and be seen, and herds of revelers jamming the sidewalks, ambling from one bar and restaurant to another. By midnight, when the scene hit its peak, it would take a half hour to crawl just a mile down the street.

Gabriel half wished he'd agreed to meet Nicole on another side of town, but she lived in the area, not far from the restaurant. Still, because parking in Buckhead was at a premium, he had to park two blocks away.

The pizzeria was located in a converted gas station, dipped in bright colors, and boasted an immense patio illuminated by strings of white Christmas lights. A multicultural crowd, lured outdoors by the warm summer evening, filled the patio to near capacity.

Gabriel found Nicole at a corner table, trying to give the brush-off to a young brother who wore a long white tee and had a mouth gleaming with an undoubtedly fake platinum grill.

"Excuse me." Gabriel cleared his throat. "This is my seat, man."

"Oh, you her man? All right, then." The guy winked at Nicole. "You got my number, shorty, a'ight?"

Nicole gave him an artificial smile, sending him away, and then she turned to Gabriel. "Thank God, Gabe. You were right on time."

"The challenges of life as a diva."

"Whatever. Where's Dana? I know you guys usually spend Friday nights together."

"She's working late." He hoped his tone did not betray the truth. He glanced at the Corona sitting in front of Nicole and, to change the subject, said, "You had a beer the other night, too. Have martinis become passé?"

"Seems like it, doesn't it?" She offered a weak smile. "You want something to eat? I ate at Mom's."

"I'll eat after we talk," he said. "So what's up, sis? I know you didn't invite me here for chitchat."

She took a sip of her beer. "You know how much I hate to admit I'm wrong, right? Especially to you."

"True. Actually, you don't like to admit you're wrong to anyone."

"Whatever." She rolled her eyes. Then she grew serious. "I was wrong about Isaiah, Gabe."

Gabriel's heartbeat stuttered. "What do you mean?"

"You know that bad gut feeling you have about him? Well, I have one, too."

"Did something happen?"

"I think so. I don't know." She twisted her fingers through her hair, laughed nervously. "Okay, that sounded stupid."

"You said it, not me."

"He gives me a nasty feeling," she said. "When I think about him, I feel nauseous. The weird thing is that I didn't feel that way when I first met him. But after Mom and Daddy said he could stay with them, I showed him to your old room. . . ."

"He's staying in my old bedroom?"

"And I don't know what happened—I don't remember anything out of the ordinary—but by the time I finished showing him to your room and then giving him a tour of the rest of the house, I couldn't get away from him fast enough."

"Really? Did he do something that bothered you? Or say something nasty?"

"Not that I can remember. But I had a dream about him last night, Gabe. A really, really sick dream. I don't even want to tell you about it."

"Good, because I don't want to ask."

"Anyway, I went to the house for dinner tonight, right? Isaiah and Daddy had gone out for drinks to celebrate him helping to close a deal or whatever. Anyway, Mom and I were the only ones at the house. So I had a chance to look through Isaiah's stuff."

"You went through Isaiah's things?" he asked.

Her face reddened. "I know, it was a terrible thing to do, but I wanted to find something that might explain why I have these creepy feelings about him."

"Actually, I wish I'd thought of that," he said. "But, sorry— please go on."

"He keeps his bags under the bed, which is kinda weird. I pulled out his suitcase and started to unzip it—and I suddenly felt dizzy. And then . . . this is where it gets really strange."

She fiddled with the beer bottle. He waited for her to continue.

"I had a vision or a flashback—I don't know what you would call it, maybe a dream while I was awake—of being in the bedroom with Isaiah. And he was making me do stuff. Sick stuff."

Gabriel's stomach performed a slow flip-flop.

"He was ordering me around as if I were a robot, and even though I didn't want to do any of the things he told me to do, I had to obey him. It was as though he had hypnotized me. I was . . . powerless. I've never felt like that in my life, ever. He could have told me to jump out a window and I would have done it."

"But you said this was a dream," Gabriel said.

"I don't know *what* it was," she said. "But I know he did something to me. I've never felt so violated. It made me sick."

Gabriel was glad he hadn't ordered any food. He was feeling nauseous, too.

"Anyway, because you don't like Isaiah either, you're the only one I could tell about this," she said. "What do you think? Do you think I'm crazy?"

He almost laughed. He was seeing snakes and visions in mirrors—how could he possibly have the nerve to call her crazy?

"No, I don't think you're crazy," he said.

She sighed with obvious relief. "Then what do you think happened? What did he do to me?"

"I don't know, sis. I'm clueless. Does Mom have any idea that you were looking through his things?"

"Are you kidding? She would've cried bloody murder. You better not tell her."

"I'd never do that. I don't think we should tell anyone about this yet."

"I'm really worried. I don't like him staying there with Mom and Daddy. I don't trust him."

Gabriel resisted the urge to gloat and declare, "I told you so." It would have been a childish thing to say, and he wasn't in a joking mood.

"What should we do, Gabe?"

"Honestly, I don't think there's anything we can do yet to get rid of him, because of Pops. Pops wants him here, and you know he runs that house."

"But you and I are having these terrible feelings."

"That won't hold any water with Pops, you know that. He deals in facts."

"Yeah." She gazed at her beer, suddenly grabbed it, and drained the rest of the bottle.

His sister didn't scare easily. For all her little-princess ways, she was a tough girl at heart with a lot of spunk. It disturbed him to see her like this.

"I want you to stay away from Isaiah," he said. "He's dangerous. From now on, let me do the investigating, okay?"

She nodded. "God, I hope he doesn't know someone was rummaging in his stuff. I tried to put everything back exactly as I'd found it, but what if he's like you? When you were a kid, if I came into your bathroom and moved the toothpaste one inch, you'd know."

"Let's hope he's not like me. In the meantime I have someone doing a background check on Isaiah."

"That's a really good idea," she said with a rare touch of admiration.

"I want hard facts that Isaiah is up to no good. That's all that will convince Pops—irrefutable proof."

"You're exactly right," she said.

A waitress walked past with a steaming pan of thin-crust pizza. Although he had been hungry only ten minutes ago, he no longer had an appetite. His nerves were taut, and food was a distraction.

What had Isaiah done to his sister?

She made it sound as though he had hypnotized her, taken control of her with some kind of mind-control technique. But was Isaiah capable of something like that? Where would he have learned how to do such a thing?

And did Nicole's experience with Isaiah have anything to do with his own schizophrenic-type issues as of late?

It seemed that there had to be a connection. But he wasn't ready to discuss it with her. She was already frightened enough. He had to get more information first.

"What're you thinking about?" she said.

"I'm thinking about how little we really know about Isaiah," he said. "But we've thrown open the doors and let this guy into our lives, and I know that he's going to keep stirring up trouble. Makes me wish for the good old days when it was just you, Mom, Pops, and me. One big, happy family."

"But no family is perfect," she said. "Everybody has skeletons in the closet, as we've unfortunately learned."

"It seemed perfect, though, for a while, didn't it?"

"It did." She looked at him, and her youthful face was weary, like the countenance of a much older, embittered woman. "But we were living a lie."

Chapter 35

Dana left the hospital at nine-thirty that night. She started, automatically, to drive the route that would take her to Gabriel's house—and then she caught herself and changed direction to head to her own place.

She hated being at odds with Gabriel. Their relationship had never been tested like this. It was driving her crazy with worry.

He was the only man she had ever loved. She was terrified of losing him. But if they could not work out their differences, she had no choice but to let him go.

On the way to her condo, she stopped by Krispy Kreme and bought three doughnuts. They contained enough sugar to keep her up all night, but they were comfort food, and if she couldn't comfort herself sometimes, who would?

She parked in the underground garage and took the elevator to her unit.

She stopped outside the doorway. The bag of doughnuts dropped out of her fingers.

Someone had spray-painted a message on the door, in neon orange and green:

GABE IS MINE, BITCH!
STAY AWAY FROM HIM
OR ELSE!!!

Gabriel and Nicole left Fellini's together. He walked her to her car.

"What's next for you?" he asked her. "Going home?"

"I have company coming over," she said.

"Company, huh? As your big brother, I think I need to know more about this 'company.'"

Nicole giggled. "I think not."

He hugged her.

"Be careful, sis. I'll keep you in the loop if anything develops. Do the same with me, okay?"

"Good night, Gabe."

As Gabriel walked to his car, his cell phone rang. It was Dana.

"Hey," he said. "Thanks for finally calling me back."

"Get over here to my place, Gabriel," she said. "Right now."

"What's wrong?"

"Now!"

She hung up sharply. He stared at the phone, perplexed. What was going on?

Isaiah was having a grand time at Club Touch. He never realized his old man could be so much fun.

They sat in the VIP section in a plush leather booth. They were the big ballers of the evening. The club's hottest dancers had been making the rounds at their table all night. Isaiah had stuffed so many dollar bills in G-strings that his fingers were getting sore.

During a break in the action, when he and his father were lounging and sipping Courvoisier, the waitress, a scantily clad sista with a tiny waist and perfect breasts, stopped by their table to check on them.

"We'll have another round of drinks," Isaiah said. When Pops started to dig into his wallet, Isaiah presented a credit card. "I got it, Daddy-O. This one's on me."

"Thanks, son."

"Start a tab, baby," Isaiah said to the waitress.

The Visa card he'd given to her bore Gabriel's name—as did all the accounts Isaiah had opened in the past month. He'd gotten hold of the credit card accounts that Gabe had opened, too.

He'd learned how to do identity theft in prison, gathering the tricks of the trade from a brainy white prisoner who taught him everything he knew, in exchange for protection from the thugs.

Don't let anyone tell you that you can't acquire useful skills in prison.

Chapter 36

Gabriel stared at the words that had been spray-painted on Dana's door.

Vertigo spun through him. It took all his strength to stay on his feet.

Still wearing her hospital scrubs, Dana stood beside the door, arms knotted over her bosom. Her face was as tight as a fist.

"Who did this, Gabriel?"

"I don't know." He spread his hands helplessly. "I'm as shocked as you are."

"Bullshit," she said. "Who've you been cheating on me with?"

"I haven't been cheating on you! I swear it."

"Then how do you explain this?" She banged her fist against the door.

"I *can't* explain it. Maybe someone's trying to get between us, someone jealous. . . ."

He clapped his mouth shut as the answer struck him.

Isaiah.

Taking it all away, little brother . . .

No one else had motive. He hadn't cheated on Dana, hadn't so much as flirted with another woman since he and Dana had begun dating three years ago. This situation reeked of Isaiah and his dirty tricks.

"Well?" Dana said. She was trembling like a lid on a boiling pot, clearly trying to hold herself together.

"Isaiah did it," he said.

"What?"

"He's trying to ruin my life, like I told you. This is just the kind of thing he'd do, to drive you and me apart."

"No, no, no." Shaking her head, Dana pressed her hands to her temples. Tears rolled down her cheeks. "Damn it, I can't trust you anymore!"

"But I didn't do anything wrong! I'm telling you, Isaiah did this."

"Stop it!" she screamed. "I'm sick of hearing you blame Isaiah for all this shit! It was you. You, you, you!" She mashed her finger into his chest. "You cheated on me!"

"Dana, please." Gabriel tried to put his arms around her. She slapped his hands away and stepped back.

"Just get the hell out of here." Sniffling, she wiped her eyes with the heel of her hand. "And tell that bitch you fucked if I see her around, I'm gonna kick her ass."

"Listen, this is bullshit. You've gotta believe me!"

"I'm through with this." She reached for the doorknob. "I'm not talking about it anymore."

"Dana, wait—"

She hurried inside and slammed the door in his face.

He knocked. "Please open up. Don't shut me out."

She didn't open the door.

He started to pound against the door again . . . and then dropped his hand to his side. He was wasting his time. She didn't believe him and she wasn't going to talk to him about it, no matter how much he beat on the door and pleaded.

"I'll call you tomorrow," he said, loud enough for her to hear him. "This is *not* over."

She didn't answer. Arms swinging, he stomped away to his car in the parking garage.

Isaiah was making good on his promise to destroy his life. Gabriel wanted nothing more than to choke the man until his eyeballs popped out.

He got in the Corvette, jammed the key in the ignition, and then stopped, thinking.

He dug a card out of his wallet. Isaiah had given him his cell number when he'd first met Gabriel at the office. Cursing under his breath, Gabriel punched the number into his cell.

Isaiah answered on the third ring. "Whassup, player?"

Pounding music and chatter flooded the line. Was Isaiah at a club?

"I know what you did to Dana's door," Gabriel said.

"Hang on, I can't hear you," Isaiah said. A few seconds passed and the background noise diminished. "Pops and I are chillin' here at Club Touch, celebrating the deal I closed today. Anyway, what do you want?"

"You know what you did to Dana's door, asshole! Don't play stupid."

Isaiah laughed. "Wasn't me," he said. "Must've been one of your chicken heads who decided to put your business out on the streets. Dana was pissed off, wasn't she?"

Gabriel clenched the phone so tightly the casing squeaked.

"I'll bet she was," Isaiah said. "She looks like the kind of girl who won't tolerate any shit. And why should she—when there's a brother like me waiting in the wings ready to tap that ass."

"That's it," Gabriel said. He flung the phone to the seat.

He'd reached his limit. He could take only so much of this shit.

He was going to the strip club. He was going to kill Isaiah.

He roared out of the parking garage. Made a wild, squealing turn onto the street.

The phone chirped.

It had to be Isaiah, calling back to taunt him.

"What the fuck do you want?" Gabriel shouted into the phone.

"Whoa, chief. Guess I called at a bad time."

It was Sean Miller.

"Hey," Gabriel said in a calmer voice. "Sorry. I thought you were someone else."

"I'd hate to be that 'someone else,'" Sean said. "You sounded ready to kill a brother."

Gabriel braked at a red light. He sucked in a breath, counted to ten.

Sean was right. Rage had overwhelmed him. He needed to cool off before he did something he regretted later. He would get Isaiah, but he had to be smart about it. Bursting into a strip club and attacking the man, while an appealing thought, would be foolish.

"Okay, I'm cool," Gabriel said. "Do you have something for me?"

"You near a computer? I sent you an e-mail. You need to read it."

Dana had a laptop, but there was no way she would allow him inside her place tonight.

"I have to get home first," Gabriel said. "Gimme twenty minutes."

Isaiah and Pops arrived home a few minutes after eleven o'clock. Isaiah had wanted to stay at the club longer, but Pops pleaded fatigue. Pops retired to bed immediately upon entering the house, exhausted from an evening of squeezing luscious titties and asses. The horny old dog.

Walking to his room upstairs, Isaiah thought about how

angry Gabriel had sounded on the phone. Gabriel hadn't told him what had happened between him and Dana when she discovered the vandalism on the door, and Gabriel didn't need to share it with him—his tone had told Isaiah everything. Isaiah had dealt a severe blow to their relationship.

Smiling to himself, Isaiah walked into the bedroom, unbuttoning his shirt. He sat on the bed and untied his shoes.

He yawned. Tomorrow would be another full day, what with the big birthday party coming up, and the other activities he had planned. He needed his rest

He slipped out of his shoes and then walked to the bathroom to shower.

A large humanoid shape was moving in the mirror.

Isaiah flicked on the light.

The shadowy vision—clearly a tall, manlike shape—remained in the glass for several seconds before melting away into nothingness.

This was the second time this had happened to him. He was no closer to understanding what it meant or who it was. A side effect of his new talent? He didn't know.

Mulling it over, he began to move to the shower stall—and then he saw something.

A long strand of reddish-brown hair lay on the vanity next to the rim of the sink. Hair from a woman.

It couldn't have been Marge. She had salt-and-pepper hair, not auburn.

He believed that the Reids hired housekeepers to clean the house, but it could not have been a maid either because the bathroom had not been cleaned. Tiny black hairs from when he'd shaved that morning littered the sink bowl.

He picked up the strand and examined it. Thinking. *Sensing.*

Nicole's pixie face flickered in his mind's eye.

Holding the hair between his thumb and forefinger, he

walked into the bedroom. He knelt and lifted the satiny bed skirt.

He had aligned his luggage in a particular way. The suitcases had been moved, maybe only an inch or two, but that was enough to trip his internal alarm system.

"Little sis," he whispered. "What were you doing in here?"

At home, Gabriel ran to his office. He turned on the laptop computer and tapped his fingers on the desk as the machine progressed through its maddeningly slow boot-up cycle.

I need something to bring Isaiah down, he thought. *This better be it.*

As soon as the computer was ready, he logged on to the Internet and checked his America Online account. There was an e-mail from Sean with the subject line *Isaiah Battle.*

He opened it.

Here's something I found that I thought you would find interesting, Sean wrote. *Read it and then call me, no matter what time it is.*

Gabriel scrolled lower in the message. There was an article from the *Chicago Sun Times* that had been published on April 13 of that year.

MURDER SUSPECT ESCAPES MORGUE

Isaiah Battle, 29, suspected of murder in a South Side home, reportedly left the Cook County Office of the Medical Examiner after being declared legally dead of multiple gunshot wounds.

A staff member reported seeing Battle leave the premises before the autopsy began, a spokesman said. Paramedics who discovered Battle at his family's home had been unable to resuscitate him and had pronounced him deceased at the scene.

The suspect's mother, Naomi Battle, 52, was killed in the gunfire, in addition to Gary Hughes, 26, a known gang member. Witnesses reported that numerous shots reportedly rang out in the residence. The incident is believed to be gang related.

Battle had been released in January from the Stateville Correctional Center, where he had served five years on an armed-robbery conviction. He is at large and is sought for questioning in connection with the homicides.

Chapter 37

Before taking action, Isaiah wanted to verify his suspicions, as any good big brother would do before assigning blame and dispensing punishment. He found Marge in the grand salon, watching a local gospel program on television—some slick, brother-man preacher pacing the pulpit in a ridiculous orange suit, probably haranguing the audience to send him donations so he could buy a new Cadillac. A humongous Bible, as big as the stone tablets Moses had hauled down from Mt. Sinai, rested on Marge's lap.

This woman carried the Bible around with her so much it might as well have been chained to her wrist. She reminded him, in that sense, of Mama. But Marge had been blessed with good fortune. Mama had been cursed.

"Hi, Isaiah," Marge said. "Did you and your father have a good time tonight?"

"We sure did." Earlier Pops said he'd told Marge only that they were going out for drinks, and mentioned nothing about where they would be enjoying said libations. Isaiah wondered if this Holy Roller woman knew her husband was a strip-club junkie—or if she knew and was living in denial.

He sat in the chair beside her. "What did you do this evening? Something at church?"

"How did you know?" She smiled. "I had a meeting with the women's auxiliary and then came home and had dinner with Nicole. By the way, if you're hungry there are leftovers in the refrigerator."

"Okay." So Nicole *had* visited. "What was Nicole doing tonight? Hanging out with her girlfriends?"

"She said she was going home. She doesn't run the streets like a lot of young folks do. She's always been a quiet, studious girl."

A quiet, studious girl who likes to snoop through people's shit.

Isaiah got to his feet. "I'm guilty of wanting to do a little street running. I think I'm going to head out again, see what I can get into."

"Be careful," Marge said. "Folks in Atlanta are crazy."

Not as crazy as I am.

He went into the kitchen. On the wall beside the telephone there was a plastic board on which Gabriel and Nicole's contact information was written: telephone numbers, home and work addresses, e-mail addresses.

He jotted Nicole's home address on a scrap of paper.

He also noted that an assortment of keys hung on a peg board. He read the labels above the hooks. Spare keys to the house, spares for the cars. Keys to his father's cabin in the Blue Ridge Mountains.

While he was out, he might as well get some copies of those keys made, too. It was late, but there had to be a hardware store or some such place in ATL that did that stuff around the clock. He dropped a few of the keys in his pocket and then he headed for the door.

Little sis had violated his privacy and he wanted to know why. Before he doled out punishment.

* * *

Gabriel read the newspaper article again. Then again.

His fingers on the keyboard were cold, as though dipped in ice water

He struggled to wrap his brain around the story. Isaiah had been declared dead of gunshot wounds, but he had come back to life. Miraculously. Like some modern-age Lazarus.

How?

Gabriel called Sean.

"I read it," Gabriel said. "This is definitely him. What do you make of it?"

"I was hoping you might know," Sean said. "'Cause I have no clue, chief. Does this information fit anything you already know about him?"

"No. I had no idea this had happened." He paused. "Wait, he did tell me his mother had been murdered, that she'd died in his arms. But he didn't say anything about getting shot or killing anyone."

"Must've been a gang war, something like that," Sean said. "Moms probably got caught in the crossfire. That happens all the time these days, man. Shame."

Gabriel felt an unexpected push of sympathy for Isaiah. He could not imagine how it would feel to see his own mother gunned down, to be there when her eyes slid shut for the final time. Although he did not endorse Isaiah's actions, he could understand why the guy was so furious.

"It's clear that they made a mistake when they declared him dead," Sean said. "That happens, too. Not often, but it happens. Sort of like a premature-burial deal. Someone has an accident and wakes up to find himself in a body bag, hollers his head off, and then they let him out. It's a good thing this dude got up before they started the autopsy and cut into him."

"You think it was a simple mistake, then?" Gabriel said. "You don't think he actually died and then came back?"

Sean made a scoffing sound in his throat. "Of course not. Do you?"

Maybe. Because I think the same thing happened to me.

But he said, "Nah, man. So, what else did you find?"

"That mistaken-death story was the most fascinating thing. Otherwise, like you said, he's got a record as long as Yao Ming's wingspan. Armed robberies, grand-theft auto, burglary—if it involves taking something that doesn't belong to him, he's done it. He's bounced in and out of jail since he was eighteen, and, judging from the pattern of criminal activity, I'm positive he was knee-deep in crime during his juvenile years, too, but those records are sealed by the courts."

"He's been a thug from the start, then," Gabriel said. "Anything else?"

"Minor stuff. Bad credit history. He took out a few credit cards back in the day, ran up the balances, and never paid them. Crashed a couple of cars, has a bunch of unpaid parking tickets for which a warrant had been issued for his arrest in Chicago. That might be part of why he's in ATL. He *is* here, right?"

"Yeah." Gabriel sighed.

"Like the article said, he's wanted for questioning in the murder investigation. Do you know where this dude is, chief? I don't want to tell you how to handle your business, but I think you need to call the cops. This guy is major trouble."

"It's not that simple, Sean," he said. "Listen, I gotta go. Thanks for digging up all this. The check's in the mail."

"Whatever you're doing, be careful. Peace, out."

He got up and paced through the house. Thinking about what he'd learned.

He had initially contacted Sean because he wanted his friend to dig up dirt on Isaiah he could present to his family as a justification for them to cut Isaiah out of their lives. What had he discovered that could cast Isaiah in a bad light? The guy had a bunch of unpaid parking tickets, and a warrant for his arrest had been issued. And he was a suspect in an ongoing murder investigation.

It was irrefutable evidence. Information that, if he shared it with Mom and Pops, would persuade them to doubt the wisdom of allowing Isaiah to hang around. They were, after all, harboring a suspected murderer.

But Gabriel was not convinced that running to his parents with this info was a good idea.

He was thinking about Isaiah being declared dead and reportedly rising from a slab in the morgue. He was thinking about what Nicole had said.

He could have told me to jump out a window and I would have done it.

If Nicole's dream or vision had actually happened to her—and Gabriel had a hunch that it had—then Isaiah was far more than a thug on the run from the law.

Isaiah might possess some kind of power.

A few days ago Gabriel would have dismissed such thoughts as ludicrous. Now, anything seemed possible. He believed he'd acquired his own telekinetic ability as a consequence of his car wreck and subsequent brush with death. Did it require a great leap of imagination to think that something similar might have happened to Isaiah?

Isaiah could only have mastered the art of hypnosis, could only have used his skill as a hypnotist to bend Nicole's will to his own. But that didn't feel right to Gabriel. Intuition told him that Isaiah had picked up a paranormal talent.

Assuming that Isaiah had gained a psychic ability of some kind meant Gabriel had to be careful. When Isaiah came to their house, he had to know that the family could easily delve into his background and learn about the murder investigation. He wasn't stupid; he simply didn't care. His mysterious skill might have given him so much confidence that he considered himself untouchable.

But what was the extent of Isaiah's talents? Could he move objects, like Gabriel? Perform telepathy? Mind control? Something else?

Gabriel decided that, until he learned more, going to his family would be imprudent. Dangerous, even.

His main advantage at this stage was that Isaiah was not aware of how much he had learned about him. Gabriel did not want to reveal his hand until he had stacked the deck in his favor.

Another question troubled him: Why had he and Isaiah undergone such similar experiences in the first place? Was it coincidence?

Or was something else at work?

Nicole was at her town house watching TV in her bedroom with Allen, her sometime boyfriend, when someone knocked on her front door.

"Who could that be?" Allen asked. He was a broad-shouldered, stout brother, an all-American wrestler in his undergrad days. They'd been classmates at Duke law school and had been seeing each other on and off since he had moved to Atlanta five months ago. Nicole would have preferred a monogamous relationship, but Allen, like so many other men she met, claimed that he wasn't ready for commitment and wanted to play the field (and, of course, sleep with her when it was convenient). Nicole knew she should have demanded more, or stopped seeing him altogether. But she got lonely sometimes and he was good company. And, to be honest, she liked Allen a lot—maybe loved him. She didn't dare tell him that or else he *would* stop coming around.

Allen lay sprawled on the bed stroking her legs, which she had stretched across his lap. He claimed that she had the nicest legs he'd ever seen and liked for her to wear shorts when they were home together. Personally, she thought he liked for her to prance around in shorts so he could get his hands on her bare flesh and gradually entice her out of her panties. But she didn't usually mind the coaxing and actually had been looking forward to a night rolling in the sheets when the visitor tapped on the door.

She looked at the clock on the nightstand. It was almost midnight.

"I've no idea who that could be," she said. She lowered the volume on the TV with the remote control. "I'm not expecting any visitors."

"You sure about that?" Allen asked.

"Whatever." She ignored the thinly veiled accusation. He was the only man she was seeing, and, hell, she saw him only once every couple of weeks. Who did he think she was, a loose woman?

"Maybe I should answer," Allen said. He cracked the knuckles of his strong hands. "Scare that buster off."

"Maybe you should start paying the mortgage here before you talk about answering my door."

"I was kidding, Nicole. Don't be so sensitive."

But she knew he wasn't. He had the nerve to be jealous. Men were a trip.

Another knock, more insistent.

"Nicole, it's Gabe," said a loud voice that sounded like her brother.

Why was Gabe coming over this late? It wasn't like him to visit without calling in advance. It was a pet peeve of his and he made sure he never did it to anyone else.

But things had been strange for their family lately since Isaiah had come into the picture.

"That's your big brother?" Worry came over Allen's face. He sat up and buckled his jeans. "Need me to leave?"

"I'm a grown woman. I don't need to hide my business from my brother." Nicole smiled a little. "Be right back."

She climbed off the bed. Allen swatted playfully at her backside as she walked out of the bedroom and she gave him a look of mock anger.

She went to the front door. She glanced through the peephole. Gabriel had his face turned away from the door and wore an Atlanta Braves baseball cap, but she recognized him from the spread of his shoulders, the angle of his chin.

She opened the door.

Gabriel turned to her.

Except it wasn't Gabriel. It was Isaiah.

"Hey, little sis," he said. "Mind telling me why you were looking through my shit?"

Chapter 38

Isaiah had intended only to question Nicole and then dispense appropriate punishment. But as often happened to him, matters quickly spun out of control.

After he said to her, "Mind telling me why you were looking through my shit?" she screamed, like the scaredy-cat, never-been-to-the-projects princess she was. What the hell? It was a simple question.

Isaiah slapped his hand over her mouth, stifling her scream. He forced his way inside and shut the door behind him with the heel of his shoe.

Nicole's eyes were huge and terrified behind her glasses.

"Hey, what's going on?" A stocky, dark-skinned brother moved out of a room and into the hallway. He had the muscular build of a wrestler and a neck as thick as a bull's.

This is going to get messy in a hurry, Isaiah thought. But he didn't remove his hand from Nicole's mouth.

Bull Neck hitched up his jeans around his narrow waist. "What're you doing to her, man?"

"This is family business," Isaiah said. "It's between me

and my little sis. Go back in the bedroom and finish whacking off, all right?"

"What did you say?" Bull Neck flexed his muscles.

"Look, man, go—"

Nicole stomped on Isaiah's foot. Isaiah snarled like a wounded beast, his hand falling away from her mouth. She slipped out of his arms.

"He's not my brother!" she cried. She stumbled away. "Please help me!"

This bitch was going to force him to do something he didn't want to do, something he hadn't planned to do.

As always, trouble shadowed him.

There was no time to focus and command. Not with the two of them to handle. He had to take care of this guy quickly before Nicole's screams drew the attention of her neighbors.

Bull Neck lowered himself into a wrestler's crouch. He charged at Isaiah like a rhinoceros, hard and fast.

Hadn't this guy watched the TV news? Brothers didn't scrap with their bare hands anymore. That shit had gone out of style like Jheri curls and MEMBERS ONLY jackets. These days you had to stay strapped with a gun or, at minimum, a knife. Isaiah *always* had something on him in case a rumble broke out. Tonight he wore his Buck switchblade in a pocket clip.

He stealthily snapped out the blade. As Bull Neck rushed him, Isaiah whisked the knife across the guy's neck with the deadly grace of a surgeon, severing the carotid artery. Blood spurted from the wound. The guy crumpled to the floor. Clawing at his throat, he croaked, like a creature in a horror flick. Blood flowed from his neck, spread like a halo around his head.

Nicole was on the other side of the living room, the telephone in her hands.

"Put that down." He hurled the knife at her. It flashed across the room in a lethal blur and sank into the sofa, barely missing her.

She screamed and dropped the phone.

"You forced me to do this," Isaiah said calmly. "This is all your fault, really. This brother's death is on your hands, you stupid, snooping bitch."

Nicole tried to run into the hallway.

Isaiah caught her by her arm. He lifted her in the air—she felt as light as a Barbie doll—and slammed her onto the sofa. Her glasses bounced off her face and clattered to the carpet.

He stepped forward, crushing her glasses beneath his heel. He planted his knee on her fragile chest, pinning her to the sofa cushions. She struggled to breathe, tried to squirm from underneath him, but he had her nailed in place like an insect on an examining board.

He yanked the knife out of the couch, and brought the blood-stained switchblade close to her face. He swept it back and forth slowly, like a hypnotist's pendulum.

"Now let's try this again, little sis," he said. "Why were you going through my shit?"

"Please don't hurt me. Please." Tears hung in her eyes. "Please don't kill me."

"I'm not going to kill you," he said. "Why would I do that? We're family, right? Just tell me what I want to know. Why were you in my room?"

"Had a . . . a bad feeling 'bout you." Snot congealed in her nostrils. "You'd done something to me . . . something sick. . . ."

How did she remember what he'd done to her in the bedroom? He'd given her the command that she would not remember the incident.

That disturbed him, but he said, "So why did you snoop around?"

"Wanted to find proof . . . that you were bad."

"Oh?" He laughed. "Shit, you could've asked Gabe that. He would've told you I'm a bad motherfucker."

"W—why?"

"Why? Why what?"

"Why'd you . . . do that to me?"

He shrugged. "Seemed like a good idea at the time. And you do have a hot bod." He nodded toward the dead man on the floor. "Can't say I blame the Junkyard Dog there for wanting to tap that ass."

She began to weep again, perhaps thinking about her boyfriend.

He rapped the knife against her nose. "One more thing. Have you told anyone else what happened?"

She stared at the blade, not answering.

He inserted the tip of the knife in one of her nostrils. She started to squeal.

"Don't make me slice up this pretty little nose of yours. Tell me the truth."

"G—Gabe," she said. "I told Gabe."

That made sense. Gabriel had made it abundantly clear to the family that he despised Isaiah. It only followed that Nicole would share her misgivings with him.

But it meant nothing. Gabriel already knew Isaiah's agenda and he couldn't do anything about it. Gabriel had no idea what Isaiah was capable of doing, the power he held.

"You did good, girl." Isaiah folded away the switchblade. He pushed off the couch.

"You're . . . you're letting me go?"

"In a way, yes, I am. I'm going to set you free."

Hope surfaced on her face.

"But I have to teach you a lesson first," he said. "You invaded my privacy, little sis. It's only fair that I invade yours."

A vein began to throb in his forehead.

Focus . . . command . . .

Twenty minutes later, Isaiah was driving through the night-darkened city.

Nicole rode beside him. She gazed out the window with a vacant expression. She hadn't spoken since they had left her town house, though her lips were slightly parted. Nothing had come from her mouth but a thread of drool that streamed down her chin like cheap taffy.

Isaiah had made good on his promise to invade her privacy—the privacy of her mind. He'd stormed into her consciousness like a hurricane, dismantling logic, reason, memory . . . sanity. He'd left her as addled as an Alzheimer's patient.

It was a particularly fitting punishment for a girl who liked to think she was so smart.

He was driving toward the hood, the cut, the trap, a crime-and-drug-infested area of Atlanta. A buppie princess like her needed to witness firsthand how the other half lived, for at least once in her privileged life.

He had never planned on doing anything like this to her. It had been his intention to tear apart Gabriel's life and then his father's. But Nicole, like women tended to do, had to stick her nose in his business. For that she had to pay the consequences.

Isaiah arrived on Bankhead Highway, now called Hollowell Parkway—though a mere name change could not transform the notorious urban jungle that countless ATL rappers waxed poetic about in their lyrics. Isaiah had never driven through the area, had only heard about it and identified it on a map. But ghettos were the same all over the country. It was a Friday night, past midnight, and the thugs and prostitutes and crack heads were out in full force. They watched Isaiah cruising by, their eyes cold, hungry, suspicious, angry.

"I bet you've never so much as driven through this part of town," Isaiah said to Nicole. "Even though you've lived in ATL all your life. Have you?"

Of course she didn't answer. Didn't even look at him. Lights washed over her face and she didn't blink, as though her vision were attuned to some blasted inner mind-scape.

Isaiah pulled to a stop across the street from an apartment complex that looked as though it should be condemned. People swarmed around the crumbling buildings like giant roaches.

Isaiah got out of the car and walked around to the passenger side. He opened the door and took Nicole by the arm. Gooseflesh pimpled her skin. On some level she was frightened.

He pulled her out of the car; she moved stiffly as though stricken with arthritis. He cupped her clammy cheeks between his hands and tilted her head upward so he could look into her eyes.

Her eyes were directed at his face, but she saw right through him.

If she were lucky—truly lucky—some compassionate soul would discover her and take her to a hospital, and they would attempt to identify her. However, Isaiah had taken care to strip her of all identification. If she ever made it back to her family, she would have to be one blessed girl.

He kissed her on the forehead like any loving big brother would do when saying good-bye.

"Bye, little sis. Enjoy getting acquainted with your people."

He climbed back in the car and drove away. He glanced in the rearview mirror and saw her standing on the curb, shivering alone.

But not for long, he thought as he cruised past the fierce hordes of young men. *Not for long*.

Chapter 39

Around half-past midnight Gabriel attempted to call Nicole to share some of the information he'd picked up from Sean (minus his admittedly far-fetched theories about psychic powers). Nicole was a night owl and didn't mind late calls. But she didn't answer her phone.

He figured she must be occupied with her "company." He left her a message asking her to call him back.

He was eager to discuss what he'd learned with someone, wanted to toss ideas back and forth with a trusted confidant. Normally Dana would have been that person. But he was the last man she wanted to talk to right now.

Yawning, he settled on the sofa in the family room.

What should he do next?

Eventually he would have to confront Isaiah. A show-down was inevitable. But he didn't think he was ready for that yet—not until he had a better idea of what Isaiah could do. He needed to learn more about him.

As Gabriel ruminated on his next step, the prickly feeling returned. He used his telekinesis to stir the contents of a glass bowl of potpourri that sat on the coffee table. Then, once he tired of that, he floated the remote control toward him and channel surfed. Finding nothing of interest on television, he used his power to juggle the remote control, spinning it end over end like a bottle.

Sometime later, bored, he drifted to sleep on the sofa.

He fell into a dream. . . .

"Payback's a bitch, ain't it, motherfucka?" a rough voice said.

He tried to raise his hand and fire a gun and discovered that he couldn't move his arm. He no longer had a pistol, anyway. He'd dropped it somewhere.

But the dreadlocked black man standing over him still had a gun of his own.

The man aimed the weapon at his chest and squeezed the trigger.

Gunfire echoing in his ears, he spiraled into darkness, deep and complete.

No matter what. . . .

Although darkness enveloped him, he wasn't dead. He was fully conscious.

What the hell is this? Is this what dying is like?

Somewhere ahead a pinpoint of pulsing white light appeared. It expanded into a beacon and steadily grew even larger, forming into a wide doorway. The brightness revealed the surrounding blackness to be the walls of a smooth tunnel.

An invisible force began to carry him toward the radiance like an otherwordly express train.

I'm not ready to die. I want revenge.

As he traveled closer to the light, he could make out, in the illuminated doorway, a tall humanoid figure, ablaze like lightning.

So an angel is waiting to greet me on the Other Side? Do I deserve this?

The doorway grew so incandescent, it was like viewing the sun at high noon. He wanted to close his eyes but he couldn't look away.

The glowing being stepped forward—and pushed him. He tumbled backward in the darkness like detritus floating through deep space.

Maybe they realized they made a mistake and are sending me to hell.

He heard noises. The squeak of shoes on tile. Muffled voices. The clatter of something that sounded like silverware on a plate.

The darkness faded. Harsh fluorescent light punished his eyes. He blinked.

He lay on his back. He was in a dreary, gray-walled room, a lab of some kind. Sharp chemical odors pierced his nostrils.

He turned his head, which demanded effort, for it felt as though his skull were cast in concrete. On his right he saw several gleaming silver tables, each large enough to hold a human body.

On his left there was a bank of what appeared to be mini refrigerators set in a wall. Beside the coolers there was a set of double doors, like you would find in a hospital ER.

But this wasn't a hospital, he realized.

He was in a morgue.

I'm not dead! What the fuck am I doing in here?

He remembered what had brought him there, however. The gunfight back at the crib. Seeing Mama die. Taking bullets from those motherfuckers.

His vow of vengeance.

No matter what, I'm going to get you for this. . . .

Fury electrified him like a cattle prod touched to his flesh.

He tried to sit up—it felt as though heavy iron plates lay on his chest. By the time he was sitting upright, sweat had popped out on his skin.

A thin sheet covered him. Underneath, he was nude.

Most of his body was numb. He'd been to the dentist once, to get a cavity filled and had gotten a shot of novocaine to deaden his tooth to the pain. His entire body felt as though it had been injected with that shit.

He grasped the edge of the sheet and tore it aside. He swung his legs to the side of the table, groaning from the exertion.

His legs were so weak that when he slid off the table, he almost crashed onto the floor. He leaned against the edge of the table to keep his balance.

There was a large desk, on the far side of the room. No one sat behind the desk but there was a wrapped sandwich and a bag of Jays potato chips sitting on the surface, evidence that someone would be returning soon.

His stomach craved food. He walked-staggered to the desk and grabbed the sandwich. He took a huge, sloppy bite.

It was only a turkey and cheese sandwich on wheat, but it was the best thing he'd ever tasted in his life.

He stuffed it into his mouth, chewing savagely, making soft, animal-like sounds of pleasure. As he consumed the food, strength and sensation returned to his muscles and nerves.

He recalled taking a shotgun slug in the shoulder and a bullet in the chest, but he didn't feel any pain in those regions of his body. Puzzled, he checked the entry points of the gunshot wounds. A snarl of fresh scar tissue covered his shoulder, and there was a puckered slash on his chest, thanks to the nine millimeter. These wounds should have killed him.

But he was alive.

It was a miracle.

He had finished the sandwich and was reaching for the potato chips when someone entered the room via the double doors. A tall, broad-shouldered white man with dark hair and glasses. He was dressed in scrubs and was bringing a can of Coke to his lips.

"What the—" the man said, eyes stunned behind his lenses. He dropped the soda on the floor.

He had to stop this guy before he got away, told everyone what had happened. After the shit that had gone down at the crib, the cops would wanna haul his ass back to the joint, and he wasn't having that.

He did the most natural thing. He shouted at the white guy, "Stop!"

As he spoke the command, electrical current seemed to sizzle up the channel of his spine and explode in his brain like a thunderclap. He blinked, feeling drunk on . . . something. Power?

The man had stopped. In midstep. He looked a figure in a wax museum.

He felt a peculiar throbbing in the center of his forehead. He touched it. It was a vein.

The white man was still frozen. Chest rising and falling. Eyes twitching. But still suspended in place.

Understanding flooded him.

He had told this man to stop, and the man had obeyed.

Somehow, surviving death, coming back from the Other Side, had gifted him with some sort of power. It made sense. That was how it happened in the movies, after all.

He grinned at this amazing discovery.

Then, finding a metal stapler on the desk, he stalked across the room and smashed the guy in the head with it, knocking him unconscious. He stripped him of his clothes and dressed in them himself.

He probably looked like a felon in scrubs, not a doctor or whatever this guy had been, but the disguise should be good enough to get him out of there and back on the street.

Once he hit the streets again, it would be time for revenge.

First, the niggas who had attacked him and his mother. Next, his father. . . .

Gabriel burst out of the dream. Chest heaving, he looked around.

He lay sprawled on the couch in the family room. The television was on, playing some Stephen King movie.

He sighed, lay his head against the cushions.

The dream had been like a film in its own right. It had been so realistic, yet so strange. He'd been in Isaiah's viewpoint, experiencing Isaiah's twisted thoughts, too.

Had his dream merely been influenced by the article he'd read of Isaiah's return from death? Stuff like that had happened to Gabriel before. Many times, he'd watched a particularly vivid film and later dreamed of some element of the movie.

Or was there another answer?

Had he dreamed of what had actually happened to Isaiah?

Much later that night, after Isaiah returned from his errands, he slept.

He dreamed, too.

He dreamed of driving a Lincoln Navigator on a highway in a blinding rain and getting smacked by an tractor-trailer. He crashed through a guardrail, tumbled down an embankment, slipped into darkness, and hurtled toward a radiant doorway . . . only to be turned away before he merged into the ethereal light.

The dream then dissolved into him standing in front of a bathroom door. He reached toward the door. But the knob twisted and the door floated open, independent of his touch.

And his palms began to tingle. . . .

Isaiah awoke from the dream shortly thereafter. He lay in the darkness, gazing at the ceiling.

He was quite sure that he had dreamed of something that had happened to Gabriel. He knew all about the accident.

But that wasn't what perplexed Isaiah. Something else did.

The door that had opened on its own.

Did Gabriel have some sort of power, too?

Chapter 40

Early the next morning, after a night during which he'd managed maybe two hours of restful sleep, Gabriel went to Lowe's to purchase paint and brushes. When he attempted to pay for the items with a credit card, the clerk, a young black woman, handed the card back to him.

"It's been denied," she said, and gave him a *you knew better than that* look.

"Denied? That's not possible. Try it again, please."

She swiped the card again. Waited, and then shook her head and handed the card back to him.

"Okay." He handed her another card. "Try this one."

She tried that one. With the same result.

What was this? There was nothing wrong with these credit cards.

"Wanna go for strike three with another one?" she asked.

This was exactly what he needed. A comedienne.

"Let's try my debit card. This one has to work 'cause I know I have funds in my bank account." He handed the card to her.

She accepted it dubiously. Swiped it. Then turned to him as if he were the most trifling man walking the earth.

"Strike three," she said.

"This can't be." He had at least a few hundred dollars in that checking account, and more in savings. "Are you sure something isn't wrong with your system?"

"It's been working fine all morning."

Gabriel flipped through his wallet. He had only a five-dollar bill and no more credit cards.

"I'm going to run out to my car for a minute," he said. "I'll be right back."

In the Corvette's glove compartment he'd stored an emergency stash of fifty dollars in cash; he'd learned to do that because sometimes computer systems could be offline when you needed to purchase something. He peeled off a twenty and returned inside the store to pay for the items.

"Handle your bidness, honey," the clerk said, bagging his purchases.

Gabriel hardly heard her. He couldn't figure out what was wrong. He'd never had a problem with his credit cards—he paid them in full each month and the account balances were well below the limits—and he knew for a fact that he had money in his bank accounts. He'd checked his statement online only a few days ago.

It was yet another problem to investigate. As if he didn't already have enough issues.

When it rained, it poured.

Gabriel drove directly to Dana's condo. He hadn't called her beforehand to announce that he was visiting. She wouldn't want to see him. But he needed to see her.

On Saturday mornings Dana usually went to an LA Fitness in Midtown to work out. He wanted to be at her home when she returned.

He approached her front door. Isaiah's spray-painted message looked even more vulgar and offensive in the daylight. Residue from the almost-murderous rage Gabriel had experienced last night stirred in him.

I'm gonna get you for this, Isaiah.

Muttering under his breath, Gabriel cleaned dust and grime off the door with a towel and then opened a can of burgundy-red paint, the same color as the door.

He was applying paint to the wood in steady strokes when Dana appeared in the corridor. She wore an Emory T-shirt and athletic shorts and her hair was pulled back in a ponytail.

Displeasure twisted her face.

"What're you doing here?"

"I'm repainting the door."

"Painting the door isn't going to change what you did. I want you to leave."

"Listen." Gabriel dipped the brush in the can. "Isaiah did this, Dana. He admitted it to me when I talked to him last night. He's trying to drive us apart—and I'm not going to let that happen."

"I don't want to get into this right now." She came forward. "Get away from my door. I'll repaint it later by my damn self."

Gabriel moved aside. He inhaled a deep breath and concentrated on summoning his energy, as he'd been practicing.

His telekinesis awakened, power sparking across his palms.

"You sure you don't want me to help?" he asked. And when Dana turned to spit another nasty remark at him, he caused the paintbrush to sail through the air, rest against the door, and slide downward in a smooth stroke.

Dana's mouth dropped open.

"Yeah, I did that," he said. "We need to talk, baby. I've got a lot to tell you."

Chapter 41

Gabriel asked Dana to sit at the dinette table. Then he told her everything.

He explained the onset of his psychic ability, including his theory for how he'd acquired the talent after his concussion; he told her what he'd learned about Isaiah from Sean's background investigation; he related Nicole's chilling experience with Isaiah; and, lastly, he described the hyperrealistic dream he'd had last night and his ideas of the paranormal talent Isaiah possessed.

Dana listened silently without interruption. As he talked, she got up, brewed coffee, poured herself a mug, and gave one to him, too. Gabriel interpreted the gesture as a small sign that she was coming around to his side again.

"That's everything," he said. "I know it's crazy, Dana, and I wouldn't believe it myself if it weren't happening to me. But, as you can see . . ." He floated a container of coffee creamer through the air and placed it on the other side of the table. Dana gaped, amazed. "This is as real as it gets."

Dana pursed her lips. She stared at a spot on the table, a

look that came over her when she was immersed in deep thought.

He waited a moment. "What do you think?"

She looked at him. "I believe you."

"You do?"

"My med-school professors would kill me if I admitted this, but I do think that some people are gifted with ESP, psychic powers, what have you." She sipped her coffee, a faraway gaze coming into her eyes. "When I was a little girl I remember people saying that my great aunt was born with a veil, which supposedly gave her second sight. I don't recall seeing her do anything to demonstrate her ability, but I remember that folks from the neighborhood would come to her house to get her advice on their marriages, relationships, children, finances, whatever. Auntie Bell was like the neighborhood treasure."

"You never told me about her."

"She passed a long time ago when I was nine. Since I've been in the medical field I've tried to adopt a more logical, scientific approach to things—and probably been a little bullheaded about it sometimes." She smiled, embarrassed. "But I've seen what you can do with my own eyes."

"How about the stuff I've told you about Isaiah? Do you believe that, too?"

"I do," she said. "You wouldn't make up anything like that. You have no reason to lie, and neither does Nicole."

Finally Dana was on his side.

She reached across the table and grasped his hand.

"Baby, I owe you an apology," she said. "I'm sorry for not trusting you. You deserved better than that from me. I never should have doubted you."

He put his other hand on top of hers and held it tight.

"I wasn't acting like the most rational man in the world," he said. "I can't blame you for everything."

"But I never gave you much of a chance. When I heard

about Isaiah, how he never knew this side of his family, my heart went out to him. I know how it feels to be abandoned, Gabe. I let my sympathy for him get in the way of me supporting you."

Gabriel kept quiet, letting her get her words out.

"I should've stood by you," she said. "God, the terrible things I said to you. . . ." She bit her lip, shaking her head. "Can you please forgive me?"

"Forgiven." He kissed her hand. "Let's put this behind us. I need you, girl."

"You've got me. I won't ever doubt you again."

Smiling at him, she brought the carafe to the table, and refreshed their coffee.

"Have you eaten breakfast yet, babe?" she asked, rubbing his shoulder.

"Nope."

"How do mushroom and cheese omelettes sound?"

"Sounds delicious to me. I'm starved."

"I need to get some food in me before I can do the heavy-duty thinking we need to do," she said. "I have a lot of questions."

"While you cook," he said, "I want to use your computer. I have some other questions, too—about my bank accounts."

Dana had set up the spare bedroom as a guest room and home office. She kept a late-model Dell laptop on the desk.

Sipping coffee, Gabriel logged onto his bank's Web site. He entered his username and password to access his account.

His checking account, which had boasted a balance of several hundred dollars earlier in the week, had a zero balance. His savings account, in which he had kept around a thousand dollars, had also been drained.

Full withdrawals had been posted on both accounts. Wire

transfer transactions, processed yesterday, had sent his money to an unidentified receiver.

Taking it all away, little brother.

Gabriel had no proof that Isaiah was responsible; he didn't need any evidence. He *knew*.

Gabriel accessed his other investment accounts, which he maintained with various financial-services companies. Diversification of his assets had paid off. He had close to thirty thousand dollars spread around, and all those funds were intact.

Then he went to the Web site of Experian, one of the three primary credit bureaus. He went to order the online credit report.

"Dana?" he called. "Can you come in here for a sec?"

She came inside a minute later, wiping her hands on a towel. "What's up?"

"I need to buy an online credit report but I can't use my credit card to pay for it. Can I use yours? I'll explain in a moment."

"Okay." She left the room and came back with her bank debit card. She stood behind his chair as he entered the payment information and hit SUBMIT.

He drummed the desk, waiting for the report to appear. "I hope this isn't as bad as I think it is."

The report finally appeared. Gabriel scrolled down the page.

His stomach plummeted.

"Oh, my goodness," Dana said. "Is that right? It can't be, can it?"

Gabriel put his hands to his face. He didn't want to look at the screen any longer.

New credit accounts had been opened in his name in the past month. Accounts for clothing stores, a classic-cars dealer, a car-stereo company, electronics stores, and Master-Card and Visa cards. Eleven accounts, in total. His existing credit cards had been maxed out, too.

The balance of the accounts was approximately one hundred and forty thousand dollars.

"Isaiah did this, didn't he?" Dana said. "He stole your identity and ran up all these bills."

Gabriel massaged the bridge of his nose. He laughed—a bitter sound. It was the only alternative to crying like a baby.

"Isaiah," he said softly. "You sneaky motherfucker."

"I'm so sorry, Gabe," she said. "This is terrible."

Gabriel only stared at the screen. Numb. Disbelieving.

Dana took his arm. "Let's go eat. We'll talk about what we're going to do next."

She led him out of the bedroom. His legs wobbled. Isaiah had been pummeling him like a heavyweight champ. Gabriel was still standing. But barely.

"Voilá," Dana said, placing plates on the table. "Breakfast is served."

The omelette looked delicious. But Gabriel only picked at the edge of it with his fork.

Dana, lifting a slice of omelette to her lips, put her fork down against the plate. "Baby, you've gotta eat."

"I'm not hungry anymore," he said.

"I know you're upset—"

"Upset? We've just found out that Isaiah has completely fucked up my credit and will force me to declare bankruptcy. 'Upset' isn't the right word. There isn't a word to describe how I'm feeling right now. How about up-fucking-set-pissed-off-as-hell furious?"

Dana waited for him to finish.

"This ruins our plans," he said. "You think we'll be able to buy anything as a married couple with a bankruptcy on my record? Not for a helluva long time."

"You won't have to declare bankruptcy. You can report it as an identity theft. They'll take those charges off your report."

"Maybe," he said. "That's what I'll try to do, but that process will be a nightmare and could drag on forever, and my credit will be in the toilet in the meantime."

"I'll help you. I'll make calls, help you with paperwork, whatever it takes. You can't let this get you down."

"He's pushing me to the edge." Gabriel made a tiny measurement with his thumb and index finger. "I'm this close to getting a gun, going to my parents' house, and blowing that motherfucker away."

"He'd want you to try something like that," she said. "You'd go to prison—just like he did. You'd be locked away for years. He wants that, Gabe. You'd be playing right into his hands. Don't you see?"

"Fuck it." High on angry adrenaline, Gabriel got up from the table. Blood pounded in his temples and sweat oozed from his pores. He'd never tasted fury like this.

Visions of Isaiah's smirking face swirled in his mind.

Taking it all away . . .

Gabriel found himself at the door without realizing he'd walked to it. He was reaching for the knob when Dana took his hand.

"Don't go," she said. "Cool down. Stay here with me."

"I've had enough of letting this guy get away with this shit."

He pulled his hand away from her and groped for the doorknob. Dana slipped around him and blocked the door.

"Dana, get outta the way. I mean it."

She crossed her arms over her chest. She didn't budge.

"I'm not letting you leave and do something you'll come to regret," she said. "This isn't just about you. This is about us, our future. I don't want my husband in jail—or dead."

Gabriel dropped his hands to his sides. He unclenched his fists and wiped his sweaty palms on his jeans.

"You're right," he said. "Isaiah's trying to play me. I can't give in."

"*We* can't give in," she said. She came forward, pulled him into her arms, and hugged him close.

"Thank you," he said.

"When I said I'd have your back from now on, I meant it," she said. "Let's go eat and figure this stuff out, okay?"

Chapter 42

Back at the table, Gabriel shoveled a piece of omelette into his mouth, chewed eagerly. With his mood change, his appetite had returned.

Dana had taken out a pen and notepad and placed it beside her plate.

"We have a lot of ground to cover," she said. "First things first: why, exactly, did your accident trigger these psychic powers?"

"I did some research on that. I think that when I wrecked, I had a near-death experience. I remember it quite clearly. A tunnel, a bright white light, just like in the movies, you know. But it seemed real."

"So you got a look at the Other Side, and when you were sent back, you were given psychic powers?"

"Seems like it. As crazy as it sounds."

Dana scribbled on the notepad and then looked at him. "But why? Everyone who survives a near-fatal accident isn't able to bend spoons. Why you?"

"I don't know. But remember that a similar thing apparently happened to Isaiah, according to my dream. When he woke up in the morgue, he made that guy freeze in place like he was some kind of puppet. Then he went out and killed some other guys, I think."

"That's so scary." Dana made quick notes. She tapped the pen against her bottom lip. "And it's weird that you would have a dream from his perspective, with his thoughts, too. I'm wondering . . ."

"Wondering what?"

"I'm wondering if Isaiah's had a dream from your viewpoint, too."

"I never thought about that." Gabriel put down his fork. "Where'd you get that idea from?"

"Have you ever heard of connectedness?"

"Never. What is it?"

She twirled the pen between her fingers. "I know about it only because I was working with twin girl patients, once. They both had lupus. They had the exact same symptoms, would experience pain in the same limbs, often even at the same time. I was fascinated and did some research and discovered this theory of connectedness. Some people—usually twins, but they can be siblings close in age, or a parent and a child—seem to have an emotional or physiological connection."

"Isaiah and I were born within a few minutes of each other," Gabriel said. "Although he was born in Chicago and I was born here. That in itself is pretty weird to me."

"It is," she said. "It's possible that, due to you guys having the same father and the same birth dates, there is some sort of connectedness phenomena going on. How likely is it that he would also have a near-death experience and then come back with psychic talent? Pretty damn unlikely—unless you and Isaiah share a link."

"Do you think he's seeing visions in mirrors, too, then?"

"It's possible."

"And having hallucinations of water moccasins?"

"Maybe he is. Unless he tells us, we won't know."

"I don't want to tell him a damn thing about what's happening to me." Gabriel said. "The less he knows about me, the better."

"I agree. We shouldn't show our hand." Dana jotted down a few other comments. She rested her chin on her palm, rapping the pen against her lip.

Gabriel cupped his hands around the coffee mug. "What're you thinking, Dana?"

"Thinking about what Isaiah can do. We're saying he's got some kind of mind-control ability, right?"

"Right. I saw him doing it in my dream and then he did stuff to Nicole."

Dana nodded. "What if Isaiah is causing *your* hallucinations?"

"You think he's behind the figure in the mirror and the snakes?"

"I'm not sure about the shape in the mirror . . . but the snake . . . well, snakes scare you to death. Does Isaiah know you're afraid of snakes?"

"I never told him," Gabriel said. He was about to sip his coffee, and then reconsidered. "Wait a minute. The first time I met him we were in my office and he made a comment about my aquarium. He told me I should keep a snake in there instead of fish, and I said something like, 'I hate snakes.'"

Dana snapped her fingers. "And that was all you had to say to him. He knew then that he could use snakes to scare you, make you doubt your sanity. He's been doing it to you from the start, Gabe. I'm willing to bet on it."

Gabriel remembered when Isaiah had distributed gifts to the family the first night he'd met them. He'd given Gabriel a wooden statue of a man entwined with a large snake.

What a sick joke.

"Jesus." Gabriel shook his head. "Those snakes . . . they look so real. How the hell could he get into my head like that?"

"Same way he got into Nicole's head. It's part of his gift."

A chill tap-danced down Gabriel's back. The possible insight into Isaiah had brought a greater, more profound fear of him.

Rushing out to confront Isaiah would have been the most dangerous thing he could possibly have done.

Dana was writing notes.

"There has to be a way to block him from screwing with my head," Gabriel said. He put his hands around his skull, protectively. "Whatever it is, I have to find it."

"I have one idea," Dana said. "Overcome your fear of snakes."

Gabriel chuckled. "That ain't happening. Hell, naw. I was bitten, remember?"

"I was in a car accident once, Gabe. That doesn't keep me from driving."

"That's different."

"Oh?" She cocked her head. "How so?"

"Snakes are deadly."

"Cars have the potential to be deadly. Look at all the fatal accidents that take place every day. You were almost killed in a wreck, babe, and yet you still drive."

"How would you act if I put a poisonous snake on the table here?" he asked.

"I'd run and scream my head off," she said. "But we aren't talking about me. This time it's solely about you and what you fear. Your fear is all up here." She touched her forehead with the pen. "As long as you're terrified of snakes, Isaiah will be able to use that against you."

She was right. He didn't want to admit that she was right, but he understood the wisdom in her advice. Fear was emotional, and, sometimes, entirely irrational.

But he could not envision himself seeing a snake—even if he knew the snake was an illusion—and not being deathly afraid. Although the fear was only in his mind, it was as palpable to him as a locked door, and just as capable of confining him.

"I'm going to have to work on this," he said.

"You do," she said. "But I have confidence in you. You'll overcome it. Honestly, you don't have any choice."

Dana was right on that score, too. He would never beat Isaiah until he conquered his fear.

"I'd like to talk to Nicole," Dana said. "At this point we need as many allies in the family as we can get. I think we should loop her in on everything we've discussed."

"I left her a message last night. She hasn't called me back."

"Why don't you call her again?"

Gabriel checked his watch. It was a quarter to ten. On weekends Nicole slept in and hated to be called before ten o'clock, but these were unusual circumstances.

He flipped out his cell phone and hit the speed dial for her home number. She didn't answer. He called her cell phone. No answer.

"She must be asleep," he said. A yawn came over him suddenly. "Speaking of sleep, I could use some. I got barely two hours last night."

"You can take a nap in the bedroom. I'm going to take a shower and do some cleaning. Saturday is housework day for me, you know."

"Wake me up in a couple hours. I don't want to sleep all day—I might miss something."

In Dana's bedroom, Gabriel removed his shirt and jeans and lay on his back on the queen-size bed. He closed his eyes for a minute, listening to Dana shower, and then he opened his eyes and contemplated the shadowed ceiling.

Fatigue lay like sand bags on his body but his mind was wide awake, turning restlessly through his conversation with Dana. He thought about Dana's theory that he and Isaiah shared a psychic link. Connectedness.

On the surface he and Isaiah could not have been more different people. It disturbed him to consider that he was in-timately connected to a violent criminal.

Because it begged the question: if he had grown up in Isaiah's rough neighborhood, would he have turned out just like him?

It was the controversial nature-versus-nurture debate. Was a human being a product of his genetic heritage or his environment? Or a measure of both?

You have this life only because Pops gave it to you, little brother.

Although Isaiah had never spoken those words to Gabriel, it was something he would say. And Gabriel couldn't help wondering if, maybe, Isaiah was right.

It was too troubling to reflect on further.

He directed his thoughts instead to the idea of Isaiah being responsible for his snake hallucinations. It seemed obvious now, but he hadn't wanted to think about it. Admitting that he was so vulnerable to an outside influence was humbling. He liked to believe he was stronger than that.

He could have told me to jump out the window and I would have done it.

What chance did they have against someone with Isaiah's ability? Could Isaiah really force someone to do anything he commanded? Or were there limitations to his talent?

As he lay there, dwelling on these questions, Dana strolled into the bedroom with a bath towel wrapped around her waist.

"You're still awake," she said. "Hmm. I was hoping you would be."

"Why?"

She climbed on the bed, lips curved in a lascivious smile.

"We haven't finished making up," she said.

"Oh." In spite of his exhaustion, desire made his body warm and eager. "That's the best part about making up, isn't it?"

Positioning herself on top of him, she lowered her head so they were face-to-face, their noses less than an inch away, her eyes so close he thought he could see his face reflected in them.

"I'll always be here for you, Gabe," she said in a whisper. "I'm sorry I left you out in the cold."

"I've already forgiven you."

"I know, but I want to tell you again. Because, well . . . I love you."

Gabriel's breath snagged in his throat. He knew she loved him, knew that as certainly as he knew his own name, but this was the first time she'd ever said it.

Watching him closely, she smiled. "That wasn't so hard. I could get used to saying that to you."

"I love you, too," he said.

She kissed him.

Gabriel traced his hand down her smooth, firm back, gripped the edge of the bath towel, tugged it free.

Dana kissed his chin and began to weave a line of soft, lingering kisses down his chest and stomach, the sensation of her moist lips sending ripples of pleasure dancing across his flesh.

Gabriel's cell phone rang.

"Not now," Gabriel said. He groaned.

"It might be Nicole calling you back," Dana said. She moved from on top of him. "Better answer it, babe."

He grabbed the phone.

It was Mom.

"Something's happened to your sister," Mom said in a reed-thin voice. "She's in the hospital."

"Nicole's in the hospital? What happened? Is she okay—"

"She's at Grady." Mom's fragile voice almost broke. "Can you come now?"

The romantic mood had passed instantly. Brow heavy with worry, Dana was already sliding off the bed and getting her clothes.

"We're on our way," Gabriel said.

Chapter 43

Gabriel loathed hospitals. To him they were palaces of pain, misery, and suffering. He could not remember a single positive experience he'd ever had at a hospital.

Now he found himself at Grady again, only a few days after he'd been a patient there himself. As he and Dana hurried down the corridor to Nicole's room, he touched the fading bruise on his head, remembering the car accident that was intertwined with so many other improbable things. Psychic powers. Visions in mirrors. Illusory reptiles. A bizarre bond with Isaiah. A veritable treasure box of mysteries.

He'd come there to visit his sister, but at this point, when every turn of events led to surprising revelations, he wondered if something else unexpected would happen.

Nicole was in a private room. Mom was already there, wearing a classy ivory dress Gabriel recognized as one of her church outfits. Mom participated in several ministries at their family church and had probably come to the hospital straight from the house of worship.

"Thank the Lord both of you made it," Mom said. She rose from a chair beside the bed, her eyes rimmed with red.

She hugged Gabriel and Dana. "Your father and Isaiah are on the way. They were playing golf this morning."

"That figures," Gabriel said.

Mom gave him a sympathetic look. Then all of them turned to Nicole.

Nicole was asleep, but she looked terrible. Her hair was disheveled. Her lips were chapped. Dark circles outlined her eyes.

"What happened to her?" Dana said.

"No one can give me a definite answer," Mom said. "She was found early this morning, wandering on Bankhead—or Hollowell Parkway, whatever they're calling it now."

"What was she doing on Bankhead?" Gabriel asked. He looked closer at his sister, searching her body for signs of injury.

"We don't know," Mom said. "But Eunice Johnson, from church—she's the lady who used to baby-sit you and Nic sometimes—she was on her way to her job and saw Nic sitting on a bench on the side of the road. Nic couldn't talk, or wouldn't talk, and Eunice knew right away that something was wrong. Eunice said she reminded her of her late husband, who had Alzheimer's."

"Alzheimer's?" Dana asked. "There's no way Nicole could have that. She's much too young."

"Eunice got Nic in her car," Mom said, "and called me, and I asked her to bring her to the hospital. Eunice left just before you got here—she was running late for work. But she was right on time for my baby, praise God."

"Amen to that," Gabriel said, disturbed at the thought of his sister wandering, incoherent, through one of the most dangerous areas in Atlanta. "It really is a blessing. Anything could have happened to her there."

Dana scrutinized Nicole. "Has she been given a physical exam?"

Mom nodded. "No one touched her. But the doctor doesn't

know what's wrong with her. She thinks Nicole is suffering from shock. She's been asleep for the past hour."

"I'll be back," Dana said. "I'm going to chat with the physician who examined her."

Dana left the room. Gabriel gently placed his hand on Nicole's forehead. Her skin was cool and dry. Her eyelids fluttered but did not open.

It didn't make any sense. When he'd talked to Nicole the previous night, she had been fine. What had happened to her?

Isaiah.

His jaws went rigid. Isaiah had invaded Nicole's mind once before. Could he be responsible for this, too?

Gabriel turned to his mother. She had settled in the chair again and was clutching a fistful of Kleenex.

"What time did Isaiah get home last night, Mom?" Gabriel asked.

"He and your father came in around eleven," Mom said. "Why?"

"They came in together?"

"They did. Why are you asking?"

"Hold on. Did Isaiah go anywhere afterward?"

"As a matter of fact, he did," Mom said. "He said he was going out. He didn't say where."

"Did he mention Nicole at all?"

Mom closed her eyes, remembering. "I told him Nicole had been over for dinner. I think he asked me what she was doing later that evening. She told me she was planning to go home. That's all I said to him."

Son of a bitch.

Isaiah had done this to Nicole. Somehow. He must have found out that Nicole had been snooping through his belongings. This was his way of punishing her.

Gabriel's fury must have been evident on his face because Mom asked, "Do you think Isaiah had something to do with this?"

Looking at his mother, stricken with worry, Gabriel no longer cared about concealing the truth.

"Yeah, I do," he said. "I can't explain how he did this to Nicole. But I know he did."

Mom tossed a handful of tissue onto the bedside table. She walked to the window.

"Shut the door, Gabriel."

Gabriel closed the door and moved to stand beside his mother. She looked out the large window at the sun-drenched city beyond, but the clouded look in her eyes made Gabriel suspect that she was seeing something else.

"I would never say this in front of your father," she said, "and please keep this between you and me. But I don't approve of how he's been handling this situation with Isaiah. He's been unfair to all of us, and especially to you."

Gabriel could not believe he was hearing this from her. She almost never took a stance against his father. And when she did, she certainly did not share her disagreement with her children.

"Yeah, I would say so," he said. "Pops has crammed Isaiah down our throats."

"I've had an uneasy feeling about Isaiah from the start," Mom said.

"You, too?"

"Yes. For many reasons. But, like you, I worried that Isaiah's intentions were less than sincere. I shared your 'gut feeling,' as you called it."

"Why didn't you say anything, Mom?"

She shifted to face him and her gaze was fierce. "Because *I support my husband.* I've always supported him . . . even when it hurt me to do so. I believe in my marriage vows, which we took before God. I submitted to my husband's headship in the household, without question."

Gabriel took his mother's hand, caressed it. She squeezed his fingers tightly.

"You have no idea what I've had to endure over the

years," she said. Sniffling, she shook her head. "You can't imagine the secrets I've kept hidden from our family. You can't imagine the secrets I've kept hidden from you, most of all."

"Secrets?" His voice wavered. "What . . . what secrets?"

Mom covered her eyes but could not hide her tears.

"Mom? What is it? Please tell me."

Mom lowered her hand. Her eyes wet, she clasped both his hands in hers.

"Gabriel," she said, slowly. "You—"

Behind them, Nicole screamed.

Chapter 44

On Saturday morning, Isaiah and his father hit the golf course. They played at Cascade Hills, a posh country club of which Pops was a long term member.

Isaiah had never played golf in his life. Brothers in the hood didn't play golf. They played basketball. There weren't any putting greens in the state pen, but there were plenty of hoops.

But Pops, a firm believer in the game of golf as a forum to lubricate business deals, had decided to teach Isaiah how to play. While the morning dew still clung to the grass, Pops drove their golf cart to the edge of the rolling driving range and they unloaded their clubs. Pops, wearing a black Kangol cap twisted backward on his head like a hip jazz cat, effortlessly whacked one ball after another into the hazy sky. He then tried to teach Isaiah how to grip the club and swing.

It was a frustrating experience. After a half hour of fumbling with the club and missing the ball with embarrassing frequency, Isaiah was ready to quit. He didn't have the patience for this shit today.

The truth was, he was worried about Nicole.

He wasn't worried about her welfare; he could care less about her well-being. He worried that he shouldn't have left her in the ghetto. Her family was too connected, like the damn Kennedys. There was a chance that someone would recognize the princess and whisk her back to the palace, and, if she regained her bearings, what if she told them what he'd done? She had remembered, after all, how he'd first invaded her mind in the bedroom, even though he'd given her the command that she would forget the whole thing.

What if she recovered and told everyone she'd seen him kill a man?

He should have found a better way to punish her. He had acted impulsively, out of anger, and he couldn't get rid of the feeling that his actions were going to come back to bite him in the ass.

It wasn't his fault, though. The bitch had had no business snooping through his things. She had forced him to do what he'd done. And then her boyfriend, wanting to be a hero like Action Jackson, had tried to tackle him, and Isaiah had been compelled to kill him in self-defense. None of what had happened was his fault.

But as so often happened in his life, he had to pay for other people's mistakes. He bore the weight of other people's misdeeds on his shoulders. When all was said and done, accusatory fingers would be pointed at him.

It was so damn unfair. But hadn't Mama taught him that life was never fair for poor folk?

Isaiah's uneasiness made focusing on that stupid golf ball even more difficult. Imagining that the ball was actually a miniaturized version of his father's head didn't help either.

Pops's cell phone rang and he took the call. Grateful for a break, Isaiah propped the club against the bag. He went to the golf cart, where they had stored drinks in a cooler, and popped the tab on a Coke.

"Come again?" Pops said. "Nicole's in the hospital?"

Isaiah nearly spat out his soda.

Someone found Nicole and identified her. The lucky bitch!

Pops listened on the phone, concern drawing his lips taut. Then he said, "We'll be there ASAP," and hung up.

"We've gotta go," Pops said. "My baby girl is in the hospital."

"What happened to her?" Isaiah asked with as much ignorance as he could manage.

"We don't know yet, but she's being kept at Grady." Pops hopped behind the steering wheel of the golf cart. "Let's move, son."

Isaiah paused. How should he handle this? If he accompanied his father to the hospital, he ran the risk that Nicole would be in full possession of her faculties and would blab to everyone what had happened, if she hadn't already. He had killed a man. Although he had evaded the cops before, he was in an unfamiliar city with no friends. Hiding out would present a challenge.

On the other hand, Nicole's brain might still be as scrambled as a platter of eggs at the Waffle House. She might not recall a damn thing. He might still have time to finish his plan.

Pops snapped his fingers. "Let's go!"

I've waited my entire life for this chance. I can't punk out now. What would Mama think of me?

He knew what she would think. She would be disappointed. He couldn't tolerate the idea of going back on his word.

No matter what. . . .

Isaiah slid into the passenger seat.

"Okay, Pops. Let's go see about my little sis."

Chapter 45

Nicole's shriek abruptly ended Gabriel's conversation with his mother. Leaving her revelation unspoken, Mom hurried to Nicole's side.

Dana and the nurse on duty, a tall redheaded woman, rushed into the room, too.

Nicole thrashed in the sheets, waving her limbs like a child terrified of water who was abandoned in an ocean. Her eyes were wide and frightened. Her lips peeled back from her teeth and a bloodcurdling, wordless keen rose from deep in her chest.

Gabriel wanted to touch her, comfort her, but he was afraid. He'd never seen anything like this in his life.

Mom, Dana, and the nurse grasped Nicole's arms and held her against the mattress. Mom spoke soft, soothing words.

"Mama's here, baby. Everything's okay, you're safe, baby. Mama's here, Mama's not gonna let anything happen to you."

Nicole gradually ceased struggling. She lay against the bed, perspiration glistening on her face. Her eyes slowly swam into focus.

Gabriel wanted to ask her to say something, wanted to question her about how this had happened, but Nicole's eyes bugged out again as though her mind had turned inward to some hellish netherworld. Speaking to her while she was in this condition would be a waste of breath.

Mom stroked Nicole's forehead, cooing to her. Dana and the nurse stepped away from the bed.

"I'll go tell the doctor she's awake again," the nurse said and left the room.

Dana came to Gabriel. She smiled wanly. "At least she's conscious."

"Isaiah did this to her," he said. "He's screwed up her mind. I know it was him."

"You're probably right, but we could never prove that. Nicole would have to tell us, and I don't think she's able to talk yet."

"What's wrong with her? Give me your medical opinion."

"I talked to the doctor who examined her. She thinks Nicole's suffering from dementia, induced by a traumatic event."

"Yeah, Isaiah bum-rushing her mind." He mashed his fist into his other palm. "Next time I see him, Dana, I'm not holding back. He's gone way over the line now."

Dana nodded tightly. She didn't try to talk him out of his anger or smooth over his feelings. She knew better, and she looked pissed off herself, too.

Mom had climbed next to Nicole on the bed. She cradled Nicole in her arms, as though she were a small child. Nicole clung to her, her eyes painfully innocent. She began to suck her thumb, something she hadn't done since she was a preschooler.

Gabriel could not stand watching anymore. "I'll be back. I've got to get some fresh air."

He crossed the room. As he reached for the door, it swung open, and it wasn't because he'd used his telekinesis. They had visitors.

His father.
And Isaiah.

Nicole wandered through the strange, remote corridors of her mind.

She was in her childhood bedroom, the room decorated in various shades of pink, her favorite color. She lay on the bed underneath a fluffy comforter. But she was cold—as cold as though an arctic gale gusted through the room. She looked and saw that a window across the room was open, wind tearing at the curtains. She had to close it. She pulled aside the comforter, swung her legs to the side of the mattress, and planted her feet on the floor.

The soles of her feet pressed against something wet and sticky.

Allen, her boyfriend, lay on the floor beside her bed, gazing sightlessly at the ceiling. Blood bubbled from a gaping wound in his neck; gore covered her feet.

She shrieked. She tried to pull her feet out of the blood, but it was like trying to escape a tar pit. The blood, clotted and gluey, clung to her soles. She finally tore away and landed on her knees on the carpet.

She was hyperventilating. Cold air poured into her lungs, spreading a deep, numbing chill throughout her body.

Gasping, she stumbled to the window. Wind buffeted her face like fists. She managed to grasp the edge of the window. As she prepared to slam it shut, she looked outdoors.

Isaiah was outside. He stood on the lawn, looking up at her. A smile twisted across his face.

You invaded my privacy, little sis. It's only fair that I invade yours.

She tried to close the window, but it would not budge.

Isaiah began to float upward as though drawn into the air by invisible wires.

No running from me.

She had to get away from him. He would violate her, force her to do terrible, perverted things.

But she couldn't close the window. He would get in and she would belong to him.

She ran to the bedroom door and flung it open.

Isaiah stood in the hallway.

Gotcha.

She opened her mouth in a silent scream. . . .

Chapter 46

When Pops and Isaiah entered the room, Nicole gave a strangled yip, like a frightened puppy.

Gabriel swung around to face Nicole. Her attention was riveted on Isaiah. Fear dilated her pupils.

He was right. Isaiah *had* done this to her.

Pops brushed past Gabriel with a perfunctory greeting and went to Nicole's bedside. But Isaiah hesitated on the room's threshold. His eyes had narrowed to challenging slits.

Although the room behind them was full of people, Gabriel was so focused on Isaiah that they might have been the only men in the universe.

The tingly psychic energy enveloped Gabriel's hands.

"You did this to Nicole," Gabriel said. "I know everything."

"You don't know jack shit," Isaiah said. "Sit your ass down, boy."

Gabriel noticed a prominent vein throbbing in the center of Isaiah's forehead—and suddenly a needle of pain punctured Gabriel's skull and stabbed into the core of his brain. He opened his mouth to scream but couldn't make a noise. His tongue was like a heavy, sodden sock.

What the hell is he doing to me . . .

He felt his eyes swelling like balloons. His arms and legs grew leaden . . . but they began to flex involuntarily. He was powerless to control his own limbs.

Isaiah's doing this to me. He's hijacked my brain.

Moving sluggishly, Gabriel staggered toward a chair beside the door.

Isaiah winked at him. He strolled triumphantly into the room.

Gabriel's body moved to obediently drop into the chair. But he gripped the armrests and straightened his arms, fighting against sitting.

"No," he whispered, sweat dripping from his brow. "No."

Tremors rattled through his arms. Staying on his feet was like trying to resist a tremendous tide of water.

Across the room, Isaiah approached Nicole's bed. She squirmed in the sheets, whimpering. Dana had stepped away from the bed, her wary gaze on Isaiah, but Mom and Pops crowded around Nicole, trying to soothe her.

I have to tell them the truth.

But the powerful force pressed down on Gabriel, commanding him to sit.

He closed his eyes and concentrated every molecule in his body on fighting back, throwing off Isaiah's iron yoke. His tendons ached. His heart hammered. His head seemed to be pulsating like a bass drum.

No!

Gabriel spilled forward, face first, onto the tile floor. The fall knocked the breath out of him. Dazed, he lifted his head, moved his arms.

He was in control of his body again.

"Are you okay?" Dana came to him. She took him by the elbow and helped him to stand. "What happened?"

"I'm fine now." He brushed dust off the front of his shirt

and jeans. Near the bed, Isaiah had his arm around Pops as though comforting him. Mom held Nicole to her bosom, instinctively turning her head away from Isaiah. Yet Nicole continued to whine softly.

Enough. I've seen enough of this shit.

Dana must have sensed the imminent explosion. She took her hand off Gabriel's arm and slowly stepped away.

Isaiah whispered something in Pops's ear. Pops nodded.

Gabriel thundered toward Isaiah. Isaiah glanced over his shoulder. Gabriel drew back his fist and caught Isaiah in the jaw with a vicious right hook. Isaiah's head snapped backward. He stumbled into the wall and slid to the floor on his butt. His head lolled, drunkenly, and he groaned. If they were in a boxing match, the referee would have started the knockout count.

Gabriel rubbed his knuckles. His hand hurt like hell, but that had been the most gratifying pain he'd felt in a long time.

Pops turned on Gabriel. "What the hell is the matter with you?"

"Isaiah did this to Nicole," Gabriel said. He pointed to Nicole, who stared at Isaiah in the corner with something approaching satisfaction. "Look at her, Pops! She was afraid of him. She's glad I knocked his ass out."

"Have you lost your mind?" Pops said. "Your brother has nothing to do with your sister's condition. I want you to apologize to him. Matter of fact, as your father, I'm ordering you to apologize to him."

"No disrespect intended, but I'm not apologizing. You should be apologizing to *us* for bringing Isaiah around in the first place."

Dana came to stand beside Gabriel. Mom, nodding encouragement at Gabriel, cradled Nicole closer to her.

Pops, observing all this, crossed his arms over his chest. "What's going on here?"

"Isaiah's been planning to tear our family apart from the

beginning," Gabriel said. "He told me that, the first night he came to our house. He's been ruining my life and he's planning to fuck up yours, too. Our whole family."

"I'm not listening to any more of this nonsense," Pops said.

"No, you're gonna listen, Pops. You've been making it too easy for him to do all this. Bringing Isaiah into the house and showing him off, trying to make up for *your* mistakes with him. It wasn't our fault you neglected him for his entire life. But how do you think Mom feels about you bragging about Isaiah and carrying on? How do you think Nicole feels? How do you think *I* feel?"

"You don't know what you're talking about," Pops said. "You don't understand."

"I understand enough. Isaiah hates you. He hates all of us. Because of what you did to him and his mother. He's not here because he wants to be a part of the family. *He's here for revenge.*"

Pops had beaten Gabriel with a belt only once in his life. Gabriel couldn't even remember what he'd done to enrage his father. But right now Pops looked angry enough to rip his belt out of his slacks and pop it against Gabriel's backside again.

Massaging his jaw, Isaiah slowly got to his feet.

Pops glared at Gabriel and then looked to Isaiah.

"So, Isaiah?" Pops said. "What do you think of these accusations? I think they're ludicrous, but what do you think?"

Eyes lowered, Isaiah stroked his chin, as though deep in thought.

"I think . . ." Isaiah said, raising his head to show his gleaming, excited eyes, "that Gabriel is telling the truth."

Isaiah flicked his hand forward. Gabriel glimpsed a sharp, metallic object leaving his fingers.

A knife.

The blade hurtled through the air toward his father, who stood as still as a paper dummy on a firing range.

By reflex, Gabriel raised his hand, invoking his telekinesis against the murderous blade.

The knife spun off course and twanged harmlessly against the opposite wall.

His eyes as huge as saucers, Pops touched his throat, feeling the flesh the blade would have ripped open.

Isaiah swiveled to Gabriel.

"You did that," Isaiah said. It was a statement, not a question. "Like in my dream . . ."

Gabriel waded forward. He swung a fist at Isaiah.

Isaiah blocked the punch and drove a cat-quick jab into Gabriel's solar plexus. Pain exploded through Gabriel's body. He dropped to his knees.

Isaiah took off running.

"Allen," Nicole said softly, her gaze resting on the knife on the floor. Her voice escalated into a shriek. "Allen . . . Allen . . . Allen!"

Allen was Nicole's sometime boyfriend, Gabriel thought. Why would the knife make her scream his name?

Unless . . .

Isaiah was near the door.

"Call Security!" Gabriel shouted at his family. They huddled together, their faces confused and frightened. "Do it now!"

Then he chased after Isaiah.

Chapter 47

Isaiah raced out of the room and plunged into the corridor. He crashed into a orderly carrying a tray of food. Dishes and silverware clanged to the floor.

"Move!" Isaiah shouted. He shoved the guy aside and kept running.

His plan was crumbling to pieces. Gabriel, just like in his dream last night, had used some crazy power to deflect the knife.

Isaiah had thought he was the only one with a gift. But Gabriel had one, too. Didn't that just figure? The golden boy still had the edge.

It didn't matter anymore. Soon, the cops would be after him. He wasn't going to prison again. No motherfuckin' way. He'd rather die.

He sprinted like a track runner down the hallway, feet slapping across the tile. Nurses and doctors and orderlies and patients—no doubt terrified at the thought of a black man on the run and probably thinking he had stolen something or killed someone—scattered like frightened mice out of his path.

He was on the fourth floor. He had to get to the exit and, somehow, back to his car at his father's crib.

The stairwell lay ahead. He couldn't risk getting trapped in an elevator. Within minutes every rent-a-cop in the hospital would be searching for him.

He glanced over his shoulder.

Gabriel was in the hallway, coming after him.

Isaiah felt in his pocket the pen he'd stolen from Gabriel's desk.

His plan might have fallen apart. But he still had a few tricks left.

Gabriel spotted Isaiah at the end of the corridor. Isaiah pushed through a door and disappeared into the stairwell.

Gabriel followed, wishing he had a gun, a knife, some kind of weapon. Then he remembered his telekinesis, which had thrown the spinning blade off course, saving Pops's life.

He already possessed the only weapon he needed.

Righteous anger pumped through his blood, juiced up his muscles. He was ready for a fight with Isaiah, had been eager for a showdown with this guy from the beginning. He didn't want to kill him. No, he wanted to beat him down, pulverize him as punishment for everything he'd done to him and his family—and then, when he was finished with him, he'd turn him over to the cops, because he was certain Isaiah had murdered Nicole's boyfriend.

Gabriel shouldered through the stairwell door. Dim light illuminated the staircase. He heard Isaiah's footsteps beneath him, clapping down the steps.

Gabriel pounded down the first flight of stairs. He reached the landing and rounded the corner for the next flight.

He almost stepped on a water moccasin.

He screamed, lost his balance, and tumbled down the stairs.

The snake was sprawled over the top half of the steps, as

though it had been dumped there out of a sack. Gabriel rolled down the stairs, having the presence of mind to shift to avoid the reptile despite his rough fall.

He crashed onto the landing below, his body knotted in pain. He'd bitten his tongue. Salty blood filled his mouth.

"Got you, motherfucker," Isaiah said.

Isaiah seized him by the front of his shirt and hauled him upright. He shoved Gabriel against the wall. Gabriel threw a punch at him but was so disoriented that his aim was off the mark. Isaiah smashed a fist into his stomach. Agony forced Gabriel to bend double, clutching his abdomen. Isaiah rammed his knee underneath Gabriel's chin and Gabriel's teeth clacked together like dry bones.

Gabriel collapsed to the floor, his head spinning.

"That's how we do it in the hood," Isaiah said with a cold grin. Looming over Gabriel, he held a silver pen in one hand, rubbing the tip with his thumb.

Gabriel recognized the pen as belonging to him. He thought he'd misplaced it. Now he realized Isaiah had stolen it. But why?

"This here pen gives me the power to hack into that fat head of yours," Isaiah said. "A personal item. That's all I need to work my magic."

Pulling himself upright, Gabriel lunged for the pen. Isaiah kicked him in the ribs. Gabriel let out a yelp, sagged to the floor again.

Coiled on the stairs above, the snake hissed. Although Gabriel had learned how Isaiah was creating the hallucinations, it made the snake no less frightening. It began to slither toward Gabriel, evil eyes hungry.

"You told me how much you hate snakes, little brother," Isaiah said.

"It's not real," Gabriel said in a weak voice. But his heart pounded so loudly the vibrations seemed to transmit to the cement beneath him, making the entire floor tremble. "Not real."

The snake undulated over the last of the steps and drew closer to Gabriel's legs. Dull light gleamed on its scales.

"Your mind makes it real," Isaiah said. "If it bites you, you might die."

Gabriel tried to scoot backward.

Isaiah grabbed him around his neck and wrestled him into a headlock. Air wheezed through Gabriel's nostrils. His stomach hurt, his ribs and jaw ached, and he struggled to maintain his hold on consciousness.

The snake touched Gabriel's foot. It rose, preparing to strike.

Isaiah gripped the pen in his free hand. Gabriel, his palms afire, strained to lift his arm. He concentrated on pushing the pen out of Isaiah's grasp.

The snake opened its mouth, exposing long fangs dressed in venom.

Move.

The pen spun out of Isaiah's fingers and clinked down the stairs below.

"Shit!" Isaiah said.

The water moccasin had vanished.

It was never there to begin with.

Gabriel drove his elbow backward, thrusting it into Isaiah's gut. Isaiah gasped, and his hold on Gabriel loosened. Gabriel dropped to one knee and flipped Isaiah over his shoulder. Isaiah hit the floor and bounced down the steps like a broken doll.

Sucking in painful breaths, Gabriel went after him.

Although he had to be hurting, Isaiah quickly got his legs under him. He retrieved the pen from the floor and scrambled to the next flight of steps leading down.

Gabriel reached the bottom of the landing and hustled around the corner.

Another water moccasin awaited him on the stairs.

Stifling a scream, Gabriel froze in midstep.

Come on, damn it. You know it's not real.

Already at the bottom of the steps, Isaiah glanced up at him and grinned. He waved the pen in the air like a victor's flag.

He was going to get away.

Hissing, the snake slithered toward Gabriel. Gabriel retreated against the wall.

He heard a door open below. Isaiah's footsteps dwindled into silence.

The water moccasin glared at Gabriel for a few seconds, daring him to make a move. Then it dissolved into nothingness and Gabriel was left gaping at the empty stairs below.

Chapter 48

While Dana and Gabriel's mother kept a vigil at Nicole's bedside and spoke to the hospital's security staff, Gabriel and his father drove to Nicole's town house in Buckhead. Gabriel had an awful feeling about Nicole's boyfriend and he wanted to verify his suspicions with his own eyes before they involved the police.

He and his father exchanged barely ten words during the drive. Avoiding Gabriel's gaze, Pops fidgeted with Nicole's house key, which Mom, fortunately, had kept in her purse.

Gabriel figured that Pops was ashamed. But he said nothing to alleviate his father's humiliation; he wanted to let him stew in it for a while, and perhaps then he'd grasp the severity of what he'd done, the damage to the family he'd allowed to occur, and how close they had come to a complete meltdown.

It went without saying that Gabriel's birthday party, scheduled to take place that evening at the 755 Club, was going to be canceled.

Gabriel parked in front of the town house. Pops tried to insert the key in the door lock but his hands trembled so badly he couldn't drive the key into the slot. Gabriel nudged his father aside, slid the key into the lock, and turned it. He began to open the door.

A rank stench seeped through the crack. Gabriel's stomach churned and he covered his mouth with his hand.

"Oh, Jesus," Pops said. He pressed a handkerchief to his lips.

Gabriel pushed open the door all the way.

Allen lay sprawled in the hallway. His skin had begun to turn blue. His eyes stared blindly at the ceiling. Dried blood outlined a gash in his neck like a grotesque collar, and more blood had congealed around his body like spilled crimson paint.

Isaiah. He hadn't even bothered to hide the guy's body.

Pops stumbled away from Gabriel's side, bent double, and vomited.

Biting his knuckle to stem his own gag reflex, Gabriel stepped inside. He was careful not to touch anything and risk contaminating the crime scene, knowledge he'd gleaned from shows like *CSI*.

Nothing on a television forensics crime show, however, would adequately explain how Isaiah was able to do the things he did. Mixing up Nicole's mind like a blended drink. Making Gabriel see illusions of snakes. . . .

Gabriel detected movement across the living room, in a mirror.

He carefully navigated his way around the corpse. He moved closer to the glass.

On previous occasions he'd gained a vision of a blurry, shadowy figure in the mirror, a phantom of indeterminate identity and origin.

Finally the mystery was unveiled. It was clearly reflected back to him, as vivid as the living room behind him.

He was looking at Isaiah.

*   *   *

Isaiah had escaped the hospital by the most conventional of means: he caught a taxi in front of the main entrance. He gave the driver, a guy from some Caribbean nation who played reggae on the car radio, the address to his father's house.

Thirty minutes later he was in his Chevy Chevelle, speeding away. He'd left his luggage inside the house. Although he'd made copies of the house keys, he didn't have time to go inside. When the cops were after you, every second of freedom was crucial.

Besides, he already had the most important things to ensure his survival: his own mind—and his loaded Glock.

He would return to the house some other time.

He drove at the speed limit on I-285, heading north. He wasn't sure yet where he was going to go. The only thing he knew for sure was that he needed to get away from ATL for a few days, maybe longer, and let the heat cool off.

As he barreled down the highway, he glanced in the rearview mirror—and saw something that nearly made him lose control of the car.

Gabriel was reflected in the mirror, and he was staring at him.

Gabriel focused so intently on the phenomena in the mirror that he had temporarily forgotten he was in the presence of a dead man, steeped in the putrid smell of death.

Gabriel had a clear look at Isaiah, as though a psychic mirror were positioned in front of Isaiah and Gabriel's eyes were embedded in the glass itself. A lucid, frontal view.

Isaiah was in his car. Driving. Sweat drenched Isaiah's brow and he wiped the back of his hand across his face.

Then Isaiah's gaze flicked upward, checking a rearview mirror.

Isaiah's eyes widened with surprise.

He sees me, Gabriel realized. *Just like I'm seeing him, he's seeing me, too.*

A sense of wonder, cool as water, rippled down his back.

Isaiah's eyes hardened to gray points. He spat out a stream of words. But Gabriel could not hear him, and he was unable to read Isaiah's lips.

Isaiah flipped Gabriel a middle finger.

"Fuck you, too!" Gabriel shouted.

Isaiah pointed at Gabriel with his index finger. He shouted something else.

"I can't hear you, idiot," Gabriel said, and indicated his ears.

Isaiah spoke more slowly, and Gabriel suddenly comprehended the movement of his lips: *This ain't over, little brother.*

Isaiah raised a handgun to the mirror and pointed it toward Gabriel.

Bang, Isaiah said.

Gabriel turned away from the glass. Pops leaned against the doorway, clearly making an effort to avoid the corpse. His face was haggard and he dabbed at his lips with his handkerchief.

"You were talking to someone over there," Pops said. "Who?"

Gabriel ignored the question. "Isaiah did this, Pops. He'll be back."

"How . . . how do you know?"

Gabriel glanced at the mirror. Isaiah's face had vanished.

"Gut feeling," Gabriel said.

Part Three

FATHER'S DAY

*It doesn't matter who my father was; it matters
who I remember he was.*
— Anne Sexton

Chapter 49

The following week, life returned to normal for the Reids . . . as normal as possible, considering the threat that had almost dismantled their family.

Nicole's health improved. She gradually regained her mental faculties, and, by midweek, her physician released her from the hospital and said she should be able to return to her ordinary activities within a week or so.

But Nicole's emotional wounds, exacerbated by Allen's grisly murder, were slow to fade, and when she slept (with the aid of drugs), she usually had nightmares.

The Atlanta Police Department issued an all-points bulletin for Isaiah Battle, seeking to charge him in the murder of Allen Tyson and the attempted murder of T.L. Reid. Forensic tests confirmed that the knife Isaiah had hurled at T.L. Reid was the same weapon he'd used to kill Allen. He was considered armed and extremely dangerous. Isaiah's former prison mug shot was plastered in the newspapers and on television, along with a list of his previous felonies—and the account of his miraculous life-after-death escape from the Chicago morgue, which officials were quick to downplay as a simple medical misdiagnosis. Allowing the public to believe that Isaiah had somehow cheated death would only incite the city into a panic.

Everyone was on the lookout for Isaiah. It comforted the Reid family to know that the authorities were working hard on their behalf, but the police department's eagerness to apprehend Isaiah had an unexpected downside: mistaking Gabriel for Isaiah, the cops approached him three times within the space of a few days. In one instance they had Gabriel handcuffed and pinned against his car before they bothered to check his driver's license.

Gabriel decided that until the situation cooled down, or Isaiah was found, he would spend most of his time at home. He telecommuted for work, and Dana brought him groceries and other items. It was a necessary measure, but he hated it. He felt as though he were under house arrest.

Even though Isaiah had disappeared, he was still making Gabriel's life miserable.

On Friday afternoon, almost a week after the incident at the hospital, Pops visited Gabriel.

"Sorry to drop in unannounced," Pops said. "I was on the way home from the office and wanted to see how you were doing."

"Been working hard all day," Gabriel said. "I was about to get a beer. Want one?"

"That would hit the spot." Pops removed his suit jacket and hung it on the coat hanger in the foyer. "It's been a long day—hell, a long week."

"Tell me about it." Gabriel grabbed two Heinekens out of the refrigerator. He popped off the caps and handed a beer to his father.

He watched Pops take a long sip.

Other than brief discussions related to company business,

Gabriel had not had a conversation with Pops all week. He sensed that Pops was still embarrassed, especially with the media attention. The media had depicted Pops as a sentimental fool for so quickly welcoming Isaiah into the family. If there was one thing Pops had always sought to avoid during his years as a high-profile entrepreneur, it was waving his dirty laundry in front of the public eye. Gabriel was certain Pops worried that his portrayal in the news as a man who lacked the good sense to run his household properly might damage his hard-earned reputation as a shrewd businessman.

But what had brought Pops to Gabriel's home? His father was a man of purpose; he didn't believe in idle chatter. He would have visited Gabriel only for a good reason.

Pops leaned against the kitchen counter. "How've you been holding up?"

"I've been picking up the pieces. It's been a headache. It's going to take months to clean up my credit."

"I'm glad you'd saved enough to buy a car. I always taught you that if you saved your money, one day it would save you."

"You were right," Gabriel said.

While waiting on the insurance payment for his totaled SUV, Gabriel had dipped into his investment funds—the only accounts Isaiah hadn't plundered—and purchased a new vehicle. A used one, actually: a Nissan Xterra. It was a big step down from the fully loaded Lincoln Navigator he'd used to drive, but he didn't care. He was past the days of trying to impress people.

"Can I see the new ride?" Pops asked.

"Come on."

Gabriel led his father into the garage. The silver Xterra gleamed, thanks to a recent wash and wax.

Pops ran his fingers across the hood. "Looks good."

"Thanks." Gabriel opened the driver's-side door and slid behind the steering wheel. "It's the first car I've ever bought on my own, you know."

"It is, isn't it?" Pops said. Hands on his knees, he studied the dashboard. "I would've bought you a new car, if you'd asked. You know that."

"I know, Pops, and I appreciate it. But I had to do this on my own."

Grunting, Pops straightened. He sipped his beer.

"How's Dana?" Pops asked.

"She's fine. She's coming over later this evening for dinner."

"Good, good. Anything else going on?"

Climbing out of the jeep, Gabriel shrugged. "Just taking it day by day."

"I hear ya." Pops took another sip of beer.

Why wouldn't his father get to the point? It was odd to see Pops so unsure of himself. In retrospect, however, Gabriel had learned a lot about his father recently—and most of it wasn't flattering.

"I haven't seen or heard from Isaiah, if that's what you're wondering," Gabriel said. "I think he'll pop up again, but I don't know when or where. In the meantime I'm staying alert."

"No more gut feelings about it?"

"Nothing I haven't already told you."

Gabriel was being truthful. Not only had he not seen or heard from Isaiah, he had not experienced another incident of viewing his brother in a mirror. He hadn't had any unusual dreams. He hadn't seen any illusory snakes. His telekinetic ability, too, had deserted him. He was once again just ordinary Gabriel Reid—like Peter Parker stripped of his Spider-Man talents.

"I think it's time for me to get to the point." Pops drained his beer and tossed the bottle in a recycling bin against the wall. Leaning against the jeep, he dug his hands deep in his pockets and bowed his head, gazing at a spot on the concrete floor. "I owe you an apology, Gabriel. I was wrong for how I treated you. I'm sorry."

Gabriel's lips parted, but he didn't speak. He was stunned. Silence hung between them, thick as smoke.

Pops wiped his mouth with a handkerchief, as though he could erase the memory of the words that had passed his lips.

Gabriel waited for his father to continue. But Pops only raised his head and looked at Gabriel questioningly, and Gabriel realized that Pops was finished. It had taken a lot for Pops to humble himself enough to offer three contrite sentences. He wasn't going to say anything else.

Gabriel would have to be happy with that.

"Okay," Gabriel said. "Let's put this behind us then."

Pops offered his hand and they exchanged a firm shake. Then Pops started toward the door and Gabriel followed him inside the house.

As he viewed his father from behind, he noticed the slump in his father's shoulders and the slight forward incline in his stance, as though Pops were walking against a strong wind. Stress, Gabriel thought, had weakened his father. He was beginning to look frail. Before Isaiah had arrived, his father had seemed, to him, like the most powerful, commanding presence on Earth. But he was only a man. He wasn't invincible, and time and circumstance were wearing him down.

It was such a sad realization that Gabriel blinked away a tear.

Pops draped his suit jacket across his shoulder. "I wanted to tell you, we've had a change of plans for Father's Day. I know it's been our tradition to go to the cabin and go fishing. But I don't think I have the energy for that this year."

"I understand. It wouldn't be a good idea for us to go away on a trip anyway, what with everything that's happened."

"That, too," Pops said. "So we're going to have a family dinner at the house on Sunday. Four o'clock sharp."

"We'll be there."

Pops opened the door. Gabriel stopped his father with a hand on his shoulder.

"Thanks, Pops," he said. "For you to say what you said, it means a lot to me."

Pops smiled tightly, clasped Gabriel's hand, and then walked outside.

Pops wasn't an emotionally expressive man, but he was Gabriel's father—and Gabriel loved him all the same.

Later that night, lying beside Dana in bed after making love, Gabriel turned to her and said, "You know, Pops apologized to me today."

"He did?" Dana propped her head on her elbow, regarded him with amazement. "What brought that on, I wonder?"

"I think it's been eating him up inside. He knew he was wrong. He wanted to do the right thing."

"You think that's it?" Dana said.

"What else would it be?"

"I don't know. But you've told me before that your dad never apologizes. Why this time?"

"Nothing this serious has ever happened to our family," Gabriel said. "It stands to reason that the old way of doing things, not apologizing or whatever, has to change. At any rate, I'm happy with it."

"That's all that matters then," she said. She laid her head on the pillow and traced her fingers across his bare chest.

"You think there's another reason why he apologized?"

"It doesn't matter what I think, Gabe. He's your father, and if you're happy with his apology, that's good enough for me."

"I still want to know what you think."

"Honestly?"

"Yeah," he said. "Honestly."

"I think your dad has a lot of secrets," she said. "Sure, I think he was apologizing partly for the disaster with Isaiah, but I also think he might've been apologizing out of guilt for what he's still keeping hidden from you."

Gabriel thought about the secret his mother had almost revealed to him at the hospital. But that didn't involve Pops, did it? It was something Mom had concealed from him and had nothing to do with his father.

Right?

He asked Dana, "What else do you think he's kept hidden from me?"

"If I had any idea, I'd tell you. But I don't know. Call it a gut feeling."

That brought a chuckle out of him.

"If you'd said that two weeks ago, I would've been insulted," he said. "But if I've learned anything after all this, it's that my father isn't perfect. He's human, he makes mistakes, and he's got skeletons in the closet just like anyone else. For all I know, you could be right. Am I going to press him about it? No. He apologized and I think he was sincere. I'm going to leave it at that."

"Wow." Dana ran her finger along his cheek. "You don't sound like the Gabriel I met three years ago."

"The Gabriel you met three years ago was a boy."

She moved on top of him. She looked down at him and smiled.

"I love you," she said. She'd told him those three words plenty of times recently, evidence that he was not the only one who had grown.

"Love you, too." He kissed her.

They made love again.

Gabriel awoke from a nightmare. He swam to consciousness, shuddering. Cold sweat filmed his face and chest.

"You okay?" Dana asked sleepily.

"Yeah, it was only a dream."

But the nightmare had been incredibly vivid. In it he'd

been standing in front of the bathroom mirror, but he didn't see himself reflected; he saw Isaiah. Isaiah shouted at him, *"This ain't done yet, motherfucker,"* and leaped through the mirror, glass shattering as if it were some kind of supernatural window. And then Isaiah grabbed Gabriel by the throat and flung him into the garden tub, which was full of hissing water moccasins. . . .

Gabriel shook his head, clearing the horrifying images from his thoughts. His bladder was full. He didn't want to use the bathroom, didn't want to look into that mirror. But he had no choice.

He rose out of the bed and shuffled to the bathroom. At the threshold, he paused. He gazed at the mirror. The glass was dappled with silvery moonlight. A shadowy figure regarded him.

Trembling, he flicked on the light switch.

Isaiah was not in the mirror. He was looking only at himself, his eyes red and anxious.

"See?" he told himself. "Only a dream."

But a chill gripped him, and it was slow to let go.

Chapter 50

Sunday was an atypical June day in Atlanta: cool, overcast, and windy. Severe thunderstorms were forecast for later in the evening, forcing families planning Father's Day barbecues to enjoy their feasts before the sky dumped its rain on their gatherings, and keeping eyes glancing warily at the thickening shroud of gray-black clouds.

"I'm a little worried about this dinner," Gabriel said to Dana as he steered his jeep onto his parents' street. Brisk wind harried leaves and debris across the road in front of them. "So much is still up in the air, with Isaiah at large and Nicole recovering. I wonder if anyone will be in a mood to celebrate Father's Day, of all things."

"Stay positive," Dana said. "We might have a great time. We deserve a little happiness after all we've been through lately."

He parked in the driveway. Pops answered the door.

"Happy Father's Day!" Gabriel and Dana said in unison. Gabriel thrust a wrapped gift and a card into his father's hands.

"Thanks, kids," Pops said. He welcomed them inside, kissing Dana on the cheek and giving Gabriel a hearty handshake.

Pops looked much better than he had a couple of days ago. His posture had improved, his shoulders once more thrown back, broad and proud. His eyes were clear and alert. His hair and beard were neatly trimmed. Dressed in a beige button-down shirt and dark slacks, Pops resembled the dignified father and CEO Gabriel loved and admired.

"Something smells good," Gabriel said. "What did Mom cook for dinner?"

"Believe it or not, I cooked dinner," Pops said. "I put some filet mignons on the grill, and we'll have potatoes, salad, a couple other dishes. I admit it's not up to your mom's gourmet-chef standards, but I wanted to turn over a new leaf this year. Why shouldn't I cook for my family for Father's Day when I'm so blessed to have you?"

"That's very nice of you," Dana said.

"No kidding," Gabriel said. "The last time Pops cooked I think I was seventeen, when Mom had come down with a bad case of the flu."

"What did he cook?" Dana asked.

"Hamburger Helper," Gabriel said, and all of them laughed.

They walked into the grand salon. Mom greeted them with hugs and kisses. Nicole sat in a chair near the fireplace and rose to hug them, too.

Nicole looked good. Her skin was radiant and her eyes sparkled.

"How've you been doing?" Gabriel asked her.

"I'm fine during the day," she said. Her face darkened. "Nights are a challenge, though. I've been taking sleeping pills or else I wouldn't get any sleep at all. Nightmares."

"I feel you," Gabriel said, remembering his dream from the other night.

"I don't think they'll end until the police catch him," she said. "Until I know for sure that he's locked away and can't get to me again."

Gabriel wished he could reassure her that Isaiah would be captured soon, but he didn't because he didn't entirely believe it. Isaiah was cunning, and with his talents, who knew how long he could evade arrest?

"Whether they catch him or not, I won't let him do anything to you again," he said. "That's a promise."

Nicole hugged him again. "Thanks, Gabe."

He pinched her cheek. "That's what big brothers are for."

"Dinner should be ready shortly," Pops said. He wrapped an apron around his waist and headed toward the patio door. "Marge, can you get drinks for the kids, please? I'm going to check the steaks."

"What would you guys like?" Mom asked. "We have sweet tea, wine, beer, and soda."

"Sweet tea's fine for me," Dana said.

"Gabe?" Mom asked. She began to walk toward the kitchen. "What would you like?"

"Let me see what kind of beer you have," Gabriel said and followed his mother.

He trailed her to the kitchen on purpose. It was the first time, since visiting Nicole at the hospital, that he had been alone with her.

They had unfinished business to discuss.

As Mom filled a tall glass with ice and lifted the pitcher of sweet tea, Gabriel opened the refrigerator, took out a bottle of Samuel Adams, and approached her at the counter.

"We never finished our conversation at the hospital," he said in a lowered voice. "You were going to tell me something important."

Mom spilled tea onto the countertop.

"Oh, Lord," she said. She snatched a roll of paper towels, ripped one off, and began mopping up the spill. She avoided his gaze.

"Mom?" Gabriel touched her shoulder. "Please. Tell me."

She shook her head, eyes downturned. "Forget I said anything, baby. I never should have brought it up."

"What are you hiding from me? If it's about me, I have a right to know."

"I'm sorry I ever said anything. Let it go, Gabe. Please. It's better that way."

You can't imagine the secrets I've kept hidden from you, most of all.

Gabriel gritted his teeth. Mom put down the paper towels and placed her hand on top of his.

"Please trust me, we should leave this alone," she said. "If you really must know—and, Lord help me, I don't think you should—then it's not my place to tell you."

"Then whose is it?" Gabriel said.

Pops bustled into the kitchen. He carried a large platter heaped with steaming filets. "The steaks are done!"

Mom glanced at his father and then gave Gabriel a look that answered his question.

They took dinner in the sunroom. Fine-mesh screen windows allowed cool air to filter inside, but kept annoying bugs at bay. Even if it began raining—and the sky steadily darkened, proof that rain was near—they would stay dry.

Dinner was delicious. They feasted on thick, juicy filet mignons. Baked potatoes. Tossed salad with blue-cheese dressing. Pops promised an equally delicious dessert, too.

As they dined, their conversation was light and sprinkled with humor. Gabriel, like the rest of them, had endured enough hardship in the past couple of weeks to give him a newfound appreciation for the joys of a good meal in the company of loved ones, and he avoided any topics—namely, Isaiah—likely to stir controversy or discomfort.

Nevertheless he was determined to have a private conversation with his father sometime that evening. In spite of Mom's warning that it would be best if he did not uncover the secrets, curiosity percolated in his stomach. What could be so terrible that he was better off not knowing about it? Although he remained an active participant in the dinner talk, the question echoed in the chambers of his mind.

Pops served dessert: New York–style cheesecake with fresh strawberry topping. It was superb.

"Wow, Pops," Gabriel said. "You really put your foot in this. I'm amazed."

"I have to confess that I didn't make the cheesecake." Pops grinned sheepishly. "I picked it up from the Cheesecake Factory."

"And I was about to give you another compliment, too," Nicole said and laughed.

"For real," Dana said. "I was about to ask you to cater the food at our wedding."

Mention of Dana and Gabriel's upcoming October wedding sparked a new line of conversation among the women. They began talking about flower arrangements, bridal dresses, food, invitations . . .

Quickly losing interest, Gabriel found himself looking out the window at the backyard. A drizzle had begun to fall, droplets rippling across the swimming pool. The strengthening wind ruffled the trees and shrubbery. Distantly, thunder grumbled.

Gabriel noticed that his father had bowed out of the conversation, too. Pops sipped coffee and, with dull interest, watched the women chattering.

Gabriel caught his father's eye. "You up for a game of pool, Pops? They'll be talking about wedding stuff for a while."

"Let's go," Pops said, rising from his chair.

Mom glanced knowingly at Gabriel as he and his father left the table. She knew him well.

He had to get to the bottom of this.

Chapter 51

Pops and Gabriel went downstairs to the recreation room on the terrace level. The rec room had stack-stone walling, a fireplace, and a professional-quality rosewood billiards table. Floor-to-ceiling windows and French doors dominated one side of the room, providing a view of the flagstone patio and swimming pool.

The rain had begun to fall in sheets; the pool now appeared to be boiling like a cauldron.

"My game is rusty," Pops said. He took a cue from the rack on the wall. "It's been a couple of months since I've played."

"Already making excuses, are we?" Gabriel said. He began placing the balls inside the wooden triangle on the woolen table surface.

"But I'm sure I can still kick your butt," Pops said, ever the competitor. Pops hated to lose, a trait Gabriel had acquired from him. When Gabriel had been a teenager living at home, they'd used to shoot pool into the wee hours of the morning, neither of them wanting to accept defeat, calling it quits only when exhaustion forced them to a draw.

"Rack 'em up, kid," Pops said. "You break first."

Gabriel lifted the rack. Then he sharpened the tip of his favorite cue, aimed at the white cue ball, and pumped a smooth stroke, scattering the balls across the table with a satisfying clatter.

"Seven in the left corner pocket," Gabriel said. He shot— and missed.

"Looks like I'm not the only one who's rusty," Pops said. He bent forward, surveying an angle for a possible shot.

"I wanted to talk to you about something," Gabriel said.

"Yeah?" Pops studied the balls.

Gabriel checked the staircase, confirming that no one was nearby. "About a week ago, Mom said something about a secret she's kept hidden from me. Something really important. But she wouldn't tell me what it was—she said it wasn't her place to say. She hinted that I should ask you."

Pops's lips were drawn in a firm line. He rose out of his crouch, clutching the cue stick as though it were a weapon.

"Your mother said that, did she?" he said. "Did she tell you you're better off not knowing?"

"She did. But I want to know."

"You don't need to know."

Gabriel laid the cue across the table. "Pops, I'm a grown man. Whatever it is, I can handle it. And if it's about me, I have a right to know."

"Shit, I thought you wanted to play pool," Pops said. He tried to rack the cue stick, ended up dropping it on the floor. Cursing, he kicked it away and snatched his handkerchief out of his pocket. He mopped his face.

"What it is?" Gabriel asked softly but firmly. "I need to know."

"Wasn't finding out about Isaiah bad enough?" Pops said. He balled the handkerchief in his fist. "Goddamn it, why the hell did Marge bring this up?"

"She wants me to know the truth."

"She should've talked to me about this first." Muttering,

Pops leaned against the edge of the billiards table. He closed his eyes and massaged the bridge of his nose, a gesture Gabriel had picked up from him.

Quietly, Gabriel waited. On the other side of the room, rain beat against the windows, streamed down the doors. Lightning ripped across the angry purple-black sky, followed soon after by a burst of thunder.

"Okay," Pops said. "Can you run upstairs and get us a couple beers? I'm going to need another one for this—and so will you."

"I'll be right back," Gabriel said.

Theo watched his son ascend the stairs. He sighed.

The truth could set you free. It also could give you a migraine.

His son wanted to know the truth. But once Theo told him, he was going to wish he hadn't asked.

Theo wanted to strangle Marge for bringing up this mess in the first place. They'd had an agreement: this was one secret they would never, ever divulge to anyone. She had broken her promise.

In spite of his anger toward his wife, Theo had to admit that he—and he alone—ultimately bore responsibility for the situation. Gabriel would realize that and blame him. The thought of his son hating him forever, so soon after they had mended fences, intensified Theo's headache.

He heard a footstep behind him. He looked over his shoulder.

It was Isaiah.

Fear clenched Theo's heart like an iron fist.

"Happy Father's Day," Isaiah said.

He swung a dark object at Theo's head.

Chapter 52

Gabriel walked down the hallway toward the kitchen. Anxiety quivered through his knees. He was so worried about what Pops was going to tell him that it was difficult to maintain his balance.

Maybe it's not as bad as I think it'll be. What could be worse than learning I have a crazy half brother? Is Pops gonna tell me I have a psycho half sister, too?

Possibilities circled through his mind, and they only made him more anxious, more eager to get this over with.

As he passed through the hallway, he saw that the women had moved out of the sunroom and into the grand salon. They were still talking about the wedding, of course. Gabriel looked away, fearing that they would try to snare him in the conversation. This was one time when he truly could not be bothered.

He walked into the kitchen. He reached for the refrigerator handle.

Before he could touch it, the door opened.

Tingles cascaded over his hands.

The last time he'd exercised his telekinesis, he'd been at

the hospital, fighting on the stairwell with Isaiah. He'd been unable to access the talent since, and, after numerous attempts, had given up, deciding that for some mysterious reason the gift had gone into remission, like a side effect of some weird medical condition.

Now it was back.

But why?

"You forgot about our father-son fishing trip, didn't you?" Isaiah whispered into his father's ear. But Pops was unconscious, his lips lolling open, saliva gathering in the corner of his mouth. "Well, I didn't forget."

Slinging his father's arm across his shoulder, Isaiah dragged him toward the French doors that faced the patio and quietly opened them. Cold rain spattered his face. He draped a jacket over his father's head to keep him dry and asleep.

After the shit went down at the hospital, the Reids, naturally, had changed the house locks as a security measure. But they'd neglected to replace the lock on the terrace doors. That was the downside of living in such a big-ass crib; it was impossible to remember everything.

Isaiah had suspected that they would have a family gathering on Father's Day. He'd hidden in the basement for hours, biding his time, waiting for the perfect opportunity.

He didn't want a confrontation with Gabriel or anyone else in the family. This time it was solely between him and his father.

"I promised Mama that no matter what, I was going to get you," Isaiah said. He pulled his father outside and toward the far side of the rambling yard, staying close to the exterior walls to avoid being seen by someone inside. Rain slanted in his eyes, forcing him to squint, but he was thankful for the downpour and the premature darkness the thunderstorm brought. It would provide cover.

"But before we get to that, we're going fishing, Pops. You never did take me fishing, but you took Gabriel all the time. We're going on a fishing trip of our own, just you and me."

The wrought-iron gate on the east side of the property was locked from the inside. He hit the lever to open it, forced the gate open wide with his shoulder, and lugged his slack-jawed father across the damp grass toward the white Ford Econoline cargo van he'd parked against the curb at the edge of the cul-de-sac, out of a direct view of the estate windows.

He'd stolen the van late last night out of some poor sucker's driveway. ROBERT'S HEATING & AIR-CONDITIONING was painted in red across the side and rear doors. An unsuspecting neighbor would assume that he was a technician visiting the community to make a service call.

He slid open the side panel door and hauled his father inside.

Gabriel stood in the middle of the kitchen, his palms crackling with psychic energy.

Why had his telekinesis suddenly returned?

Dana entered the kitchen carrying an empty glass. She picked up a pitcher of sweet tea but put it down when she noticed the look on his face. "Something wrong, baby?"

"The power's back." Gabriel flexed his hands.

A mirror, he thought. *Look in a mirror*.

As Dana watched him, curious, he rushed into the hallway. A large mirror hung on the wall in the foyer.

Heart drumming, he moved in front of the glass.

He saw Isaiah.

Isaiah was pulling his father inside a van. Fishing poles and tackle boxes covered the floor behind him.

"Oh, shit," Gabriel said.

"What is it?" Dana said. "What's wrong?"

Gabriel scrambled to the basement door. He pounded

down the stairs, leaping over the last five steps and landing on the hardwood floor with a bone-knocking thud, he barely felt in his rising panic. From a distance, Dana followed.

"Pops!" he shouted, running into the rec room. "Pops!"

The patio doors were open. They swung in the rain.

His father was gone.

Chapter 53

After Isaiah had stolen the van last night, he'd cleared all the technician's tools and junk out of the cargo area and remade it into a work space to suit his purposes. There were no rear or side windows, but he'd suspended a heavy, dark blanket from the ceiling, behind the front seats, to keep his work and captive hidden from anyone who might peer through the windshield. Then he stored his own tools on the floor: a coil of rope, duct tape, a utility knife, and fishing gear.

With his father lying unconscious on the cold metal floor, the first thing Isaiah did was remove his father's gold Rolex. He laid it beside him. The watch, much like Gabriel's pen, would prove useful.

Moving quickly, Isaiah knotted a length of rope around his father's wrists. He tied his ankles together, too.

As he was bending over his father, preparing to slap a piece of duct tape on his mouth, Pops's eyes fluttered open.

"Isaiah," he said in a garbled voice. He blinked, groggily. "What're you doing?"

"I'll tell you in a minute. We've gotta roll."

Driving the heating-and-air-conditioning van offered him a

reasonable amount of cover. Nevertheless, being parked so close to the Reids' crib made him antsy. The cops were still on the prowl for him.

"Help," Pops said. He rocked back and forth, struggling to break free from the ropes. "Someone, help me!"

Isaiah dug into the tackle box beside him and extracted a large barbed fishhook. He waved it in front of his father's eyes.

"I'll thread this through your lips like a catfish if you don't shut up and stay still," he said. "You want me to do that?"

A fat drop of sweat rolled down his father's temple.

"Please don't do this," Pops said. "This isn't the way, son—"

"Shut the fuck up!"

Flinching as if struck, Pops fell silent.

Isaiah pressed the duct tape across his father's mouth. Pops's chest rose and fell rapidly as he breathed through his nostrils in a petrified wheeze.

"Now, to answer your question: we're going fishing," Isaiah said. "You told me that you and Gabe would always take a father-son fishing trip on Father's Day at your cabin in the Blue Ridge mountains. I decided it was my turn to enjoy the tradition with you. That's only fair, right?"

Pops said something unintelligible. He shook his head wildly.

Check out the big-time CEO now. He looked like a frightened old man. He'd probably pissed on himself. If he hadn't yet, he would soon.

Isaiah picked up his father's Rolex. He rubbed his thumb across the fine Oyster band and sapphire crystal face. His father wore this watch, a Yacht-Master model that listed for something like twenty grand, all the time. It was perfect for Isaiah's purposes.

This was going to become more fun very soon. He was just warming up.

* * *

Isaiah had abducted Pops. The vision in the mirror had told Gabriel as much, but he'd needed to go to the terrace to confirm with his real eyes—his *physical* eyes—that it was true.

"Wasn't your father down here?" Dana asked. "Where'd he go?"

Gabriel didn't answer. He hurried to the far corner of the recreation room. A large closet was set in the wall, the double doors made of sturdy oak, a keyhole in the center. Gabriel dug out his key ring, found the right key, and jammed it into the slot.

"Damn it, Gabe," Dana said. "Tell me what's going on!"

"Isaiah was here. He took Pops." He pulled open the closet doors; they were so wide it was almost like opening a bank vault.

A tall gun cabinet stood within. Several rifles and shotguns gleamed darkly behind the tempered glass.

Dana looked from the firearms to Gabriel, shock and worry taking turns on her face. "How do you know? Did you see him?"

"I saw it in a mirror." He inserted another key into the gun-cabinet lock. "Isaiah was pulling him into a van. He's taking Pops to the cabin."

"How do you know that?"

Gabriel opened the cabinet doors. The bracing yet oddly comforting smell of well-oiled steel and gunpowder penetrated his nostrils. The guns, comprising his and his father's hunting collection, stood like soldiers at attention.

"I saw fishing poles and tackle boxes in the van," he said. "Isaiah knows Pops and I would normally have a Father's Day fishing trip, so he's taking him up there himself. He never got to go on a fishing trip with Pops, you know. That's how the crazy bastard thinks."

"So what're you doing?" she asked. "Don't tell me you're going after him."

"That's exactly what I'm doing. I promise you Isaiah isn't

taking Pops there to drink beer and catch perch—he's got something else in mind. I'm not gonna let it happen."

Gabriel selected a Mossberg 500, twelve-gauge, pump-action shotgun outfitted with a scope and a nylon sling. He'd purchased the gun—well, Pops had purchased it for him—the previous year. The shotgun was ideal for hunting and home defense, and he was about to embark upon a little of both.

"Please, Gabe, don't go," Dana said. "I'll call the police."

Gabriel pulled open one of the cabinet's lower storage areas. Boxes of ammo lay inside. He ripped open a box of shot shells and began to load the gun.

"Don't call anyone," he said. "This is family business."

She crossed her arms over her bosom, shuddering. "Are you sure about this?"

"As sure as I've ever been sure of anything." He rose, touched her arm. "Dana, you've got to trust me on this. Okay?"

Trust. The same principle that, only a week ago, had knocked them flat on their backs and left their relationship in tatters.

Dana hesitated for a beat, gnawing her lip. Then she nodded.

"All right," she said. "I'm scared but I'm going to trust that you know what you're doing."

"Thank you." He turned back to the closet. A camouflage hunting vest hung on a hook beside the gun cabinet, along with a few jackets. Gabriel grabbed the vest and slipped it on. He loaded the front pockets with extra rounds of ammo.

Mom, trailed by Nicole, appeared at the rec room doorway.

"What's all this commotion?" Mom asked. "What are you doing with that gun?"

"I'm going to save Pops." He strapped the Mossberg by its sling over his shoulder. "I don't have time to explain everything else. Dana will fill you in."

As they gaped at him, Gabriel moved past them, and

mounted the staircase. He halted on the steps, struck by an idea.

"Dana, can you give me your makeup compact, please?"

Dana gave him a puzzled look, but she rushed upstairs to get her purse. He followed her. She dug out the compact and handed it to him.

He snapped it open. He examined the small rectangular mirror.

He saw Isaiah behind the wheel of the van, eyes squinted in concentration as he navigated through the rain. Windshield wipers ticked back and forth. A dark curtain fluttered behind Isaiah, separating the cabin from the cargo space.

Gabriel was willing to bet that Pops was imprisoned on the floor behind that sheet. Pops might be safe, for the time being.

"How about your pepper spray, too?" Gabriel asked. A gift from Gabriel, Dana carried the weapon on her key ring. It could be useful in tight quarters.

Nodding, Dana removed the small canister of pepper spray from her key ring and handed it to him.

Gabriel stuffed the items in his vest pocket. He quickly kissed Dana, and then Nicole and Mom, ignoring their protests and pleadings.

"I promise, I'll bring back Pops," he said. "Alive."

He opened the front door and ran into the storm.

Chapter 54

My son's gone crazy and it's my fault.

Theo lay on the floor, bound at the wrists and ankles. The ropes were so tight that, after a halfhearted effort to break free, he had given up. His hands and feet had grown as numb as bricks from his constricted blood flow.

Beneath him the cold floor thrummed; rain hammered the walls and ceiling. It was like being trapped in a tin drum; it was so loud he could scarcely hear himself breathe.

Fishing rods and the contents of a tackle box clinked and rustled around him. The sight of outdoor gear, and its promise of tranquil days spent on a sun-spangled mountain lake, usually had the unfailing ability to relax him. Now he viewed the stuff as potential torture equipment. The fishing line could be looped into a garrote around his neck; a hook, as Isaiah had already threatened, could be used to puncture his flesh; a casting rod could be used to beat him. There were dozens more painful uses for the implements, and Theo could not stop thinking about them.

And you deserve it, Theo. You deserve every lick of pain and suffering he gives you.

Theo could not argue with that soft voice; it was his conscience. The same conscience that, over the decades, had counseled him to do the right thing by his son.

He should have moved Isaiah and his mother out of their crime-ridden neighborhood and into a more peaceful community. He should have communicated with Isaiah on a regular basis, invited the boy to Atlanta during the summers and introduced him to a different side of life. He should have sent Isaiah to college, should've prepared a job for him in the company.

He *knew* he should have done those things. His conscience had told him so.

But he'd ignored the voice, as he ignored most advice when it was something he didn't want to hear. He'd been too concerned with what his colleagues might think. Worried about what people in church would whisper behind his back. Fearful of earning the scorn of his friends, and eavesdropping on conversations in which they would say, "Yeah, T.L. has a kid out of wedlock. Negro cheated on his wife, uh-huh. He's no different than any of the sorry brothers out there—he just looks better on the surface."

He'd hoped Isaiah would eventually go away. Even after the chaos of a week ago, during which he had foolishly opened up himself and the family to the boy, he had hoped that the madness at the hospital would be the end of it, that he'd never see Isaiah again.

Denial had protected him in the past, but it was, ultimately, merely a comforting fiction. Gabriel had warned him that Isaiah would return. Gabe had an unerring sense of what Isaiah would do.

He wondered if Gabriel realized Isaiah had abducted him.

He wondered if Gabriel would come to save him.

He wondered if, after all the wrongs he had done to his wife and children and so many others, he deserved to be saved.

Chapter 55

Plowing through the rain, Isaiah took I-285 North, looping around the northwest side of metro Atlanta, and connected with I-75 North at the top of the Perimeter. I-75 North would take him to I-575, which turned into the Georgia Mountain Parkway. The Georgia Mountain Parkway would carry him into the Blue Ridge Mountains, where his father kept his cabin, and where they would get down to serious father-son business.

Isaiah had slipped the old picture of Mama and Pops out of his wallet. He imagined that Mama had to be proud of him just then. He had promised her he would get his father for how he'd treated them, and he was keeping his vow. If there was one thing Mama had always held sacred, it was the importance of being true to your word.

Don't be one of them sorry-ass Negroes, baby, promising folks the sky and the moon. Keep your word and God'll keep you.

Admittedly, Isaiah hadn't been concerned much about God lately, but it seemed Mama was right. A week ago his plan appeared to have fallen apart. But he'd gotten away. He'd found a safe refuge. He'd pulled himself together.

And he'd gotten in his father's shit for real this time, no more fucking around with Gabriel. He despised the golden boy and had wanted to make his life miserable, but his real beef was with Pops, and he couldn't get sidetracked anymore.

Although the curtain hanging behind Isaiah's seat had made the rearview mirror useless, Isaiah glanced at it out of habit—and almost swerved and hit a car in the next lane when he saw who was staring at him.

Gabriel.

The weird psychic connection of theirs that had been dormant for the past week had returned.

Gabriel was driving, too. Worry spun through Isaiah's mind. Was Gabriel following him? Did Gabriel know where he was going? How could he know?

Isaiah checked the side mirrors but he didn't see a Corvette—the last vehicle he'd seen Gabriel driving—on his tail.

He returned his attention to the rearview. Gabriel looked upward, presumably into his own mirror, and spotted Isaiah. His eyes glared hatefully.

Isaiah flipped him the bird.

Gabriel looked away at something out of sight. A few seconds later he put a cell phone against his ear.

Isaiah's cell phone beeped. He answered it.

"I see you, little brother," Isaiah said. "I'd say you were ugly if we didn't look so much alike."

"You'd better not hurt Pops," Gabriel said. "If you lay a hand on him, I'll kill you."

"Pops and I have some personal business to discuss. It has nothing to do with you. Stay home with your girlfriend and mind your business."

In the mirror, Gabriel's jaws bulged with anger. "I'm warning you."

"You're warning me? What? You spoiled motherfucker . . ."

Isaiah veered off the highway onto the shoulder of the road, the tires spitting up gravel and mud. Holding his cell phone in one hand, he grabbed the rearview mirror with his other. He ripped the mirror away from its base, plastic snapping.

He flung aside the makeshift curtain. Pops lay on the floor, eyes panicked. Sweat glistened on his face.

Isaiah flipped open a tackle box. He removed a hook and a pair of pliers.

Pops watched him, terrified. Gabriel was shouting at him, tinny voice barking from the phone. His face swam crazily in the mirror.

Isaiah knelt over his father. Pops screamed against the tape gag, attempted to roll away. Isaiah braced him between his knees. He threw the cell on the floor nearby.

"I know you can see me," Isaiah shouted in the direction of the phone. "Watch this."

He yanked away the duct tape from his father's lips.

"Please," Pops said. "Don't hurt me, I'm sorry, please . . ."

He clamped the pliers over Pops's bottom lip. Pops emitted a distorted shriek, his tongue squirming like an earthworm, his teeth clacking together.

Peeling down Pops's lip, Isaiah sank the hook deep into the flesh, driving the metal all the way through until the tip broke the skin on the other side.

Pops was screaming, beating his legs against the floor. Warm blood flowed.

Carefully—almost tenderly—Isaiah taped his lips shut again.

Pops's eyes had rolled back to reveal the whites. A pinkish mixture of saliva and blood dripped from the edges of the duct tape.

Isaiah looked in the rearview mirror. The color appeared to have drained from Gabriel's face, and he had fallen quiet.

Isaiah picked up the phone.

"Warn me again, all right?" Isaiah said. "Go ahead. I'm listening."

Gabriel was silent.

"That's what I thought," Isaiah said. "Stay the fuck out of my business. And you better not call the cops. If I so much as smell a cop on my ass, Pops is gonna be cruisin' in that big Cadillac in the sky. Hear me?"

Chapter 56

Via the mirror, Gabriel saw everything Isaiah did to his father. He was so sickened that his stomach heaved, threatening to regurgitate the dinner he'd eaten less than an hour prior. He pulled over to the shoulder of the road to calm his nerves.

Lightning opened a rupture in the bruised sky, and a riptide of thunder crashed across the land. Rain washed down the Xterra's windows, blurring the world beyond, and Gabriel wished he could be washed away, too, carried to a better place where he would not have to deal with a psychopath like Isaiah. Seeing Isaiah torture his father had shaken him to the marrow.

Gabriel looked at the shotgun on the floor beside him. He felt like a fool. Hunting deer and quail was one thing; hunting a man was something altogether different and required more fortitude than he possessed.

What did he know about murder? Isaiah had *killed* people. He was a hardened criminal and would slit someone's throat as casually as he would shake his hand.

Nothing in Gabriel's background had prepared him for

this. He'd had a privileged childhood, had gone to Jack & Jill summer camps, top-flight private schools, and ski trips to Vail with college friends. He was a buppie, his survival instincts softened by dinners in posh restaurants, nights at the theater, cocktail hours with buppies like him, wine tastings, museum openings, golf outings, and jazz festivals. He was a man of culture and creature comforts, a businessman, an intellectual. He wasn't a fighter. Wasn't a killer.

He had to admit the truth: maybe he couldn't save his father. Isaiah had taken this situation to an unprecedented level of violence and terror, and Gabriel couldn't go there with him.

Massaging the bridge of his nose, he contemplated his cell phone. It was time to call the police. The professionals.

If I so much as smell a cop on my ass, Pops is gonna be cruisin' in that big Cadillac in the sky.

Isaiah had warned him about involving the police, and Gabriel believed he meant what he'd said. But what was his alternative?

As he considered what he would say to the police, the phone rang.

"Gabriel," Mom said. Her voice was firm. "Where are you?"

"I'm on 285. I pulled over to the side of the road for a little while."

"Why are you sitting on your behind? You said you were going to help your father."

Gabriel paused. "Mom, I think I'd be better off calling the police."

"You said you were going to bring your father back. Alive. You promised me."

"Mom, I . . ." He wiped his sweat-filmed forehead. "Listen, I'll just call the cops, okay?"

"You're giving up?"

"I didn't say that. You don't understand how dangerous Isaiah is, Mom. You have no idea."

Mom was quiet.

"You're right," she said. "Isaiah *is* dangerous. But I don't want anyone to get hurt, including your brother—but especially your father. If we call the police, Lord only knows what might happen to our family."

Gabriel mulled over her words. Although Isaiah was out of control, he was still family. Their flesh and blood. And though he had caused a lot of harm to them, Gabriel didn't really want to kill him. He wanted to get him away from his father, yes, and put him in prison for a long time, surely. But he didn't want to kill him. Killing him would be an absolute last resort.

He doubted the police would be as sympathetic. What was Isaiah to them? He was just another troublesome felon on the run from the law, who'd humiliated them by managing to elude capture for a week now. If Isaiah resisted arrest—and his volatile behavior suggested he would—it was almost a certainty that they would gun him down.

And Pops might die in the crossfire. It was the classic hostage situation that had filled a hundred Hollywood action movies.

If I so much as smell a cop on my ass . . .

He hadn't told Mom about Isaiah's threat, but as she often did, she had an intuitive understanding of what was at stake.

"You're right," Gabriel said. "We can't risk calling the police."

"Thank the Lord you understand." Mom expelled a heavy sigh. "Where is Isaiah taking your father? Do you know?"

"He's going to the cabin."

"Do you know how to get there?"

"You know I do."

"Then what are you waiting for?"

Gabriel had to smile. He had never loved his mother more than he did at that moment. She'd given him just the proper dose of tough love to kick his ass in gear again.

"Thanks, Mom. Tell Dana I love her."

"You'll tell her yourself when you and your father get home safely," she said. "We're praying for you, baby."

"I appreciate that." Gabriel's gaze fell on the shotgun. "I'm going to need it."

Chapter 57

Upon leaving the Georgia Mountain Parkway, Isaiah took a series of winding roads that carried him deeper into dense forest land. The storm clouds looked as though they had merged with the peaks of the mountain range, creating a womb of blackness.

He took a right turn onto a maple-shrouded, gravel driveway. A spacious log cabin with a wraparound porch stood at the end of a long, curving path: Pops's mountain home.

How many black men owned a crib in the mountains, of all places? You knew you had money to burn when you could afford some shit like this.

Isaiah had parked his Chevelle on the side of the cabin, underneath the boughs of a tree; the vehicle concealed it beneath a black car cover. Even though he'd been on the run, there was no way he was going to give up that whip. Purchased with money and credit he had stolen from Gabriel, it was like the spoils of war he read about in military history books.

He parked the van at the end of the driveway. He shut off the engine.

Behind him, Pops groaned. The old man's joints, bounced about by the rough ride, were likely as stiff as the wood of the cabin walls.

Isaiah pulled his Glock out of his hip holster. He climbed out of the van. Rain drizzled onto the canopy of trees, cold droplets running off the leaves and spattering his head. He turned his face skyward, parted his lips, and flicked out his tongue to sample a raindrop—something he loved to do as a kid—and got a thrill of pleasure from the sweet, woodsy taste.

Where he'd grown up in the hood, the rain had tasted like acid and pain.

As raindrops trickled down his cheeks, he looked around. Although other homes occupied these mountains, the cabin stood alone, smack dab in the middle of several picturesque acres of maples, elms, and pine. Other than the patter of the rain and the distant gurgle of thunder, the woods were completely quiet.

He walked around the perimeter of the house, checking for footprints in the mud, tamped-down grass, snapped branches, discarded cigarette butts, and other signs of intruders. The cops might be on to him, and he could ill afford to get careless, especially now, when he was so close to finishing.

He circled the entire cabin. Nothing was out of place.

Satisfied, he unlocked the front door. He stepped inside, holding the Glock with the muzzle aimed at the ceiling, finger on the trigger.

Weak gray light filtered through the partly opened wooden blinds but left much of the interior swathed in shadows. He tapped a wall switch, flooding the room with light from an ornate ceiling fan. The living room, kitchen, and dining area were empty, surfaces clean and devoid of clutter. The scent of lemon disinfectant hung in the cool air.

He moved into the short hallway and glanced in the three bedrooms. Vacant.

He walked inside the bedroom at the end of the hallway, went to the bed, and pulled up the bed skirt. His luggage lay exactly where he'd left it, hidden underneath.

He was safe. No one knew he was here.

His plan had worked perfectly.

He'd seen a talk show on TV, years ago, about teenagers who were drug addicts in spite of their parents' best efforts to convince them to just say no, and he remembered the story of a particularly clever white boy who used to hide his drugs in his parents' bedroom. In his parents' bedroom! Who would've thunk it?

Isaiah had been hiding out at the cabin all week. They had flashed his mug all over TV and the newspapers, but no one had ever thought to look for him at one of Pops's area properties. It was a childishly simple idea, and that was why it had worked.

Still, he had to take precautions. Gabriel, with their mysterious mirror-link thing, might have figured out where he was hiding and be stupid and send the po-po after him, in spite of Isaiah's warning.

The house, however, appeared to have been untouched since he'd left that morning. Holstering the gun, he returned to the van and slid open the side door.

Pops lay on his shoulder, facing the doorway. The blood streaming from his wounded lip had dyed his goatee a deep crimson.

Pops's gaze zeroed in on Isaiah's Glock.

"This isn't for you, Pops," Isaiah said. Relief passed over Pops's face. Isaiah added, "But it's for anyone who tries to stop me from doing what I want to do with you."

Screws of fear tightened Pops's face.

Isaiah hopped into the van. He gripped the edge of the duct tape covering his father's mouth and ripped it away, a fleshy, tearing sound.

Pops bleated like a kicked pig.

The fishhook hung from his bottom lip like a crude tribal

piercing, dried blood congealing on the tip. His lip was swollen to an almost comical degree and beginning to turn purple.

Isaiah roughly yanked the hook out of his father's lip. Pops cried out.

"Be glad I didn't tear your lip to shreds with this thing," Isaiah said. He tossed the hook toward the back of the van. Fresh blood had begun to seep from his father's wound.

"Please, son," Pops said. His voice was slurred, ragged. "I'll do anything you want, pay you any money you want, just tell me what it is you want me to do."

"Right now I want you to shut up. We'll get settled first, then talk. Cool?"

Without waiting for an agreement, Isaiah flipped his father onto his stomach. He removed a knife from a sheath he wore strapped to his calf. He cut the ropes binding his father's wrists and then freed his ankles.

"Get up," Isaiah said. He kicked his father's thigh with his Timberland. "Don't even think about running either, lest you wanna make my day. I'm like Dirty Harry with this motherfucker." He slipped the gun out of the holster and made a show of aiming it.

Pops slowly sat up, swinging his legs over the side of the van. He rubbed his bruised wrists tenderly and then touched his lip. A grimace contorted his face.

Isaiah jumped onto the driveway. "Let's go. We're heading inside."

Moving like a much older man, Pops slid off the van's floor and stood. Hunched over, he looked at the house in front of them.

"How'd you know about this place?" Pops asked.

"Research, Pops," he said. "You think I came to you not knowing anything about you and what you had? If you spend a little money, you can get all the dirt you want on somebody. And if you'd checked up on me, you would've known better than to let me into the family."

Humiliation reddened Pops's face. He was a proud man, and the most difficult thing for a proud man to accept was that he had made a foolish, easily preventable mistake.

Isaiah poked the Glock's snub-nosed muzzle into the small of Pops's back.

"Go on in," Isaiah said.

Pops trudged toward the house, dragging his feet as though they were weighed down with sandbags. Isaiah opened the front door and nudged his father inside.

"This way," Isaiah said. He directed his father down the hallway into one of the bedrooms.

It was a small, squarish room with ivory walls and a hardwood floor. Isaiah had shuttered the two windows that normally overlooked the forest beyond. He flicked a switch, releasing harsh white light from a conical ceiling fixture.

When Isaiah had arrived at the cabin, a twin bed had occupied the room, along with a wooden dresser and a desk. In preparation for Pops's visit, he had removed all the furniture, stacking the pieces in another bedroom. A wooden chair was one of only two items in the room. It sat in the center under the light, like a display in a museum of torture.

The other thing in there was a red toolbox, lying in the corner.

"What's this?" Pops asked. "I thought you wanted to go fishing."

Isaiah barked a laugh. "Come on, man. I put some poles and tackle in the van, stuff I found in the shed up here, but I was only fooling. I don't give a damn about fishing with you. The time for that happy father-son shit has long since passed."

"Then why'd you bring me here?" Pops warily eyed the chair.

"I'm going to kill you," Isaiah said. "But first I'm going to make you suffer for a while. Mama and I suffered for thirty years, you know. Least I can do is torture you for a few hours before I put you out of your misery. Mama would say that's fair, don't you think?"

Chapter 58

Sitting in his jeep on the shoulder of the highway, Gabriel learned how to turn off his psychic connection to Isaiah. It was too distracting and troubling to see Isaiah's crazed face every time he glanced in the rearview mirror. Closing his eyes, Gabriel counted to ten, telling himself that when he reached ten, he did not want to see Isaiah's face in the glass.

At the end of his count, he checked in the rearview. Isaiah had vanished.

He felt a sense of satisfaction. He was learning how to control his talents, or whatever you wanted to call them. It would be crucial for later.

He started driving again. The rain continued to fall, but it had slackened to a persistent drizzle, which meant that the Atlanta drivers once again felt safe barreling down the slick highway at the speed of sound. Gabriel stayed in a middle lane and drove at a moderate speed. He couldn't save his father if he died in a car wreck on the way there.

And what was he going to do when he arrived at the cabin? March to the front door and demand that Isaiah release Pops? Conduct surveillance from the forest and wait for a chance to make a move? Kick down the door and attack Isaiah?

He didn't have any training in this sort of thing. He had no idea what his next step would be.

He took I-75 to I-575, which became the Georgia Mountain Parkway. After an hour of driving on the highway, he reached the exit for the cabin.

He turned into the parking lot of a gas station and parked in the far corner.

Closing his eyes, he drew deep breaths. Then he opened his eyes and studied the rearview mirror, which, at present, gave him a view of a rain-smeared phone booth behind him.

Show me Isaiah, he thought. *I want to see him now.*

Fog curled and twisted across the mirror's surface as though it were a fortune-teller's misty crystal ball teeming with visions.

Slowly, Isaiah materialized in the murkiness.

Isaiah stood in a small bright room. A man sat in front of him; ropes bound the man to the chair. Shoulders slumped, the prisoner shook his head from side to side, as though in severe discomfort.

Gabriel recognized the man from the back of his head. It was Pops.

Isaiah was speaking, but Gabriel was unable to read his lips. Isaiah wore a snide expression.

I've seen enough, Gabriel thought. *No more.*

The vision faded.

He'd learned what he wanted to know. Pops was still alive.

But time was running out.

Chapter 59

Roped to a hard chair, a hot white light bulb above him searing his eyeballs, Theo, pushed to the boundaries of his sanity, tried to talk sense to his son in hopes of convincing him to set him free. Theo had led countless sales meetings in his career, had employed his golden tongue to coax hundreds of millions of dollars out of the accounts of multinational corporations and into his own coffers, had used his gift of gab to catapult himself from poverty to prominence—but all those experiences paled in importance to this one.

For the first time, he was talking to, quite literally, save his life.

Sweat poured from his face and armpits, ran cold down his back. He had perspired so much in the past couple of hours that he was certain he was dehydrated. His lip throbbed painfully; drool inched down his chin, too and—though it embarrassed him, made him feel like a demented old fool—he was helpless to stop it.

Indeed it was a struggle just to stay coherent. But he hadn't forgotten Isaiah's promise of torture, and averted his gaze from the red toolbox sitting in the corner. He didn't want to know what terrible instruments it might contain.

Listening to Theo's plea, Isaiah paced back and forth in front of him, his boots creaking across the floorboards. He had put away the gun. He held Theo's Rolex in his right hand and gently fingered the band. His actions perplexed Theo, but, then again, Isaiah was not exactly dealing with a full deck. His boy was crazy as a wood lizard, as Theo's mother liked to say.

Nevertheless, he had to talk him out of this.

"You're a smart young man," Theo was saying. "You've got your entire life ahead of you. You don't need to ruin it by doing something like this. I . . . I can help you, son. Since you came to me, I've been trying to help you."

"Who said I want your help?" Isaiah said. "When Mama and I needed you, you weren't there. It's too late to be offering help now. We're past that shit."

"It's never too late to change course. Did I ever tell you about one of my VPs? Thomas Robinson. He didn't graduate from college until he was thirty-five, went and got his MBA, and didn't show up at our office until he was forty-one, and he has one of the sharpest business minds I've ever—"

"I don't want to hear one of your rags-to-riches stories, all right? None of that pull-yourself-up-by-your-bootstraps bullshit! You ain't Booker T. Washington, man." He glared angrily at Theo.

"No, I'm not," Theo said softly. "But I know your potential. You can do great things, can accomplish something wonderful. When I look at you, I see a diamond in the rough. All you need is a little polish, a little time, and the world can be your oyster."

"My oyster?" Isaiah scowled. "I hate oysters. Damn things taste like snot."

"Bad analogy." Theo thought quickly. "The world can be

like that Chevelle of yours. You can drive it wherever you want. All you need to learn are the rules of the road."

"Like my Chevelle?" Isaiah smirked, but something in his eyes seemed to stir. He looked away.

Theo's heart picked up speed. He dared to hope that he was touching a sympathetic nerve.

Isaiah slipped the Rolex on his wrist. He admired it as though imagining what it would be like if he'd purchased the luxury watch on his own with legitimately earned money.

"The world can be yours," Theo said.

"Give me a motherfucking break, Pops. It's too late for me." Isaiah threw the watch across the room. Wiping his eyes, Isaiah went to one of the windows and peered through the blinds. His shoulders trembled.

I've gotten through to him, Theo thought. *Now if I can talk him down, maybe I can convince him to let me out of here.*

"All yours," Theo said, close to a whisper. "I can help you. It's my duty to you, as your father, to help you reach your fullest potential. I'm sorry it's taken so long for me to say this, but I'd like for you to accept my offer."

Isaiah didn't respond. He rubbed his chin.

"Son?" Theo asked, worry creeping into his voice. Isaiah's mood had changed.

Isaiah turned away from the window and strolled to the corner. He retrieved the watch from the floor. Dusting it off, he grasped it in one hand, running his fingers across the crystal face.

"I don't want to talk about this anymore," Isaiah said. "Why don't you talk to Mama?"

"Huh?" His son had truly gone off the deep end. Naomi, may she rest in peace, had been murdered months ago— ironically, in a gunfight that Isaiah had likely provoked.

Then a voice from the grave spoke from behind Theo.

"Hey, baby. Did you miss me?"

An icy wind seemed to blow through the room.

Shuddering, Theo looked over his shoulder.

Naomi Battle, resplendent in her youth and beauty, smiled at him.

Chapter 60

Cruising slowly on the curving mountain lane, Gabriel passed by the mouth of the driveway that led to the cabin.

He saw, through the dripping trees and shrubs, a white van parked in front of the house. Electric light, mostly masked by blinds, glimmered from one of the bedroom windows.

Isaiah and Pops were still in there.

Rolling past the driveway, he pulled to the muddy shoulder of the road. He parked far out of view of the house, under the wide arms of an elm. He hoped that he had the element of surprise on his side; he couldn't risk Isaiah checking out the window and seeing his jeep.

Gabriel turned off the engine. He looked at the shotgun on the floor beside him.

This was the point of no return. Once he climbed out of the Xterra, he couldn't turn back—not without forever seeing a coward when he looked in the mirror.

He took Dana's makeup compact out of his vest pocket. He passed it underneath his nose. Her sweet scent clung to it, making his pulse run faster.

He prayed that he would see Dana again.

He snapped open the case to reveal the small mirror. He had turned off his link with Isaiah, so he saw only his own face reflected in the glass. But he wondered if Isaiah had psychically tuned in to him, saw him sitting there in the jeep, and was prepared to tangle.

It was a risk he had to take.

As tongues of lightning tasted the fringes of the mountains, Gabriel slipped the compact into his pocket, grabbed the Mossberg by its sling, and opened the door.

The rain had subsided to a slow drizzle. But the sky, swollen with thunderclouds, kept a lid of premature darkness on the day. That might be to his advantage.

He quietly closed the door. The soft *thunk* still seemed loud to him.

No other vehicles or people were on the road. He might have been the only man alive.

He pulled an Atlanta Braves cap low on his head, went to the back of the jeep, and opened the trunk.

The cargo area contained a bag of brand-new golf balls and a set of clubs. He'd been keeping them in there in anticipation of playing golf with Pops sometime soon.

He loaded his pockets with several golf balls and then closed the cargo door.

Crouching, he crept into the woods on the same side of the road as the cabin. The forest was thick, damp, and fragrant. Armadas of bugs buzzed around him, bombarding his face, and he swatted them away from his eyes and slogged forward. He headed in a direction that would carry him toward the side of the cabin that housed the lit bedroom.

During the last leg of his drive Gabriel had hatched a plan of attack. His ultimate goal was to rescue Pops without risking his father's life. His best chance of accomplishing that objective was to draw Isaiah out of the cabin. It meant that he and Isaiah would have a showdown in the forest.

He couldn't think of anything else. If he attacked Isaiah

while he was inside, Isaiah could hole up in a room and use Pops as a hostage. The crazy asshole already had demonstrated that he was willing to hurt Pops to make a point. He had to get Isaiah out of the cabin. Only then would he be able to deal with him.

He didn't want to kill Isaiah. He just wanted to slow him down, disable him, perhaps. If he could shoot Isaiah in the leg, or blast Dana's pepper spray in Isaiah's eyes, it would incapacitate Isaiah sufficiently for Gabriel to assume control of the situation.

Branches snapped beneath his shoes. He cursed under his breath. He didn't want to make any sounds that would alert Isaiah to his presence before he wanted to make himself known. He advanced more carefully, placing each footstep with maximum stealth.

Through the trees and shrubs, the cabin came into view. He glimpsed the twinkling light in the bedroom.

What was Isaiah doing in there, anyway? Was Pops okay? Alive?

Gabriel's anxiety prevailed. He slipped the makeup compact out of his pocket, snapped it open, and gazed into the mirror.

I want to see Isaiah. . . .

Chapter 61

*"**D**id you miss me, baby?"*

Naomi, looking as beautiful and youthful as when Theo had first met her thirty-some years ago, seductively wrapped her lithe arms around his neck. She slithered onto his lap. She wore a tight-fitting black dress as though ready for a night on the town.

"Huh?" Theo blinked rapidly and repeatedly. *Naomi is dead.* How could he be seeing her so young and alive?

She even smelled like he remembered from his youth. She wore a spicy fragrance, like jasmine.

Isaiah must have slipped him some kind of hallucinogen, though Theo didn't recall Isaiah puncturing him with a syringe or feeding him anything. But a drug was the only explanation. Naomi could not possibly be real.

However, he felt her weight on his lap, felt a feathery, tickling sensation as she traced her fingers across the back of his neck, could feel even her warm, minty breath on his face.

She was so real that he'd forgotten all about Isaiah. The boy had retreated to the shadowed corners of the room, Theo's Rolex glinting in his hand.

"Talk to me," Naomi said in the low, throaty voice that had seduced him the first time he'd met her. "Ain't you got something to tell me after all these years?"

Although Theo worried that talking to this illusion would give it an even firmer toehold in his mind, he found his lips forming words.

"I . . . I don't know what to say," he said. "You look so . . . so young."

Her smile bent into a frown. "That all you got to say to me? After what you did?"

His heart slammed.

Naomi dug her fingers into the meat of his neck. Her nails felt like talons. Pain sizzled down his spine and fanned through his shoulder blades.

"Ain't you gonna apologize to me?" she asked. "Don't you know what you did to me and my baby, you sorry nigga?"

"I was married!" Theo shouted. "You knew that when you met me. I told you from the beginning that we could never have a life together."

"But you left us. You living the good life down in Atlanta, kicking up your heels with your family, and we was starving. We might as well been dead to you."

"That's not true," he said.

She rose off his lap. She brushed off her dress as though being close to him had soiled her.

"Ain't no excuse for what you did," she said. "You wear them nice suits and use big words, but you just like all the other ones. A low-down, dirty dog."

He couldn't argue with her. In fact, he shouldn't argue with her. She wasn't real. In essence, he was arguing with his own guilty conscience.

"My baby here, he all growed up now." She smiled with pride. "You left him, but he made it. My baby's a survivor."

"I want to help him," Theo said. "He's lost his way, and I take the blame for that. I want to help steer him in the right direction."

Naomi sneered. "He don't want that. He came to take care of your sorry black ass. He promised me he would."

"Before you were gunned down—a situation you were dragged into because of him?"

"Fuck you!" Isaiah exploded out of the shadows. "I didn't kill Mama. You did!"

Naomi vanished as quickly as an image cast by a film projector. One moment she was there, fuming; the next heartbeat, she was gone.

Isaiah thundered forward.

"I didn't mean that," Theo said. "I shouldn't have said that, I'm sorry—"

Isaiah punched him in the face. Theo's head rocked sideways and he tipped backward in the chair. The chair lost its balance and he crashed against the floor, landing hard on his shoulder, agony biting deep into his body.

Salty blood flooded his mouth, clogged his windpipe. He spat it out, sucked in a gasp of air.

Isaiah leveled the gun at Theo's head.

"Don't you ever say that again," Isaiah said.

Theo spluttered. "I'm sorry."

Glaring at him, Isaiah turned and walked to the toolbox in the corner. He dug inside.

Whatever he was getting out of there, it would mean trouble for him, Theo thought. A minute ago his heart hadn't seemed capable of beating any faster—but now it whammed against his rib cage at a more frenzied rate than ever.

Isaiah returned. Theo squinted at the small, pistol-like device in his son's hands. Was that a . . .

"Taser gun," Isaiah said. "You ready for fifty thousand volts of electricity to snap, crackle, and pop through those wrinkled veins of yours?"

"Don't continue this." Theo was panting. "Whatever lesson you're aiming to teach me, I've learned, I swear it."

"I'm not trying to teach you anything. I'm doing this because I want to see you in pain. This is punishment for what you did to us."

"Please, no—"

Isaiah pulled the trigger. Two probes, trailed by wires, zipped from the gun's muzzle and hooked on the front of Theo's shirt.

And then the agony began.

Chapter 62

Gazing into the makeup compact's mirror, Gabriel had once again seen enough.

He closed the mirror with a loud clap and stuffed it into his pocket. Pops had made some terrible mistakes, had mistreated Isaiah, but he didn't deserve to be punished like this. Isaiah had gone way too far.

Adrenaline flooded Gabriel's bloodstream, tightening his muscles, quickening his pulse. He was thankful that he hadn't called the police.

Because he wanted to handle Isaiah himself.

Power popped across his hands. But there would be no need to use his talent against Isaiah. Instead, he double-checked that the shotgun was loaded and ready to fire. He had not fired the gun since last fall during a hunting trip with Pops and some family friends, but he was a good shot, with reliable aim from a respectable distance.

Gabriel scrambled through the wet, clotted underbrush. As he drew closer to the cabin, moving in a circle around the perimeter of the property, thunder bellowed through the woods, the rumble echoing Gabriel's booming heartbeat.

He found a spot to hide. Near an immense pine tree, about twenty yards or so from the cabin's front door. Hunched between the pine and a thick grove of shrubs, he had a line of sight to the porch and a partial view of the bedroom in which Isaiah was performing his sick deeds.

Now he had to draw Isaiah outside.

He dipped his hand into his pocket and grasped a golf ball. Focusing on one of the front windows, he flung the ball toward it.

The ball fell several feet short of the window, bouncing into a heap of leaves and twigs beside the porch steps.

He fished another ball out of his pocket. He threw it.

The ball hit the window with a loud *crack!*

That'll bring the asshole out of there.

Gabriel lifted the Mossberg to his shoulder, slid his finger to the trigger, and waited.

Chapter 63

Crack!
Isaiah was in the bedroom standing over his father, who twitched on the floor like a crack head suffering a serious jones, when the noise rang out from the front of the cabin.

"What the fuck was that?" he asked no one in particular. It sounded as though someone had broken a window with a rock.

He retracted the Taser's electrodes. His eyes rolling drunkenly, saliva foaming from his mouth, teeth locked in a grimace, Pops's limbs continued to spasm. He'd been thrashing so hard that he'd loosened the ropes that bound his ankles and wrists to the chair.

Isaiah hated to be distracted from his quality time with his dad. But he had to investigate the noise. It could be the police. Or Gabriel.

Whoever it was, God help them. Isaiah was in no mood for nonsense.

Turning from his father, Isaiah went to the toolbox and dropped the Taser inside. He retrieved the Glock, ensured that it was loaded, and jammed another magazine in his pocket. He headed toward the doorway.

"Be back soon, Pops," he said. "Sit tight."

But Pops was unconscious, a puddle of spit spreading on the floor underneath his head.

Isaiah's suspicions were correct: one of the living room windows was cracked. A spiderweb of fractures spread outward from a small rupture in the glass.

Someone had done this deliberately. It could have been a bunch of kids playing pranks, but he doubted it. He'd been living in the cabin for a week and he'd seen fewer than a dozen people moving around the mountain paths near the house, and none of them had been children.

Intuition told him that Gabriel was responsible.

Isaiah moved down the short hallway to the bathroom. He popped inside and looked at the mirror.

At first he saw only his own reflection. Then he concentrated on seeing Gabriel, thinking maybe he could summon the vision on demand.

Several seconds later he was rewarded with a clear view of little brother.

Gabriel was hunkered between a tree and some shrubs. Dressed in a camouflage vest like a black Rambo, he had balanced a shotgun on his shoulder.

"You must think I'm stupid," Isaiah whispered. "Think I'm gonna walk outside to check out the window so you can pop me? You gotta be better than that to smoke the kid."

But he had to give it to Gabriel. His little brother had balls, coming up here like this, all alone. It was stupid, but brave. Isaiah could respect him for that.

All the same, he had to take care of Gabriel once and for all. It was time to show little brother what the real world was all about.

Isaiah smashed the butt of the Glock against the mirror. Shards fell away from the frame and clinked into the sink.

Being careful not to cut himself, he picked up a crescent-shaped sliver of mirror. It would help him keep tabs on Gabriel.

He darted into the kitchen. At the far end of the room, a door gave access to the backyard.

Isaiah opened the door and slinked outside.

Chapter 64

Hidden between the pine and the bushes, shotgun held at the ready, Gabriel waited for Isaiah to emerge from the front door.

About a minute or so after he threw the ball, he saw a faint shadow move behind the broken window—as though Isaiah was assessing the damage—and he tensed his trigger finger, expecting Isaiah to storm onto the porch, a perfect target. But after another minute, nothing had happened.

"Damn," Gabriel said. "He knows something's up."

He fumbled out the makeup compact. Focused on seeing Isaiah in the mirror.

"Shit."

Isaiah was no longer in the house.

He was outside. Creeping through the forest.

He'd seen through Gabriel's lame ploy and had flipped the script. Gabriel looked closely in the mirror and thought he saw Isaiah carrying a jagged mirror in one hand, too.

Damn it! I underestimated him.

In Isaiah's other hand, he gripped a mean-looking pistol.

From what Gabriel saw, he was unable to determine from

exactly where Isaiah was walking, or where he was going. He could be twenty feet away, sneaking up on him. Or in the woods on the other side of the driveway.

Gabriel whirled around.

The only noises were the drizzling of rain against leaves and brush, the soft sigh of the wind, and his own frantic breathing.

Where was Isaiah?

Gabriel glanced in the mirror, hoping to catch a clue.

Gunfire rang out. Splinters exploded from the pine tree beside him.

Gabriel took off running.

Chapter 65

Theo woke up—and immediately wished he hadn't. He was in a universe of torment.

His muscles felt as though they had been shredded in a blender. His jaws ached from clenching his teeth. Even his eyes hurt; they felt puffy and tender.

He couldn't believe that Isaiah, his own son, had done this to him. The boy didn't possess an atom of compassion. He was singularly cruel.

For the moment, Isaiah appeared to be gone. Theo vaguely recalled having heard Isaiah leave the bedroom. He didn't know how long ago that had happened. Pain had warped his sense of time.

But Isaiah wasn't finished with him. He'd promised to kill Theo, and Theo fully believed that his son would make good on his threat. Theo had tried to talk reasonably to him, but he now realized that was a lost cause. Isaiah was a pure psychopath, beyond the reach of logic and fundamental morality.

What was Naomi? Had his encounter with her all been a dream? He wasn't sure. Nothing that had happened felt real since Isaiah had captured him in the basement at home. This entire experience was like the most vivid nightmare Theo had ever had in his life.

The cabin was mostly silent. Rain ticked on the roof and against the windows. But he didn't hear Isaiah moving around in another section of the house. Maybe he had ventured outdoors for some reason.

Theo had to get the hell out of there while he had a chance.

He lay on his side on the hardwood floor, his limbs strapped to the chair. The mere thought of moving sharpened his pain. But he had to try. He was certain Isaiah had stored more implements of torture in the toolbox and he didn't want to be around to give him another opportunity to use them.

He tested the strength of the ropes. They had loosened, probably due to his wild flailing when he was being shocked, but there wasn't enough give in the knots for him to work free.

He craned his head to look behind him. Pain lanced into his neck and he gasped, nearly blacked out. He maintained his tenuous hold on consciousness only by sheer force of will—the same iron will that had enabled him to rise from a roach-infested shotgun shack in east Texas to a mansion in Atlanta.

He spotted the toolbox in the corner, perhaps ten feet away. The lid was open, but he couldn't see inside.

He wondered if there was a knife in there. Something he could use to cut himself free.

He gritted his teeth against the expected pain. Then he began to wriggle across the floor.

Chapter 66

Gabriel fled through the woods.

He believed the gunfire had come from somewhere near the cabin, so he did the logical thing and ran away from the house, delving deeper into the forest. He had explored these woods many times over the years, knew them as well as he knew the lines of his own face. But in his frenzied state, he might as well have been running blind through a blackened room. He was completely disoriented, thinking only about survival.

He ran hard, the shotgun on the sling jouncing hard against his ribs. A mist of buzzing insects obscured his vision and clotted his nostrils and he quickly raked his hand down his face.

The rain had abated but the day had grown darker and every patch of darkness seemed to conceal a threat; he imagined a hundred Isaiahs closing in on him, aiming for a fatal head shot.

If I can just get to the lake, Gabriel thought. *Then I can make a stand.*

The lake was—or should have been—not too far away. A few hundred yards. If he could reach it alive, he could take cover among the big rocks and clumps of dirt scattered along the shore and have a clear shot at Isaiah when he ran out of the woods.

But Gabriel had to get there first.

Isaiah's gun barked again. Gabriel turned, half expecting to catch a round in the head. But the bullet shaved bits off a tree several yards behind him.

He saw Isaiah back there, too, a dark shape lurking in the brush. But he saw him for only a microsecond, not long enough for Gabriel to get off a good shot. Isaiah weaved and bobbed like a boxer as he ran, making himself a difficult target.

He was so much better at this than Gabriel that Gabriel felt an onrush of anxiety that almost tangled his legs as effectively as a snarl of weeds.

I can do this, Gabriel told himself. *Just get to the lake before he does. Do that, and I'll have him in my sights.*

Gabriel's second wind arose and he hustled through the brush with increased speed.

The trees and shrubs began to thin. Ahead, at the bottom of a hill, he glimpsed the darkly rippling lake.

He lowered his head and willed all his remaining energy into his leg muscles.

As he burst out of the woods, Isaiah's gun boomed.

Pain tore into Gabriel's shoulder. He roared.

Oh, shit, I'm hit.

His body stunned, he lost his footing. He tumbled down the rocky embankment, rolling end over end.

Memories of his car accident flashed through his thoughts; hurtling through the guardrail and down the steep hill, bouncing around in the seat like a crash test dummy.

I'm gonna die this time. . . .

He banged onto the lake's shore, slamming against an outcropping of rock. Something in his pocket—had to be the makeup compact—crunched, and he thought of how angry Dana would be when she found out he'd broken it.

But as he raised his head, groggy, he found that he was in a far worse predicament.

He'd lost the shotgun somewhere along his tumble down the hill.

And a huge water moccasin lay coiled on the rocks, staring directly at him.

Chapter 67

As Gabriel ran out of the forest and into a clearing, Isaiah fired at him—and scored a hit.

Gotcha, little brother!

Struck in the shoulder, Gabriel whirled like a mad dervish, lost his balance, and fell down the slope beyond, plummeting out of sight.

Isaiah sprinted forward. Breaking out of the woods, he halted at the crest of the hill.

Gabriel's shotgun was snagged in a stand of weeds halfway down the embankment. Farther below, sprawled on the rocks near the lake, lay the golden boy himself. Gabriel was alert—and when Isaiah looked closer, he saw why. A water moccasin was on a nearby shelf of stone, within striking distance.

Isaiah grinned. The irony was delicious.

The snake was not an illusion; in his haste, Isaiah had not thought to bring Gabriel's pen and mess with the guy's mind. The reptile was real.

But would Gabriel realize that?

If the water moccasin did not finish off Gabriel, Isaiah would.

Isaiah checked his Glock, verified that he had a few rounds remaining. Then he began to walk down the hill, taking his sweet time, savoring the thrill of final victory.

Chapter 68

Gabriel heard Isaiah at the top of the ridge. But he didn't look at him.

He didn't dare take his attention away from the water moccasin. The snake watched him with its evil, slitted eyes. It flicked out its tongue, tasting the damp air.

He wondered if it could taste his blood in the air, too. Warm blood seeped from the shoulder wound, but the initial pain had faded. Had the bullet penetrated his flesh or merely grazed him? He wasn't sure.

The snake hissed.

Was the snake another illusion, engineered by Isaiah? Or was it real?

He didn't know the answer to those questions either. However, cottonmouth water moccasins were common in this wilderness. When a snake had bitten him several years ago, it had happened around the shores of this same lake.

Indecision had frozen him. He was afraid to move, for risk of upsetting the snake. But if he remained in place, the snake might bite him anyway.

He had to do something.

"This is gonna be interesting," Isaiah said above him. Slowly making his way down the slope, he glanced at the snake and laughed. "Talk about being stuck between a rock and a hard place, eh?"

A realization hit Gabriel like a kick in the stomach: the snake was real. Isaiah saw the creature, too, which wasn't the case with an illusion.

His terror hit a new, higher peak.

If the snake didn't strike, Isaiah was going to kill him. He had no way to defend himself.

Then he spotted the bottle of pepper spray. It had fallen out of his pocket and landed on the rocks, the cylinder partly concealed by the snake's tail.

He saw, about seven or eight feet away, a loose stone the size of a tennis ball.

As a plan stirred in his mind, his palms began to tingle.

The water moccasin, as if sensing his building energy, began to slither toward him. It hissed malevolently.

Immobilizing fear cramped Gabriel's stomach. He visualized the snake biting him in the throat, saw himself lying there, helpless, as deadly venom invaded his veins, and then Isaiah would stand over him and press the gun's cold muzzle against his forehead. . . .

No. I have to fight this, and I have to fight it now.

The snake rose.

Gabriel opened his right hand, which was angled toward the stone. He was right-handed and, thankfully, his right shoulder was unhurt.

Energy leaping across his palm, he concentrated on the stone.

As though catapulted from a slingshot, the rock darted into Gabriel's grasp. Springing upright, Gabriel lifted the stone high and brought it down on the water moccasin's head.

The snake's skull collapsed with an audible crunch. Its tail twitched like a live wire.

"Hey!" Isaiah closed in on Gabriel.

Gabriel thrust his hand underneath the writhing, dying reptile. He grabbed the pepper spray. Spun.

Isaiah started to raise the gun to shoot, but Gabriel was faster.

He fired a blast of pepper spray in Isaiah's face.

Chapter 69

In the bedroom, after an agonizing and seemingly interminable crawl-scoot journey across the floor, Theo finally reached the toolbox.

He laid there for a minute, taking in shallow, painful breaths. Every pressure point in his body pulsed as though he had been mashed in a giant sandwich press. Considering the fantastic stresses his body had endured in the past hour, it was a miracle he hadn't suffered a heart attack. Jogging three miles a day on a treadmill apparently had paid off.

He continued to listen for footsteps in the house. He heard only the dull patter of rain.

Isaiah had been away for several minutes. What was going on? Had someone come there to make a rescue attempt?

It was such an optimistic thought that Theo quickly put it away. He didn't want to give in to naive hope. He had to get out of this mess himself.

He twisted his neck, raised his head. Looked over the lip of the toolbox.

The box contained rope, a roll of duct tape, cotton rags, a

hammer, several long, glistening nails . . . and a utility knife with a retractable blade.

Hope—real hope—bloomed in Theo's chest.

The knife, the sharp blade jutting from the metal casing, lay atop the rope. Within reach.

But he didn't have use of his hands. That left only his teeth.

Stretching his head forward like a giraffe extending for a piece of fruit atop a tree, Theo moved his lips toward the knife. He clamped his teeth over the blunt end of the handle.

Got it.

He snapped his head sideways, flinging the tool to the floor. It landed less than a foot away.

Now for the hard part.

But, first, he waited perhaps ten seconds, panting, wrung out by the exertion.

The floorboards outside the bedroom creaked. He paused. Listening.

No one was in there. It was only the cabin making settling sounds, as older homes tended to do.

Back to work. Using his heels, he turned himself around, dragging the chair, positioning himself so that his hands, bound behind him, faced the utility knife. He wriggled his fingers, feeling for the blade. The tip of his index finger brushed against the metal, the sensation sending excitement coursing through him.

Stay cool, Theo. Focused. You haven't closed the deal yet.

His galloping heartbeat slowed.

He inched backward. Reached. Took hold of the knife.

And promptly dropped it. His fingers were sweaty, as though soaked in grease.

Concentrate.

He plucked the knife off the floor again. Held it tight.

And, after taking some time to level the blade firmly against the rope, he began cutting.

Chapter 70

White-hot tongues of fire attacked Isaiah's eyes, exploded up his nostrils, seared his lips. He couldn't see. Couldn't breathe. He could still hear—and all he heard was a terrible shrieking, more like an animal's cry than a man's.

It was coming from him.

Gabriel, that motherfucker, had sprayed him with mace or some shit like that, and it was the most incredible agony Isaiah had ever experienced in his life. Like sticking his head in a barbecue pit. It was worse than dying.

Although he was screaming, some deep instinct of his mind that was still plotting survival kept his grip fastened on the Glock. He charged forward, not sure where his legs were taking him—it was as though they functioned independently, commanded by the sheer drive to live—and when he felt cold water splashing across him, he was grateful. The lake. Of course. Water might counteract or shorten the incapacitating effects of the spray.

He dove in headfirst.

Chapter 71

As Isaiah howled and rushed into the lake, Gabriel scuttled up the hillside to retrieve the shotgun. Due to his rough fall, his muscles protested at the effort, each step bringing a fresh jolt of pain. But he pushed on. Isaiah was helpless for the time being, but Gabriel wasn't sure how long the pepper spray's effects would last. Isaiah had once averted a violent death; he would surely conquer the pepper spray, with perhaps superhuman vigor.

Gabriel wasn't feeling quite as heroic. His shoulder, still oozing blood, grew number by the minute, which made it difficult to raise his arm. And the blood loss was sapping his strength. If he did not get medical attention soon, he would be of no help to Pops at all—assuming he ever made it back to the cabin.

Behind him, Isaiah thrashed in the lake, shrieking. It was impossible to tell whether he was in pain or enraged. Probably both.

Gabriel ran harder.

The Mossberg was tangled in weeds. Gabriel grabbed the

gun. Raising it to his shoulder was like lifting a hundred-pound barbell. He almost fell underneath its weight.

He swiveled toward the lake, where Isaiah continued to flail. Although Gabriel used to believe in a crude code of honor, believing you had to look a man in the face as you shot him, he disregarded all those noble notions. This was a life-and-death struggle, past the time for any of that code-of-honor crap. Isaiah surely would not have paid him the same respect.

Gabriel fired at Isaiah.

Wings of water sprayed upward. Isaiah beat the surface once, with his hand—and then his movements ceased and he sank underwater.

"I got him," Gabriel said, unable to believe it.

Except for a few outward ripples, the aftereffects of Isaiah's desperate struggle, the waters had become tranquil once more.

He had killed Isaiah.

He dropped to his knees. He wanted to weep. But he was in too much pain to even cry.

He looked out to the lake. He expected to see Isaiah's corpse float to the surface. But it did not appear. His clothes could have become caught on rocks. Or . . .

Make sure he's dead, Gabriel.

That quiet voice of intuition, which had not steered him wrong yet forced him back to his feet. Drawing in heavy breaths, he trudged to the shore. He looked for Isaiah's corpse.

He did not see it.

Slinging the shotgun over his shoulder, he waded into the cold water. After a dozen footsteps, it was up to his waist. He saw dark material bobbing below the water's surface. He fished it out.

It was Isaiah's torn shirt.

But where was the rest of him?

Chapter 72

Isaiah was swimming.

He'd learned to swim as a child at the local YMCA on summer breaks from school. The big Olympic pool would be sparkling clean in the morning and polluted with piss by afternoon, the result of the bad-ass neighborhood kids who thought it was funny to urinate in the water. Those same knuckleheads, older than him, would throw him, screaming, into the deep end. He learned to swim under duress. For survival.

Just like now.

When Gabriel fired the shotgun at him, Isaiah immediately went under. The slug smashed into the water near him, narrowly missing his thigh. Still blinded by the pepper spray, knowing that Gabriel would keep shooting until he'd killed him, Isaiah tore off his shirt, dove deeper, and began to swim away in a direction he saw from memory, not from sight.

His lungs yearned for air, but he stayed underwater until he'd swum a good distance and then quickly poked his face above, pulled in a deep breath, and went under again.

As he swam, eyes open, his vision slowly returned. The water was murky, vegetation rippling like tentacles around him. Several fish peeled by, darting out of his path as though he were a great white shark, there to invade their peaceful habitat.

They could sense a predator.

Isaiah quietly broke the surface. Treading water, he looked around.

He wasn't far from the shore. Maybe twenty feet. Turning back, he saw Gabriel, far behind, wading in the water just offshore, searching the lake for Isaiah.

His little brother was a helluva lot tougher than he'd thought. The guy would not quit.

If their lives had turned out differently, if they had grown up together, they would've made quite a pair, would've terrorized the block. As it was, one of them was probably going to die before this was all over.

First Isaiah had to take care of his main responsibility: their father.

As stealthily as possible, he stroked back to land, where a rocky outcropping provided cover. He rose out of the water.

His eyes and nasal passages were clear of the pepper spray. He checked the Glock, which he had stuffed in his waistband. A few rounds left.

For Pops, he needed only one.

He ran into the woods. Back toward the cabin.

Chapter 73

Gabriel could not find Isaiah.

He'd swept through a section of the lake, perhaps twenty feet in diameter, and found only Isaiah's mangled shirt.

It didn't make any sense. He had shot Isaiah. Hadn't he?

He thought about what he'd seen.

He'd fired into the water directly at Isaiah. Isaiah had thrashed once and then the waters had calmed. Which meant Isaiah's corpse should be nearby.

Unless he had miraculously escaped. Eluded Death. Again.

But where had he gone?

Gabriel looked farther down the shore. He didn't see Isaiah.

He sloshed back to dry land. As he shuffled, the makeup compact crunched in his vest pocket. He pulled it out.

A jagged crack ran down the casing. Great. This was Dana's favorite compact. She'd be pissed.

He opened the compact. As he'd worried, the mirror was smashed to pieces. But one of the shards, perhaps an inch long, and shaped like a crescent moon, might be able to give him a look at Isaiah.

He concentrated.

He fully expected to see Isaiah in another region of the lake, a waterlogged corpse, eyes bloated and mouth hanging open.

But Isaiah was running, shirtless, through the forest. He had his gun. His face was drawn and resolute. He didn't appear to be wounded at all.

The cabin, Gabriel thought. *Pops.*

Gabriel looked to the peak of the hill and the wall of forest beyond.

His wounded left shoulder was completely numb. His left arm, which he could barely move, felt like a lead weight, pulling down the side of his body. He was no longer bleeding, but he felt light-headed.

He wanted to lie down there on the rocks. Relax. Take a nap. He had never been so exhausted.

But he couldn't. This wasn't over yet. He had to tap into a reserve of energy and get moving.

He stood still for a few seconds, head bowed.

Then he lifted his feet and started walking.

And, soon after, running.

Chapter 74

Theo had almost cut himself free.

His work on slicing the ropes progressed at a slow pace,
he fumbled the utility knife to the floor every few seconds.
But each time he dropped the knife, he tried to pry his wrists
apart to test the strength of the bond. As the rope grew increasingly slack, his heart soared.

He was going to get out of here. Alive.

In his excitement he'd nearly forgotten the pain that
throbbed at a hundred different points in his body. Lips
pressed together, stinging sweat leaking into his eyes, he
worked the blade against the rope, making small but steady
movements. His fingers ached but he labored relentlessly.
Back and forth. Back and forth. Back and forth.

As he cut, he thought about his family. Marge, Nicole,
Gabe. He badly wanted to see them again, wanted to hold
them in his arms and tell them how much he loved them. If
one good thing had come from this horrifying experience, it
was his newfound appreciation for his family. He wanted to
be a better man for them.

The knife slipped out of his fingers and clinked to the hardwood.

Theo attempted to pull apart his wrists.

The rope resisted, for a beat—and then loosened, threads shredding. He twisted his arms out of the slot in the back of the chair and swung them around in front of him. He examined his hands and wrists. His skin was chafed from the rope, but he didn't care.

He was free.

He reached behind him, grasped the knife, and bent to cut through the rope looped around his ankles. It took less than a minute to free them.

He kicked the chair aside.

He lay there on the floor, panting. He was so exhausted he didn't want to move, and getting free had brought a fresh awareness of the injuries that riddled his body. His lip was sore from the fishhook, his jaw throbbed from when Isaiah had punched him, and every other part of him hurt from the electrical shock Isaiah had delivered.

But he wasn't out of this madness yet. He had to push on.

He slowly got to his feet, dizziness blowing through him and nearly causing him to lose his balance. He swung toward the doorway, paused, and then dragged his feet toward the toolbox.

Underneath the rope and duct tape, he found pliers, a hammer, and a screwdriver. The stun gun lay inside, too, but Theo didn't want to fuss around with that. He was hoping to find a real gun. But he didn't see—

A door banged open at the front of the house.

Isaiah, he thought, fear spinning through him. *That psycho son of mine is back.*

Footsteps hurried inside.

Frantic, Theo grabbed the utility knife off the floor.

He hid behind the half-opened bedroom door.

* * *

Isaiah ran inside the cabin. He had a feeling—one of those unquestionable gut feelings—that Gabriel was going to realize he was still alive and come after him.

Little brother could come if he wanted. It was going to be too late for Pops.

Isaiah ran down the hall. The door to the bedroom in which he'd tied up Pops was partly open, harsh white light spilling outside and onto the hallway floor.

"I'm back, Pops," Isaiah said, approaching the doorway. "I know you missed me."

Isaiah shoved the door open with his shoulder.

The chair lay toppled on the floor. Empty. Cut ropes lay nearby like shorn hair.

"What the hell. . . ." Isaiah said.

His father popped from behind the door like a jack-in-the-box.

"I'm sorry," Pops said.

He thrust something metallic deep into Isaiah's exposed abdomen.

Fuckin' utility knife, Isaiah realized as the blade bit into his flesh.

Isaiah grappled with his father to pull the knife out of his body. But Pops, in a shocking show of strength, pinned Isaiah against the wall and drove the blade deeper.

"I'm sorry," Pops whispered. Tears ran down his weathered face.

Groaning, Isaiah felt as though he were gushing blood. But he wasn't going out like this. Fuck that. He'd gotten out of tighter spots than this, had survived a bullet in the chest. He refused to die, and especially at the hands of this man.

No matter what. . . .

Growling, he closed his fingers around his father's neck. He squeezed.

Pops gagged. His eyes bulged. He stumbled away from Isaiah and fell to the floor, choking and coughing.

Isaiah pulled the knife out of his stomach and threw it away. Dark blood flowed, covering his hands.

Damn, he got me good.

His legs weakened. He leaned against the wall for support. He dug into his waistband for the Glock, pulled it out, was reassured by its lethal weight.

Lying on the floor, Pops looked at him. His face said it all: Game over.

"I promised Mama," Isaiah said. He raised the gun.

Something cold pressed against his temple.

"Put it down," Gabriel said. He held a shotgun to Isaiah's head.

Gabriel didn't want to kill Isaiah. But to protect his father, he would.

Isaiah, still aiming the gun at Pops, cut his gaze toward Gabriel.

"Knew you were coming, little brother," Isaiah said. He sounded short of breath, and Gabriel noticed that a wound in his abdomen bled profusely. "What took you so long?"

"Drop the gun," Gabriel said.

"I need to do this, man." A tear slid down Isaiah's cheek. "Don't stop me."

"How much do you wanna bet that I can blow your brains against the wall before you pull the trigger?" Gabriel said. "I don't want to kill you—but I will, if you force me."

"Both of you, please put away the guns," Pops said. His voice was slurred, likely due to his swollen lip. He drew a chair toward him, set it upright, and settled into it heavily. "There's something both of you need to know."

"What're you talking about?" Gabriel asked. Isaiah, too, was frowning.

Pops wiped his lips.

"I'm talking about what I was going to tell you at home today before your brother here abducted me," Pops said.

"He's not my brother," Gabriel said. "Doesn't act like it anyway."

Isaiah sneered.

"Yes, he is your brother, Gabriel," Pops said. "Not your half brother either. Your full-blooded brother."

"What?" Isaiah said.

Gabriel couldn't gather enough air to speak.

"You and Gabriel," Pops said. "You have the same mother, too: Naomi Battle. May her soul rest in peace."

Gabriel lowered the shotgun. Isaiah dropped his pistol and slid to the floor, pressing his hand against his stomach. Blood continued to seep between his fingers and his breaths came shallow. He was fading.

Gabriel sat on the floor, too, but it was due to shock. He felt as though he'd been whacked over the head with a sledgehammer.

"H—h—h . . . how?" Gabriel said.

"Naomi gave birth to twins," Pops said. "You and Isaiah are identical twins. Isaiah, you were born first. Gabe, you came a few minutes later. What a handsome pair of boys you were." A wistful look came into his eyes.

Gabriel looked at Isaiah. Not wanting to believe. But knowing it was true.

"Why'd you separate us?" Isaiah asked. Pain pinched his face. Speaking seemed to demand all his energy.

"Marge—who Gabe grew up knowing as his mother—wasn't able to have children," Pops said.

"But Nicole—" Gabriel started.

"Nicole was a miracle baby," Pops said. "Before her, Marge and I had tried for years to have a child. We got frustrated with the situation and then with each other. I got involved with Naomi during a business trip to Chicago when Marge and I were on the brink of filing for divorce. I never planned for Naomi to get pregnant, but it happened. And when I found out that she was carrying twins . . . well, I got to thinking this could be the solution to our desire for children. After Naomi gave birth, I offered to take both of you and raise you as my own children in Atlanta." He looked at Gabriel. "Naomi named both of you boys, by the way. She insisted."

"She did?" Gabriel said. He'd always thought Pops had given him his name.

"And Mama was okay with you . . . you taking him?" Isaiah asked, glancing at Gabriel.

"It was a compromise," Pops said. "I wanted both of you, as I said. She was willing to give me only one. So she gave me Gabriel. I promised to take care of you, too, Isaiah."

"But you didn't!" Isaiah shouted, and then he stopped, delicately holding his stomach. "You left us."

"I *tried* to pay child support, Isaiah. She never told you that, did she? I've never wanted to tell you this, because I know how much you loved your mother, but soon after I took Gabriel home with me, I sent her money. Three times. A few thousand dollars each time. She sent the checks back to me. I called her and demanded to know why she refused the money. Do you know what she said? She thought if she took the payments, I would use that as leverage to take you away from her. She was afraid I would go to the courts, have her declared an unfit mother, and demand custody." Pops chuckled bitterly. "As though I wanted my personal life raked over the coals in a courtroom. I was trying to do the right thing and provide for my child. But Naomi . . . I always think she was frightened of the influence she thought I wielded. She told me she'd rather raise you herself in the ghetto than lose you to me."

"You're lyin'," Isaiah said, but his face didn't back up his words. Doubt had crept into his eyes.

"What about Mom?" Gabriel asked. "She knew all this?"

"When I brought you home, Gabe, she just fell in love with you. I think you're the only reason she didn't demand a divorce from me, because she loved you so much. You're her baby, in the truest sense of the word."

Tears had begun to fill Gabriel's eyes.

"Why him?" Isaiah said. Tears wet his cheeks, too. "Why the fuck did he get to go live with you? Who chose?"

"Naomi made the decision." Pops had slipped out his handkerchief. He blotted his eyes. "She gave me Gabriel. You were her heart, Isaiah. She wanted to keep you."

Sobbing, Isaiah lay on the floor. Gabriel noticed that blood had spread like an oil spill around Isaiah's body.

Gabriel crawled to him.

Only a couple of minutes ago, he had been ready to kill this man. Now he felt a kinship with him he'd never felt in his life with anyone.

His twin brother.

It explained their psychic connection. It explained everything.

He cradled Isaiah's head in his lap. He looked at Isaiah's face, so much like his own—yet Isaiah's features had been hardened by such cruel experiences, and Gabriel's softened by such good fortune, that neither of them had been able to see that they were much more than brothers, were really twins.

Gabriel pried Isaiah's hand away from his stomach. The wound was deep and ugly.

"I never meant for this to happen." Pops said quietly. "I didn't want to hurt him, but he had gone crazy. . . . I was only trying to defend myself. . . ." Pops began to sob.

Gabriel pulled off his shirt and pressed it to Isaiah's wound to stem the flow of blood.

"Just grazed your shoulder with that bullet, little brother," Isaiah said. He smiled bitterly. "You'll be all right. You always were the lucky one."

"We'll get you to the hospital. You've just gotta hang on, okay?" Gabriel said. "Pops, can you call an ambulance?"

"I'm on it." Pops stumbled out of the room.

Isaiah watched their father leave and then turned his head to Gabriel.

"Dig in my pocket," Isaiah said. "Right, front pocket. Get . . . wallet."

Gabriel slipped his hand into the pocket of Isaiah's jeans, being careful not to move him too roughly. He retrieved a brown leather wallet.

Isaiah took it from him, unfolded it open. A faded photograph slid out: the photo of Naomi and Pops, taken so many years ago at a Chicago hibachi restaurant.

"Don't care what Pops says," Isaiah said. "Mama was . . . good woman. You . . . you would've loved her."

Isaiah pressed the photograph into Gabriel's hand. Gabriel studied his mother, a woman he had never known—and never would. Grief kicked in his chest and fresh tears pushed at his eyes.

"You keep it now," Isaiah said, closing Gabriel's fingers over the picture. "Take care of it."

"You aren't gonna die," Gabriel said. "You've lived through worse stuff than this. Just hang on, man."

"Sorry for all the . . . fucked-up shit I did," Isaiah said.

"Hang on, Isaiah!"

"See you . . . little brother . . ." Smiling dreamily, Isaiah closed his eyes.

He was dead.

Gabriel wept. He wept for the mother he had never known, and the twin brother he'd known far too briefly and tragically.

Most of all, he wept for the terrible, cruel hand life had dealt them.

You always were the lucky one. . . .

But to go on living with the truth seemed the worst luck of all.

* * *

Again, Isaiah was in total darkness, traveling toward an uncertain future.

He'd vowed to get revenge on his father, but his father had proven wilier than he had ever counted on. Bastard had stabbed him.

And then there had been Gabriel. His damned twin, caught in the middle of the mess, none of what had happened to either of them his fault.

Why hadn't he figured it out? He remembered how Mama would sometimes study the photos of Gabriel, well dressed and prosperous, that Isaiah would clip from business magazines. At the time, he'd assumed she was questioning why Isaiah had not managed to plot a similarly successful course in his own life. He'd never imagined the truth: she was looking at pictures of her other son.

Mama, I'm sorry, I failed.

A pinpoint of brightness appeared far ahead. As he rushed toward it, helpless to change direction or slow his speed, the light grew larger and brighter, expanding into a gigantic doorway.

Mama's face spun through his field of vision like a moon. Her sad, tired face. But then her lips turned up into a soft smile of approval and he wondered: had he truly failed?

Mama actually looked proud.

No, he thought. *I did the best thing I could have done. It was better than killing Pops.*

T.L. Reid would live the remainder of his life with the knowledge that he had murdered his own son.

Isaiah merged into the light and the fate that awaited him on the other side.

Twenty minutes later an ambulance and policemen arrived. Gabriel and Pops explained what had happened. The police did not arrest Pops. His claim—and Gabriel corroborated it—was self-defense.

Driving, Gabriel followed the ambulance from a distance. He half expected Isaiah to return miraculously from the dead, to burst from the back doors of the vehicle.

Nothing happened.

Isaiah Battle was gone forever.

Chapter 75

A week later, they buried Isaiah in the family plot in a cemetery outside Atlanta. Gabriel, Pops, Mom, Nicole, and Dana were the only ones in attendance at the funeral.

After the burial they returned to the house of Gabriel's parents for dinner. It was a somber gathering; their conversation was subdued, as though they worried about disturbing someone who slept in a nearby room.

The death of a family member, even someone as misguided and troubled as Isaiah had been, had a sobering effect on all of them.

Gabriel, for his part, had been in a melancholy mood all week. Trying to piece together his shattered life. Trying to absorb the truth. Trying to move on.

Gabriel's telekinesis had gone into remission. He suspected, this time, that it would never return. He no longer glimpsed any spectral figures in mirrors either.

Without Isaiah, the other half of him, there was no need for such things.

After dinner Mom excused herself to go to the bathroom. Gabriel waited for her in the hallway outside the bathroom door. Mom emerged a few minutes later and looked at him with concern.

"What's wrong, baby?" she asked.

He had been waiting to discuss this subject with her again. Waiting for the opportunity, and waiting, most of all, until he was ready to talk about it. Now was the time.

"Pops told me everything, Mom," he said.

"I know." She sighed. "Come sit with me for a little bit, okay?"

They went upstairs to her private study. Mom removed a familiar volume from one of the bookshelves: a large, leather-bound photo album. Opening it, she sat on the sofa and patted the cushion beside her, inviting him to join her. After a moment's hesitation, he did.

Mom turned to his newborn-baby pictures. He was a honey-skinned baby with a smear of dark, curly hair.

"You were such an adorable baby," Mom said. "The first time I laid eyes on you, I fell in love. While I didn't agree with what your father had done, I realized you were a gift. I promised the Lord I would raise you as my own."

"I'm not angry with you," Gabriel said. "You'll always be Mom to me."

"But you have questions," Mom said.

"Yes," he said. "Like my birth certificate, for instance. You're listed as my mother, and my birthplace is listed as Grady hospital, here in Atlanta, not someplace in Chicago."

"Part of the agreement between me and your father," Mom said, "is that we would have to create a background that could stand up to scrutiny. Your father is a well-connected, successful businessman. A man like him can get any paper-work you need."

Gabriel had expected as much. Pops never had any problem using his status to pull strings.

"But didn't family and friends question it?" he asked. "I mean, one day you suddenly show up with a newborn baby. Someone had to ask you about me."

"Although your father and I met in college here in Atlanta, shortly after we married we moved back to Texas, where both of us are originally from, and where our families and closest friends resided. Well, soon after you were born, we decided that returning to Atlanta would diffuse the controversy and the prying questions. So we moved here almost immediately after we took custody of you. Things were better that way."

"Did you know about Isaiah, too?"

"Your father never told me the woman had twins. That's why I was so shocked when Isaiah arrived. I had no idea he existed."

"Then Pops lied to you for years, too."

"He could have done the righteous thing and given me the *whole* truth, yes," Mom said. Her face reflected years of repressed pain.

"I risked my life to save him." Gabriel clenched his hand into a fist. "But he's been lying to all of us from the beginning. This is all his fault."

Mom placed her hand atop his, loosened his fist with soothing rubs. "Your father is a complex man. Full of contradictions. You were correct to go there to help him. He needed you then, and he needs you now, more than you realize."

"What does he need me for? I'm starting to really doubt that I need him at all."

"Our children are our conscience," Mom said. "They remind us of the values we're supposed to hold dear. Sometimes we fail—but so long as our children are in our lives, we never forget our responsibility to them and ourselves."

"I'm not sure I understand that, Mom, but thanks for the words of wisdom anyway."

"You'll understand once you have your own children," she said. "Now, hold on one moment, lest I make a liar of myself."

Mom walked across the room and opened a file cabinet. She took out a manila folder and gave it to him.

It contained an obituary for Naomi Battle.

"I must counsel you to do the proper thing," Mom said. "Pay your respects to your birth mother, Gabriel."

Clasping the folder to his side, Gabriel left his mother's study and went downstairs.

He located his father in the grand salon. His back facing Gabriel, Pops stood silently at the large window, sipping cognac.

Ever since the events at the cabin, the past couple of times Gabriel had seen his father at home, a glass of liquor was always within his reach, and Gabriel wondered if his father had resolved to heal himself—or kill himself—through the bottle.

Your father is a complex man. Full of contradictions.

Pops turned, noted Gabriel's presence. He nodded slightly.

Gabriel nodded, too.

He loved his father. He hated his father.

But through it all, T.L. Reid was still his father. And he always would be.

A week later, Gabriel and Dana took a flight to Chicago. They visited Mt. Olive Cemetery, on the Southside.

Kneeling, Gabriel placed a bouquet of fresh carnations on his mother's grave. He lowered his head.

"Thank you," he said softly to the mother he had never known.

In October, Gabriel and Dana wed.

Although they already had been together for three years,

when they married, they discovered new depths in their love for each other. Gabriel found unexpected strength and security in loving someone, unconditionally, and knowing in his heart that she felt the same about him—with no lies and illusions clouding the air between them.

At home late one evening, about a year into their marriage, Dana sat next to Gabriel on the sofa and told him, with tears glittering in her eyes, that she was pregnant. Jubilant, he swept her off her feet and carried her across the room, making such a joyful ruckus that their new dog, Nia, a rambunctious yellow Labrador, regarded them as if they had lost their minds.

The following summer, nine months after Dana's announcement and a surprisingly easy labor, Dana gave birth.

To twin girls.

SUBSCRIBE TO BRANDON MASSEY'S
TALESPINNER

Readers of Brandon Massey now can subscribe to Brandon Massey's free Talespinner newsletter by visiting his website at www.brandon massey.com. Talespinner subscribers receive access to free short stories, an electronic newsletter, opportunities to win prizes in exclusive contests, and advance information about forthcoming publications. Go online today to www.brandonmassey.com and sign up. Membership is free!

Grab These Other
Thought Provoking Books

Check Out These Other
Dafina Novels

Look For These Other
Dafina Novels

If I Could
0-7582-0131-1

by Donna Hill
$6.99US/**$9.99**CAN

Thunderland
0-7582-0247-4

by Brandon Massey
$6.99US/**$9.99**CAN

June In Winter
0-7582-0375-6

by Pat Phillips
$6.99US/**$9.99**CAN

Yo Yo Love
0-7582-0239-3

by Daaimah S. Poole
$6.99US/**$9.99**CAN

When Twilight Comes
0-7582-0033-1

by Gwynne Forster
$6.99US/**$9.99**CAN

It's A Thin Line
0-7582-0354-3

by Kimberla Lawson Roby
$6.99US/**$9.99**CAN

Perfect Timing
0-7582-0029-3

by Brenda Jackson
$6.99US/**$9.99**CAN

Never Again Once More
0-7582-0021-8

by Mary B. Morrison
$6.99US/**$8.99**CAN

Available Wherever Books Are Sold!

Check out our website at www.kensingtonbooks.com.

Grab These Other
Dafina Novels
(trade paperback editions)